NO GOOD DEED

By Auston Habershaw

The Saga of the Redeemed
The Oldest Trick
   Consisting of: *The Iron Ring*
                          Iron and Blood
No Good Deed

NO GOOD DEED

Saga of the Redeemed: Book II

AUSTON HABERSHAW

HARPER
VOYAGER
IMPULSE
An Imprint of HarperCollins Publishers

EPub Edition JUNE 2016 ISBN: 9780062369192

Print Edition ISBN: 9780062369208

10 9 8 7 6 5 4 3 2 1

Dedicated with love to my wife, Deirdre—the steady voice of reason and the skeptical eye every dreamer needs. You should all be so lucky.

"Any emotion, if it is sincere,
is involuntary."

MARK TWAIN

PROLOGUE

The main courtroom in Keeper's Court, Saldor's hall of justice, had five sides, one for each of the arcane energies that made up the world. The accused stood in the center, chained by the wrist to a large squat stone at the center of the floor. Dull, black, and trapezoidal, "the Block" was so old that the courtroom itself was several centuries its junior. It was said that, in the old days, the condemned would have their heads struck off the moment the verdict was read. Those were primitive times, however—blood was no longer spilled in the Saldorian courts. They had other ways of making the condemned regret their actions. Ways that would not stain the woodwork or upset any children present.

There were four judges for any major trial—one for the Ether, one for the Lumen, one for the Dweomer, and one for the Fey. They each sat in a pulpit that loomed over the Block, as staring down one's nose at the accused was an ancient custom that even this modern, enlightened age wasn't keen on abandoning. The fifth pulpit, the Astral one, was occupied by a rotating cast of witnesses, accusers, defenders, and officers bound to present physical evidence to the court. Between these five pulpits and elevated a dozen feet above the floor was the gallery, where citizens of Saldor were encouraged to come and witness their justice system operate. They were even encouraged to bring things to throw sometimes, and jeering was understood as good form. It was surprising, honestly, the frequency with which persons present could shed illumination on a matter with a simple threat or insult, whether by prompting the accused into a rash reply or bringing new evidence to light. Justice in action, as it were.

Today, the gallery was in a rare mood, and eager to speed justice along. Beneath them, standing tall and graceful in her gray robes, a Mage Defender was about to hear her sentence. Kari Dempner looked at her, big eyes heavy with what might wind up being tears, despite her best efforts. "It's not fair," she muttered beneath her breath. "It just isn't."

The question, of course, was whether Kari, runaway merchant's daughter turned ink-thrall, would do anything about it. Could she stand up there, in court, with all those eyes on her, and speak what she knew to be true? Did she have the courage? Her knees shook beneath her skirts and she wished she had some Cool Blue to calm her. "It's not right," she muttered again.

The howls of the mob drowned out her whispers.

She doubted the rabble had even the slightest clue what the charges were, but to them it didn't matter. Corruption trials always brought out the worst sorts— there was no shortage of criminals in the gallery, as well as a smattering of moon-faced idealists and bitter conspiracy loons. To see their biases confirmed by the courts was too rich a confection for them to abstain. They were here to wallow in it.

"Myreon Alafarr." The voice of the Lumenal judge echoed through the chamber, amplified by the enchantments placed upon the pulpit itself. He was a frail old man in a white robe too large for him and a wig that seemed likely to slide over the front of his crumpled face at any moment. Arthritis had bent his hands into claws that could barely cling to the white orb he bore. *"You will stand, please."*

A scent wafted past Kari's nose—cologne, probably of Akrallian make, expensive and too liberally applied. Its cloying odor sent icy needles dancing down her spine. It meant one thing . . .

"Why, Ms. Dempner, what a pleasant surprise." A voice, soft and gentle as a baby's hand, whispered breathily in her ear. A man's hand—also soft and powdered, bedecked with jewels and well-manicured—fell upon her shoulder and lay there, limp and heavy. "Enjoying the show?"

Kari knocked the hand away by instinct and turned to see Gethrey Andolon, her former lover (though the term applied only loosely). He grinned at her with teeth buffed and polished to an ivory shine, which marked a stunning contrast to his rouged lips and dyed blue hair. It was a fashion popular among young men, but Andolon was too old by almost twenty years to wear it. He ought to have looked ridiculous. Instead, his soft brown eyes made Kari's heart shrivel up like a raisin in her chest.

Meanwhile, the Lumenal judge had interrupted the proceedings in order to have a coughing fit, the sound magically cast about the room so that all could hear the phlegm in his throat with the juicy clarity afforded someone sitting next to him at a dinner table. When it passed, the judge proceeded with the rituals of justice. *"You stand accused of fraud, improper sorcerous conduct, and conspiracy to traffic in illicit magecraft, to which you have pled innocent. You have heard the arguments brought against you in the case and have been confronted by the evidence collected by the Defenders of the Balance. Do you wish, at this point, to change your plea and throw yourself upon the mercy of the court?"*

Kari looked back at the accused. All it would take would be for her to stand and make herself heard, and the world would know Myreon was innocent. "I could do it," she said over her shoulder. "You couldn't stop me."

Andolon chuckled quietly and motioned to the taciturn Verisi with the crystal eye sitting beside him. "So I've been told, Ms. Dempner. Why do you think I'm here?"

Kari glanced at the Verisi—an augur. Of course. She should have known. Anything she might do, Andolon's pet augur could predict, assuming he had scryed the outcome of this proceeding. Nothing about to transpire was a surprise to Gethrey Andolon. He had set it up all too well.

Andolon tsked through his teeth. "Don't be so glum, my dear. Perhaps Magus Alafarr will change her plea, eh? Maybe none of this will be necessary."

"She won't." Kari hissed. "She'll never. That woman has balls bigger than you'll ever have, Andolon." All about them, the gallery howled for Alafarr's blood.

"She won't do it," the augur stated, his real eye far off, scanning the strands of the future.

"She'd better not." Andolon snorted. "Otherwise we'd have come across town for nothing."

Alafarr had to think she might win. Kari knew the mage had a lot of friends come forward in her defense—staff bearing magi, Captain-Defenders, and so on. Her alibi was strong, too, and her accusers had no motive they could clearly articulate. It was agony to think all that evidence was going to count for nothing. Finally, the Mage Defender's voice echoed up from below. "I will retain my original plea, your honor."

Andolon snickered, adjusting his lace ruff collar. "Perfect! *Perfect!*"

The gallery loved it, too—a chant of "Stone her good' began in one corner. Others threw rotten vegetables her direction. They missed. Kari felt her heart sink, weighed down by the slippery, limp hand of Gethrey Andolon creeping back onto her shoulder, finger by finger.

"Don't do it," he whispered in her ear, the heavy

scent of his cologne making her cough. He rubbed her shoulder again, slowly, gently—a man stroking a prized possession. "I can make it worth your while, Kari. Ink enough to swim in. Think about it."

The Lumenal judge raised his orb and it flashed with sun-bright brilliance. Order fell over the court. "Does the accused wish to address the court prior to hearing our verdict?"

Kari trembled. The temptation of the ink was like a physical force—she could scarcely breathe with the thought of it. Andolon could afford it, too—that was why she first latched onto him. He was the first educated man who had spoken to her in months and he didn't mind her vices—even approved of them. It wasn't until later that she realized the price she had paid for his company. The price to her pride; the wearing out of her soul. Gethrey Andolon wanted to consume her, just as he wanted to consume everything around him. He was like ink given human form.

Alafarr's voice was firm, even in the face of her disgrace. "I wish to say only that I am innocent of these charges. I am being framed for a crime I did not commit . . ."

Now was her last chance. Kari glanced over her shoulder and saw Andolon, watching her carefully, his augur whispering in his ear.

" . . . the evidence is faulty or tampered with, and I ask the court to reflect upon my service to the Defenders of the Balance, to Saldor, and to the Alliance of the West when considering my guilt in this matter."

Kari saw in Andolon's eyes her future—her long, slow slide into oblivion, cheerfully abetted by her one-time lover. She saw herself winding up in some Cross-town whorehouse, barely aware of the world around her, her blue-stained fingers wedged forever in a series of little glass jars.

Andolon rubbed her shoulder some more. "Don't, Kari. Be smart for a change."

Alafarr's voice did not waver; she did not shout nor sneer. She was the picture of dignified poise. "I did not do it, there is no reason I would have done it, and I would not have been able to do it at the time my accusers claim. I have shown you as much when preparing my defense. The guilty parties are likely in this room as we speak, here to gloat over my misfortune. Were I not forbidden from naming them, I could tell the court exactly where to find them."

She knew! Adrenaline surged through Kari's legs. She shook off Andolon's hand with a glare and stood. She was going to do it. She, Kari Dempner, was going to do the right thing for the first time in a long, long time.

She opened her mouth to speak, but the words were cut short by a bright, sharp pain across her throat. She clutched at her neck, eyes wide—a wire, thin and strong, lay across her windpipe. Strong arms dragged her back to her seat. She writhed, but the man with the garrote held her still, dragging her backward.

The Lumenal judge was reminding Alafarr of the complicated legal justification for her gag order while a low rumble of furtive conversation percolated through the gallery. Kari kicked her legs, flailed with her arms, striking people around her. She got a few annoyed glances but nobody seemed to notice anything amiss. Blood thundered in her ears, laced with panic. How did they not see? How could no one notice her being murdered, right *here*?

Andolon's face floated into view. "I would introduce you to my little angel of death, but he's the quiet type, you see. Nobody can hear you, Kari, and nobody will notice you are gone until the crowd clears."

The orb was raised and flashed again. The gallery grew quiet, still oblivious of the woman being strangled in their midst. *"Is that all?"* The old judge asked Alafarr.

"Yes, your honor."

The judge nodded. *"Will the judges please stand to deliver their verdicts?"*

Kari felt her limbs grow heavy. The fight in her was gone. She looked back, trying to see her killer. All she could make out was a shadow of a man, nondescript save his mouth and a small tattoo of a button just above the corner of his lips. A Quiet Man of the Mute Prophets; a man with no soul.

Andolon tsked. "Such a shame, Kari. I would have liked just one more tumble with you. You always were so . . . so *pliable* in bed."

One last jolt of energy surged in Kari—anger, shame, fear, all rolled together—and she threw her head backward at the Quiet Man, causing him to lose his grip for a second. She gasped one more breath of air, honking like a half-dead goose, only to have the garrote slam home again.

Her last attempt at escape was drowned out as the gallery hissed and booed at Alafarr. The Mage Defender stood stock-still as three hundred people shouted all manner of insults. A rotten apple squelched against the Block not more than a foot from her leg.

The Lumenal judge raised his orb and restored order again. Everyone settled down; the theatrical portion of the event was over. The old judge's voice came to Kari as though in a dream. *"The Judge of the Lumen finds the accused to be innocent."*

The judge to the Lumen's left, the Fey judge, nodded. *"So noted. Do you affirm it seven times?"*

"I do so affirm."

Kari felt her thrashing heart thrill at this small victory—maybe Alafarr would be innocent after all, maybe Andolon wouldn't have her killed this way . . .

Andolon cocked an eyebrow at her. "Is she still alive? Dammit, man—finish the job. We're almost done here."

The Dweomeric judge was next. She was an older woman with iron-gray hair and a severe demeanor. *"The Judge of the Dweomer finds the accused to be guilty."*

"She better," Andolon grunted under his breath. "She cost a bloody fortune."

The Lumenal judge asked for her affirmation, and the Dweomeric judge affirmed three times, as was traditional. A tie. For Kari, the world began to fade away.

Her brief moment of escape and the seconds it bought her were almost at an end. She scarcely heard what followed.

"*The Judge of the Ether finds the accused to be guilty.*"

"*So noted. Do you affirm it thirteen times?*"

"*I do so affirm.*"

Kari's mind drifted to her childhood in Ihyn, playing with her mother aboard her father's ship, telling tales of selkies who stole naughty children. The sun on her hair and the smell of the sea . . .

"*The Judge of the Fey finds the accused to be guilty.*"

There was a cheer from the gallery. The chant of "STONE HER GOOD" began in earnest, so loud it almost drowned out the final formalities. Gethrey felt buoyed by their petty hatred. He began to chant along, a grin splitting his face.

"*So noted. Do you affirm it once?*"

"*I do so affirm.*"

Alafarr did not sink to her knees, or faint, or quail. If anything, she seemed more rigid than before. Her face was a mask of serenity. Gethrey grinned at this, knowing how the woman must have been raging inside. He nudged DiVarro, his augur, in the arm. "It's too perfect. Too perfect by half!"

He spared a look at Kari—she had stopped twitching, finally. Gods, strangling people took forever, evidently. He'd had no idea.

The old Lumenal judge spoke over the crowd. "*Myreon Alafarr, you have been found guilty of the crimes of*

fraud, improper sorcerous conduct, and conspiracy to traf-
fic in illicit magecraft. You are hereby stripped of your staff
and expelled from the Defenders of the Balance from this day
forward. Furthermore, you are to be petrified and confined
to a penitentiary garden for a period not exceeding three
years. May your time as stone allow you to contemplate your
crimes with the depth and gravity such acts deserve, and
may your ordeal strengthen your resolve against such mis-
deeds in the future. This is the finding of this court, under
Hann's guidance, and with the blessing of Endreth Beskar,
the Lord Mayor of Saldor, and Polimeux II, Keeper of the
Balance. Court is hereby adjourned, and the accused's sen-
tence shall be set to begin immediately."

Gethrey applauded with gusto as Alafarr was led
away, giggling like a boy. Around him, the mob howled
and jeered even as they headed for the exits. Nobody
raised any alarm about any dead woman beside him.
The plan had worked perfectly. "There, DiVarro," he
said finally, "that's settled. We can proceed."

"There is a complication." DiVarro said.

He threw an arm around DiVarro's waist and
steered him toward the exits, drifting along in a river
of human flotsam, all high on what they perceived to
be justice. "You augurs—always so dire. Alafarr was
our last obstacle, understand? I had all the other angles
covered. Now, she is disgraced, Kari is dead, and you
know what the best part is?"

DiVarro said nothing, frowning at his hands.

Gethrey laughed. "There is no one in all of this
world who will bother trying to help Myreon Alafarr."

CHAPTER 1

THERE'S ALWAYS THREE

"I'm telling you there has *got* to be another trap." Tyvian's legs ached as he crouched in the shadowy entrance of the old temple's holy sanctuary. The place reeked of rotting vegetation, which, predictably enough, was due to the massive piles of rotting vegetation scattered all over the place. The Forest Children took their religion seriously enough to dump all their best fruits and vegetables into a dark hole for their false god to feast upon, but the god, as it happened, wasn't much of an eater.

Artus held his nose against the sickly sweet stench.

When he spoke, it was in a nasally whisper. "Where the heck would they put a trap in here? Why would you booby-trap a church anyway?"

"It's not a church, Artus, it's a pagan temple. And since we've already evaded two such booby traps, I'm telling you there's a third, and it's somewhere between us and that enormous statue." Tyvian pointed at their target.

The holy sanctuary room was circular, perhaps fifty yards across, and the floor was convex, its carefully carved flagstones forming a perfect dome. At the apex of this dome, and at the center of the chamber, was a massive statue of some kind of polished white rock. It was roughly humanoid, but instead of arms it had branches and instead of hair it had leaves. Its head was thrown back, looking up through a circular chimney that rose twenty feet up to the forest floor above them. Vibrant green moss grew over the statue's shoulders and up its sides, and from its open mouth poured a pure white light that shot up the chimney and into the open sky above. It was this statue that Tyvian was pointing at—the great idol of Isra, the false god of the Forest Children, and the Ja'Naieen, the Heart of Flowing Sunlight, the Source of Life.

Or, as Tyvian liked to think of it, the Five Pound Enchanted Diamond.

Artus pulled a small stone out of his pocket and skipped it across the flagstones between them and the statue of Isra. It bounced at a wild angle and skittered off into the shadows. "Well I don't see no traps. What makes you so sure there's three and not just two?"

Tyvian shifted position, causing his muddy clothing to creak. "Artus, these are superstitious people. They like patterns, and patterns are most often dictated by the disposition of the five energies, whether we know it or not. Now, the Fey's number is one and the Dweomer's number is three. The chances of them going about making just two traps to protect their god would be slim."

Artus frowned. "Well, why wouldn't there be five traps or seven or thirteen? Those are magic numbers, too."

Tyvian rolled his eyes. "Artus, where on earth would they hide *eleven* other booby traps in one room? They're superstitious savages, not paranoid civil engineers."

Artus sighed. "Fine, then—where is it, smartypants? My rock didn't trip nothing, and I don't see no touch plates or trip wires or trap doors or anything. Is your magic whats-a-madoo doing anything?"

Tyvian looked down at the magecompass he'd placed on the threshold of the sanctuary. He had it tuned to the Astral currently, as that would give him the best reading regarding the overall sorcerous energy trapped or flowing through the place, but the orbs were spinning slowly and the needle was indecisive as to direction. He swapped out the granite orbs for ones of iron and then hardwood and then bone and then glass, running through all the energies. The only ones that spun with any urgency were the bones (the Ether) and the wood (the Lumen), which was exactly what he expected from a chamber full of rotting vegetables and a statue enchanted with a Lumenal spell of some kind. He sighed. "I don't see one, honestly. The room seems clean."

Artus shrugged. "Well, okay then—let's nab the thing before those priests come back."

Tyvian nodded. "You first." The ring gave him a pinch, but he barely winced. He'd gotten accustomed to many of its lesser jabs over the eighteen months or so he'd been forced to wear it, and it didn't approve when he put his fifteen-year-old apprentice in harm's way.

Artus shouldered his pack, drew out his machete, and walked slowly across the curved floor toward the idol. When the floor didn't fall away and no rocks fell on him, Tyvian followed, folding up the magecompass and stuffing it into his coat pocket. He kept his hands free and his eyes open.

The curved flagstones were slick with the accumulated gunk and slime of years of rotting vegetable matter. Green-and-white mushrooms grew in big clumps here and there and the buzz of flies was everpresent. Artus slipped once, his hand sinking through the hide of a greenish-yellow pumpkin and emerging covered with slimy, moldy filth. "Uhhh . . . gross . . ."

"Focus, Artus," Tyvian cautioned, and stepped past him. Tyvian couldn't shake the feeling that they were being watched but he knew that was essentially impossible. They had staked out the temple for weeks before actually going inside, and they knew the comings and goings of the priests perfectly. Right now the two men and three women who were dedicated to the temple were indulging in their weekly bath, which involved a lot of praying and, oddly enough, an enormous amount of sexual intercourse. Artus had been noticeably keen to observe that particular ritualistic habit. Tyvian guessed it was the most attentive Artus had ever been during a stakeout.

In any event, the priests wouldn't be back for another hour at least, and given the intricacy of the deadfall traps and dart trip wires both he and Artus had evaded to get this far, Tyvian didn't think the priests would be able to rush in and stop them without falling on a bed of dung-encrusted spikes or being injected with some kind of unpleasant poison.

Tyvian reached the base of the statue of Isra, where he could see up the chimney to the sky above—it was just after midday and the sky was clear of any rain clouds. Good. He was about as filthy and damp as he was willing to get, no matter how big a diamond this was. He wondered how likely it was that he'd be able to clean all the mud and dirt out of his breeches without having to resort to sorcerous means when this affair was over and done with.

Artus was beside him. "Great, now how do we get it out?"

Tyvian climbed Isra's tree-bough arms so he could look inside the statue's mouth. The Heart of Flowing Sunlight was there, set into the gullet of the Forest God's statue. It was just as enormous as the rumors had claimed—a raw, uncut diamond the size of his two fists pressed together.

Having judged the size of the statue's mouth and the diameter of the diamond, Tyvian looked back at Artus. "Hammer, please. If we're going to commit sacrilege, why settle for half measures?" He took the hammer from Artus, tested its weight, and then broke Isra's jaw apart with one good swing.

The Heart of Flowing Sunlight tumbled out of the idol's half-destroyed head, glowing like a piece of star-light, and bounced off the curved floor. Artus flailed his arms to catch it but missed, the jewel skittering away into the field of rotting plants.

Tyvian groaned. "Dammit, Artus! Get it!"

Artus nodded and slid across the floor toward the massive jewel, trying not to fall into the muck again. Tyvian watched him go, shaking his head. Typical Artus. The last year had seen the boy shoot up five inches in height, but nothing appreciably in weight. Artus was now a jumble of arms, legs, sharp elbows, and bony shoulders who ate as much as five men and topped Tyvian by a full inch and a half. He could scarcely walk down a corridor without bumping into something, tripping, or making noise. It was like part-nering with an animated, three-legged hat rack.

Artus slipped one last time, just in front of the jewel. "It's okay!" he yelled, his voice echoing through the chamber. "I got it!"

Then the nearest pile of rotting plants picked itself up and threw itself at him. Artus vanished into its slimy, smelly innards with a half-startled yelp. The Heart of Flowing Sunlight likewise sank into the confines of the green-black, oily mass, winking out as both it and Artus were engulfed.

Tyvian blinked, barely believing what he had just seen. "Kroth."

Glancing around him, he noted that *several* of the rotting piles of sacrificial vegetables were performing a kind of flopping, oozing locomotion, and mostly in his direction. "Kroth's teeth!"

Tyvian set his pack down and began to rummage. "Rope, rope, need the rope . . . *ouch!*" The ring bit down on his hand as hard as if Tyvian had slammed it in a door. He glared at it. "*I know!* I'll get him in a second!"

A wet, brownish-green tendril of something wrapped itself around Tyvian's ankle. Before it could pull, though, he drew a knife and cut himself loose, then went back to the pack. "Dammit, where the hell is the damn thing?"

"Tyvian!" Artus's voice was breathless and panicked. "Help! Hel-*mphhfhhfhhh*." Tyvian looked up for a moment to see Artus's head emerging from the pile of animate vegetable matter only for it to vanish again as *another* pile of partially gelatinous muck hurled itself on top of him.

Tyvian's own situation was not improving. There were three big oozing masses of glop closing in on him from three separate directions, waving their half-solid tendrils at him. Standing with his back to the statue of

Isra, he hauled out a coil of rope and looped it over the vandalized head.

A tendril grabbed Tyvian around the waist. He cut it with the knife, but a second tendril seized his weapon by the hilt and dragged it away, consuming it within the mushy confines of a hungry plant-matter blob. Tyvian skipped between two of the encroaching things, only to now find himself surrounded by four of them. Rummaging frantically in his pack, his fingers suddenly closed around something thin, hard, and uneven. "Ah-ha!"

He pulled out the wand and spun to see the green-black bulk of a trash-thing looming over him, ready to pounce. He pointed at the center of the beast and pronounced the activation word, *"Ghrall!"* A ball of ruby-red flame burst from the tip of the wand and consumed the plant creature in an unnatural fire of pure Fey energy. The tip of the wand glowed like a coal in a furnace. "There! How do you like the taste of that, eh?"

The rotting piles of plant matter, evidently, had no opinion one way or the other. They continued to shamble toward him, reaching out with thin tentacles of rotting vine or ivy. Tyvian blasted three more, buying himself a little breathing space, and then looked for Artus. He couldn't see the boy, per se, but he did spot a particularly enormous patch of seething plant matter that seemed to have swallowed something very displeased to be ingested.

Tyvian ran, almost slipping on the uneven floor,

and skipped past another two plant monsters before reaching the pile under which Artus struggled. He turned and blasted the two things he'd passed and guessed, judging by the speed of the creatures, he had about seven seconds to get Artus out of there before being consumed himself. He glanced at the wand—immolating Artus was probably not the best solution. Hmmm . . . what then?

Artus's foot thrust out of the pile, sans boot. Tyvian reflexively grabbed him by the ankle and tried to pull, but the boy's skin was coated in slippery, smelly ooze and he was engulfed anew by his captors. If he was going to drag Artus out, Tyvian knew he would need a much better grip, ideally around the lad's waist.

That meant getting dirty. Really, really dirty.

Tyvian took a deep breath. "Kroth's bloody teeth, it's come to this, has it?" He looked at the rope and snapped his fingers. "Here!"

The rope's Lumenal and Dweomeric enchantments blazed to life; it tied itself around the waist of the Isra statue, and then its free end flew through the air and into Tyvian's hand. Securing the rope around his own waist, Tyvian took a deep breath, closed his eyes, and dove in.

The experience of wading through an animated mass of rotting vegetables was one that he did his very best not to record. He could feel the slimy ooze soaking through his shirt, he could hear it squishing and sloshing in his ear canals, and he was certain it was trying to crawl up his nose. Tyvian pretended he was receiving a mud bath in a Verisi spa, which helped diminish his inherent sense of disgust right up until Artus accidentally kicked him in the chin. This caused Tyvian's mouth to open, and the whole illusion was ruined forever.

He roared silently and groped until he found Artus. It wasn't difficult—the plant-things were piling on top of them, crushing them together, seeking to drown them in a seething morass of moldy fruit rinds and deliquescent lettuce. Tyvian grabbed Artus around the waist with one arm and began to pull on the rope with the other. In any other situation this would have been a physical impossibility for Tyvian or even for a man three times Tyvian's size and strength, but he had the ring, and the ring liked it when he rushed to the rescue.

The sun-bright power of the iron ring pulsed on Tyvian's right hand, sending waves of superhuman strength through his arms and legs. Artus wrapped his arms around Tyvian, which freed the smuggler to pull the rope bit by bit, hand over hand. The plant-things tried to stop him, they threw all their weight over him, but they couldn't prevent Tyvian's inexorable escape. Suddenly, as quickly as he had gone in, Tyvian found himself emerging from the rotting depths of the creatures. He and Artus broke free with a pop.

Artus fell to the ground, coughing and gasping for air, but Tyvian grabbed him by the belt and pulled him to his feet before the plant-things could swallow him up again. Tyvian pushed him toward the statue. "The chimney! Climb out!"

Artus snatched up Tyvian's pack as he ran to the center of the room; he was still wearing his own. Tyvian cast about for the blasting wand but didn't know what became of it—probably somewhere in the depths of those *things*. The whole chamber seemed awash in them now, all of them oozing and shambling and crawling slowly toward the two thieves. Tyvian darted to Artus's side and, freeing the rope around himself, ordered it to the top of the chimney, where it dutifully flew and secured itself to an exposed root. Tyvian pointed up. "Go! Quickly!"

Artus climbed with both packs as fast as Tyvian did with none—something to be said for the power of terror—and soon both of them were on their hands and knees at the top of the chimney, coughing, wheezing, vomiting out the disgusting remnants of their would-be killers.

Tyvian wiped a film of green slime off his face and gasped in the clean, fresh forest air. "I . . . I told you there was a third trap."

Artus rolled over on his back. "Saints . . . I thought I was a goner . . . I thought I was dead . . ."

Tyvian shook his head to try and get the gunk out of his ears. "Would have been, were it not for my heroic efforts. I hope you appreciate the lengths I go to." Slowly, he got to his feet, letting his eyes adjust to the midday sunlight.

Artus opened his pack and pulled out the Heart of Flowing Sunlight. "We got it."

Tyvian, though, didn't react. "Artus," he said calmly,

"You know how you thought you were dead a few moments ago?"

Artus sat up. "Yeah?"

Tyvian put his hands up slowly. "You might still be right."

"What?" Artus rubbed the goop out of his eyes and looked around.

The only thing he saw were the arrowheads of a score of drawn bows and the angry, filthy faces of the Forest Children surrounding them.

CHAPTER 2

A LOW-DOWN DIRTY GETAWAY

The Forest Children, also known as the woodkin to those of a more Galaspiner bent, or the Vel'jahai, if you happened to be one of them, were barbarous savages who lived within the vast confines of Isra'Nyil, or, more simply, the Great Forest. Tyvian had heard an awful lot of rumors about them over the years, and none of them had been flattering. His observations of their movements during the last few weeks had confirmed more rumors than they dispelled. They were superstitious, violently territorial vegetarians who "lived in harmony with nature," which evidently meant sleeping in burrows like human badgers, bathing infrequently, and rutting like wild animals in open daylight, where any passing fifteen-year-old farmboy might gawk at them and ask his partner/mentor extremely inappropriate questions about human anatomy.

Tyvian prepared to be shot with at least a dozen arrows immediately. When it didn't happen, he found himself talking. Talking, he had found, usually got him out of a lot of sticky situations. "Greetings, friends I have wonderful news!"

Tyvian's smile and cheery tone took the savages temporarily aback. They muttered among themselves in their slippery, silvery language. It sounded like pigeons trying to coo at each other with polysyllabic words.

Tyvian kicked Artus out of his open-mouthed shock. "Bow-wards!" he hissed, and then kept turning on the charm. "My partner and I have performed an in-depth investigation, and we have discovered that your god is false!"

Artus slowly took off his pack and began to rummage around.

Tyvian shot him a withering look. "My pack, fool In my pack!"

The arrows quavered in their bows as the petite wiry builds of the Forest Children struggled to hold them. They looked confused, perhaps even afraid Tyvian just kept smiling. "Now, I know this comes as a shock to you all—I understand. However, consider the advantages! No longer must you pitch your hard-earned fruits and vegetables down a dark hole in the midst of a forest—Isra isn't eating them, believe me—and you can now devote that time to more productive pursuits such as, for instance, the knitting of pants. I mean, let's face it, gentlemen—some of you fellows are one misguided falcon's dive away from compulsory celibacy!"

Artus was elbow deep in Tyvian's pack. "I don't see them anywhere."

The Forest Children had stopped muttering among themselves. Their faces were now grave. Tyvian kept smiling, but growled out the side of this mouth, "Artus, bow-wards now, please."

"I'm looking!"

The savages were parting, allowing someone at the back to push their way to the front. Tyvian knew whoever it was probably wasn't there to bail them out. "Look much, *much* faster."

"They in the big pocket or the side pockets?"

"Big pocket, dammit. *Big* pocket!" Tyvian kept his eyes fixed on the person approaching, though all he could currently see was a mop of matted red-orange hair drawing close. He heard Artus fumbling around inside the pack, cursing under his breath.

Tyvian found himself looking at a young woman clad in only a loincloth, a few elaborate tattoos, and a colossal mane of hair that spilled over her shoulders and fell almost to her knees. Were she cleaner and not flanked by men who planned to kill him, Tyvian might have spent a good minute ogling her rather taut, compact frame and athletic curves. He reflected, suddenly, that he usually seemed to meet the most attractive women the exact same way—just before they tried to kill him.

The woman drew a spike from her hair that looked like a very large thorn with a crossbar that allowed her to hold it, with the "blade" portion poking between her middle and ring fingers. She pointed it at Tyvian. "You Destroyers have defiled the holy temple of Isra. Why?" Her voice was clear and penetrating—the voice of an orator.

Tyvian looked back at the hole. "Is *that* what that was? Honestly, we were just looking for somewhere to—"

"Lies!" she snarled, showing her teeth.

"Got them!" Artus announced, slapping something into Tyvian's hand—a smooth, elliptical amulet fashioned from an alchemical mix of lodestone and steel.

Tyvian slipped the amulet over his head. "We were robbing you of your giant enchanted diamond—there, happy now?"

The woman's green eyes seemed to glow with anger. "Your blood must be used to cleanse the temple space! Surrender to the Ja'Naieen and we will only kill one of you!"

Tyvian shrugged. "Hardly tempting—I need Artus to carry the packs."

That did it. The woman chirped something angry at the Forest Children archers, and they loosed their arrows in one terrifying salvo.

Tyvian, of course, knew that the Vel'jahai's weapon of choice was the bow, which was why he had invested in bow-wards for both himself and Artus. The thing was, however, that bow-wards were designed to stop only a few arrows at a time, working under the assumption that you weren't, say, standing less than five paces from twenty archers who had nothing else to shoot at but you and your friend. So, when all of those razor-sharp projectiles came whistling straight at Tyvian's torso and struck the boundary of the ward more or less at the same time, the result was a complete overload of the ward's capacity. This, of course, meant Tyvian's ward exploded with a flash of blue light and a thunderclap roar that caused everyone present to hold their ears and fall to their knees.

Everyone, that was, except Artus and Tyvian.

"Time to run!" Tyvian grabbed his pack and sprinted, Artus just behind him. He kicked one of the Forest Children in his skinny, beardless chin as he rose to stop them but otherwise didn't break stride. They dove into the forest like a pair of big dogs through a hedge, eschewing dexterity and stealth for sheer, brute speed.

Arrows began to zing past their ears shortly thereafter, embedding themselves in trees or sticking in their packs as they ran, bobbing and weaving among the broad mossy trunks of the deep forest.

"Where the hell is Hool?" Tyvian snarled, more to the air than to Artus.

Artus answered anyway. "She's probably by the temple entrance. We came out the back!"

Tyvian leapt over a dead stump and ducked back into a hollow, Artus just beside him. This bought them a few seconds from the arrows. "Which way is the temple entrance?"

Artus looked around. "I dunno! I don't even know where we are!"

Tyvian poked his head up, only to have an arrow embed itself in the tree stump no more than three inches from his face. "Gods! I hate the gods-damned forest!"

"Which way do we run?"

Tyvian threw up his hands. "Away! Does it really matter? Go, boy, go!"

Artus took the lead. Tyvian wished he had the time to dig out his sword, Chance, from his pack as he ran, for the thought of being overrun by savages and having no blade to stab them with was among the most depressing ends he could think of. He couldn't, though, since his pack was doing a good job doubling as a pincushion for errant woodkin arrows.

Their lead, small to begin with, was vanishing every second. The Forest Children were on either side of them now, trying to flank. Tyvian imagined they had no more than a few more seconds before they were surrounded again.

They broke out of the trees, and Tyvian saw a form of salvation—a canyon, perhaps fifteen feet wide, with a large tree fallen across it. Tyvian pointed toward it breathlessly, but Artus had already seen it. The boy engaged reserves of energy only a teenager seemed to have and pulled ahead of Tyvian, bounding across the fallen trunk like a squirrel.

Tyvian was a few seconds behind him, with a half-dozen Forest Children, including Red-hair, nipping at his heels. He leapt onto the trunk and tried running across but stumbled halfway. He flailed around at errant branches to regain his balance and tried to stand up when a sweating, dirty Forest Child jumped on his back, grabbing him around the throat.

Tyvian estimated the little man to weigh no more than one hundred ten pounds, soaking wet, and therefore the smuggler found himself in the rare circumstance of being both larger and stronger than his opponent. He stood up, gagging against the man's forearms locked over his windpipe, and threw himself backward atop the trunk. Tyvian heard the man shriek as a particularly sharp broken end of a branch pierced his back. The Forest Child loosened his grip, after which Tyvian found it a simple matter to disentangle himself and kick the fellow over the side.

This marked the first time Tyvian had looked down. The canyon was more than twenty feet deep, and the rushing white water looked exceptionally rough. The thought of falling suddenly made him dizzy.

Another Forest Child lunged at him with one of those punch-spike things. This was more in line with what Tyvian was used to—he deflected the blow and, grabbing the man by the scruffy hair, pulled him off-balance and pushed him off the tree again. Two down, at least—he looked up—thirty-five or so to go. Wonderful.

Red-hair was next to step onto the tree, but she was more cautious than the others. She kept her distance. "There is no escape for you, Destroyer."

Tyvian pointed over his shoulder. "I was under the impression that I could escape *that* way."

Red-hair laughed. The laugh seemed remarkably genuine—a deep belly-laugh that made her breasts shake and her mouth open all the way.

Tyvian didn't like that laugh one bit—what was wrong with crossing the canyon? He cast a look over his shoulder.

Artus was running back in his direction. His face was deathly pale. "Run! Run!"

Tyvian looked behind Artus to see what, for a split second, he thought to be some kind of shambling hay-stack the size of a dray wagon. He was wrong.

It was a bear.

"Kroth's bloody teeth!" he swore. "Can this *possibly* get any worse?"

Red-hair roared incoherently in the direction of the bear, tipping her head. The bear answered in kind, nodding its massive head in similar fashion. It stopped at the edge of the tree trunk and roared at Artus and Tyvian, who were now standing back to back over a drop to certain death.

Tyvian sighed. "She can talk to bears. Right. That's worse."

Artus was clearly one more surprise away from total panic. "What do we do? What do we do? Saints, we're dead! Dead!"

Tyvian looked at Red-hair and the rows of Forest Children lining the edge of the canyon, bows ready. He looked back at the bear, its head low and its black eyes fixed on him and Artus. He looked down. "I've got a plan, Artus."

Artus blinked. "Really?"

"Hold your breath."

"What?"

Tyvian pushed Artus off the tree trunk. The boy screamed the whole way down. Red-hair was agape, her mouth hanging open. Tyvian gave her a wink and followed Artus down. *He* remembered to hold his breath.

It didn't do a hell of a lot of good.

Some eighteen hours later Tyvian crouched at the edge of a lake in his underclothes, watching the dawn mists slowly burn off in the face of the sunrise. It looked like something out of a poem: the water was a deep blue-green and spotted with the pristine white of countess-lilies; the grass glittered with dew beneath the full boughs of the trees. Somewhere nearby a loon whistled for its mate. When Tyvian had selected this place for their rendezvous point, the idea had been to cap off his stunning heist with a beautiful sunrise picnic. He had even preselected what they would have for breakfast—it was packed up in Brana's satchel.

Unfortunately, Brana's satchel was now at the bottom of a river, lost when the gnoll pup and his

mother, Hool, had dragged his and Artus's floundering
arses from the rapids and deposited them on the shore.

The four of them had spent the better part of last
night scurrying through the woods like weasels, trying
to put distance between them and a host of woodkin
that wanted them dead with a religious fervor. Even
now, Hool and Brana were out making false trails to
throw off pursuit. Tyvian was using the time to recu-
perate from having to swim in filth. Artus was using
the time to complain.

"I mean, seriously—how many times are you going
to throw me off a bridge into a river?" Artus had Tyvian's shirt on a rock and was absently rubbing it with
another rock—his peasant version of "doing laundry,"
apparently.

Tyvian tried not to look at the mauling of a good
tailor's work, focusing instead on the charming natural environs of Isra'Nyil's outer edges. "No doubt you
are teeming with alternative escape plans from that
situation, tactical mastermind that you are."

"Oh, that's rich!" Artus snapped, brandishing his
laundry-rock at Tyvian. "I don't remember you asking
me nothing, so how do you know? You just pushed me
off a damned log without even a wink!" He returned to
pummeling the clothes. With gusto.

Tyvian couldn't help but snort. "Artus, we were
about to become pincushions for poisoned arrows or a
light snack for a bear *or both*. It wasn't exactly the time
to have a conversation. Besides, you were busy soiling
yourself. I think the only "plan" you might have sug-

gested would have involved the fetal position and a lot of weeping for our mothers."

Artus leapt to his feet and cocked the rock over one shoulder as if to throw it. "You leave my mother out of this, you—"

He was interrupted by the great, golden-furred mass of Hool emerging from the nearby underbrush and fixing him with a coppery glare that could probably kill a bird dead. "Shut up, Artus! You are making too much noise again!"

Tyvian nodded. "Thank you, Hool. I've been trying to—"

"You shut up, too. You make almost as much noise as he does." Hool brushed a few stray brambles from her mane. "Me and Brana just worked very hard to hide your stupid human footprints and you are going to spoil it by shouting all the time. Be quiet."

Brana tumbled out of a tree, yipping cheerfully. He had almost quadrupled in size this year, going from less than forty to nearly a hundred fifty pounds of fur, muscle, and teeth. His mane had thick streaks of white in it and his eyes were pure gold to his mother's copper, but he was without a doubt his mother's son . . . pup . . . whatever. They seemed to share the same joy of criticizing humans. "Noisy! Very too noisy!" he barked.

His Trade needed some improvement.

Artus said nothing, but he was still glaring at Tyvian when he sat back down to continue assaulting the smuggler's clothing. The process was becoming

more and more nakedly metaphorical by the second.
Tyvian knew the argument was far from over, but he
was too tired, filthy, and hungry to consider pursuing
it on his own.

The gnolls had with them an impressive collection
of dead birds and squirrels—already plucked and prepared to cook—hanging from the lanyards they wore
about their torsos. Leave it to gnolls to take a harried
escape into the wilderness in the dark of night and
turn it into an opportunity to collect breakfast, lunch,
and dinner.

Hool handed her portion of her catch off to Brana
and crouched next to Tyvian. "We saw only two or
three of the little people this morning, but they were
going the wrong way. They are good trackers, but
they are scared of something, so they make stupid decisions."

Tyvian nodded. "They're afraid of the open—if an
Eretherian patrol spots them, they're good as dead.
After we eat, we move south a few more miles and
we'll be out of the forest entirely. Nothing to worry
about then."

Artus grunted sarcastically and opted to abandon
Tyvian's shirt in order to assist Brana with setting a
campfire.

Tyvian couldn't let it pass. "Oh, what's your problem now?"

Artus rolled his eyes.

Tyvian sat up straighter. "Out with it!"

"Nothing." Artus groaned, breaking a stick over his knee. "Nothing is wrong. Everything is super fine and dandy-like."

Hool laid her ears back. "Stop being sarcastic."

"Stop sarcazamazy!" Brana said, punching Artus in the arm.

"Ow!" Artus rubbed his arm and then hooked Brana's ankle with his leg and swept the gnoll pup off his feet. He then leapt on top of him and the battle was begun. Artus worked on getting a headlock while Brana scrambled around on the ground, working his leverage to try and make for a reversal.

Hool was on her feet in an instant, offering advice. "Artus, get his arm behind him! Brana! Quick now! Use your legs! *Brrghh! Roof! Whrraggh!*"

The two juveniles rolled around, crushing the budding campfire and scattering their supplies. Artus got on top of Brana, straddling the gnoll's stomach, and planted a few good punches into Brana's chest (punching in the nose was off-limits except in real fights, Hool insisted). Brana, though, caught Artus's forearm in his jaws and immobilized him without breaking the skin or his arm (since actual biting was off-limits except in real fights). They struggled in this impasse for a moment or two.

"Groin!" Hool barked, leaning down beside the pile. "Go for the groin!"

Tyvian watched the impromptu hand-to-hand combat lesson progress with a sigh, noting how his shirt remained filthy and wet, his breakfast lost, and the prospect of a campfire and a meal in the near future was becoming more slight. "This is my life now," he said, putting his head back against a tree trunk. "This is what it's all come to."

He held up his ring hand, where the simple iron band seemed to glower at him.

He glowered back.

CHAPTER 3

CIVILIZED COMPANY

Tyvian didn't say much as they made their way from the outskirts of the forest and southwest into the Eretherian Gap, following a worn, wagon-rutted highway called the Forest Road, which would take them to Derby—the closest thing the northern reaches of Eretheria had to a city. It was there that Tyvian planned to fence the Heart of Flowing Sunlight. It was also there that Artus expected Tyvian to blow that money on buying old and rare books. Again.

They had strung their still soaked clothing between them on a rope to dry as they walked. The sun was hot on Artus's shoulders as he followed Tyvian, but he didn't complain. Tyvian was always accusing him of complaining, so he kept his mouth shut just to prove him wrong.

Artus could tell by the way Tyvian walked that he was wrestling with something and that it wasn't a time to ask questions. Anytime the smuggler had his shoulders tight and his head down meant he was "upset," and if he was looking at his ring hand a lot, that meant he was currently arguing with himself. Then there was the fact that he was mostly naked, wearing only a pair of underbreeches and soggy boots. Disturbing him in this state was a good way to get a tongue-lashing.

Artus knew to read Tyvian's body language because of Tyvian himself. The smuggler had spent months teaching him to understand what he wanted without any words, saying that such information could likely save both of their lives someday. Artus found the instruction immensely confusing, since only a few mistakes would result in Tyvian being so frustrated that Artus had trouble seeing anything else in the way he held himself. He never did get the hang of "worried," "cautious," "happy," or "relaxed," but Artus had become a master of noticing frustration and anger. He could tell if Tyvian was angry from the front, from behind, from above, from beneath, in the dark. He could see frustration in the way he held his shoulders, his sword, the way he moved his hands, the way he held his feet—if nothing else, Tyvian had trained him well in being able to notice when he shouldn't bother the smuggler.

So, Artus spent his time watching the scenery as they walked. He had to say that of all the places he'd been in his life, Eretheria was the prettiest. The great pasture of the gap, stretching from the forest in the north to the farms of Lake Country in the south, rolled golden-green across the gentle swell of low hills. There were small copses here and there, clustered around natural springs or ancient rock formations. The trees were of species Artus didn't know—tall, broad-leafed, with yellow and white flowers blooming under the summer sunlight. In the distance he could make out cattle ranches—long, clean buildings with colorful shingled roofs and glass windows, completely lacking in the fortifications seen on every ranch in his homeland. "This is Eretheria," the pretty little buildings proclaimed, "there is no danger here."

Artus knew that wasn't strictly true, though. He thought back to their escape from Draketower a month or so before—the riders atop the griffons, their enchanted bolts screaming through the air. He thought of poor Saley—the girl Tyvian had tried to "rescue" from the lord of Draketower—now lying beneath a cairn of stones by the side of a nameless lake.

Draketower had been Tyvian's last refuge in Eretheria, and burning his bridges with Sir Cameron had put them all out in the woods. They'd been eating like gnolls, sleeping under trees, and scrambling just to stay alive, and all because Draketower had been such a gods-damned fiasco. And it was all Tyvian's fault.

Artus knew it, Hool knew it, Brana *probably* knew it, but Tyvian *certainly* knew it.

Artus had wanted to bring it up before breakfast, but he didn't. That was a fight he wasn't itching to repeat. It was coming, though. Sooner or later, Tyvian Reldamar had to admit that he could be wrong.

"Art!" Brana butted Artus from behind with his head. For Brana, no communication was complete without some kind of physical contact. Well, assuming he liked you, of course.

"What? Hey, quit it!" Brana was fumbling with Artus's pack—the only one still usable after their escape from the woodkin—and Artus tried to push the gnoll pup away. Brana, though, saw it coming and retreated from the push, letting Artus get off-balance. Before Artus could recover, Brana kicked him in the knee and Artus found himself flat on his back. "Ow!"

The rope holding their drying clothes fell to the ground. Tyvian whirled, his eyebrows pinched together in his *I'm not messing around* face. "Dammit! Don't soil the clothes, you juvenile louts!"

Brana had his tongue hanging out the side of his mouth and was grinning wildly. "Horses!"

Taking off his pack, Artus rolled into a crouch, rubbing his head as though he were stunned, but then lunged at Brana's feet and knocked him down. Artus pressed his advantage by grabbing a great fistful of Brana's mane just at the base of his skull and yanking so the gnoll's head went back and Artus could wrap an arm around the his neck. He squeezed for all he was worth, well aware that he couldn't hurt Brana's twenty-inch neck from this angle even if he wanted to; he was about to go for what he called a "gnoll-ride." Brana kicked and bucked and rolled, trying to knock Artus off, and Artus simply held on for dear life, his legs wrapped around Brana's midsection and his arms around his neck, laughing wildly. "I got you! Got you! You . . . *oof* . . . can't win this time!"

"Will you two idiots stop that!" Tyvian snapped. He stood over them, frowning, as he pulled on his mostly dry shirt. "There's somebody coming! Artus— get dressed! Quickly now!"

Brana grunted a bark that indicated a mixture of the sentiments *obviously* and *I just said that* and then added "Horses!" in his usual enthusiastic Trade.

Artus let Brana go, and the gnoll gave him a punch in the arm that hurt far more than the Brana probably thought. "Ow! Will you cut it out?"

Tyvian hoisted Artus to his feet. "Brana, where's your mother?"

Brana jerked his head northward. "Watch for little people." Hool had been carefully keeping an eye out for any Forest Children coming out of the woods for them, but none had materialized, just as Tyvian had predicted.

Tyvian nodded, kicking off his boots and shaking the dust off his breeches. "Go and find her and tell her there are some people coming and that the two of you should stay hidden. Understand?"

Brana didn't say anything and was already scampering off in the direction his mother had gone before Tyvian had stopped talking. The smuggler watched him go, grimacing. "You know, I have really no idea what that gnoll is thinking most of the time."

Artus smiled. There honestly weren't a lot of things he did better than Tyvian, but this was one of them. "He was probably looking for an excuse to ditch us for a while now. He was getting pretty bored on this road."

Tyvian grunted as he laced his shirt. "It's about time we ran into something interesting. Gods, but this shirt is an abysmal ruin! My kingdom for a bloody tailor!"

Artus looked ahead on the road. A cloud of dust was rising into the pale sky and getting closer, but not very rapidly. "Riders?"

"Heralds. Something's going on." Tyvian shook his head and cursed at the wrinkles in his cravat. He muttered something about having to "tie it Verisi style" in a way that made it sound a lot like a curse.

"Heralds for who?" Artus scratched his head.

Tyvian glared at him. "For *whom*. Are you going to get dressed, or what? Move, boy—those riders could be on us in minutes, and I don't want to have to disavow you as a traveling lunatic I met on the road."

Artus scowled. "What's the big deal?"

"Provincial nobility. Have to be on our best behavior, look our best." Tyvian pulled on his socks, cursing at a hole that revealed his big toe. "Gods, why does this nonsense always happen to me?"

Artus shook his head and began to pull on his breeches. "But you hate provincial nobility. You think they're stupid wannabes or something, right?"

Tyvian had on his jacket and was adjusting his sleeves. "They also have *money*, Artus, which we currently lack and of which we need a great deal. Now get on your damned clothes and act like a manservant before that herald,"—he pointed to the silhouette of a rider on the horizon who was carrying a pennant of some kind—"gets here and thinks we've just waylaid some merchants and stolen their clothing."

"I'm going, I'm going!" Artus snarled, hastily pulling on his shirt. "This has bloodstains on it."

Tyvian threw his hands in the air. "We were attacked, all right? Hurry!"

Artus got himself presentable (by his standards, not Tyvian's) by the time the herald was within earshot. Tyvian waved him down. He was a man in light mail—a man-at-arms, not a knight—and wearing red and yellow, with the head of a boar on the pennant and also on his tabard. Artus didn't bother puzzling out the heraldry.

"Halloo, the travelers!" the herald called.

Tyvian waved back, showing both his hands. "Halloo, the rider! May I approach?"

"What are you doing?" Artus whispered. "What are you going to tell him?

Tyvian sighed. "My depleted state has reduced me to wheedling favors from provincial nobility as a matter of course these days. Don't worry about it—I'll be back shortly, I shouldn't wonder."

Tyvian set off to meet the rider, who stayed mounted during their conversation. Artus folded his arms and watched, wishing he could hear what was going on. He *never* got to know what was going on. It was Tyvian's life, and he was just the damned help—his opinions were completely irrelevant, his ideas were stupid, and saints forbid he actually be *told* anything useful! He took to kicking over anthills while he waited.

In a few minutes Tyvian came back, riding behind the herald in the saddle. "Ronger here will take us back to the camp of his master, Sir Banber Galt of Korthold."

Artus looked around. "Where do I ride?"

Tyvian laughed. "Artus, you run, obviously." He nudged the herald. "Where do I ride? Eh?"

The herald laughed, his handlebar moustache quivering. Artus glared at them both. "Yeah," he muttered, "har har."

The herald nudged his horse into a slow trot, but Artus still had to jog to keep up. He had to keep it up for miles, too. All the while, Tyvian and Ronger the Herald entertained each other with pointless gossip and obviously exaggerated anecdotes. Artus noted that Tyvian wasn't bothering to conceal his identity. Ronger had a lot of questions about the life of a famous outlaw, apparently, and was duly impressed with Tyvian's answers.

They never once inquired how *he* was doing, though. The more he ran and sweated and stumbled, the darker his mood became. He figured the *least* Tyvian could do was offer to switch on occasion—

have him run for a bit while he rested. Of course not, though. He was Tyvian Reldamar, famous smuggler and criminal mastermind, and Hann forbid he should soil his precious shirt with some actual physical labor. Artus would have spat, but his mouth was like a desert. Any residual sympathy he had for Tyvian over Drake-tower dried up along with it.

Eventually they crested a rise and found themselves looking down at a small encampment. It involved a series of brightly colored tents and pavilions flying various heraldic symbols that Artus knew Tyvian had tutored him in at some point in the past but that he had immediately discarded as pointless information and forgotten about. There were at least thirty people milling around, and Artus counted a few dozen horses staked out to graze. He suspected Tyvian was going to stake him along with them and tell him to eat grass.

Tyvian dismounted at the edge of camp and saluted the herald. "Thank you for the ride, Ronger. Please tell Lord Bamber that I will attend him presently, should he wish it."

Ronger saluted back and rode off.

Artus was leaning over with his hands on his knees, forcing air to wheeze in and out of his burning lungs. "You . . . bastard."

Tyvian slapped him on the back. "Cheer up, Artus—the exercise is good for you. Once you've sufficiently recovered yourself, get some water and meet me at the big red-and-yellow tent at the center of this whole affair."

"Why? You need me to carry you in on my back?"

Tyvian rolled his eyes. "Oh, yes—poor Artus, so abused. Let's forget that I dragged your unconscious body out of a lake no more than a month ago, or that I saved you from plant monsters *yesterday*, or that I—"

"Fine, fine! I get it!"

Tyvian nodded and then prodded at Artus's sweat-soaked shirt. "Hmmm . . . I'll have to get this replaced. Have to have you dressed your best, after all."

"Why?" Artus blurted, sitting down. "What the hell are we doing here? Just bloody tell me!"

Tyvian smiled. "We're going to a battle."

Artus nodded, but it was a full second before the words actually sank in. "Wait . . . what?"

But Tyvian was already gone. Artus was left to dip his head in the horse trough all by himself . . .

. . . with the other pack animals.

CHAPTER 4

THE BATTLE OF THE SEASON

Eretheria was a patchwork land of petty fiefdoms—small earldoms and peerages and counties all in a constant game of intricate and ancient diplomacy that stretched back all the way to the fall of the last Warlock Kings and the end of the Second Age of the world. Tyvian had heard it argued that modern day Eretheria was, in essence, a better picture of what the world was like at that time than any other place. Essentially, everywhere *started* with Eretheria's brand of convoluted feudalism, and over the centuries everywhere *else* in the world had refined and improved that system.

Eretheria was a throwback, a political relic, a bizarre fossil of the ancient world here in this age of sorcerous enlightenment.

Tyvian found the place delightful.

One of the best things about Eretheria (in Tyvian's opinion) was its complete lack of any kind of unified law. What was legal in one little provincial earldom could be illegal in the next one over and never even addressed in the backwater peerage up in the hills. Officially, of course, there was the High Law, which was decided by the Congress of Peers and was theoretically enforced by the Defenders of the Balance. The High Laws themselves, however, were primarily designed to safeguard the station of the nobility and of their ancestral lands.

That morning, Tyvian and Artus were astride borrowed horses on their way to witness one of the most common ways the High Law was settled between disputing nobility—a pitched battle on the field of honor. It was another beautiful morning, the sun spilling pink light across the dew-coated grass as far as the eye could see. There was a soft breeze coming from the south, making the pennants of those in the spectator party display their colors with rampant flair as they all rode together toward the town of Derby.

Yesterday afternoon Tyvian had presented himself to those going to watch the battle with the introduction of his new herald friend, Ronger. There was one peer, Sir Banber Galt of Korthold, and one peeress, Dame Margess Vane of Teller Valley, each from small holdings in the surrounding territories. They had with them a collection of their retainers, ensigns, heralds, and champions who were charged with the pitching of tents, the carrying of flags, and the fighting of duels, should any of those things prove necessary. The two low-ranking nobles were delighted to have Tyvian along in the same way children were delighted to find a raccoon living under their porch stairs—he was an entertaining oddity, both fascinating and a bit dangerous, and they couldn't help but wonder about everything he did. Tyvian, conversely, was delighted to have their company in that it meant two things: firstly, that the food he would be eating for the next day or so would be a grand improvement over Hool's roast squirrels, and secondly, that these people had the connections he needed to acquire money, favors, and gossip that could prove crucially useful to him in his diminished state.

Tyvian, therefore, was doing his best to appear dashing, heroic, and fascinating. Even in borrowed clothes and astride a Corrissar mare that had a tendency to bite, he felt he cut a dashing figure. Artus, in his stained servant's garb, looked the part of rough-and-tumble man-servant pretty well while astride a big Benethoran Red that was as mild as the Eretherian summertime and strong as a bull. Together, they looked every bit their reputation. Tyvian only wished his clothes fit better and that Artus were a bit less skinny and had more than patches of scraggly facial hair.

Artus was a surprisingly good rider, and sat so

easily in the saddle that Tyvian wondered why they hadn't used horses much before. Then he remembered Hool and Brana, and remembered why. Gnolls and horses didn't get along very well, in the same way that wolves and sheep were disinclined to keep each other's company. Tyvian found himself recalling his gnoll-free existence rather fondly, even if it seemed only dimly memorable. Gods, had it been so long since he was civilized?

A trumpet sounded on the road ahead, and Tyvian could see a horseman in green livery and mail watching their approach while a fellow on foot in the same livery, minus the armor, was sounding the horn. The fellow on foot was also holding a banner bearing the tree-and-sword device of Sir Mardan Pherielle—one-half of that day's scheduled military conflict.

Artus sidled up beside Tyvian, causing his horse to skip sideways a pace and snort. Tyvian did his best to make it look like she had done that on purpose. "You sure about that horse?" Artus asked.

Tyvian scowled. "I only need her for the afternoon."

Artus nodded ahead, where advance riders from their spectating party were heading to meet the Pherielle men. "Is this trouble?"

"No, Artus, just a formality. The fellow up there is just informing our party of the battle that will be taking place nearby, while our friends' retainers are telling *him* that we're here to watch and not participate. The rest of their conversation, I imagine, is going to be a discussion of where we can pitch our tents."

Artus cocked an eyebrow. "Are you *sure* we aren't going to be fighting?"

Tyvian nodded. "Of course. Eretherian warfare is the most civilized example of the art in the world. We're neutral parties of good breeding, and so long as we don't go charging off to support one side or the other—which would be an unpardonable breach of etiquette, mind you—we've nothing to worry about from either side."

Artus mulled this over for a second. "Are people going to get hurt?"

"Obviously. It's a battle, Artus, not an equestrian competition. I expect that the Lord Pherielle and His Grace the Earl of Derby have consented to all the standard rules of combat. People will die, but probably not as many as you would expect."

"And why are they fighting?"

Tyvian shrugged. "Money, ultimately—everything's about money. Evidently there's a natural spring a few miles from here that once was part of the Pherielle fief but was annexed by the current Earl of Derby's grandfather in a dispute over debt. The current Lord Pherielle has declared the current earl's claim over the spring to be expired, citing some law dating back forty years, but the earl has refused to relinquish his rights."

Artus scratched his head. "Is fresh water rare around here or something?"

"Hardly. This is more an issue of family credit history than it is of necessity."

"Why don't they settle it with a duel?"

Tyvian sighed. "The Earl of Derby is an old man. Lord Pherielle can't very well challenge him to a duel without looking quite the cad at court, which means the next time the earl petitions the congress for a law pertaining to . . ." Tyvian shook his head. "Look, it's complicated, all right?"

Artus was frowning. "So these two rich guys are gonna get a bunch of peasants killed for no reason and . . . and then they're going to shake hands and that's *it*?"

Tyvian nudged his mount away from a retainer's horse that was drawing too close. "You'd rather they fought an *actual* war, then? Should the Earl of Derby sack Pherielle's castle and murder all his servants? Should Pherielle set fire to Derby, pillage the elderly earl's granaries, and then poison his wells? Would that be better?"

"I think they should just leave the small folk out of it," Artus countered. "Don't seem fair to die for some lord who don't give a care about you over some stupid spring you don't even need."

Tyvian was about to open his mouth to respond but thought better of it. Artus was still angry with him for . . . for whatever reason—existing, apparently. It wouldn't do to have an argument here. A peasant boy snarling at his betters would *not* be well-received among the peerage.

Truth be told, Tyvian didn't especially approve of the comparatively recent inclusion of peasant levies in

Eretheria's little squabbles either. In the pre-Illini War age, it had all been handled by professional mercenaries. *It's not why I'm here*, he reminded himself. Well, perhaps not himself—perhaps he was simply reminding the ring to mind its manners.

The observation area was the flat top of a hill that stood a quarter mile from where the forces of Pherielle and of Derby were arrayed. The pavilions and tents of the spectators were erected in a matter of minutes, and Tyvian found himself sitting on a folding chair beside Sir Banber and Dame Margess, plus an array of their servants and Dame Margess's champion, Sir Denoux Collierre. They had a viewing glass—a simple crystal set with a modest enchantment designed to magnify distant objects—that was passed back and forth as the group remarked upon the look of certain men-at-arms and speculated as to the maneuvers each side might employ to secure victory.

"Mardan has more light and medium cavalry," Sir Banber said, popping a cherry in his mouth and spitting the pit. He had been dropping Pherielle's familiar name consistently since they sat down, and Tyvian imagined it was because Banber expected Pherielle to win and wanted to appear close to him. "I expect he'll flank Derby's infantry blocks and send the whole column into disarray."

"Pardon me, milord." Collierre nodded his deference to Banber even while squinting through the viewing glass. He had a face that did squinting well, Tyvian thought—it complemented his unusually long nose. "I do not mean to disagree, but it appears as though Derby has employed several blocks of mercenary pike-men. A charge of cavalry against that would be very costly and likely unsuccessful."

Banber grunted. "Galaspiner riffraff. A rank of Eretherian knights in armor will scatter them, pikes or no. Didn't Perwynnon do as much at Calassa?"

"Those were Dellorans, milord, not Galaspiners," Tyvian said. "And Perwynnon had the advantage of surprise, not to mention the fact that Finn Cadogan—a mercenary and a Galaspiner, mind you—had secured that surprise by his raid the night before."

Banber and Collierre glared at Tyvian for a moment, and Tyvian let them do the mental arithmetic about his surname on their own. Collierre got there first. "Are you a relation to Lyrelle Reldamar, the archmage present at Calassa?"

"The *Earless* Lyrelle Reldamar is my mother, sir. I've been hearing stories about Perwynnon and Cado-gan and the rest of them since I was a child."

The mention of his mother's rank was sufficient to change the posture of Tyvian's noble companions almost immediately. He found it rather amusing that while they weren't impressed with his mother's status as one of the world's most powerful sorcerers, the fact that she held the title "Earless" was sufficient to make them sit up straighter.

The Dame Margess spoke up next. She was a

woman of perhaps his mother's age, maybe a bit older, but she clearly couldn't afford the *cherille* necessary to keep her hair from graying and her hands from looking brittle. Her eyes, though, were sharp and as dexterous as they probably had been in her youth. "How would your lady mother deal with this battle, then, Master Reldamar?"

Tyvian weighed his options and decided to answer truthfully. "My mother has always found battles to be tedious affairs, milady. She would prefer to pepper her enemy's camp with so many spies that her victory would be assured without the need to loose an arrow."

Sir Banber snorted. "Typical womanly behavior. Give me a good horse and a lance in my hand any day over spies."

Tyvian shrugged. "I believe Banric Sahand shares a similar opinion, milord."

Banber's beetle-black eyebrows lowered, but the knight let the slight pass. Tyvian guessed the fellow wasn't entirely sure whether he had just been insulted or not. "Well, Sahand was quite the general, you have to admit."

"Why're you talking like Sahand ain't around?" Artus asked, his voice a little too loud. As Tyvian's manservant, he'd been standing behind Tyvian's left shoulder the whole time. Everybody stopped what they were doing to stare at him.

Tyvian gave Artus a private glare. "Artus, would you mind seeing how well our porters are catching up?"

"Porters?"

"You know—the *porters* we have *following* us carrying a number of our *things?*" Tyvian clenched his teeth and opened his eyes as widely as possible. If the damn fool boy had bothered learning all the nonverbal cues he'd been trying to teach him all these months, gaffes like this could have been completely avoided by now. It was enough to make Tyvian scream, but rather than do so verbally, he did it with his eyes.

Understanding, or a reasonable facsimile thereof, dawned over Artus's face. "Ohhhh . . . right. Porters. Okay—I'll be right back."

"Don't rush." Tyvian smiled as his eyes kept screaming.

After Artus had left, Banber cleared his throat. "A Northron boy, correct?"

Tyvian nodded. "I believe he's from Benethor, sir."

Banber nodded and grunted as though that explained things.

The sound of drums beating an advance was carried to them on the breeze. One could see the organized ranks of white-and-green Pherielle's peasant levies marching at a slow clip toward the massed blue-and-yellow ranks of Derby. Tyvian could just barely make out the glitter of arrows in flight raining down on the advancing Pherielle forces; he saw some men fall, and those that had shields raised them.

Banber, peering through the viewing glass, nodded his approval. "Pherielle is looking to test the resolve of the Derby line. Good, good—nice and straightforward. If the mercenaries hold, they'll be caught up fighting with the ranks and won't be able to stop the flanking maneuver."

Tyvian nodded, squinting against the sunlight to watch the little shapes of men in ranks marching on each other. He judged it would be another minute or two before the battle was joined and, from the weak showing made by Derby's peasant archers, that battle would be ugly for both sides. His ring began to tingle a bit; it shared Artus's objection to sitting back and watching peasants kill each other over their lords' pride. He pointedly ignored it and held up a silver chalice to one of the various servants standing about. "Wine, if you please."

"There goes the cavalry!" Banber hooted, passing the viewing glass to Collierre. "A flanking maneuver, just as I said!"

After inspecting the battle, Collierre handed the viewing glass to Tyvian, who held it before his eyes and let the images coalesce in the crystal rather than trying to squint through it like some Kalsaari spyglass. He could see the advance blocks of Pherielle's peasant levies now charging full-bore at the massed Galaspiner pikes. At that moment, Pherielle's reserve line of mail-clad men-at-arms on horseback was thundering off to the left flank and beginning to wheel so that they would smash into the Galaspiner formations from the side as the mercenaries were fighting off the levies to the front. Tyvian tsked. "Pherielle's lost it—sprung the trap too soon."

"I beg your pardon, sir, but that's poppycock,"

NO GOOD DEED 59

Banber countered, chuckling. "Even Collierre here agrees with me now—look at how well Mardan's cavalry are wheeling! They'll hit those pike blocks all at once, and nary an arrow feathered in them!"

Collierre nodded. "It looks bad for Derby, I must say."

"Have you watched many battles, Master Reldamar?" Dame Margess asked, accepting the viewing glass from him with a grateful nod.

"Not especially," Tyvian said, shrugging.

"Yet you still think Pherielle will lose?" Collierre squinted at Tyvian, who wondered if Collierre's eyes actually didn't open all the way.

Tyvian grinned at him. "Care to make it interesting?"

"Do I detect a wager?" Banber tore into a roast chicken leg and popped a few grapes in after it.

Tyvian sipped his wine and narrowly avoided making a face; gods, the swill was as sweet as mead. Why was it so damned hard to find a decent wine? That bottle he'd shared with Cam at Draketower would likely be the last decent bottle he'd have until he reached Saldor. He missed the taste of decent wine every day. Every damned day.

"Well?" Banber asked, rubbing the chicken grease off his hands and onto the doublet of one of his valets.

Tyvian pushed the memory of good wine out of his mind. "I say Derby and his mercenaries hold the line and win the day, and you say Pherielle routs the sellswords and drives the earl from the field. Shall we say a hundred marks to whomever is correct?"

"Done." Banber nodded.

Collierre paused, squinting at his mistress. Dame Margess smiled and nodded. "Oh, go on, Denoux. I agree with you—I think poor old Derby is going to have the worst of it."

Tyvian grinned. "Settled, then."

They sat back to watch, with Artus getting back a few minutes later. The peasant levies pressing the Galaspin mercenary front not only failed to break through the line, but broke themselves on the merciless yard-long tips of the sellsword pikes. This part of the battle was going in that direction even before the cavalry made their charge. There was a complex trumpet call from the mercenary lines, and the block reformed into a pike square that deployed its weapons to both flank and front at the same time. The result was the cavalry not so much riding the Galaspiners down as crashing into them and making an awful mess. In short order, the screams of horses and men could be faintly heard over Sir Banber's chewing.

"See—I told you. They'll break," Banber announced, looking pleased.

Dame Margess was pale. "Sweet Hann, why don't they ask for quarter?"

Artus pointed at the rear portions of the Derby line, where the archers were mostly standing around chatting with each other and Derby's smaller force of cavalry was deployed in a line and motionless as trees. "Isn't that where the earl is? What's he doing?"

"Getting his money's worth." Tyvian felt the ring begin to squeeze him—not the burning pain from some terrible act of his own, but rather the steady pressure of a wrong he was allowing to happen.

As he understood, Artus's face turned red, then green. "That's awful."

Tyvian wiped sweat from his forehead. He had gotten pretty good at tolerating the ring's lesser jabs, but it was still damned uncomfortable. He kept his voice cool and even. "It's their job. Derby paid them to hold the line, so they're holding it. The company purser will charge Derby a silver crown per man wounded and two per man dead. I will bet you anything that there's an accountant at the earl's side calculating figures for him at this very moment. Better mercenaries bleed than his own retainers, but as soon as the price gets too high, the horses will be sent in."

"Unless they break," Banber added.

The Galaspiner mercenaries didn't break. After another minute of ugly combat that was difficult to follow even with the viewing glass, the Derby cavalry got the signal to charge. They swept down upon the disorganized horsemen of Pherielle and broke them in a single maneuver, then swept back to clear the field of those peasant levies who had rallied to their banners and were making another advance on the beleaguered pikemen. By the time the Pherielle standard was struck from the field, the whole battle had taken about a half hour.

Tyvian pulled Artus aside as the battle was ending, "Go tell Hool and Brana to meet us outside Derby in about an hour." Artus nodded and went, though he muttered about it. With that done, there just remained the pleasant business of collecting his winnings.

Tyvian was gracious in victory—it *always* paid to be gracious when winning a bet. Sir Banber, cheeks red from too much sun, ran a hand through his thinning hair and said he'd be damned. "You're not a soldier. How did you know they wouldn't break?"

"While I might not be a soldier, milord, I am a keen judge of human nature. Consider this: you're a mercenary who works in Eretheria and you've been told a group of noble spectators will be watching the battle. Assuming you wish to keep making a living at this and further assuming that you would like to be well paid, what do you do?"

Light dawned on Sir Banber's sunburned face. "I'd stay! I'd hold! Damn, a performance like that means I can charge any price I please to the next fellow who needs some pikes. Astute, Master Reldamar, I must admit. I'll send the money along tonight. Where can you be reached?"

Tyvian eyed Dame Margess, who was deep in intense concentration with a man in her livery who looked very much like a financial advisor of some sort. A little ways off to the side, Collierre was busy squinting at his feet as he kicked a few clumps of sod around aimlessly. It was the very picture of a woman worried about her finances and a champion worried about his job. "We'll be staying in Derby—I'll give your man Ronger the name of an inn before I leave. I'm afraid I can't just say where at the moment, given my—"

Banber waved off the explanation. "Of course, of course! Naturally, a man of your station has unusual living arrangements. Quite to be expected—very dashing, in its way. The women must love it, eh?"

Tyvian tried to smile, but all he could think about was the girl, Saley, smiling at him mere minutes before he got her killed. He felt briefly ill.

"Are you perfectly all right?" Banber blinked at him.

Tyvian forced a laugh. "Yes, yes. Too much sun, is all."

"That reminds me," Banber went on, grinning broadly, "I have just the thing that might cheer you up."

"Oh?" Tyvian tried to conjure hopefulness in his eyes, but didn't quite pull it off. The things that cheered Sir Banber up and the things that were likely to cheer Tyvian up at just that moment weren't likely to intersect.

"Caravan came up through my territory last week, by way of Saldor. Brought the most interesting gossip."

Tyvian sighed: gossip, of course. To the Eretherian, juicy gossip was the cure for almost every malady. Were Tyvian pierced through the heart with a Forest Child arrow, Sir Banber would probably come in to tell him what kind of underwear the Count of Ayventry wore to bed. The arrow would consequently be expected to remove itself from his chest out of outrage and embarrassment.

"I recall hearing you were once pursued by a Mage Defender by the name of Alafarr, is that not correct?"

The mention of Myreon almost made him jump.

He nodded, trying to look neutral. "She was some-thing of a nemesis of mine, yes."

Banber continued, his enthusiasm building. "It seems that your old nemesis has been convicted of a crime. Very serious, from what I was told."

Tyvian stiffened. "What? That doesn't sound like Myr—like *Alafarr* to me. What crime could it possibly be?"

"Well *that's* the interesting part, it seems." Banber chuckled, his eyes twinkling, "*Smuggling!* Would you believe it? How's that for irony—you must have rubbed off on her, old boy. Ha!"

Tyvian blinked. "That doesn't make any sense at all. What possible reason would she have to smuggle something?"

Banber shrugged, still chuckling. "Oh, just a bit of rumor—seems to have struck you the wrong way, eh?"

"I beg your pardon, sir." Tyvian wiped the sweat from his brow. "Too much sun, as I said. It was a plea-sure meeting you."

Banber favored Tyvian with the slightest of bows. "And you, sir. Give my regards to your noble mother."

"I will," Tyvian lied, and was pleased that the ring had the wisdom not to pinch him for it. If Sir Banber knew what his mother would say to Banber's greet-ings, the rest of the man's hair would fall out.

After Banber headed off, Artus came jogging back from his errand. "Is that it, then? Can we get out of here? These people give me the creeps, no matter how much money they've got." Artus got a good look at Tyvian's face and froze. "You okay?"

Tyvian shook himself. "Yes, yes. Fine. Hold on." He pushed Banber's gossip from his mind and tried to refocus his attention on the Dame Margess. The focus wouldn't come.

Myreon? Smuggling? It just wasn't possible. He couldn't believe it.

"Master Reldamar?" Dame Margess called to him just after she had dismissed her accountant. Tyvian stepped forward and bowed to her as gracefully as he could manage, which was to say he imagined he bowed more gracefully than any man the dame had met outside of an Eretherian noble court.

The gesture was not lost on her. She blushed ever so slightly. "Master Reldamar, you flatter me. I have come to settle the issue of my champion's wager."

Myreon had to have been framed—that was the only possible explanation. *But why? By whom?*

"Master Reldamar?" Dame Margess cocked her head. "Are you all right?"

Tyvian nodded, trying to shake off the idea of Myreon Alafarr in a penitentiary garden. "My apologies, milady—too much sun for me, it seems." He cleared his throat. "It occurs to me that I have put you and your champion in an awkward position. As Master Collierre seems a gentleman of utmost quality, it would pain me to put a strain upon your trust in him, no matter how slight. It is for this reason I beg you to void the terms of our wager."

Dame Margess blinked and put a hand to her chest. "Such a thing is absolutely unnecessary, sir! You have won the wager, and so I shall see it paid, be it one hundred marks or one thousand!"

The response was practically scripted; it was like the peerage were made to rehearse the same speech by the same army of stern Akrallian tutors. "I must insist—I will accept no gold from you, milady. I regret making the wager in the first place; it was the work of my pride and vanity, nothing more, and such base emotions have no place in genteel society."

Behind him, Tyvian heard Artus mutter, *"Gimme a break . . ."*

The dame was not so cynical, however. "Well, there must be *something* I can do to settle this debt. Even if it is not gold I owe you, I feel I owe you my goodwill and thanks for your most honorable behavior, especially for a foreigner. In this regard *I* must insist—what may I do for you?"

The original plan had been to request access to the dame's private library—she had the look of a reader, if not a scholar—but Tyvian found that idea flying out of his head in favor of a different one. A new and probably crazy idea. A plan was forming around it, even as he stood there, constructing itself in its full complexity so quickly it was as though it had always been there, waiting to be uncovered.

Tyvian bowed to Dame Margess and took a deep breath, "Well, now that you mention it, do you have any good courtly enchanters you could recommend?"

CHAPTER 5

SHROUDS

Artus peered through the curtains of the Gentleman Bastard's second-floor window. It was a good inn and a good room—the windows were lead-paned glass and relatively new, the curtains thick and clean, and the three beds had freshly stuffed straw mattresses with thick linen sheets. A small iron stove squatted in the corner of the room, more than sufficient for cold nights.

Even after living in the West for several years now, Artus still found himself bug-eyed at its wealth. A room like this was fit for your average Benethoran knight, and all Tyvian did was slap a pair of silver crowns on the owner's desk downstairs and it had been theirs, no questions asked. Artus was fairly certain they didn't even *have* inns like this back home.

The streets of Derby were quiet, finally. The celebration of the earl's victory had breathed its last, with the remaining drunken stragglers of the day's merrymaking slowly weaving their way home in pairs of twos and threes. Artus found himself scowling at them all. What in Hann's name did they think they were *celebrating,* anyway?

"Come away from the window," Hool barked. Artus glanced behind him to see the big gnoll's eyes gleaming in the candlelight. "You will be seen!"

Artus shrugged. "Who cares if I'm seen? Nobody knows who I am anyway."

Hool's coppery gaze remained fixed on him. "I know who you are. You are Artus and you are mad at Tyvian for a stupid reason and so you're doing a stupid thing."

"I'm not mad at anybody."

Hool snorted. "If someone sees you from the street and tries to kill you, I will not help. I do not help stupid people."

Artus let the curtain fall closed and laid back on his bed. Hool and Brana never used beds, so he had one all to himself. This beat some of the roadside inns in Galaspin where he and Tyvian had one bed to share between them, which naturally meant he had to sleep on the floor. "Nobody's after us, Hool. We ain't seen an assassin, a bounty hunter, or a Defender in the better part of a year. Reldamar's just paranoid, is all."

"Just because you don't see something, that doesn't mean something isn't after you." Hool settled herself into a ball on the floor right next to Brana, who was currently snoring away. It sounded as if somebody were sawing boards. "When I hunt, do you think my prey sees me before I kill it?"

Artus scowled—he hated it when Hool used hunting analogies, and she used them all the time. "That's different."

"It is not."

Artus threw up his hands. "Look, even if you're right and everybody in the world is after Tyvian, that don't mean they're after *me*! Nobody even notices I'm here when Tyvian's in the room. You didn't see it, but them fancy folk we watched the battle with didn't even know I was alive, but they looked at him like he was . . . I dunno . . . something pretty fancy anyway. It's like that everywhere! Saints, I'll bet that Kalsaari princess or whatever—the one whose hair I pulled?—I bet she don't even remember what color my hair is. I'm a nobody, so what's it matter if I look out the stupid window?"

"Not being noticed is good," Hool said, yawning. "If nobody sees you, you can do whatever you want."

Artus grunted and thought, You'd think that, wouldn't you? He didn't say it, though. Arguing with Hool was a waste of time. She had no conception of what it was like being human, let along being *him*. She just thought everything she said was right and that was it, no arguing allowed. Even Tyvian had to give in to her eventually.

Artus tried not to think of just how similar that made Hool to his own, real mother. The very idea was sobering. What would his real mother say? He thought about it for a number of minutes before giving up. Every time he tried to imagine it, he discovered that she was speaking with Hool's voice. He tried not to think about that too hard.

"What are we doing here anyway?" Artus asked. Hool didn't immediately answer, "Hool?"

"We are trying to sleep. You are making noise." Hool made a hissing noise that was the gnoll version of *Shhhh*.

Artus crossed his arms and stared up at the ceiling, which was barely illuminated by the flickering candles. Tyvian never told him what was going on, and it was starting to grate. In the beginning there was some novelty to it all—him, a farmboy from the middle of nowhere, hobnobbing around with the suave, educated, capable Reldamar—why wouldn't he be impressed? That had faded, though. Now he just felt like manual labor—a manservant, a page, a boot-black (though, in fairness, Tyvian never made him polish his boots. That he never made him because he claimed Artus would "ruin perfectly good leather with his farmer's hands" was beside the point). Just once he wanted to be let in on the plan. He wanted to offer up his own ideas and not look stupid. Just once. Instead it was always like this: left minding the gnolls (or the gnolls minding him) for hours and hours and hours while Tyvian did gods-knew-what.

There was a knock at the door—three times, then four times. It was Tyvian. When the smuggler came in, he was whistling to himself. "Ah, Artus—you're awake. Excellent."

Artus stood up. "I've been up all night! Where did you get off to?"

Tyvian lit a few more candles and a lantern hanging from the crossbeam. "My, my, Artus, if I'd known you were so worried about me, I might have had my companions walk me upstairs and offer their apologies."

"What companions?"

Tyvian rolled his eyes. "Gods, Artus—you're like a jealous fishwife. Look, the business I had to attend to involved a lot of time and needed to be done after dark. Did you smuggle Hool and Brana in here all right?"

"Nobody saw us," Hool announced, standing up to stretch. Her body and arms were so long they temporarily blotted out most of the candlelight. "Most of the humans in this place were sick with poison. Brana and I could have stolen their shoes and they would not notice."

Brana, stretching to mirror his mother, yipped. "Shoes! Ha!"

Tyvian nodded. "Excellent—good work everybody. Now, for the reason we're here." The smuggler pulled a small box from under his cape and upended it on one of the beds. Out fell a pair of belts—wide leather things with simple brass studs, but etched all over with an intricate array of minute, blocky runes. "Courtesy of Dame Margess's favorite enchanter."

"Those things are magic," Hool said, her ears going back.

"It won't hurt, Hool—I promise." Tyvian held one out to Hool. "Here, try this on."

"No." Hool folded her arms.

"Don't be a baby—just try it on."

"What if it sticks like your magic ring?" Hool was eyeing the belt in Tyvian's hand like it was a snake.

"Then we'll cut it off. Belts are easier to cut off than rings."

Brana was already fishing his belt off the bed. "I try!"

Hool slapped the belt out of Brana's hand and pushed him on the floor. "No! Me first!"

Brana stayed on his back and whined twice, to which Hool responded with a single guttural *"Huruff."* Artus was fairly certain it meant "for your safety," but he had an imperfect ear for the gnoll language, as Hool was fond of telling him.

Tyvian sighed. "Go on, Hool. I just spent about five hundred marks and the better part of all day getting this damned thing for you, the least you can do is try it on."

Artus's mouth popped open. "Five hundred? Where the hell did you get—"

"Not now, Artus," Tyvian snapped, his eyes fixed on Hool as he held the belt out to her.

Hool ran her nose along its length, sniffing rapidly. She concluded the investigation with a snort and then snatched the belt from Tyvian's hand. She wrapped it around her waist, clipped the buckle . . .

. . . and disappeared. Standing in her place was a tall, svelte woman wearing a finely made bodice of green silk with black embroidery and a voluminous dark green skirt that ballooned out to a full four feet across. Her sun-streaked, auburn hair was piled atop her head with a series of golden pins and barrettes; her face powdered to be pale in contrast with her red, red lips. Only Hool's copper eyes were still there, except of a more human shape and size—the effect made her a singular, heart-stopping beauty. Artus was struck dumb. "What . . . what . . ."

The woman spoke, but it was Hool's voice. "What are you looking at? Why do the two of you look crazy?"

Tyvian laughed. "Hann's boots, I figured an Erethe-rian enchanter would be good at this, but I had no *idea*. Hool! You look positively stunning!"

"What does that mean? Why do you—" Hool held up her hands and then froze, staring open-mouthed at the delicate, manicured things in front of her. She then howled something in the gnollish language, which was a sight to behold issuing from the elegant throat of the tall, curvaceous woman. Artus was in the process of laughing himself silly when Hool stepped forward and grabbed Tyvian by the shirt. She hoisted him in the air like he was made of straw, but while Artus had seen Hool manhandle Tyvian hundreds of times, the image of a thin red-haired woman in a fancy dress yanking Tyvian off his feet with one hand was nothing short of ridiculous. Artus went from simply laughing to openly guffawing.

Tyvian tried to pry Hool's hand from his shirt. "Hool! Hool, if you please! This is conduct unbecoming a lady!"

Hool threw Tyvian on the bed. "WHAT DID YOU DO TO ME?"

Tyvian held up his hands. "It's an illusion, Hool! A trick! Just take off the belt and you'll see!"

Scowling, Hool reached down and fumbled with something Artus couldn't quite see. An instant later Hool was standing right where she had been, her usual golden-furred self. She held the belt out like it was on fire and dropped it on the floor. "That was disgusting!"

"Me try! Me try, too!" Brana barked, bouncing over to the bed and picking his up.

Hool moved to intercept, but Tyvian interposed himself. "It's harmless, Hool—don't worry."

The mother gnoll hesitated, which was just enough time for Brana to hook his belt on and vanish. Standing in his place was . . . Artus himself. "What?" Artus blinked. Looking more closely, he could see certain differences—a broader chin, flatter cheekbones, darker hair. Brana's illusory self was an inch or so taller than Artus and broader, too, with thickly muscled shoulders that Artus himself wasn't even close to acquiring. He wore a similarly fine set of clothing as Hool, except with more maroons than greens. "You look like my brother Balter, a little."

Brana held out his human-looking hands and then stuck out his tongue. "Ha! Brothers, yes!"

Tyvian pursed his lips, "Yes, perhaps it's best if you didn't talk much while wearing your shroud, Brana."

Artus recognized the word. "Is this like that time you disguised me and all those Defenders to look like you?"

"It is indeed, though a bit more elaborate and less prone to failure. We'll need our gnoll friends to wear these shrouds pretty consistently from now until we get to Saldor. This will let us move more easily and blend into society."

Artus blinked. "Wait a second—did you say 'Saldor'?"

Tyvian grimaced as though he knew this was coming. "Yes, we're going to Saldor. All of us."

Artus couldn't believe what he was hearing. "That's crazy! We can't go there! That's . . . that's where all the damned mirror men *come from*! That's like, like their *home!*"

Tyvian nodded. "Indeed, which is why they would never expect to find us there."

Hool was frowning. "This is a bad plan. Very stupid."

"After Draketower, the majority of my Eretherian contacts are now spent. My only friends close enough to get to with our current funds are somewhere in the domain of Saldor." Tyvian winced. "We don't really have a choice."

Artus knew that wince. "You're *lying*! You're lying to us *right now*!"

Tyvian scowled, rubbing his ring hand. "This stupid trinket . . . okay, fine—I'm lying. We're still going to Saldor."

"I don't like it," Hool said.

"I realize that, Hool, but there are no acceptable alternatives. I have a lot of old friends in Saldor. They can help us."

Artus shook his head. "It's suicide! I won't go! Why do this?"

Tyvian had his eyes fixed on his ring hand, which lay in his lap. He looked as though he wanted to jump out the window rather than have this conversation, but he stayed where he was. "I already told you."

"No!" Artus yelled. "Not good enough! Why would we walk into the place where you're the most noticeable, with the most Defenders of anywhere in the West? I'm tired of just following you around everywhere!"

Tyvian's upper lip curled back in a snarl. "Nobody's making you stay, boy! Feel free to leave if you hate my leadership that much!"

"That *isn't* what I said!" Artus punched his own palm. "I'm just saying that everywhere we go, *you* come up with the plan, *you* tell us all what to do, and we never have any idea what's coming next, and . . ."

"And what? You're saying you should get a vote or something?"

"I'm saying that you keep almost getting us *killed!*"

Silence.

Tyvian froze, staring at Artus with an expression that he was certain had *never* come up during their nonverbal communication lessons. The smuggler said nothing, so Artus found himself talking. He didn't yell. "First there was Freegate, then Galaspin last year, then Haldasburg after that, then the crypts, then Draketower . . ."

"Draketower." Tyvian nodded. "That's what this is about, eh? You can't let that one go, can you?"

"We coulda *walked out the bloody door,* Tyvian! We coulda been *gone.*"

"What makes you think Draketower was *my bloody idea?*" Tyvian waved his ring hand in Artus's face. "This! This Kroth-spawned anchor of a ring made me do it! I had no goddamned *choice!*"

Artus got in Tyvian's face. He was tall enough now that they were nose-to-nose. "No! That's not it! We coulda just rescued those girls—we coulda just lit out with Saley, but no! *You* had to be goddamned clever, didn't you? You thought we needed to nick the family jewels, too! And you know what happened?"

Tyvian turned away. "She died. Is that what you want to hear? She died, and it's my fault?" He walked to the woodstove and stared at it. "Does that make you feel better?" He nodded. "I get it. Fine. Point taken. I have a tendency to get . . . get people killed."

Artus did not feel better. Not one bit. His stomach was wrestling with itself. He felt angry and sick and tired and miserable all at the same time. "Why are we going to Saldor?"

Tyvian stiffened. "I don't have to justify myself to you! I've got a plan—I've *always* got a plan—and if you don't like it, you can run off and do whatever you want. You're a fifteen-year-old boy, Artus." He jabbed a thumb at his chest. "Me—*my plans*—have fed you, clothed you, and passed more silver through your hands than you've ever had in your life. Are you trying to tell me that the danger is too much for you? Well then, *fine*—go off and be a farmer. Marry some rosy-cheeked Eretherian farmgirl, settle down, and till soil for the rest of your damned life."

Artus clenched his fists. "That's not what I meant!"

"No? Then what? Maybe you want to suggest running away, up into the North, and meeting your lovely 'Ma'? A grand plan, except going north means crossing the Dragonspine and that means passing through Freegate, which is even more dangerous than Saldor right now. Maybe you think we should stay here, living like feral cats in the bloody woods?"

"We should go west, to the Taqar," Hool announced. "There are almost no humans there to bother you."

Tyvian rolled his eyes. "I can see how that might be a selling point for *you*, Hool, but as humans, I'm not certain we'd be well-adapted to life among the gnolls."

Hool snorted. "I did not say you would live with gnolls. Brana and I would live with gnolls; you would live by yourselves." After a moment, she added, "Probably in a hut."

Tyvian closed his eyes and pinched the bridge of his nose. "Hool, I will never, ever live in a hut. Not so long as I breathe. Saldor is where we're going. That's final. Take it or leave it."

Nobody said anything.

Tyvian let out a long, slow breath. "None of you understand the danger we are about to encounter—*none* of you. Nowhere are the Defenders more powerful than in Saldor, and you have only the barest notion of how powerful they are. Everything we do—everything we *think* we want to do—from now until the moment we cross the Vedo, could be the difference between being caught and going unnoticed. Even my *explaining* this to you changes things. I don't expect you to understand, and I'm not going to bother teaching you. Suffice to say we are playing a game now—a very dangerous game against very dangerous players. We don't get to *not* play, and I'm the only person who knows the rules. You're going to have to trust me, understood?"

Artus said nothing. He could only mutter dark complaints beneath his breath.

Tyvian went to the door. "Now, as I have adequately *explained myself* for the evening, I'm going downstairs to have a drink. In the morning, be ready to go. Hool and Brana, wear your shrouds when you leave this room and in public from now on. As Artus is fond of mentioning, I have a tendency to put us in danger, so let's not draw any more attention to ourselves than needed."

The door slammed behind him. Artus didn't look at Hool or Brana. He kept staring at his feet, waiting for the churning tempest in his stomach to subside. He took long, slow breaths.

Brana's head butted him gently from behind and he felt the gnoll's tongue lick the back of his neck. "Ah! Brana!" He turned around to see the spitting image of his older brother smiling at him with his tongue hanging out. "Gods! What the hell?"

Hool nodded. "See—I told you those things were disgusting."

CHAPTER 6

THE FIRST MOVE

Tyvian sat in a corner booth of the well-maintained taproom of the Bastard. It was high-backed, solid oak, and about as comfortable as a church pew. Still, it kept his back to the wall, made it hard for people coming in to see him before he saw them, and it was not, at present, coated with any kind of errant fluid originating from carelessly handled tankards or, as case may be, carelessly treated human bodies. Given the celebrations following the Earl of Derby's victories in the field, this was no mean feat. Even now a barmaid with a mop and a bucket was making the rounds, giving each patron a quick assessment of their current state of inebriation and their likelihood of baptizing the floor with their vomit. As mentioned, it was a well-maintained taproom.

Tyvian hated ale and didn't feel up to drinking oggra, but this was not a night for wine. This was a night to get quickly inebriated and forget about his problems for a few hours. He ordered Verisi rum and they brought him a cup of something no doubt *labeled* as Verisi but with all the flavor of the conjured swill packed up in Ihyn and shipped all over the Syrin at bargain prices. Tyvian scowled but drank it anyway.

Artus complaining wasn't new—the boy was desperate for more independence. Tyvian might not have been the boy's father, but he wasn't an idiot. If he were looking out for Artus's happiness, he probably would have extended the lad a bit more consideration, but he wasn't in the adolescent-development business. He was in the staying alive, free, and wealthy business—three things that the ring seemed intent on ruining for him.

Even though the Defenders weren't pursuing him as aggressively anymore, there were any number of bounty hunters looking to collect Sahand's reward for his capture, dead or alive, not to mention those assassins in the employ of Angharad tin'Theliara, who would love nothing more than to stab him in bed. If word got out about his involvement in robbing Cameron Thystal of Draketower, he could even imagine complicated political machinations that would make him a wanted man in any peerage or county in Eretheria, which of course meant all the good camping spots this side of Akral were now off-limits, even assuming camping was an acceptable state of existence in the first place.

Then there was the money. All of it, more or less, sunk to the bottom of a damned lake in the middle of nowhere. They were paupers. He now had a little shy of one hundred marks to get them from the north of Eretheria to the city of Saldor on the shores of the Syrin. He'd just pawned the Heart of Flowing Sunlight—for all the grief and effort it had caused him—so he could get a pair of Eretherian party shrouds for two gnolls from an enchanter who never would have given him the time of day had he not waved letters of introduction from a backwater peeress under his pointy nose. It seemed each day brought a new kind of low.

Worst of all, his quest to excise the thrice-damned ring from his life had also hit a dead end. He'd spent a king's ransom on every ancient book of history, mythology, and sorcery he could get his hands on, searching for some mention or clue as to the location or identity of the Yldd, and he'd come up completely empty. Granted, he hadn't finished all those stupid books, but still, if he hadn't found any reference yet he was beginning to think no such thing as the Yldd existed. The Artificer had probably been lying to him.

That brought him back to Sir Banber's gossip, and *that* brought him back to Myreon. He could still remember the feeling of her cold lips against his as the ring poured him into her, bringing her back from the brink of death. The memory was always there, not far from his thoughts.

Myreon, it seemed, had taken up permanent residence in his thoughts and made herself as obstreperous and frustrating as possible. How very like her.

Nevertheless, the Myreon rumor still bothered him—it seemed too convenient, too tailor-made for him. It was as though somebody had planted it as a ploy to draw him back to Saldor, and he could think of only one person in Saldor who would go to such lengths. For that reason alone he should have had every intention of steering well clear of Myreon's petrified prison, assuming it existed.

The thought of it burned, though. Tyvian could picture her on the floor of Keeper's Court, head held high, while the rabble booed. He remembered the icy calm of those blue-gray eyes—the eyes of a woman that always knew what should and should not be done. He imagined her staring injustice in the face, knowing she was soon to become so much stone in some penitentiary garden. It made him surprisingly angry.

And knowing somebody had done that to her on purpose just to lure him made him want to stab something. Maybe several somethings.

Then again, maybe he could turn this Myreon lure to his advantage. Maybe there was a way to turn the scheme back upon the schemer and perhaps restore a little bit of his self-respect. Maybe . . .

While he sipped his bad rum and thought dark thoughts, a man slid into the booth across from him. At first Tyvian scarcely noticed—the man was without clear edges, without recognizable form. A shadow shaped like a man. Gradually, though, Tyvian's mind caught up and he dropped the rum, a dagger flying into his hand.

The man did not move or react. He wore a thick black cape with a heavy hood that covered half his face in darkness. His chin was poorly shaven, his skin sallow in complexion. He wore fingerless gloves; above the corner of his mouth was a small tattoo of a button. The rest of him seemed to drop away from Tyvian's notice, no matter how he tried to focus. He was wearing . . . clothes. He was of average height and build . . . maybe. It was hard to say.

The hair on the back of Tyvian's neck stood up. He kept the dagger in his hand and tried to focus on the man's hands as best he could. They had callused, chipped fingernails—the hands of a back-alley cutthroat. Tyvian took a deep breath. "You're far from home, aren't you?"

The hands folded together and then opened, as though the man were about to release a trapped butterfly. Instead, nestled in the hands was a paper note. It read, in a blocky, functional script: *Do not go to Saldor.*

Tyvian used the tip of his dagger to clean beneath his thumbnail, doing his best to appear nonchalant, but his pulse was racing. "Pardon me, sir, but since when do the Mute Prophets send a Quiet Man to an Eretherian bar to advise me on travel plans?"

The Quiet Man's face revealed nothing. His hands closed again and then opened. The note had changed: *There is nothing you can do to help her.*

Tyvian froze. That statement had many implications, none of which he liked one bit. "Do I strike you as the kind of man who rescues damsels in distress?"

The filthy hands closed and then opened: *We know what you plan to do.*

Tyvian frowned, running dates in his head. How long would it take a Quiet Man to get all the way up here? A week, at minimum, probably closer to two. Very few augurs could scry individual behavior that far out—they were acting on a hunch, not actionable prophecy. "Just because your masters think they see the future, that doesn't mean they're right. Auguries aren't destinies. After this conversation, I might change my mind."

Another note, the writing much smaller this time: *We are prepared to make you a generous offer to stay here instead.*

Tyvian's spine literally tingled. He cast an eye around the room, checking if there was anybody else watching him. Nobody. They were completely ignored. "And if I refuse this offer?"

Death. Right now.

Tyvian grimaced. "You can't kill me here. Even with your . . . *talents*, let's call them, you couldn't stab a man in a crowded bar without attracting attention. Don't you think I'll cry out?"

The Quiet Man's lips pulled into a rare smile, the button tattoo tugging up almost into the shadows of his hood. He presented another note. *Your drink is poisoned.*

Tyvian felt his blood pounding in his ears as he looked down at the cup. He'd watched the barkeep pour the cup himself, watched it as it was brought to his table.

NO GOOD DEED 87

The Quiet Man wouldn't have had any chance to poison it until it was sitting in front of him . . . not until he had slipped into the booth across from him. He must have poisoned it right under his nose, and he'd been too blinded by sorcery and his own dark musings to notice.

Still, he wasn't dead. He wasn't even distressed. It could be a bluff. "I suppose you're offering the antidote, then? This old dance? Say I don't believe you. Prove it—let me see the poison and let me see the antidote."

With a flourish, the filthy hands produced a small pouch from which he shook some finely ground black leaves. Then, in the other hand, a small vial of blue liquid suspended by a lanyard around his neck. Tyvian recognized both materials immediately. He pointed at the poison. "*Arbol de sombra,* correct? Very nasty, indeed. A full dose of that and I should be dead in an hour."

The Quiet Man let the antidote drop back into the invisible obscurity of his clothing. He laid a note on the table and pushed it towards Tyvian. It read: *Decide.*

This time Tyvian did smile. "You know, I *almost* feel sorry for you." He caught up his knife in a flash and slammed it through the closer of the Quiet Man's two hands—the one holding the poison. The knife pierced him between the tendons of his index and middle fingers and bit deeply into the thick wooden table beneath, pinning the hand in place.

The Quiet Man's mouth opened into a perfect O, but no sound came out. No sound could. His free hand dropped the antidote and struggled to remove the knife, but Tyvian grabbed him by the wrist and forced his hand to the table. Around them, nobody seemed to notice. Tyvian chuckled. "You see, the problem with becoming a silent sorcerous abomination is that you can't call for help. Now, I know what you're thinking: I just have to hold out a few minutes and Tyvian Reldamar will be on death's door from the *arbol de sombra,* right?"

The Quiet Man tried to wrestle himself free, but Tyvian used his body to push the table back against him, pinning his torso between it and the high-backed booth. The button-tattooed mouth continued to scream silently. Nobody noticed.

Tyvian tsked through his teeth. "What a very rotten poisoner you are. I'm drinking *rum,* you dunce. It is no doubt pretty terrible rum, but it is *rum* for all that. While *arbol de sombra* works fine in ale and water and even certain weaker wines, the alcohol present in rum would neutralize the poison before I ever drank it. That's the trick with *arbol*—very deadly, very subtle, very quiet, retains its potency for weeks, but you can't poison a drinker worth a damn. That antidote you've got there? It's just pure grain alcohol with a bit of blue tincture to make it look special. It's the oldest alche-mist's trick in the book."

The Quiet Man struggled again, but Tyvian had him. Unless the man decided to rip the knife out with his teeth, he was stuck holding hands with Tyvian until he opted to let go.

Blood ran across the table in little crimson rivers. Tyvian took care not to dip his shirt in it. "Enough lecturing, though—let's to business. I choose to *decline* your invitation to remain here in this dreary old town on the edge of nowhere. I'm certain your masters will get the message—they hear and see what you hear and see, don't they? Goodness, your fellow Quiet Men are experiencing this pain at this very moment, aren't they? How unfortunate for them."

The Quiet Man did not respond. He thrashed and tugged at Tyvian's grip but couldn't get loose.

Tyvian shrugged. "Well, I'm sure they'll get over it. Now, what to do with you? I can't very well have you trying to poison me every day from here to Saldor, now can I?"

Holding onto the sorcerous assassin's free hand with his left hand, Tyvian used his right to scoop up the pouch of *arbol de sombra*. The ring pulsed a warning. Tyvian knew he *had* to kill this man, right here and now, but he couldn't so long as the ring thought he was in no danger. Damned thing. The two of them sat there for a moment, holding hands like lovers.

"I'll make you a deal," he said at last. "I let go of your free hand, and we'll see who grabs my knife first, right? On three: one, two, *three*—"

Tyvian released the Quiet Man's free hand, which darted over to the hilt of the knife and began worrying it out of the table, his mouth frozen open in agony while the blade ate at the flesh of his injured hand. Tyvian merely opened the poison pouch wide and got ready. The ring kept pulsing in warning; he wouldn't be free to act until the Quiet Man was on the verge of attack, and so he waited.

The knife came free with a fleshy squelch. The

Quiet Man slashed at Tyvian's throat, mouth still open wide.

Tyvian ducked the attack; the ring fell silent. Quick as a viper, he leaned across the table and stuffed the entire pouch full of poison into the assassin's open mouth.

There was no sound, no gurgling or spitting. The Quiet Man put his ruined hand to his throat, but too late. Enough *arbol de sombra* to poison twenty people had slipped down his throat, undiluted by any liquid. He was dead in a matter of seconds.

Nobody noticed.

Tyvian got up and left a gold mark on the table, for when the waitstaff eventually discovered the body—whenever that would be. Even as he stood up he found it difficult to focus on the slumped, shadowy form of his would-be killer. He left the rum, too—he didn't feel like drinking anymore. He felt like getting the hell out of there.

He retrieved his knife, rubbed his face. *Gods—a Quiet Man.* That settled things: Myreon *had* been framed.

The game of *couronne* he had just described to Artus had begun. The pieces were on the board, and his opponent had just made her first move. In a way, it clarified things for him. He was thankful for it. He was going to Saldor and he was going to beat her at her own bloody game. He was going to teach her to never meddle in his affairs again.

And this time his mother was going to listen to him.

CHAPTER 7

A (MOSTLY) PLEASANT JOURNEY

The journey south through Eretheria was a pleasant one, especially now that the gnolls could be taken with them anywhere they pleased and Tyvian didn't have to worry about the constabulary being called out and Hool eating anyone. They traveled in the daylight, stopping at roadside inns when they wished, and were able to pass for country gentry without anybody raising any eyebrows. The money from Tyvian's wagering got the best food most places could offer, and the best rooms, too. There were a few featherbeds along the way and it didn't even rain very much. If he believed in such things, Tyvian would have thought that Hann was smiling on him for once.

Hool, unfortunately, was not as well pleased. She despised wearing her shroud, and every compliment paid or hat tipped by a passing traveler made her angrier. "It's just because they want to mate with me," she grumbled, her rich baritone thundering up from her elegant human neck.

Tyvian frowned. "Now Hool, give these gentlemen some credit. They're simply being polite to a lady, not trying to seduce you."

Hool snorted. "Then why aren't they as polite to the ugly ladies?"

Tyvian considered this. "You may have a point there, I suppose. Of course, all that is different if you have money; money trumps looks every time."

"That just makes humans stupider." Hool wiggled her head a bit, which Tyvian inferred might have been her shaking her mane were she a gnoll. In her shroud, it simply looked like she was having a seizure.

"Remember your poise, Hool," Tyvian said, yanking on his horse's reins to keep his mount on the trail. Even with the shrouds in place, the horses still didn't like Hool much. There was something about a human being that could run as fast as them that they found disconcerting.

Hool grumbled something unintelligible but held her head high instead of low and thrust forward, as was her typical gnollish preference.

While Hool grumbled over her human appearance, Brana found the entire affair to be hilarious. He spent a lot of time mimicking men he saw on the road and listened in on human conversations intently. His Trade improved a good deal, though he was still prone to peppering his speech with a variety of barks, growls, and yips. He squatted on chairs rather than sat in them, and his table manners remained atrocious. It wouldn't have been so bad if Brana didn't bother using utensils—half the Eretherian peasantry ate with their hands anyway. The problem was, he didn't even eat with his hands—he simply pressed his face to the plates, wolfing the food down in alarming gulps. Once, at an inn near the border of the Viscounty of Courmalain, onlookers had watched in horror as Brana cleaned a turkey leg to the bone in a matter of three bites. After that, Tyvian took to telling people Brana was an escaped circus performer. Disgusted by the whole affair, Hool was constantly scolding Brana and did her best to keep the pup away from people. Brana, of course, took his mother's disapproval with an obedient whine, but then would sneak off to do somersaults for people at the next possible opportunity.

They traveled south along the Laiderre Road, which led from Derby across the gap to Courmalain and through the Whispwood before it turned east into Lake Country. If northern Eretheria had been scenic and pastoral, Lake Country was like something out of a fairy tale. Here, the lush vineyards and orchards of some of Eretheria's richest fiefdoms clustered around pristine, royal-blue lakes and glittering castles of alabaster and gold. Knights in armor so heavy with magecraft they *glowed* more than shined could be seen riding along the roads on a regular basis, embarked upon this or that quest or fulfilling all manner of oaths to their liege.

They frequently stopped to pay homage to Hool, as etiquette dictated. Tyvian found this richly amusing and wondered how many overglamoured Eretherian peers would press their lips to Hool's graceful hands before she took it upon herself to rip one of their arms off. Hool, to her credit, never said anything and never attacked anyone, but she also never smiled or gave the least indication she was pleased at being fawned over—a fact that perplexed more than one handsome young knight. Each evening, she would insist on ditching her shroud to go hunting for mice in the woods. Tyvian guessed it helped her feel normal again.

Tyvian was easily able to pass himself off as a provincial noble's second son, which meant he could glean a fair amount of gossip from each of the knights who happened by. On some occasions he was even invited to dine with the knight in his pavilion. They all had pavilions, since no self-respecting Eretherian knight was likely to sleep in an inn, and not every self-respecting knight was so well-respected by *other* knights to secure himself a bed in the local castle. These pavilions were elaborate affairs, Astrally expanded and with a whole array of expensive magecraft allowing them to transport rather exorbitant amounts of food, drink, and furniture in containers that easily fit on the back of their squire's horse.

One such evening they were just outside of the Viscounty of Alouna and dining with a Sir Jenwal Esthir, a vassal of the Count of Hadda. He was a young man—probably only older than Artus by a half-dozen years—well-spoken, educated, and clearly wealthy. His taste in wine, for a rarity, was actually good, and he was sharing with Tyvian and Hool (whom Sir Jenwal had insisted dine with them) a bottle of Otove '24—a good year, and it had enough time to mature the flavor into something more complex, with overtones of caramel. Tyvian noted, with some distress, that Hool wasn't even touching hers. She sat very still in the brightly lit tent, arms folded across her chest, and glared at Sir Jenwal. To her, Tyvian imagined this entire meal was a dominance game, and she was playing to win. Blissfully unaware, Sir Jenwal ignored her and focused his attention on Tyvian, as a gentleman who didn't want to get into a duel should. Tyvian knew, though, that any second the idiot would find an opening and, in a flash, he'd be on one knee yowling poetry to Hool as earnestly as any tomcat on an alley fence.

Tyvian decided to take his wine and get the hell out of there. Before he went, though, he gave Jenwal a wink and a significant look. "Careful, sir—she bites."

He found Artus and Brana sitting around the campfire outside the pavilion—Jenwal's squire had been sent on some kind of errand, or perhaps was answering nature's call. Tyvian sat himself on a log and sipped his wine.

Artus, who had been sullen pretty consistently

since Derby, roused himself from his adolescent doldrums to ask a civil question. He was sipping something out of a cup made of silver and inlaid with rubies. "Where do they get it all?"

"Get what?"

Artus motioned to the elaborate camp setup and the pavilion. "We've passed, what, fifteen guys like this since we been on this road? I've seen more fancy castles than I can count, too. And these weren't defensive keeps neither, or watchtowers—these were castles of rich knights in rich clothes." Artus shook his head. "Where do they get all the money, is all I wanna know. I mean, these are fertile lands, sure, but all *this*?"

Tyvian grimaced, but in truth welcomed the return of an Artus who didn't actively despise him. "Loans. Investments. It's all very complicated, Artus, but basically it's like this: Eretheria has been fertile farmland for thousands of years. There hasn't been a drought of any significance for almost a century. Now, what does that mean?"

Artus frowned. "Lots of crops, I guess."

"Correct—lots of crops. Lots of crops means guaranteed income. Guaranteed income means the capability to take out loans against your future prosperity."

Artus nodded. "Yeah, I heard about that—but then you gotta pay it back, right? You've gotta pay back more than you borrowed in the first place. Why would you do that, when you could just wait a bit longer?"

Tyvian shrugged. "You're not thinking like an ambitious Eretherian peer, Artus. Why wait when you can borrow money to invest in your land to make it worth *even more* money? Then, you can refinance your loan for even *more* money, which you can then reinvest."

Artus laughed. "You're kidding me, right? That's crazy—you can't do that forever."

"Of course not." Tyvian grinned. "When things get tight, though, you can just invade your neighbor's land and seize a particular part of it—say a well, for instance—and then you can pay off the loans with the new income that land generates."

Artus shook his head, considering the implications. "That still sounds crazy to me."

Tyvian nodded. "It is, in fact, crazy. I assure you of that. Such Eretherian financial gymnastics also happen to be the basis of the entire economy of the West. That, Artus, is where they get all the money." Tyvian motioned to the smoke climbing into the night sky. "From everywhere and nowhere in particular."

Hool stalked into the firelight and threw Jenwal's squire onto the ground and sat on him. He was unconscious. She said nothing, but took to examining her human nails with some curiosity. Her illusory hair was mussed, and not in a wind-blown kind of way. Tyvian sighed. "Hool, what did you do?"

Hool glared at him, and in her copper eyes Tyvian could see every inch of the man-eating beast she was. "That man touched my breasts."

Tyvian swallowed hard. "Did you . . ."

"I didn't kill him. I just hurt him," Hool said simply. "We should leave now."

Tyvian looked down at the velvet-wrapped object in Hool's hands. "Fine," he said. "But we don't steal anything."

Hool shrugged. "Who would want all this stupid stuff anyway?"

Tyvian ducked back into the pavilion to check on Sir Jenwal's injuries, but the knight was nowhere to be found. He looked everywhere in the Astrally modified tent—under the table, under the cot, behind the weapon stand—until, finally, there was only one place left to look: the chest.

Tyvian took a deep breath and opened the lid. There, folded up like a pocket handkerchief and stuffed inside, was the bruised and barely conscious body of the young Sir Jenwal. Tyvian sighed and shook his head. "Perhaps I should have been more specific, sir. Of all the things the Lady Hool does to overeager suitors, biting is only the most common."

He reached into the chest and removed Sir Jenwal's signet ring; the knight only moaned in protest. The ring was much less understanding—it seemed to hiss on his hand, but Tyvian ignored it. Just to spite it, Tyvian decided to nick the wine, too. Life was too short to pass up good wine, ring be damned.

Three days later the four of them were crowded inside a private compartment aboard the Eretheria-Saldor express. They had been riding for almost twelve hours, the spirit engine screaming past the green pastures and

NO GOOD DEED 99

azure ocean vistas of southern Eretheria at top speed.
The sun had set while they wound their way into the
Tarralle Mountains, and now, as they picked up speed
heading down the other side, the Sovereign Domain of
Saldor and its titular capital city was no more than an
hour or so in their future.

Tyvian felt a certain dryness at the back of his throat
that he had come to associate with unease. The Quiet
Man back in Derby still unsettled him—it was only
raw luck that he had survived, honestly. Indeed, this
entire enterprise—his decision to return to Saldor, his
plan for crossing the border, everything—was almost
entirely based upon luck. Tyvian felt as though he was
going mad, somehow. He wondered—not for the first
time during their trip—if Artus wasn't right about
him. Maybe his judgment was off. Maybe the damned
ring had finally robbed him of his edge.

"The border between the counties of Eretheria and
the southern end of the Saldorian domain is the Vedo
River, which we are crossing right about now." Tyvian
pointed to a map he had laid out across the table in their
cabin, indicating a major branch of the Trell River that
split off from just north of Bridgeburg and ran all the
way south to the Sea of Syrin.

Only Artus was looking at him. Brana had stuck
his head out the window and was letting his tongue
loll, inhaling the seaside air in great gulps. Hool was
growling at him, just an edge of fear in her voice. "Get
back inside! You will fall out and die! Brana! BRANA!"

Artus looked worried, "Won't they catch us once

we get there? I mean, we aren't stowaways, but we *are* smugglers, sort of, and . . . well . . ." Artus looked at the gnolls haplessly; Hool was dragging her pup inside by his belt while Brana howled.

Tyvian sighed. "Hool and Brana definitely count as contraband, yes. The shrouds they're wearing aren't technically illegal, but they're definitely frowned upon and will attract attention if detected. Saldor is a place that takes security very seriously, as you will soon see. What's more, the Defenders will be using auguries to scry the future to a limited extent, so they will know within a reasonable degree of accuracy what is going to happen and who they are going to find when they search the train, before they actually search."

Artus looked like he had just been stabbed. "Wh-What? Seriously? They can see the bloody *future*?"

Tyvian shrugged. "To a certain extent. Scrying has its limits."

"I am waiting for your stupid plan to start making sense," Hool said. She picked up the teapot from the end of the table and drank from the spout. "I am tired of having to act like a human. It hurts my back."

"Unfortunately for you, Hool, acting like a human is an integral part of the plan. I've gone to some lengths to make this work, now, so don't let your negative attitude get in the way."

Artus shook his head. "How can we avoid them if they already see the future? I don't get it—how will Hool acting like a human fool anybody? Won't they be using magic—won't she be detected?"

Tyvian grinned. "Of course she will. My plan relies upon that fact, actually.

This time both Artus and Hool spoke in unison. *"What?"*

"In fact," Tyvian said, delighted at their reaction and not quite willing to let them off the hook, "in Derby I sent letters ahead of us to people I know to be Defender informants, saying that I and my companions intend to cross into Saldor via spirit engine, and that we will all be wearing shrouds, so they will *definitely* be looking for us, and what's more, I've already furnished them with a description of all three members of our party."

There was dead silence for a few moments as Tyvian waited for them to catch up. Hool got there first. "There are four of us."

Artus was a close second. "We aren't *all* wearing shrouds."

Tyvian nodded. "My mother perhaps said it best: a little misinformation will go a long, long way. Furthermore, by letting them *know* who they think they are looking for, they won't bother to scry the future, since scrying is an inexact science, at best."

Hool narrowed her eyes at him, which on her shroud Tyvian thought was a very fetching expression. "Explain. Don't make it confusing."

Tyvian took the teapot from Hool and held it over the map. "When I pour this, which way will the tea go?"

Artus frowned. "It could run in almost any direction, I guess. Whichever way is downhill."

Tyvian nodded, "And, given the rocking of the train on its tracks, what constitutes 'downhill' at any moment is subject to random chance. So . . ." Tyvian let a drop of tea fall on the oilcloth map. It beaded up and ran toward Hool. He repeated the process, and this time it ran toward himself. "It could be different every time. Scrying works similarly—the future is wide-open, not predetermined. Auguries are not destinies, my friends. *However,* they are pretty good predictors of *likely* events. Somebody unaware that they were being scryed and contemplating murder can be predicted as committing the murder sometime in the future—that much is easy—but predicting *when* they will murder and *how* is far less precise, since those things rely on chance as much as planning. Furthermore, if the murderer is *aware* people are trying to predict his behavior, he can alter it, therefore making it even *harder* to scry accurately. This means that even talented augurs—such as the ones employed by the Defenders—will only be able to predict an action with any specificity sometimes less than an hour beforehand. This makes interception a rather dicey proposition."

"So, I still don't understand what we're going to do." Artus rubbed his head and stared down at the map as though it might have Tyvian's plan scrawled into a corner somewhere. "Don't telling them where to find us still kinda screw us over?"

Tyvian sighed. "The description I gave in the letters depicts me as a middle-aged man with a spreading paunch, a nice jacket, and a guild medallion around my neck. Now, Artus, how many such gentlemen are currently aboard this spirit engine?"

"A lot—at least six or seven, I think."

"There are seven, and good for you for noticing—it's those eyes of yours that make me keep you around. It's no accident it's that many either—what I've just described is at least fifty percent of the fellows who ride spirit engines at any time, day or night. The Defenders know this, too, which is why my disguising myself like that will make perfect sense to them. So . . ."

"So you're gonna make the Defenders think you're some other guy, while we slip right past them disguised as somebody else entirely." Artus straightened, his face glowing. "I got it, right? That's it, right?"

Tyvian nodded, and motioned to a small box he'd been lugging around since Derby. "You'll find stage makeup and a variety of wigs in that box—we'll be arriving in Saldor in under an hour, so get started."

CHAPTER 8

HOME PRETTY CLOSE TO HOME

The Saldorian Spirit Engine Terminal was a massive, gleaming construction of marble, mageglass, and polished brass. Here, spirit engine lines running from Freegate by way of Galaspin and from Akral by way of Camien, Eretheria, and Daventry, both terminated beneath a vast dome inlaid with glittering mageglass starbursts and the bas-relief visages of every Keeper of the Balance since the dawn of the modern age.

Even now, late into the night as it was, the place bustled with activity. Pallets of cargo levitated by, under the guidance of teams of uniformed warlocks fiddling with enchanted rods; guildsmen and traders of every size and description, their guild-pins and trading-house livery forming a heraldic structure every bit as complex as the lineage of the Akrallian kings, shoved, jostled, and shouted at one another in their haste to be on with their errands. Then there was the nobility and minor gentry—floating along the platforms at a stately pace, their retainers and champions and valets caught in their orbit like so many moons, carefully and reso-lutely aloof from the hustle and racket of the largest city in the West. It was in this last group that Tyvian, Artus, Hool, and Brana arrayed themselves.

Defenders were all over the platform when their spirit engine arrived, searching compartments and pat-ting down merchants and guildsmen with mechanical efficiency. Tyvian, dressed in the finest clothing they could still afford, wore Sir Jenwal's signet ring on his right hand, a fake beard on his chin, and the affected air of placid superiority common to Eretherian nobil-ity on his face. Behind him, Brana wore Chance at his side—taking on the role of champion—while Artus, laden with baggage, his hair dusted to look near-black rather than brown, took on the role of manservant.

Hool lay on a baggage cart. If her eyes were weap-ons, Tyvian was pretty sure he would have been bleed-ing. "I hate you."

Tyvian gave her a tight smile. "Just clutch your stomach and start screaming."

Hool folded her arms. "That's stupid. I won't scream."

"Hool, women scream when they're having a baby."

Hool snorted. "How many babies have *you* had?"

Artus shifted his weight beneath all the luggage. "If you two is gonna argue, can I put some of this down?"

Tyvian grimaced and looked over his shoulder. Two Defenders had spotted them and were drawing close. "Kroth! Hool, just act like you're having twins, dammit—do it however you like!" He pointed to Brana, "Push your mother and don't say a damned thing, understand?"

Brana wiggled his hips a bit and nodded.

Tyvian took a deep breath. "Everybody ready?"

The lead Defender—a sergeant, judging by his mageglass armor—pointed at Hool and Brana. "Sir, I'm going to have to ask your associates to remove their shrouds."

Tyvian looked at Hool. "Now!"

Hool grabbed the sides of the luggage cart, put her head back, and began to grunt like a ninety pound hog. She then put her knees up and spread her legs and began to thrash and snarl, baring her teeth at the distant, domed ceiling.

Tyvian waved everybody forward and adopted a look of extreme distress. "Thank goodness you're here, Sergeant! We need a doctor at once!"

The sergeant blinked at the grunting, thrashing Hool. "Is she all right?"

Hool glared at the Defender. "I AM HAVING PUP—" She paused at Tyvian's grimace. "BABIES! AR-ROOOOOOOO!"

The other Defender made the sign of Hann on his chest and followed it up with, "Kroth's teeth—she's dyin'!"

The sergeant frowned. "Sir, I need the shrouds to come off, please."

Hool kept howling. "AROOOOOOOOOOO!"

Tyvian puffed himself up in true noble fashion. "Sir! My wife is in great distress! We must be allowed to pass *immediately*!"

People from all over the platform were watching them. Hool had her tongue hanging out the side of her mouth now and was breathing so rapidly, Tyvian thought she might actually pass out. The sergeant shifted in his boots. "Yes . . . well . . . surely removing the shrouds would take only a moment, and then you and your wife could—"

Tyvian stepped close to the man and whispered in his ear. "But then, sir, everyone would see that she is *not* my wife."

The sergeant's eyebrows shot up under his helmet. "Oh? OH! Oh . . . oh my . . ."

Tyvian nodded even as Hool began to snarl behind him again. "Surely, sir, you can see the *delicacy* of my situation, yes?" The ring was pinching him pretty hard at this point, but Tyvian let the pain work its way into the kind of anguished expression he was hoping for. "Surely there is some manner of arrangement we can reach?"

"AAAAAROOOOOOOOGAAAAAAAAARA-AAAAA!" Hool arched her back and snapped her teeth at the air.

That settled it. The sergeant produced a notepad. "Just . . . just tell me where you'll be staying, sir. We can check in with you tomorrow."

Tyvian smiled. "My servant will fill you in on the details. For now, we must go with haste."

The sergeant looked pale. "Welcome to Saldor, sir. And . . . and congratulations."

Tyvian didn't stop to respond; he, Brana, and Hool rushed from the station like any expectant parents should. A few brief lies later, Artus wasn't far behind.

Tyvian spent one of their last silver crowns to hire a cab. It dropped them in a densely populated neighborhood. He and Artus left their disguises inside and they all got out. "We walk from here," Tyvian announced. He tipped the driver a copper.

The street was narrow and claustrophobically so. Wood-and-stucco houses were piled upon one another, each building cantilevering itself with its neighbors, the result a series of buildings that looked like blind men holding hands on a long walk home. As Artus followed Tyvian through the labyrinth of tunnels, narrow alleys, and oddly placed gardens, he marveled that this mess was considered the greatest city in the world. It felt more like a rat's warren.

"Where are we anyway?" he asked, looking up at the seemingly interminable series of laundry lines strung across the street, impeding any ability he had to see the stars or the moon. Were it not for the healthy orange glow of the feylamps set into the lampposts on nearly every corner, they would have been wandering in pitch-darkness. Even at this time of night people were about, walking in twos and threes here and there. Unlike Derby, where the only reason the streets were filled so late was due to wanton merrymaking, these people seemed to be busy somehow. They had places to go, people to meet. Artus spotted a man calling for a car-raige, dressed as though he were about to attend a duke.

Tyvian stopped to pump a few swallows of water out of a brass pump built into the side of a building. "This is New Crosstown. It's been technically part of Saldor since the Akrallian Wars about two centuries back, but you'll still find a few throwbacks who see this section less as a part of the city and more as the moss that grows on the true city's arse."

Artus peered at the buildings in the dark, trying to figure out how tall they were. Each had to be four sto-ries, at least. Many windows glowed with candlelight. "How many people live here?"

Tyvian shrugged. "Most of them."

Hool and Brana stuck close behind Artus. They were still wearing their shrouds, but Artus could tell that it was wearing on them. They had abandoned all pretense of human posture and stalked behind Artus on all fours as much as on their two feet. Weirdly enough, this didn't seem to attract any attention. Hool sniffed the air. "This is a bad place. I can't breathe here. How do all these people live so close? How do they not go crazy?"

Brana yipped his agreement. "No space."

Tyvian shrugged. "They get used to it, I suppose. The civil infrastructure here is marvelous—pumps or wells everywhere, magically purified to prevent disease, we've got parademons that eat the trash in an elaborate sewer system, we've got specters that clean the streets, feylamps everywhere. Honestly, I'm surprised *more* people don't live here."

"Does your mother live here?" Artus asked.

"Goodness gracious no!" Tyvian led them through a small garden festooned with various sculptures, mostly surprisingly life-like figures in a variety of bizarre poses. "I strongly suspect my mother has never set foot here in her adult life, which of course made it a very attractive place to go when I was a boy."

Artus frowned, trying not to look too hard at a statue of a man with his hands outstretched and his face contorted in a grimace of either anguish or anger, though it was difficult to determine which. "Are we going to see your mother?"

Tyvian snorted. It sounded a bit like a laugh. "It's very possible. Not yet, though—one does not simply walk into my mother's parlor and say, 'Hi, Lyrelle, what's for dinner?'"

Artus couldn't quite wrap his mind around a statement like that, so he tried to forget he heard it. His own mother would lose her mind if he walked in the door. Artus could only imagine how excited his sisters would be, too. If his ma found out he had snuck into town and not come to her straightaway, he was fairly certain he'd get paddled. He decided to change the subject. "What's with these weird statues anyway?"

Tyvian glanced at the figure Artus was looking at—that of a young woman hugging herself, her head bowed in sorrow. "This is a penitentiary garden, Artus. These people are criminals, though with sentences short enough that the transmuters didn't bother altering their original form." He kicked back some of the ivy that had grown around the statue's base. There, just barely visible in the faint lantern light, was a brass plate. It read: *Annika Morosten, Arsonist.*

After sounding out the words, Artus whispered, "Saints alive. Are they . . . are they really in there?"

Tyvian nodded. "Until a warlock utters the Rite of Release specific to the prisoner in question, yes."

"This is a bad place," Hool growled, pushing Artus along. "Stop looking and move."

Tyvian rolled his eyes. "Hool, to you *everywhere* is a bad place."

Tyvian led them to a cul-de-sac at the end of which was a taller building than most, with a painted facade that must have once been green, but the years and weather had led it to peel and crack, revealing a pale, bone-white beneath. In the flickering lamplight the paint looked like black flesh, rotten and cracking off the bony carcass of some long-dead animal. The silhouettes that moved behind the thick red curtains were indistinct, but numerous enough for Artus to get the sense there were a lot of people here. It wasn't until they got closer that he made out the sign—a weather-worn wooden thing in the rough shape of a cook pot with the words *The Cauldron* painted on by a shaky hand.

"A tavern?" Artus asked, walking toward the front door.

Tyvian grabbed his arm and steered him toward the alley besides the building. "The classiest dive bar and whorehouse this side of the West Mouth, and a favorite spot for the young gentry to slum it from time to time. For many of my teenage years this was my home away from home. Now, everybody mind your manners; I was popular here once, but it's been almost fifteen years since I've been here, so . . ."

Artus had been in enough dive bars to know what this meant. "No eye contact, hands on the purse, knife at hand."

Tyvian smiled and slapped him on the shoulder. "Good boy. Now, follow my lead."

The alley had a brick stairway that sunk into the earth and terminated in a heavy, iron-studded door. Tyvian trotted down the stairs with a spring in his step and knocked with the kind of force one usually reserved for occupied outhouses in emergency situations. After a second an eye-slot slid back, spilling yellow light onto Tyvian's face.

A pair of black eyes with black, beetly eyebrows blocked that same light a moment later. "What?" The voice behind the door was heavy and sluggish. Artus conjured up images of every thick-necked bouncer at every bar he'd slummed around in Ayventry. He thought it was amazing how they all seemed to be the same.

Tyvian smiled. "It's been a long time, so I don't remember the password."

The bouncer grunted. "Then go—"

Tyvian cut the bouncer off before the slot could be closed. "I do remember *you*, though, Maude. A man never forgets eyes like that—they haven't aged a day."

Those same eyes narrowed for a moment. "Kroth damn me. You're Tyvian Reldamar, ain't you?"

Tyvian shot Maude a wink. "That entirely depends on whether or not you've got a troop of Defenders hidden under your skirts, darling."

The slot snapped closed. Artus grunted. "Maybe they're mad at you or something."

Tyvian ignored him and spent a moment straightening his jacket and taking a deep breath. The second he'd finished, the door-bolt snapped back and the door swung open. From it emerged the largest woman Artus had ever seen—as broad and thick and tall as an arahkan war-priest—wearing a studded leather jerkin, iron bracers, and a big, snaggle-toothed grin. She snatched Tyvian up like he was a daisy and gave him a hug that probably could have broken his back had it been given in anger. Maude spun Tyvian around, which was when Artus noted that she was, in fact, wearing a skirt. And heavy black boots with spiked steel toes.

Hool grunted approval. "Let's go in. I like this woman."

Maude set Tyvian down. There were tears in her

eyes. "We heard rumors you was coming back but never believed it. Been talk about how the mirror men would pay a hundred marks for giving you up. Kroth's bloody teeth, boy, it's good to see you. Look at you, all grown!" Maude giggled, "I remember you when you was hanging around with that skinny fella—the Verisi, whatsit . . ."

"Carlo," Tyvian offered.

"That's the chap! Kroth, you weren't more than fourteen then, were ye?"

Tyvian motioned toward Artus and the gnolls. "Maude, allow me to introduce my associates: Artus, Lady Hool, and Brana. Friends, this is Maude Telversham, co-owner of the Cauldron, and one of the people directly responsible for my corrupted youth."

Maude's eyes fixed on Hool and she gave a low whistle. "Hann's boots, girlie, but you're a looker." She winked at Tyvian, "Always had good taste, eh?"

Hool's nostrils flared. "We are not having sex. He is disgusting."

Maude laughed so hard her face turned red. "Oh . . . oh my, I see you've got good taste, too, eh darling? Well, don't stand there in the dark—come in, come in!"

Inside, the Cauldron was smoky and overly warm, with low-beamed ceilings and not quite enough lanterns. It was crowded, too, even though Artus judged dawn to be no more than an hour or two away. Maude had to duck under the beams as she led them to a big round table in a corner. Sitting around it were a trio of half-drunk young men in waistcoats. She slammed one fist on the table three times, making their tankards shake. "Off you go, gents—this table's reserved."

The men offered not a word of protest before moving off, and Artus tossed his pack under the table and sat down. Fatigue hit him like a wet blanket. He yawned. "Well, I guess they remember you."

Tyvian nodded. "I guessed she might. I don't see too many other people here I recognize. None of the barmaids, not the bartender, and I haven't spotted any patrons I know either."

"Is that a problem?" Artus eyed the other patrons. It was hard to make out faces in the smoky half-light.

Tyvian shrugged. "Maybe, maybe not. The same faces might mean somebody might want to turn me in, I suppose. Different people means we don't know what we're getting into, and it's concerning that Maude heard we were coming."

"You should have kept on your old man disguise," Hool said.

"Then we couldn't have made it through the door, Hool," Tyvian countered.

"*I* still have to wear this stupid magic disguise."

"Hool, for the last time: there is a difference between disguising my human self as another human and you disguising your gnollish self as a different species altogether."

Hool snorted. "Easy for you to say—you don't have stupid knights wanting to mate with you all the time."

Maude reappeared bearing four tankards of something that smelled like beer, but not very strongly. She set them down on the table with a clank, spilling some. Artus noted that the table was already sticky with . . . something. He hoped beer. "There you are, my darlings," Maude said. "I take it you'll need a room, then?"

Tyvian put a gold mark on the table—their very last one. "And discretion."

Maude slipped the gold off the table and it seemed to vanish in her hand. "Claudia will set aside a room for you and the lady; the boys can sleep here. Last call is sunup, and nobody'll bother 'em after that. As for discretion, well, there's only so much I can do. Things have changed a bit since you've been here."

Tyvian arched an eyebrow. "How so?"

Maude sighed and ran a hand through her thin iron-gray hair. "We're owned by the Prophets, now. And *lucky* to have them." The hard stare she gave Tyvian didn't indicate any sense of fortune.

"They're fine fellows, in their way," Tyvian answered, also cool.

Artus blinked at this. "Who are the Proph—Ow!" Tyvian's kick to his shin made his eyes water, and it was all he could do to not start crying. "Why'd you—"

"Who are the Prophets?" Hool asked. Artus noted, with some degree of bitterness, that Tyvian didn't kick *her* in the shin.

Tyvian smiled at her. "Don't worry about them. Old friends."

Hool snorted. "You aren't acting like they're your friends."

Maude cocked her head—somebody was banging

on the door. "Catch up to you later. Good to have you back."

When Maude had gone, Tyvian leaned in toward the rest of them and motioned that they lean close. Artus, his leg still smarting, half wanted to refuse out of spite, but he was too curious to resist. "The Mute Prophets," Tyvian whispered, "are *the* crime syndicate in Saldor. I've not always been on the best of terms with them. They made contact with me back in Derby."

"What did they want?" Hool asked.

"For me to stay away from Saldor." Tyvian shrugged. "When I said no, their messenger tried to kill me, so I killed him first."

Artus's mouth popped open. "You never said anything about that!"

Tyvian grimaced. "If I had told you then, would you have furnished a cogent plan of action that would have capitalized upon the time between then and now?"

"Well . . ." Artus scowled. "You still shoulda told us."

Hool folded her arms and flared her delicate human nostrils. "I agree with Artus. I think Artus has been right all this time. We should not have come here. Let's leave."

Artus grinned. "Finally! I've been saying that since forever!"

Tyvian scowled. "We can't leave."

"Yes we can." Hool snorted. "We just go back to that awful place with the monster machines and ride one away. Easy."

"We haven't got any money, Hool, and we *just* defrauded a pair of Defenders there, remember?"

Artus scowled. "Fine, then—how about we walk? Get a horse? Stow away on a ship?"

"No boats!" Hool growled.

Brana grinned. "Boats! Yeah!"

Artus shrugged. "Anything's better than staying here, where *everybody* wants us dead or turned to stone in one of those creepy gardens!"

Tyvian sighed and ran a hand through his hair, dislodging some of the dust from his earlier disguise. "Myreon is in one of those gardens, you know."

Artus froze. "What?"

"Maybe." Tyvian shook his head. "It's a rumor, is all—I heard it back in Derby. It said that Myreon has been convicted of smuggling and petrified."

A collective gasp. Artus looked at his hands; Brana also looked at Artus's hands. Hool nodded. "I will get our things. We will go and save her."

"No," Tyvian snapped. "We will do nothing of the kind. It's a trap—somebody framed her to get at me."

"Then we will kill them and *then* save her," Hool countered.

Artus blinked. "Who did it?"

Tyvian took a deep breath and then smiled faintly. "My mother."

A million questions bubbled to the surface—Artus wanted to ask them all, but he found himself tripping over his words. He was about to stand up and start yelling at Tyvian for keeping this from them all, for taking them this far only to lead them into a self-admitted trap. He didn't get the chance, though.

"Tyvian Reldamar! As I live and breathe! Is it really you?" Artus looked up to see a pale powder-cheeked man in an expensive cloak standing over the table. He had on a hat with a lot of feathers tilted at an angle that seemed to indicate it was either falling off or the wearer couldn't decide whether his hat or his hair was more impressive and decided to display both. This seemed likely, since the fellow in question had blue hair the color of the sky, fashioned into ringlets that fell down on either side of his face.

Tyvian smiled broadly. "Gethrey Andolon. Been a long time, my friend."

"That's *Master Andolon,* you fiendish vagabond, you." Andolon gave Tyvian a wink. "I heard a rumor you were coming back to town. The fellows down the club haven't stopped talking about it for weeks. Weeks, I tell you!"

Tyvian put his hand behind his head and leaned back. "For me? Surely not—I doubt the boys even remember my name."

Andolon pulled a chair from another table and sat himself down beside Brana. Brana sniffed Andolon's shoulder surreptitiously. "Are you kidding, Tyv? We've got a whole bloody wing devoted to you! You have no idea what a draw you've been to new membership! Tyvian Reldamar, greatest duelist in the history of Saldor, wanted criminal, master smuggler, wealthy family—oh, my dear boy, I daresay I've dined off our friendship for well over a decade."

Artus looked at Tyvian. "I thought you were just making up that 'greatest duelist' stuff. Is that real?"

Andolon chuckled. "When Tyv here was sixteen, he bested three men *at once* when he not only got in a duel, but managed to insult both his opponents and his *own* second to the point where they decided to have a go at him. Never seen such a thing. Gods, I still have the scar where you stuck me!"

"*You* were one of them?" Artus's mouth dropped open.

Andolon jerked his head in the direction of Artus. "Who's the scrub?"

"My assistant," Tyvian said. "What he lacks in grace he makes up for in enthusiasm. Artus, what you fail to realize is that most duels are *not* to the death. First blood is sufficient, and in this case I managed to stick Gethrey in the calf before he ran me through."

Andolon shrugged. "That's what I get for defending the honor of a lady."

Tyvian laughed. "Just because she agrees to top you for no less than a crown and four, that doesn't make her a lady. Didn't she wind up bedding Squire Fundreth's famulus that very night?"

Andolon nodded, chuckling. "Ah, the madness of youth."

"Tell me," Tyvian said, "what brings you down here? Still slumming with Claudia's ladies? Would've figured you for married by now."

Artus had been wondering the same question. He had noted a few fops and dandies—the kind of young gentlemen that he and some other boys had occasionally picked clean while they were drunk in some Ayventry bar, but this fellow was Tyvian's age.

Andolon shrugged. "No woman would have me, what with that hideous calf-scar." He laughed. He had a face that looked like he laughed a lot. Artus found himself liking him, even if he was a bit of a dandy. "Honestly, I only come down here once in a while, mostly to maintain my 'dangerous' reputation at the club." Andolon yawned, stretched. "It's so good to see you, Tyv, but I've had a long night. Look, come by the club when you can—would be a treat, seeing you there again. Be good for you to get away from this rabble for a bit and reacquaint yourself with persons of quality. What say?"

Tyvian nodded and shook Andolon's outstretched hand. "Certainly. I look forward to it."

Andolon nodded and adjusted the jaunty angle of his hat. "See you soon, then. Ta."

Artus watched his blue-haired head bob out the door with a wave to Maude and turned to Tyvian. "He seems nice."

Tyvian's lips were pursed. "Yes, he seems it, doesn't he? Did you notice he had blood on his ring?" He held up his hand—there was a streak of red on his palm.

Artus frowned. "What's that mean?"

Tyvian grimaced. "It means you and Brana are going to follow him. Right now."

Artus felt the fatigue of their journey hit him all at once. "Now? It's the middle of the night!"

"I am well aware of the time, Artus—go. Now."

Artus dragged himself to his feet, scowling. "I need my machete from my pack."

"No. No weapons. No fighting—go."

Artus looked around for support from Hool or Brana. Hool was glaring at him—no help there. Brana was already standing and wiggling his arse as though wagging his tail, save that the tail was currently invisible. Artus found himself back to Tyvian, whose expression hadn't changed. All Artus could come up with was, "This ain't fair!"

Tyvian threw up his hands. "Fair isn't part of this conversation, Artus. Do what I ask—you can sleep when you grow up. I need your eyes open tonight. Our welcome at this place is rapidly eroding, and if you don't want to wind up like that fine young arsonist we met earlier, you will *get your arse into the street and follow him!*"

Artus went, purposely dragging his feet as he walked out of the Cauldron. Maybe, if he took his time, he'd lose Andolon before he even began. Then he could come back, sit down, and sip his weak beer and sleep on a bench in a cozy corner of the taproom.

When he got to the street, though, there was no such luck—there was Andolon, strutting down the shadowy street, twirling a cane as he went, as conspicuous as a gods-damned drum major in a parade. Artus looked over at Brana. "Can you believe this?"

Brana wasn't listening, though. Brana was too busy lapping water out of a rain barrel. Artus sighed. It looked like another bang-up evening of excitement for him, Tyvian Reldamar's favorite stooge.

CHAPTER 9

NOBODY'S HERO, NOBODY'S FOOL

Claudia Fensron was Maude's co-owner of the Cauldron. Where Maude was large, she was petite. Where Maude was angular, Claudia was curvy. For those who bothered to compare the two, it went on like this for some time; they were like a pair out of a storybook. For Tyvian, though, the most important point of comparison was this: where Maude Telversham was kindly and caring, Claudia Fensron *wasn't*. Tyvian would have bet a substantial sum that Claudia was the brains behind the sale of the Cauldron to the Prophets, but he guessed nobody would take such a bet.

In her youth Claudia could have turned heads in the dark. She had midnight black hair, alabaster skin, and lips that could make the kind of smile that made men bleed. Now, well over a decade since Tyvian had last seen her, Claudia's age had become apparent in her eyes. Light brown to the point of being gold, the wide-eyed faux-innocence she had used to part men from their money for decades had been replaced by a flint-hard squint designed to scathe more than entice. These eyes were ringed with the wrinkles and shadows; one of them was black and near swollen-shut, a livid cut resting just above the brow and only partially cleaned up. Claudia looked at Tyvian as though she knew this change in herself, and as though she knew he knew. "You actually came back."

Determined to be pleasant, Tyvian put on his most genuine smile. "Why Claudia, no kiss?"

Claudia didn't need to frown, as she was already, but she made it deepen a bit. "I see you brought that wit with you. Just what this place was missing."

The upper floors of the Cauldron were a mixture of different rooms for lease. Some rooms contained pliant and morally suspect women, while others were simply empty; the former were leased by the hour, the latter by the night. The locks were high-quality mechanical types and the walls were thick and insulated. What happened inside the rooms of the Cauldron was the business of the occupants and the occupants alone. At least, Tyvian mused, that had been the case before. With the Prophets owning the place, he suspected that may have changed.

Claudia led them to a room on the third floor. She gave Hool an appraising glance but made no comment and didn't address her, which to Tyvian was an encouraging sign that at least Claudia wasn't apt to pry into his business without being asked to do so. "Here is your key. I assume you settled up with Maude?"

Tyvian shrugged. "You won't believe me if I tell you, so why don't you just go and ask Maude."

"You plan on stabbing anybody tonight?"

Tyvian made a show of thinking it over. "Hmmm... well, not just now."

Claudia looked about as amused as a tar shingle might be by a mime. "Anything else?"

"Yes—who hit you tonight, and why hasn't Maude killed them yet?"

Claudia didn't answer. Giving him a hard glare, she slapped the iron key into Tyvian's hand and left with the candle.

This left Hool and Tyvian alone in the near-blackness of the Cauldron's main corridor. Hool sniffed the air. "I smell blood."

Tyvian fumbled with the lock in the dark. "What kind?"

"The blood of a new mother."

Tyvian could have asked for clarification of what this meant but decided to take it in its most positive sense. Prior to the ring being affixed to him, the inherent morally suspect realm in which the whorehouse existed had never bothered him in the least. Now, just standing in these halls was making his hand throb with that kind of low-grade ache that told him he ought to be more proactive in his goodie-goodie behavior. He desperately hoped to avoid asking questions that might lead to answers that would necessitate any kind of drastic action.

The room inside was furnished with a single large four-poster featherbed, a scuffed but solidly build armoire, and the kind of crimson wallpaper that made a person think of warm lovers cuddled together in warm places. Turning up the small oil lamp, he saw Hool pluck off her shroud and throw it on the bed. The transformation was instantaneous and truly jarring, as he had grown used to tall, svelte redheaded Hool over hulking, golden-furred monster Hool. In the blink of an eye the gnoll suddenly occupied almost twice the space as before. When she stretched, Tyvian watched as her arms reached almost far enough to touch both walls of the room. She then seized one end of the bed and pushed the entire thing over so there was more room in front of the small fireplace, wherein were smoldering a few embers. "There. Good night." The big gnoll curled up on the floor in the manner of a giant dog.

Tyvian nodded. After a moment he decided to add, "You don't have anything to ask me?"

Hool's ears perked up and she looked at him steadily. "If I ask you questions, will you lie to me?"

Tyvian thought about it. "That depends on the questions you ask."

Hool's ears went back. "Sometimes there is no point in talking to you."

Tyvian shrugged. "I'm doing you a favor, believe me."

Hool snorted. "Your mother is a sorceress?"

"Yes. A very powerful sorceress."

"More powerful than Sahand?"

"By several orders of magnitude, yes."

"Are we going to kill her?"

Tyvian blinked. "What? No. Of course not."

Hool stared at him for a few moments, her copper eyes glittering in the dim lamplight. "Why does she want to trap you?"

Tyvian sighed. "That's what I'm here to find out."

"*Then* will we save Myreon?"

"I told you, we are not saving Myreon. She wouldn't want me to and it wouldn't be a good idea."

Hool cocked her head. "But you love her."

Tyvian snorted out a laugh. "Of all the ridiculous—"

Hool snorted once to demonstrate her opinion of that comment, turned around a few times and then buried her head in her own fur and fell asleep immediately. How the gnoll could do that was beyond Tyvian; of all the various ways in which Hool was physically superior to him, that was the skill he envied the most. If he could fall asleep in under a minute and wake up at the drop of a hat, he would be a much better rested criminal.

Tyvian stripped to his drawers and slipped under the quilts, Chance under his pillow, and lay awake, staring at the ceiling. Above him, he could hear the telltale rhythmic creaking of a prostitute earning her keep. He found himself wondering how the girl came to be in this place and why. He knew Claudia wasn't the kind to be overtly cruel or abusive to her girls, but she was hardly a loving or caring employer. Claudia tossed girls out on the street for myriad reasons, and she would look the other way if a man was rough so long as he paid for the medical fees. Tyvian had never liked that, not even when he was a spoiled, disaffected youth. He had fought at least five duels with young nobles who had roughed up a whore. He had stopped fighting such duels, though. They had never made anything better.

"The world isn't that simple," Tyvian grumbled to himself, fiddling with the ring on his hand. "Good and bad aren't as easy as up and down. Damsels aren't so easily rescued. Say I did save all the women in here. Say I stuck a sword through whatever lout the Mute Prophets have supervising this place and carried the women out on my back, showering them with gold? What would that get me, exactly? What would that get them? I bet you more than half of them would wind up in another whorehouse before the day was out, and the rest would get themselves killed, raped, kidnapped, or married to some arse of a cooper with big fists and a mean drinking habit."

Tyvian was holding the ring up in front of his face, hissing at it in the dark. He knew it was ridiculous, but he kept doing it anyway. "It's like Draketower all over again. I did what you wanted, didn't I? I freed them, I killed the man who had abused and enslaved them, I showered them with riches—what goddamned good did it do? It ended with a poor girl drowned and left for the wolves in the wilderness. Some goddamned hero I am."

Hool stirred. "Shut up. Stop whining about everything. You are keeping me awake."

Tyvian jumped at the sound of her voice. "Sorry. I got carried away there."

"Stop thinking so much. Do what is right when it is time to do it, and everything else will be fine."

Tyvian frowned at this but didn't answer. Hool couldn't be expected to understand; Hool was a creature of the moment, a champion improviser and one who thought and acted in straight lines. She didn't see the complexity in the world because it was too much for her to comprehend. Tyvian knew this made what she said easily confused with wisdom, but he was too old a hand at the confidence game to be taken in by it. For every simple man the world produced, it had to come up with a dozen complex ways to keep him alive and happy, lest all the simple men of the world fall upon one another with whatever crude clubs and pieces of masonry they could find and cover the ground with a thick layer of their simple, simple brains.

Hool grumbled and shifted her position. "You think I'm stupid, but I'm not. Go to sleep."

Tyvian scowled and rolled away from Hool. On his hand the ring throbbed slowly—a gradual build of pressure, just short of pain, and then a sudden release, like the ponderous beating of a massive heart. It had been doing that for weeks; he had grown so accustomed to its petty tortures, he only seemed to notice while in bed. This was, he imagined, just as it was intended to be.

It was prodding him over Myreon. Myreon, who he *knew* was innocent with every fiber of his being, but whom he had promised himself he would not save.

That was why he had left off telling Artus and Hool and Brana about her for so long—they wouldn't understand. Rescuing Myreon wouldn't do anything other than put himself *and* her in more danger than they already were. She'd also hate him for it. Hell, once made whole again, she'd probably just turn him into the authorities. That was Myreon's style, after all: stubborn, loyal, and utterly incorruptible.

If not Myreon, then what *was* he doing here? The smart thing to do about a trap was walk away, but here he was—summoned as effectively as if he'd had a leash and someone had yanked. His reasoning back in Derby— buoyed by hot-blooded anger and indignation—seemed foggy to him now. What had brought him here?

The kiss.

The memory—Myreon's cold lips beneath the mountains, suddenly blooming with a fire created by his kiss—flared up, making him catch his breath for a moment. He pushed the memory away. Sentimental garbage, the whole lot of it. As though there were any possible way to steal her Rite of Release and rescue Myreon from a penitentiary garden without winding up there himself! What the hell had he been thinking anyway? Slowly, cursing himself and the world and everything else, he fell into a restless sleep.

In his dreams he sat on a throne of glass, his right hand burning with unholy fire, and a darkened sky overhead. Before him marched an array of the weak, the powerless, and the aggrieved. They howled at him, but he said nothing. He had no idea what they wanted him to say.

CHAPTER 10

ALL SLEEP AND NO PAY . . .

Artus wiped the sleep out of his eyes and bent back just far enough to work the crick out of his lower spine. Three hours following some blue-haired friend of Tyvian's as he wandered about New Crosstown was not what he had been looking forward to that evening. Were he not in the middle of one of the more interesting things he'd gotten to do in the past month, he might have just told Tyvian where to stick it and crawled into a haystack in some stable somewhere to sleep.

"He moves. Let's go!" Brana grunted, slapping

Artus on the shoulder and then darting out of the alley on all fours. He was wearing his shroud, but it wasn't making much of a difference. A giant dog running around wouldn't have attracted more attention than a young man in gentleman's clothing jumping around like an animal in the middle of a slum. Fortunately, those wandering the streets just before dawn looked to be various kinds of clerks, couriers, and porters running errands and making early deliveries, and therefore most had their bleary eyes too firmly affixed to the cobblestones in front of them to care much.

Artus ducked out of the alley, pulling the hood of his traveling cloak far up over his head, and walked casually in the direction Brana had darted. There was no sign of the gnoll-boy at the moment, but their target was clearly visible. Andolon came out of what Artus had originally assumed was a defunct barbershop but turned out to be still functional, just only if you knew the proper knock. When he went in, he was swinging his cane and whistling, and when came out he was doing the same thing. His hair, Artus noted, looked exactly the same, and Andolon didn't look like the kind of guy to need back-alley surgery. Artus didn't know what he had done there—or any of a half dozen other places he had visited—but whatever it was didn't seem to dampen his mood any.

Artus didn't really see the need for as much stealth as he was using, but Tyvian's words floated up at him from the depths of his memory: *Just because the man you're tailing doesn't see you, that doesn't mean the other person tailing doesn't. Always assume you're being watched, always assume you're being listened to, and you can't go far wrong.*

It was good advice, obviously, but Artus felt irked by it nonetheless. He was actively mad at himself for stopping every dozen paces or so and looking behind him. His time with Tyvian had made him paranoid and joyless. He could scarcely remember the last time he'd had fun, and he thought that a damned shame, given how much money he sometimes had at his disposal. He wasn't sure what he'd *do* for fun, really, but anything was probably better than being Tyvian Reldamar's human donkey.

A pebble hit Artus in the head, and he looked up to see Brana perched on the third story balcony of one of Saldor's frighteningly tall apartment blocks. "The water!" Brana chirped. "We're going to the water!"

"Get down here!" Artus waved at the gnoll, who was balancing on the railing of the balcony in a way no sane human would. "Somebody will see you!"

Brana cocked his head to the side and then jumped off. Artus almost screamed, but stopped himself. Brana slid down a clothesline and hit the ground, collapsing into a roll, and sprang back to his feet in one smooth motion. This display caused one man to jump in surprise and two others to hand him a few coppers for the show. Tongue hanging out like an idiot, the gnoll aped a ridiculous approximation of a bow and skipped off after their quarry.

Artus sighed—at least somebody was enjoying this.

Despite Brana's enthusiasm, he didn't get closer than twenty paces from Andolon. Since Tyvian had sent him off unarmed, he wasn't exactly spoiling for a fight. Evidently Andolon had, at one point, been a duelist, and furthermore this city had Defenders who could see the future and arrest you immediately after (or even sometimes before) you did something wrong. It was a harrowing thought—it made Artus question Tyvian's sanity for the hundredth time since he had brought them to Saldor. Why the hell would Tyvian's mother frame Myreon? Why would that encourage Tyvian to bring them all into a trap? They were all going to end up petrified in one of those terrible penitentiary gardens, he just knew it.

Andolon never looked behind him—not once—so the tailing was easy. So easy, in fact, it made Artus unreasonably suspicious of what was *really* going on. All kinds of Tyvian's warnings came flooding back: a person who never looks behind them after committing a crime is never alone, never assume a man is drunk unless you see him drink, never assume you are in control of a situation unless you have vetted all the angles first (he wasn't clear on what that last one meant, actually, but assumed it had something to do with having eyes in the back of your head). Artus put his hands in his pockets and sighed. He kind of hoped Andolon *would* turn around and start something. Getting in a fight would be a lot more interesting than this cloak-and-dagger nonsense, Defenders or no Defenders.

He and Brana followed Andolon to the docks. From

Tyvian's primer on Saldorian geography, Artus knew they were somewhere along the West Mouth of the Trell River, nearing Crosstown Harbor. Across the glass-still waters he could see the colored lanterns of a hundred ships bobbing at anchor out beneath the setting quarter moon. "Boats!" Brana said, pointing. "Big ones!"

They hid themselves behind a stack of empty barrels outside a cooper's shop and watched as Andolon marched himself out onto a pier and was met by some kind of large skiff with a fancy little house where Andolon could sit as two men wearing lace ruffs and shiny helmets rowed the boat. Tyvian's friend settled himself amid a few cushions and, from there, the two helmeted oarsmen took to their oars and they began to slide out into the harbor.

"Saints!" Artus swore, "How will we follow him now?"

Brana's eyes got wide for a moment before his grin followed suit. "Boat?"

"I don't know how to row a boat! Do you?" Artus asked, but it was a stupid question. Hool wouldn't let Brana so much as dip his toe in a pond larger than she could jump across.

"Boat!" Brana repeated, hitting Artus in the arm.

"No, Brana! I can't row . . . or swim. It's a bad idea."

Brana pushed him and snarled in gnoll-speak, *"Coward!"*

Artus pushed him back. "I am not! It's a stupid idea!"

"Let's go!" Brana barked. *"Let's go or you're a rabbit!"*

Artus pushed Brana again. "I am not a rabbit! You're stupid!"

Brana sucker punched Artus just north of his groin. Artus, though, had enough experience with Brana that it didn't catch him completely flat-footed. He caught Brana's arm with his and twisted it behind the gnoll's back. Brana slammed his heel down on Artus's instep hard enough to force Artus off-balance, and then the gnoll simply twisted in such a way that Artus found himself falling toward the cobbles, shoulder first.

Now it was Hool's voice in Artus's head. *If you're going to fall, fall. Let the power of the fall fill you and then change it into something good.*

Artus tucked his shoulder and rolled, letting go of Brana but allowing himself to roll to his feet. He turned to face the oncoming attack, but it wasn't coming. Brana had abandoned him and was running out on the pier. "Dammit! You stupid . . ."

Artus ran after him, but Brana had a head start and was ten times as fast anyway. By the time Artus caught up, the gnoll had skipped down a gangplank to a dock at which a half-dozen small skiffs, coracles, and long-boats were tied up. Brana was pacing the dock, sniffing at each boat's bow, his legs spread wide to adjust to the odd movement of the water beneath him.

"Brana, I said no! This is a really bad idea!" Artus descended to the dock as well, his hands gripping the guiderails on the gangway for dear life as he felt the sway and bob of the dock. "Saints, Brana—you're going to get us drowned!"

Brana gave him a devilish grin and then hopped into an eight-foot skiff. "Rabbit!" he said.

Somewhere behind them a dog barked. Artus turned to see the lights inside a shack by the pier light up. The sign above the door took a moment for Artus to sound out. "Dock . . . mast . . . er. Dockmaster."

He had five seconds to determine what a "dockmaster" was before the man himself appeared at the door to his shack, a knobby cudgel in one hand and the leash of an angry dog in the other. "What's about down there! Hey, you boys—you know what I does to boat thiefs on me dock? Eh? Come away from there!"

Artus waved Brana out of the skiff. "C'mon!"

Brana was busy untying the rope that held the skiff to the dock. "Rabbit rabbit rabbit."

"Stop! Thiefs! I'll knock yer stinkin' brains, ye Kroth-spawned tits! Varner, boy—have at them! Go!" The dockmaster loosed his hound, and the big dog shot down the gangway with all the speed of a crossbow bolt. Artus felt his arse tighten at the thought of the beast's jaws clamped onto one of the cheeks. He jumped in the boat, lost his balance immediately, and nearly fell overboard save for Brana, who pulled him to safety.

Assuming, of course, by "safety" one meant "a boat they couldn't pilot."

The force of Artus's jump had pushed them away from the dock. Varner the hound stopped short at the dock's edge, barking until foam flew from his jowls. The dockmaster was behind his dog, shaking his cudgel and spitting almost as much. "I know your faces, ye stinking ragamuffins! I'll find ye! I'll have yer arses!"

Artus managed to get himself right-side-up, but the thought of standing in the boat was too terrifying for him to contemplate, so instead he found himself peering over the gunwale at the receding form of the dockmaster. It took him a few seconds to fully realize what they had done, but when he did, all he could do was swear. "Kroth. Kroth's bloody teeth. We just stole a boat, didn't we? We stole a bloody boat."

Brana's tongue was lolling out. "Yeah! Fun!"

Artus sighed. "Right. Fun."

Whether it was the current, the tide, the wind, or some other nautical phenomenon Artus wasn't aware of, something was drawing their little boat away from the dock and out into the harbor among the hulls of the big oceangoing ships. Artus, whose firsthand experience with watercraft was limited to riding on a river barge a few times, found himself marveling at the sheer size of most of the vessels that surrounded them. He knew terms like "galleon" and "brig" and "galley" were used to describe ships, and suspected that some or all such terms could be correctly applied to the watery castles of lumber that loomed over them, but there was no way he would be able to tell which was which. All he knew was that their little boat floating amid such massive ships felt an awful lot like a leaf on a stream floating amid rocks and whirlpools.

Brana barked at some of the vessels they passed,

which made Artus want to strangle him, for fear that they'd be turned in to the dockmaster as the obvious boat thieves they were. Besides the odd curse shouted at them from windows and rigging far above them, nothing came of it. Their forward progress was slowing as well, but they were still moving, languidly and calmly, on a collision course with a big ship with two masts directly ahead of them.

"Dammit!" Artus snarled, snatching up an oar. "If we hit that boat, we'll sink! Row! Row!"

Brana picked up the other oar and the two of them did their best to change the course of their little vessel. The thing was, though, they had no clear idea how this was to be achieved. Oars, it turned out, were less intuitively used than one might imagine. Artus and Brana thrashed about, slapping and stabbing the oars against the water in a variety of ways but never with quite the desired effect. About the only thing they managed to do was make themselves rotate around backward for a second before turning back the way they started. Then Brana dropped his oar.

"Kroth!" Artus yelled. "You idiot gnoll! You've killed us!"

Artus could see Brana's teeth gleam in the moonlight. He howled in mock dismay and then cuffed Artus across the head. "Rabbit!"

The big ship now loomed over them, blocking out the moonlight, blocking out everything with its midnight-black bulk. Artus found a rope and wrapped it around his hands, not certain if by so doing he was guaranteeing his survival or just the opposite. If a boat fell apart, did its pieces sink to the bottom or did they still float? He closed his eyes. He could hear the water slapping against the sides of the ship's hull; he could smell something fishy and salty at the same time. Brana gave off a little whimper just before they hit.

. . . bump. . .

They struck the side of the great ship gently, causing their boat to shudder slightly, but nothing else. Nothing cracked, nothing leaked, and Artus did not find himself dumped in the harbor. Slowly, he exhaled and opened his eyes. "Oh."

Brana was glaring at him, he could tell. *"Stupid rabbit,"* Brana muttered in gnoll-speak.

Artus scowled back. "Oh yeah, like you knew we wasn't about to die, huh? I heard you whimper! I know that whimper—that was your 'call for mommy' whimper."

"Shut up."

Artus stuck his chin out and mimicked Brana's gravelly voice. " 'Waah, waaah! I'm Brana and I miss my *moooommy!*' "

Brana took a swing at Artus, but the boat rocked and he missed. The gnoll lost his balance and almost fell over. He was only saved when he reached out and touched the hull of the ship they were floating beside for balance. It pushed them off that ship and sent them slowly drifting toward another one.

This gave Artus an idea of how to get around the harbor, if not back to shore. Using the oar, he pushed against the hull of the next boat that came close, thereby bouncing them off in another direction. The two of them spent the next quarter of an hour taking turns bouncing themselves from anchored ship to anchored ship, trying somehow to get closer to a dock somewhere.

The sun was rising, pink light spilling across the calm waters of the harbor. Above, the calls of sailors and the cries of seagulls began to fill the early morning air. In the distance a spirit engine wailed its way out of its berth. Ships rang their bells, and the harbor, virtually dead a few moments before, was slowly coming to life.

It was in this early dawn light that Brana pointed out the boat Andolon had taken from the dock. It was tied up to a gilded, polished abomination of wood and lacquer, with four big masts and a bowsprit so elaborate, Artus worried that the figure of the selkie clinging there might actually jump down and come after them. The ship was longer and taller and broader than any they'd seen so far, but it had more of the look of a floating palace than a ship built for the sea. On its back side (stern?) were written the words *Argent Wind*.

Artus looked at Brana, and Brana nodded enthusiastically. Taking a deep breath, Artus pushed them off the next vessel and made directly for the big ship. "If anybody talks to us, let me do the talking, okay?"

Brana nodded and yipped his agreement.

"No gnollish either! And stop sitting like that—stick your legs out in front of you and sit like a human. Pretend."

Brana frowned, slowly dumped himself on his arse and stuck his legs out in front of him like a human sitting down. In that position he was nearly passable as a real person. If only he'd stop sniffing the air.

The *Argent Wind* looked even more ostentatious the closer they got to it. Artus spied gold fittings on almost every part of the ship, from the spokes of the ship's wheel to the knobs on the balustrades. The windows, which ran along the entire length of the vessel rather than just at the back, had the strange, oddly still translucence that indicated mageglass. There were two men on deck, both dressed in the same stiff lace ruffs, colorful red-and-yellow livery, and gleaming steel helmets they had seen in the skiff. They stood at attention, barely sparing Artus and Brana's little boat a look, though Artus got the sense they were more alert than they appeared. Of Andolon, there was no sign.

"Excuse me?" Artus twisted his head to see the face of a man with a thick moustache and a crystal eye above them. He had poked his head out of a porthole. "Are you in need of assistance?"

Artus looked at Brana, only to find Brana looking at him the exact same way. Artus shrugged. "Uhhh . . . we lost an oar."

The mustachioed stranger nodded as though this was the least surprising thing in the world. "Stay right there."

Artus clung to the side of the *Argent Wind*. "What do we do now?" he hissed at Brana.

Brana let his tongue hang out. "Tricky tricky!" He

nodded, as though that was somehow useful information.

A second later a rope ladder unfurled over the side of the big ship, landing quite near their little boat. The man's voice echoed from somewhere above, though they couldn't see him. "Climb aboard, please!"

Artus looked at the ladder—it was a trap. It had to be a trap. Right? What if Andolon had seen them stealing the boat and knew he was being followed? If they climbed up, they could be captured. Of course, if they *didn't* climb up, they might just float out to sea. Even if they *did* get back to dry land, Tyvian might be pissed if they didn't capitalize on this opportunity to investigate.

While Artus was still mulling this over, Brana climbed the ladder. "Wait!" Artus scowled. "Idiot gnoll."

Artus followed him. The deck was broad and spotlessly clean. Up close, the guards had the sun-browned, spotted complexions of sailors more than soldiers, but their garb was no less impressive. Artus found himself standing before a small, potbellied man in expensive velvets and a lot of gold chains. His bearing was stern and professional—something like that of an accountant or government minister. His crystal eye shone in the dawn light like a piece of ice. He put a hand on his stomach and another behind his back and gave them a shallow bow. "I am Ito DiVarro. Pleased to meet you."

"Artus. Just Artus." Artus extended a hand to shake. DiVarro ignored the hand and motioned toward a pair of liveried guards. "These gentlemen will escort you below. Mr. Andolon would like to speak with you."

Artus eyed the men suspiciously. "Aren't you coming?"

DiVarro shook his head. "I already know what you are going to talk about and I am very busy. If you'll excuse me . . ."

Artus nodded slowly, trying to look confused. "Who is this Andolon guy anyway?"

DiVarro shrugged. "The man that you followed from the Cauldron this evening, of course."

Artus's breath caught, but before he could ask any follow-up questions, a rough hand grabbed him by the elbow and escorted him away. They went down some stairs and a hatch was closed behind them, to Brana's soft whimper. It was the boom of the wooden hatch over their heads that finally settled it for Artus. "Brana," he whispered, as they were escorted down a narrow corridor. "I'm pretty sure we're prisoners."

CHAPTER 11

APPOINTMENTS WITH IMPORTANT (RICH) PEOPLE

Artus and Brana were led to a sumptuously appointed room that had to occupy a full third of the length of the huge ship and was probably two decks tall, assuming it all hadn't just been Astrally expanded—something that Artus had grown so used to that he hardly even reflected upon. It was done up as an audience chamber for some kind of royalty, though he didn't see any coat of arms displayed anywhere that would have indicated as much. The floor was carpeted in plush vermillion wool, save for the center of the room, which was tiled in white alabaster around a fountain that bubbled pure freshwater from the mouths of carvings of full-breasted, pointy-eared selkie women. This fountain was set between two sweeping staircases, also carpeted, with gold-lacquered balustrades carved in the elaborate shapes of other nautical beasts—great eels, serpents, and kraken. Along the walls, mageglass windows gave a grand view of the harbor; above, skylights filtered the dawn sun through unlit crystal chandeliers.

As Artus and Brana gaped at this opulence, Andolon appeared and descended one of the stairways. He had changed his lacy, ostentatious attire for clothing somehow even more lacy and so bedecked in jewelry so that he sparkled to outshine the stars. His golden doublet was studded with diamonds, his hands flashed with gemstones, and his long cape was embroidered with even more glittering things. He proceeded down the stairs on his four-inch heels with all the haughty confidence of a king arriving at a party in his honor.

"Ah!" he said to them. "My young guests! How good it is to see you again!"

Artus managed a half-graceful bow. "Milord."

"Yeah" Brana added, wiggling his hips.

Andolon waved an emerald-studded hand at them. "Pish-posh! Call me Gethrey, yes? Any friends of Reldamar are friends of mine!" He motioned to a trio of thick Kalsaari-style cushions that had been set out by a few servants. "Won't you sit down?"

Artus sat. Brana turned in place three times and then sat on the floor. "Gethrey" gave him a deadpan look for a moment, and then focused on Artus. This close, Andolon looked unusually young—maybe in his mid-twenties, if that—but Artus knew that couldn't be right. He realized, suddenly, that he was being looked in the eye. Like a man. Like an equal. He squared his shoulders and focused on keeping his voice from cracking. "So, what do you want from me, milord?"

"Gethrey, please." Andolon clapped his hands and three women entered the room bearing bowls full of fruit. Artus caught a glimpse of enough female leg to make his brain reorder all his current priorities into watching the three beauties saunter across the unusually large floor. They were wearing gowns with slits up the side practically to their hips and necklines practically to their navels, and had pinned to their faces broad smiles full of white, perfectly rounded teeth. One of these incredible creatures—a woman with dark curly hair and eyes of onyx—knelt beside Artus, the bowl of fruit under her arm. She smiled and nodded a greeting.

It was at this point Artus realized that Andolon had been talking to him this entire time. " . . . and so you see that I am not, unfortunately, a lord of any kind."

"I'm sorry—what?" Artus forced himself to snap his attention back to Andolon, who himself had another dark-haired beauty kneeling beside him. Trying not to look at her and instead meet the gaze of a skinny man with blue hair and diamond earrings was enough to almost cause him physical pain.

Andolon shrugged. "My family ran out of money,

Artus—that's what I'm trying to tell you. Unlike in other realms, the nobility of Saldor essentially *buy* their titles. I had to build up all this," he motioned to their environs, "on my own."

Artus frowned, eyeing the sheer ostentation of the room.

Andolon laughed. "Hard to believe, I know. Want to know my secret?"

Artus shrugged, trying to feign indifference. "Sure, I guess."

The Saldorian held up three fingers and ticked them off, one by one. "Motivated. Self. Interest. I learned a long time ago that if you look out for yourself first—if you follow your own heart, if you seek your own goals—nothing can stop you."

Artus snorted. "Money helps."

"Money *is* motivated self-interest, Artus. It's the same thing. You know who has money? The people who want it the most." Andolon shrugged. "That may sound cruel, but . . . well, life is pretty cruel, wouldn't you say? But, of course, you know all this, don't you? Tyvian is a pioneer of such thinking, isn't he?"

Artus grunted. "You can say that again."

Their conversation was disturbed by a muted squeak and the clatter of a metal bowl on the deck. Artus turned to see Brana with his head inside the bowl of fruit, wolfing it all down in giant bites. His female servant stood over him, frozen in place and so pale she looked ready to faint, but her smile still affixed where it had been when she entered. Artus, catching

Andolon's skeptical eye, said, "He's the muscle, I'm the brains."

Andolon chuckled at that. "Would you care for a grape?"

Artus blinked and looked over at the bowl of fruit (and *only* the bowl of fruit, he warned himself). "Umm . . . sure. I guess."

The serving girl picked a grape and dangled it before his mouth. In a thick Illini accent, she purred, "For *you*, my knight."

Artus looked at her, just to confirm that this was actually happening. She kept smiling and nodding, those dark eyes fixed on his face. Cautiously, he opened his mouth. The girl placed the grape inside and Artus chewed. They were ripe and just the right mixture of sweet and tart. It was, arguably, the best grape he had ever had.

Andolon was watching him, smiling the whole time. "They're from Rhond."

"Uhh . . . the girls?"

"The grapes, Artus." Andolon opened his own mouth to have a grape placed inside. "Seedless—did you notice that? A country abjurer will go around to various vineyards, warding off the development of seeds from the vines the viticulturist designates to produce table-grapes."

Artus didn't take his eyes off the Illini girl. She offered him another grape. He ate it. He found himself unable to relax on his cushion, but also wholly unwilling to move. "Uh-huh."

"Had enough grapes?" Andolon asked.

Artus nodded. The women withdrew, and suddenly Artus felt like he could breathe again. He turned back to Andolon to see that he was being offered a flute of champagne from a servant in a silver wig whom he did not hear enter. He took it. Brana got one, too.

"Thanks!" Artus said. He sipped his champagne—it was fruity and bubbly and tickled his tongue. He liked it. He liked drinking it. Hell, he liked being *offered* it. He was enjoying this—it was a feeling of . . . of control, of self-importance. Was this what Tyvian felt like all the time?

"Sorry about following you and everything," Artus heard himself saying before stopping himself. Wait—was that a good idea?

Andolon shook his head. "Not at all, not at all—I was counting on it. The fellow you met up on deck—DiVarro—he's a Verisi augur. Do you know what that is?"

Artus shook his head. "No."

"It is a mage, actually—a staff-bearing mage who attended the Arcanostrum and earned his staff with the endorsement of the Baron of Veris with the understanding that said newly minted mage would return to Veris and serve the baron. They are among the most talented augurs in the West. You have no idea the lengths I had to go to in order to secure his employment—scandalous amounts of money were spent, let me assure you."

Artus looked over at Brana. The gnoll-boy was lapping his champagne out of the flute at a steady, flapping rhythm. "Brana . . ." he hissed, "cut it out!"

"Anyway," Andolon went on, without stopping, gesturing with his own champagne flute in broad arcs, "the point is that I knew you were coming—because of DiVarro, *I know everything* before it happens. Pretty special, eh? So, I set up this little reception. I wanted a chance to speak with you alone."

"Just what, exactly, are we supposed to be talking about, then?" Artus leaned back and tried to relax, but he still felt on edge. Something about this, nice as it was, seemed . . . off.

Nah, he told himself, *that's just Tyvian talking—he's made you bloody paranoid.*

"To be honest, Artus," Andolon sighed heavily, "I'm worried for Tyvian. I'm worried that he's back in town—he's taking an awful risk being here, you know."

Artus laughed. "I know—I've been telling him that for weeks!"

Andolon grinned and leaned forward on his cushion so that his hands were on his knees. "As well you should! You and I, Artus, we're some of Tyvian's only friends, right? We've got to do what's best for him, don't we?"

Artus arched an eyebrow. "I guess so." He checked on Brana—he was curled up in his cushion, fast asleep. "What do you mean?"

Andolon shrugged. "Look, Artus—Tyvian won't listen to me, and I bet he won't listen to you either."

"Damn straight."

"You know what he *will* listen to, though?" Andolon grinned.

Artus shrugged. "No, what?"

Andolon held up three fingers. "Motivated. Self. Interest."

Artus frowned. "What, you're gonna . . . bribe him?"

"Not *me*, Artus—*we*. We are going to bribe your friend into listening to sense, and then all of us are going to wind up filthy, stinking rich. We'll be drinking champagne and eating grapes from the hands of pretty girls for the rest of our days—hell, we'll go on a cruise, see the world. How does that sound?"

Artus cocked his head. "Oh yeah? And what do *I* gotta do? Run errands? Carry stuff? Pretend to be your manservant or something?"

Andolon laughed. "Artus, that's the beauty of it—all you need to do, my boy, is sit back, relax right there with your little friend, and just wait for Tyvian to come to you."

Artus knew something about this seemed wrong, but he was damned if he could figure out what it was. He shot Andolon a big grin. "So . . . does that mean I can get some more grapes?"

"I still think we should find them. They could be hurt." Hool growled, clutching a paper fan as though it were a creature that needed throttling. Her nostrils flared at the perfumed interior of the fine Saldorian tailor shop. Had she not been wearing her shroud, Tyvian supposed her ears would be plastered back across her head.

"I told you, Hool—they need their space," Tyvian said while examining himself in the mirror—a new doublet, breeches, fine silk shirt, a powdered wig, cane, shoes. He was a vision in gold and burgundy. "No cape? Are you certain?"

The tailor nodded slightly, smoothing one side of his handlebar moustache. "Yes, sir. Capes are out of fashion for the summer. Were it autumn, well . . ."

Tyvian nodded. "Very well, very well. I will eschew the cape, though the doublet is tight about the shoulders."

"I don't like it," Hool went on. "Brana is too little. Artus is too stupid."

"I could let it out. It would only take perhaps an hour . . ." The tailor pursed his lips and whipped his measuring tape from his neck.

Tyvian relaxed his shoulders to let the tailor do his work. "Hool, I know more or less exactly where they are and I strongly suspect I will be seeing them later on today. You smother them too much."

Hool scowled. "Where are they? Do not lie!"

Tyvian smiled at her. "They're on a boat in the middle of the harbor somewhere."

Hool's eyes practically leapt from her skull. "My Brana would never go on a boat!"

The tailor placed his index finger on Tyvian's shoulder blade with steady, insistent pressure but paused before making a mark with a piece of chalk. "You wish it tailored for dueling, yes?"

Tyvian looked over his shoulder and caught the man's eye. There was no judgment there, no ridicule—he was a man tailoring a customer, nothing more. That he knew who his customer *was* didn't matter. Tyvian grinned. "No time today, I'm afraid. On all the others, though, tailoring for dueling is a must. Oh, yes, and one doublet—the black one with the long sleeves—treat that to be fire resistant."

Hool managed to collect herself, though her fan would never be the same. "Why are they on a boat?"

The tailor nodded as he made some notes on a pad of paper. "Might I suggest fireproofing, sir? No flame will catch—assuming your account can bear the extra expense."

"No, no—resistant. I want it to burn, just not me." Tyvian gave him a wink. The tailor did not react.

"Answer me!" Hool snapped.

"Because on the water is the only place criminals can safely practice their trade in Saldor." Tyvian sighed as he swung his arms in his doublet from side to side— yes, totally unsuitable for dueling. If a fight was going to happen today, he hoped his opponent had the good form to let him take it off first.

The tailor completed his note-taking, apparently hearing none of their conversation. "How do you intend to pay, sir?"

Tyvian produced his family signet ring and waved

it in front of the tailor's nose. "I'll wear the clothes out, thank you. Send the rest to Glamourvine."

The tailor stared at the ring for a moment as though mesmerized. Had there been any doubt about Tyvian's identity before, it was now dispelled. The man recovered himself and favored Tyvian with a stiff bow. "The Reldamars are always welcome in my shop, sir."

Tyvian grinned. "Then you and I, sir, are likely to become fast friends." He belted on Chance in a brand-new belt and scabbard that was a very fetching gold-studded number of Eddonish make. While he didn't technically *need* a scabbard for his mageglass sword—he could always "banish" the blade back into the hilt until he needed it and summon it again with a word—a fine sword on the hip sent certain messages to onlookers that he wanted delivered, today in particular. Satisfied with his ensemble, he trotted out to the street.

Here, behind the ancient ivy-clad walls of the Old City, the cobbles were more even and the willow trees that lined the carriage lanes provided much needed shade from the sun. The stench of the press of humanity in Crosstown had given way to clean, cool breezes and the sound of birds twittering from the flower-draped windowsills of stately town houses. Here also, though, were columns of Defenders, marching through the streets on maneuvers. All it would take would be one cry from one person who recognized him, and Tyvian was as good as captured and petrified. He took a deep breath—the high stakes games were the ones he was always best at. That didn't make them any safer, though.

Beside him, Hool grimly put on a just-purchased broad-brimmed hat of green with a white ribbon to match her dress. It was clear she was thinking about throwing it under the nearest coach. "Why do we need new clothes?"

Tyvian pointed across the street to the stately facade of a building a full story taller than its neighbors. It had a colonnade front of gray stone and broad steps of the same material leading up to a heavy door worked with elaborate wrought-iron devices of arcane and ancient description. "Because we are going in there to see my brother and, very possibly, start a fight. Are you ready?"

"Is your brother like you?"

"No. He's an archmage and a paragon of the community."

Hool frowned. "That's too bad. I would like to punch somebody who is like you right now."

Tyvian smiled and offered her his arm. She didn't take it, and instead stomped along behind him, glowering at his back.

CHAPTER 12

THE FAMULI CLUB

Technically, Saldor was a swamp. All around it, for miles in every direction, marshy ground and muddy waters clung to the roots of ancient trees, producing little other than frogs, mosquitoes, and disease. It was, by all conventional measures, a terrible place to build a city.

It was, however, an excellent place to place a magical citadel, sitting as it was at the conjunction of three massive ley lines. Sorcerers had made the place their home for millennia—long before even the Arcanostrum had been constructed—and powerful sorcerers had a way of drawing people to themselves, even unintentionally. Over the ages, the magi of the Arcanostrum transmuted the swampland into solid ground, piece by piece. The city grew in stages, starting with everything inside the perfectly circular walls of the Old City, and then with all the other appendages that had been pasted on in the centuries since.

In the modern era, however, the Arcanostrum was no longer the driving force behind this ever-increasing rate of growth. That distinction lay at the feet of the Saldorian Exchange. Money, not magic, was what made Saldor—and by extension the West—turn.

The exchange was a massive, many-columned building a full third of a mile long—a soaring edifice of marble and mageglass, gilded with all the gold filigree and fluttering angel sculptures avarice could afford. It lay in the exact heart of the Foreign District, which lay at the southern edge of the Old City, just within the city's ancient walls and a hop, skip, and jump from the docks that saw so much of the world's material wealth dragged across it.

Each and every morning ships sailing from Ihyn, Illin, Eretheria, Akral, Rhond, and even Eddon pulled into Saldor's harbor and unloaded goods along the piers. Gold, spices, steel, furs, timber, livestock, jewels, karfan, wines—if it had a value, it would be drawn toward the exchange and the Grand Bazaar with all the inexorable strength of gravity itself. Even Freegate, sluicegate as it was to the vast territories of the North, saw its gold drain south toward Saldor, not north toward itself. If Freegate was an artery of commerce, Saldor was the heart through which the lifeblood flowed.

At this time of day—mid-morning, judging by the sun—Tyvian knew the floor of the exchange would be bustling with the frenetic activity of every merchant or shipping agent with two silvers to rub together and a grand, get-rich-quick scheme. The exchange made mulch of such persons on a daily basis, and from the steaming wreckage of their burgeoning shipping empires and wild-eyed efforts to corner the market, a whole new batch of gold-mad traders was fertilized and grew to maturity in order to be cut down in their turn.

Tyvian had no intention of going there. The floor of the exchange was for fools. Instead, he and Hool were aimed at the place where the truly powerful of Saldor made and maintained their stupendous wealth—the Famuli Club.

The Venerable Society of Famuli had existed for a little over four centuries, dating back to the time when magi were more like cloistered monks and the wealthy merchant families of Saldor wanted a way to curry influence with them. It had begun as a charitable organization—raising money for Arcanostrum magi for their housing, their clothing, their food, and their research. Over the centuries, it morphed into a kind of social club for magi and their families. The original building had been burned down immediately after the Queens' Wars almost four hundred years ago. The only part that remained was the door.

Tyvian stopped before it and thrust his elbow out at Hool. "Take it."

Hool glared at his arm. "Why?"

"We are about to enter a nest of predators, Hool. They are going to look fat and old or young and stupid, but these people are among the most powerful people in the world, do you understand?"

Hool slipped her shrouded hand lightly between Tyvian's arm and his body. "What's the arm have to do with it?"

"I'm about to make an impression." Tyvian smiled, and then threw open the door.

With Hool on his arm, he blasted past the doorman before the fellow could quite unlimber his lips to form a protest. The entryway was all dark wood paneling and deep carpets. An ecclesial hush seemed to hang over the place. Expensive portraits in gilded frames eyed them as they passed by, and here and there a suit of antiquated plate armor was propped up on a stand or a bust of this or that fellow from who-knew-when. There were even a few tapestries. The doorman toddled after them, attempting to gain their attention with a few meek "Excuse me's."

At the foot of the stairs to the main floors, the fellow caught Hool by the hand. "My lady!" he said, breathless. "This club is for members only!"

Hool glowered at the short man in the powdered wig until he seemed to wither beneath its heat. "Let. Go."

The man let go and then bowed deeply—a kind of apology. Tyvian said nothing. Up they went.

The second floor was sitting rooms and smoking parlors. Fat men in expensive clothes lounged in leather armchairs so deep it seemed a corkscrew and a lever would be needed to pry them out again. The smell of good Rhondian tobacco was embedded in the tapestries and the carpets beneath their feet; the rumble of avuncular conversation drifted through open parlor doors. There were coldfires in the hearths, their unnatural blue flame pulling the summertime heat from the rooms, allowing a soft draft to blow in from the open windows.

Tyvian and Hool marched in like they owned the place. Heads swiveled in their direction and then locked on, following the sight of Hool's show-stopping shroud as much as trying to puzzle who the fellow sporting the mageglass rapier and the rakish grin might be. Tyvian smiled to a few old fellows he remembered from his youth—men who might as well have been sitting in these same seats for the last fifteen years, for as little they'd changed. If they recognized him, he couldn't tell. They nodded politely, tapping the ash out of their pipes into levitating ashtrays, and probably started calculating how Tyvian's appearance might affect the markets.

"Remember faces, remember scents," Tyvian hissed under his breath, knowing full well that Hool could hear him perfectly.

"Why?" Hool asked. She was eyeing a levitating tray silver tray that was following them.

Tyvian turned to it. "A bottle of Haubert '26,

please—unopened." The tray whisked away. Then he said to Hool, "I'm shaking some trees and seeing what falls out. I'm the target, you're the observer—got it?"

Hool nodded. "This is going to end with you jumping out a window, isn't it?"

Tyvian smiled, and then they were headed to the third floor. He figured he had maybe five minutes before every person in the club knew a stranger was here—a stranger who looked alarmingly like Xahlven Reldamar, only shorter and with ginger hair. Within ten minutes the mirror men would be all over him. The only question was who would bring them and how.

The third floor was mostly open, with cavernous, vaulted ceilings. Fifteen-foot mageglass windows that ran from the carpet nearly to the chandeliers covered one wall, affording club members a panoramic view of the Foreign District and the Saldorian Exchange itself, which stood only two hundred yards or so to the southeast. The wide floor of the hall was filled with men and women deep in hushed, hurried conference. The energy in the room, even in the early afternoon, was intense and frenetic. Most of those present had the look of someone chased by a wolf, and having been chased by wolves before, Tyvian knew the look well.

These people, when they looked up, did not, of course, look out the windows at the exchange, but rather at the opposite wall, where stood a series of mirrors of similar height and dimensions as the windows that faced them. These mirrors were uncommonly dark, as though reflecting something dimmed and distant. Words and symbols floated up from the depths of each mirror, reflecting prices of certain commodities as they were traded on the floor of the exchange or reporting on deals struck between major trading companies, firms, or individuals. At the end of the room, beside an open window, stood a basin of pure lodestone—Dweomeric energy mixed with base earth to form a solid. From this basin darted courier djinns, each bearing a message for the club member's representatives on the floor of the exchange.

"What is going on here?" Hool asked in a very poor stage whisper.

Tyvian scanned the crowd for someone he recognized. "These people are attempting to remain wealthy at the expense of others."

"They are stealing things?"

"Not exactly."

Hool snorted, apparently abandoning any attempt to understand the activity in the room. "The blue-haired man from last night is here. He is getting closer."

Apparently, Gethrey was no longer the kind of man to sleep past noon. He was wearing a hat decked out to appear like a sailing ship in a storm, its sails billowing in an invisible wind. His blue hair formed the waves. "Hool," Tyvian whispered, "stay long enough to meet him, then make some excuse and make yourself inconspicuous. We'll meet up later."

"Where?"

"The waterfront. Somewhere."

Gethrey was beside him, shaking his hand. "Tyvian! I must say I'm flattered—didn't think you'd take me up on the invitation!"

People were beginning to take note of them. Rumor from downstairs had trickled up and interrupted some of the action on the trading floor. Tyvian caught a glimpse of a few people whispering about him. He saw a woman give him the kind of physical inspection usually reserved for horses at market. He saw two or three young dandies grin. He saw five or six older fellows frown deeply.

Five minutes before trouble. Maybe six.

Tyvian smiled at Gethrey. "Good to see the old place again, is all. Tell me, is Xahlven in?"

Gethrey grimaced. "He's . . ." He looked left and right and then let his eyes travel upward.

"I see."

"Feel free to wait—I'm sure he'll be back soon. Can I get you and your lovely companion some refreshment?"

"No," Hool said.

Gethrey blinked and produced a half laugh, but when Hool didn't join him, he stopped. "Tyvian? Your lady companion is being rather . . . well . . . rather rude." He bowed to Hool. "I don't believe I've made your acquaintance, madam—you are?"

Hool favored him with a withering glare. "You smell funny. I am going to go stand somewhere else."

Gethrey's mouth fell open as Hool walked away. "I . . . well . . . I . . . did she just . . ."

Tyvian put an arm around Gethrey. He could feel Gethrey's shoulder through his coat—it was bony, thin—the shoulder of a man who had slacked off in his fencing. "Walk with me, my friend."

Gethrey recovered himself, smiled, and put his arm around Tyvian's shoulders as well. "Where are we going?"

"Across the hall, to the open window over there. I believe my coming has been expected." Tyvian began to guide them both through the crowd. A few people came up to Gethrey to say hello; Tyvian found himself smiling and shaking hands with various dandies and kissing the knuckles of giddy dandizettes.

If trouble was going to come, there was no way to avoid it—he didn't even *want* to avoid it—he only hoped Hool would get a good look or whiff of what happened and how. Hool had disentangled herself from the press of polite society by simply pushing people out of the way. There were a rash of "Oh my"s and "Can you believe that"s in her wake, but none of it slowed her a pace. Tyvian could see her standing at the other end of the hall—she was a full head taller than the other women present, her hat serving as a marker in the crowd.

Then they were at the window. Tyvian was shaking hands with a portly fellow with more beard than face. "I remember saying to my wife this once—'you know that Tyvian Reldamar,' I said, 'I can't imagine he's half so bad as the Lord Defender says.' You know Trevard, don't you? He and I are like siblings, understand? No sense of humor, has Trevard. Comes from upbringing—his father—"

Tyvian extricated his hand. "I'm sorry—would you excuse me for a moment?"

The man, his anecdote interrupted, underwent a kind of conversational collapse. Disjointed syllables tumbled from his mouth. "Well . . . ah . . . yes . . . but . . . um . . ."

Tyvian jumped out the open window.

He would have preferred to do it when no one was looking, but it probably only served to enhance his reputation among those who seemed to believe him some kind of folk hero. Were the fact of it not so annoying, the whole situation would have been hilariously funny.

In any event, he had been "jumping" out of this particular window since he was old enough to enter the club. Just outside was a cornice that was just within reach if you got a good jump from the sill. Then it was simply a matter of pulling oneself up onto the roof and walking.

Most members of the Famuli Club assumed the club had but three floors. They were wrong. There was a fourth floor—a secret floor. It was a domed chamber at the center of the club's roof, invisible from the street thanks to the simple architecture of the building. From other tall buildings, it just looked like a dome with windows that would pour sunlight down into a central rotunda, but it was not. The only people permitted to access the fourth floor were staff-bearing magi. Tyvian had no idea how *they* got up here—he had always climbed on the roof and slipped the catch on one of the windows to get in.

Today, though, the window stood open already. Tyvian found himself grinning despite himself. "Xahl-ven. Of course."

The Secret Exchange had existed on the fourth floor of the club for almost forty years. What appeared to be a small dome was actually Astrally expanded into a vast domed space of white and black tile and alabaster walls some fifty yards across. Rather than mirrors reflecting the action on the floor of the mundane commodities exchange down the street, here was a flat, five-sided reflecting pool at the dome's exact center filled with silvery, utterly still water. About its edge were a number of magi, their staves in hand, peering into its depths and muttering things to invisible scribes or self-writing pens that floated beside them. Numerous any-gates were situated around the borders of the room, each flanked by golems carved from white marble and gilded in mageglass and silver. Tyvian knew most of those anygates would have their output within or very near the Saldorian Exchange itself, should a mage find it necessary to go there in person.

Where the Saldorian Exchange dealt in the prices of fungible commodities—things like rice and grain and karfan beans—the Secret Exchange did something infinitely more complex. On a basic level, it was engaged in what Tyvian's brother called "derivatives"—

essentially contracts between parties to exchange particular goods at particular times in the future. For instance, a mage would purchase a derivative guaranteeing to pay a trading firm a certain value for a shipload of oranges by such-and-such a date. In theory this would serve to guarantee the trading firm a price and would also guarantee the mage a shipload of oranges (which could then be sold to others at a presumed profit or, perhaps, to allow the mage unlimited orange juice for the foreseeable future). Altogether, the idea was to safeguard the Saldorian Exchange (or, as the magi called it, "the Mundane") from the risk of collapse by guaranteeing fair prices and making Saldor a reliable place to do business. The magi had established it because they felt they had an obligation to secure the well-being of their home city and, furthermore, since many magi had the ability to see the future to a limited extent, such derivatives were a reliable and functionally foolproof way for them to make money.

That the whole affair had been corrupted less than a decade after its founding would surprise no one if, in fact, the average person knew anything about it. Even the members of the club a floor below only had the barest notions of what the magi (acting collectively as the Arcanostrum) actually did with the money they received and invested through their Secret Exchange. The old policy of hedging against loss with conservative derivatives had been more or less abandoned by those magi who traded here (who were, by definition, those magi most interested and talented in the sorcerous disciplines of augury, scrying, and conjuration). Since Tyvian had been alive, the magi who acted as brokers for the five colleges of the Arcanostrum were engaged in a kind of educated speculation that boggled the mind. Rather than trading directly on specific goods or companies, their investments had transformed into a variety of amalgamated "commodities." What they traded on most often now were things like Hope, Fear, War, Joy, Anger, and a half-dozen other things that were simply stand-ins for a whole series of industries and goods. Invest in War, and the derivatives would speculate as to the price of iron, leather, horses, and even things like the harvests of grain that might not come in or the public works project that would not be completed and affect trade as a result of regional conflict. Money from the magi's coffers would trickle down to the Mundane, and if their auguries had been good (and they almost always were), the profits would roll in.

Tyvian reflected for a moment that if Sahand had known how much money the Secret Exchange was making around the time of the Battle of Calassa, he would have known his bid to conquer Saldor was doomed to failure long before Varner sallied from the gates. It might have saved everybody a whole lot of trouble.

A clear, well-enunciated voice called out from the shadows. "The man who would rule must understand that iron is not his inspiration, nor is silk. Rule like water, and understand the hearts of men ebb and flow like the tides."

Tyvian scowled and turned around. "Valteri, *Meditations on the Disposition of Souls*. Book . . . nine. No, ten."

"Book eight." Xahlven emerged from behind a pillar. He was older than Tyvian by seven years, taller by four inches, and more handsome by at least two or three degrees. His golden hair was wavy without looking mussed, and the years had blessed him with just the hint of silver at his temples. He had chiseled, masculine features—the face of a hero on the cover of a chapbook, with dimples in all the right places and a little curl that came down at the center of his forehead. His eyes, like Tyvian's, were a sharp, incisive blue. He was smiling now, as he often was. "You need to brush up on your philosophy."

Tyvian shrugged. "I've been traveling a lot. Turns out lugging books around is quite a bear."

Xahlven nodded. "You look good. Very rugged, for a change. A life of adventure has roughened your edges just enough to make you look dangerous."

"They're called scars, Xahlven, and they weren't a fashion choice." Tyvian eyed Xahlven's black robes and elaborate, onyx-topped magestaff. "Archmage, now? Mother must be overjoyed."

"With mother, how would one ever know?" Xahlven smirked.

The conversation died for a moment. The two brothers stood three paces apart, regarding each other with the silent expectation that the other would make some kind of sudden move. Tyvian had no interest in shaking hands, and Xahlven, knowing this, didn't offer. The time for pleasantries had apparently ended. "What's your hand in all this?"

Xahlven laughed. "You'll need to be more specific."

Tyvian rolled his eyes and gestured to himself. "Do I really? The brother you haven't seen in over a decade is here, standing in front of you, and you're claiming not to know why?"

His brother shrugged. "I can imagine two minor reasons and one major one, though only you know which is the truth. You are here because you have run out of money, you are here because of Myreon Alafarr, or you are here because of *that*." Xahlven pointed at Tyvian's ring. "Actually, it is *mostly* because of that, isn't it?"

Tyvian felt the edge of his mouth tighten before he could prevent it. Dammit. He wasn't surprised that Xahlven knew about the ring, of course, but he took no pleasure in being correct. When dealing with his family, he was dealing with people who used others like most people used currency—they invested, they saved, they guided, they spent. Every piece of information Tyvian gave them was a weapon in their arsenal, and every piece of information they provided in return was a lure, a trap. It was very much like dealing with himself, actually.

Xahlven, though, was smarter than he was. He knew it and Xahlven knew it. Tyvian liked to think his life outside of Saldor had allowed him to come to terms with that, but it hadn't. The fact that he had gotten the wrong book for the Valteri quotation burned in his guts for no good reason other than Xahlven had corrected him about something, and he *hated* being corrected by Xahlven. When they were children—Tyvian no older than ten and Xahlven a teenager just entering the Arcanostrum—Tyvian had tried to stab his older brother in the hand with a letter opener for criticizing his handwriting on a card he was writing to his mother for her birthday. Xahlven laughed at him. So had his mother, come to think of it. The thought of it still made him angry, as did every stupid trivia question his brother had ever asked. Xahlven knew this, too, and had asked him the idiotic Valteri question anyway.

Tyvian took a deep breath. "What does she want with me?"

"Mother, as you well know, does not share her plans with me, Tyvian." Xahlven waved his staff for a moment and gazed into the distance—the motion was too subtle and clever for Tyvian to divine what kind of spell it was. "If you're here to get a leg up on whatever she has planned, I won't be much help. I suppose you'll have to ask her yourself."

Xahlven didn't "suppose" anything—he knew and was being deliberately obtuse. "Mother has never had a plot whose aftermath you didn't seek to exploit, Xahlven. Just tell me."

Tyvian's brother sighed and gave him a long look, as though trying to decide something. Tyvian imagined this display was meant to imply that Xahlven was making a gut decision to trust him with some kind of information, but Tyvian knew his brother too well.

Xahlven had probably planned to tell him this weeks ago. "Very well," Xahlven said, "but if I tell you, will you leave? You've already been noticed by three magi so far, and I can only feasibly erase the memories of two of them without causing a fuss."

Tyvian snorted. "I certainly wouldn't want to cause a fuss, now would I?"

Xahlven rolled his eyes. "Do grow up someday. So far as I am aware, Mother has some manner of disagreement with your old friend, Gethrey Andolon who has become *quite* active on the Mundane these past years. He seems to be trying to angle some kind of leverage here as well." Xahlven cast his eyes across the floor of the Secret Exchange to the central pool and those clustered there. "There are whispers he seeks to affect a crash."

Tyvian laughed. "Impossible. How?"

Xahlven's gaze never wavered from the cluster of magi in the distance. "Auguries aren't destinies Tyvian—aren't you fond of saying that? Nothing is ever guaranteed."

Tyvian followed Xahlven's gaze to find his brother was looking more or less directly at a specific mage—a dour-looking, iron-haired Verisi with a crystal eye very much like Carlo diCarlo's and wearing the tight hose and blooming breeches in fashion in the Verisi court. Whoever he was, he was a Verisi augur, probably bonded to the baron's service after earning his staff, and he was wearing sufficient gold jewelry to show that he was well-compensated for his craft.

"His name is DiVarro—he is Andolon's creature by way of enormous sums of money." Xahlven turned back to him. "I'm sure you noticed the patsy downstairs, correct?"

Tyvian said nothing for a moment—would it be better to feign knowledge or admit ignorance? He made a snap decision. "I did, yes."

Xahlven gave Tyvian one of his trademarked *aren't I so smart* grins. "Did you? Well, anyway, you'll probably meet him in a few minutes. You'd better go. Shall I tell mother to expect you?"

Tyvian thought of the shipment of clothing he'd already had sent to Glamourvine. "No, don't bother. I'm sure she's expecting me already, just as you were."

Xahlven shrugged. "You are my brother—if I can't predict your behavior, whose *can* I predict?"

Tyvian scowled. "Good-bye, Xahlven." He then ducked back out the open window and went back the way he came.

Back on the roof, he peered over the edge to see the front of the club. There was a coach pulling up sporting the scales and stars of Saldor, followed closely by a troop of mirror men marching in a double rank. Firepikes and everything. Tyvian sighed. "Great."

CHAPTER 13

NOT FRIENDS

A "patsy" was somebody who had been egged into a duel—usually a fellow with an inflated sense of pride and a poor sense of mortality. This fellow, whoever he was, had spotted Tyvian on his way through the trading floor on the way in and taken umbrage at his presence because somebody had intentionally been whispering nasty things in his ear about Tyvian for some period of time for this very purpose. Tyvian knew that it meant that this idiot was essentially a weapon—a weapon timed to go off exactly when he laid eyes on him and began to plot his intention to challenge him to a duel. The effect of the weapon, though, was not to get Tyvian stabbed, but rather to get him arrested. Duels were illegal in Saldor. The precise moment the patsy drew his sword, the Defenders would be kicking in the doors and arresting both of them, as had been foreordained by the Mage Defender in command of this section of town. When Tyvian was younger, all manner of precautions needed to be taken in order for a duel to actually happen. The patsy, being an idiot by definition, would not have taken any such precautions.

Tyvian considered jumping off the roof, but it was at least a twenty foot drop to the nearest roof, and almost fifty feet to the cobblestone street below—not especially encouraging. "Kroth take it." He sighed and, grabbing the cornice again, swung himself back into the open window.

There were so many gawkers by the window, wondering what had become of him, that Tyvian nearly kicked a woman in the teeth and in actual fact bowled over the portly bore who had been aggressively name-dropping to him a few minutes earlier. They fell together onto the lush carpets, the fat man's hands wrapped round Tyvian's waist like a lover. The fellow was so flustered that he seemed unable to function, flapping about beneath Tyvian like a half-dead fish. Tyvian somehow got the man's beard tangled in one of his buttons. So much for a graceful entrance.

He was still struggling to extricate himself from the fleshy clutches of that tubby gossip-hound when he felt something soft slap against the back of his head. "What the hell?" He looked up.

There was a man there holding a glove. He was young—no older than his early twenties, dressed in a rakish hat and wearing his hair in pink ringlets on either side of a hairless, earnest face. "Tyvian Reldamar, I challenge you to a duel."

Tyvian rolled his eyes. "Now? Can't you see I'm busy?"

The fellow straightened his doublet and threw his shoulders back. "You are a blight upon the good name of the Society and a poor influence on the younger membership. I am prepared to allow you to submit to my request that you relinquish your membership and, thereby, satisfy honor. If you refuse, it must be swords, and it must be now."

Tyvian planted a hand on the fat man's face and pushed the fellow away so that his beard left a substantial portion of its growth knotted around Tyvian's buttons. The old man squeaked in pain, but Tyvian ignored him, despite a slight twinge from the ring. "Who the hell are you, boy?"

The patsy blinked. "I am Malcorn DeVauntnesse of Halmor."

"Your uncle is Faring DeVauntnesse?" Tyvian straightened his clothing. He couldn't be certain, but he imagined the Defenders were in the process of setting a perimeter around the club as he spoke. Time was not on his side.

"My uncle has that distinction, yes." Young Malcorn rested his hand on the hilt of a very elaborate rapier—it had clearly been fashioned by more jewelers than it had bladesmiths.

The crowd parted around Tyvian as he took up a position across from the young man and took off his doublet. "Did your uncle ever tell you about how I cut off his balls once?"

The crowd gasped. Young Malcorn's expression darkened. "He told me you fought with dishonor. I take it you will not yield?" The boy drew his sword. Tyvian thought he could hear shouting coming from the second floor. From the corner of his eye he saw the levitating silver tray he had spoken to earlier arrive bearing the bottle of wine he had ordered.

Tyvian stepped forward until the boy's rapier was a hand's breadth from his chest. "The day I yield to a DeVauntnesse is the day I put on waders and fish for eels like a marsh-born urchin."

"En garde, then."

Tyvian rolled his eyes. "Not hardly." With a quick sweep of his arm, he tossed his doublet over the patsy's face. Young Malcorn lifted his free hand to pull it off, but in that time Tyvian snatched his wine bottle and threw it overhand at the idiot's head. The heavy glass bounced off Malcorn's temple with a low-pitched *bong* and the dandy dropped like a string-cut marionette.

At this point a Defender's magically amplified voice was shouting *"EVERYBODY DOWN!"* and everyone around Tyvian was dropping on their faces. Entering the hall were a trio of mirror men with a Mage

Defender in tow. They weren't wielding firepikes, though—it wouldn't do to set the Venerable Society of Famuli on fire—so instead they had their rapiers drawn. In an even match, Tyvian could have dispatched all three in short order, but the Mage Defender was the real threat—he was already weaving bladewards and guards around his three men and urging them forward with enchantments that let them skip across the long room with all the speed and grace of Taqar gazelles.

"Okay," Tyvian muttered, "out the window after all."

He turned and rushed back toward the open window beside the lodestone fountain from which issued courier djinn—his ticket out. Spying a note in the hand of one prone gentleman investor, Tyvian snatched it up and threw it into the fountain.

"Here now!" The man looked up, "I wasn't ready to send that!"

Tyvian didn't respond, but instead drew Chance in time to parry two thrusts from two separate Defenders. He backed up and, just as the cube of black Dweomer formed in his peripheral vision, leapt out the window.

He timed it almost perfectly—both Tyvian and the construct exited the window at the same time, but Tyvian was too late to land atop it, as had been his hope. So, instead of straddling the black cube as it zoomed off on its errand, he wound up hanging from it by one hand. The surface of the thing was perfectly smooth and so cold it burned.

They—Tyvian and the djinn—rocketed over the

neighboring building and then dropped to ten feet above the street beyond. The only reason this didn't knock Tyvian into space was the fact that his left hand seemed to have frozen to the surface of the construct as firmly as a tongue to a steel pole in wintertime. The pain was unique, and Tyvian expressed its novelty in a series of colorful profanities.

He was now zooming above the busy Saldorian streets, making a beeline for the Mundane, which was about as far as this escape plan had resolved itself before he threw himself out an open window. He now had to figure out how to get off the damned thing without breaking his neck *before* he arrived in the Mundane and was promptly arrested by the Defenders no doubt waiting for him there.

And, if possible, he was hoping to keep the skin on his left hand intact in the process.

It was then that a large and well-appointed black coach-and-four galloped beneath him. The coachman had to be a madman—he was whipping his team into a frenzy in his effort to match the djinn's speed. He kept shooting looks over his shoulder at the escaping smuggler, his eyes wild. "What the . . ."

From the side window of the coach, Gethrey Andolon's blue-haired head emerged, the ridiculous ship-hat on the verge of foundering in the face of the coach's frantic pace. He motioned to the roof of the coach. "Drop here! Hurry!"

Tyvian looked ahead—the djinn was less than two hundred yards from the exchange now, and he was about to get smashed against a flying buttress if he didn't jump now. With a grimace, he twisted his numb and frozen hand. It came free from the surface of the courier djinn with a disconcerting tearing noise and Tyvian fell a few feet to the roof of the coach, which immediately made a sharp turn down a narrow side street. He felt himself fly off the top of the coach and only had time to roll into a ball before bashing against the cobblestones and rolling. The wind was knocked out of him; stars danced in his eyes.

The coach rolled up beside him and the door opened; a strong, rough hand yanked him from the cobblestones and deposited him on the floor of the cab in the blink of an eye.

"Drive!" Gethrey's voice barked out a window, and drive they did. The coach rumbled out of the alley and onto the street with all the haste a team of four horses could muster.

Tyvian pulled himself off the floor and into the luxuriously cushioned seats of the coach across from his old friend. Gethrey was sitting with a flute of champagne clutched primly between two fingers. "My, you haven't changed a bit, Tyv! Still swinging from chandeliers and the lot of it, eh?"

As Tyvian regained his equilibrium, he found himself wondering who it was that had dragged him off the street—certainly not Gethrey, who was soft as butter. Then who? He shook his head, trying to clear it.

"Relax," Gethrey smiled, offering him some champagne, "you're safe. Nothing to worry about."

Tyvian took the glass but said nothing. He got the eerie sensation that somebody was breathing down his neck—somebody close and not friendly at all. He tried to block out all distractions to isolate the feeling, but it was difficult—the rumble of the coach, the taste of the champagne, the stench of Gethrey's cologne, the throbbing of his sore hand . . .

. . . but then he had it. There was a third figure in the coach—a figure made of shadows and nothingness. A figure who had a button tattoo just above the corner of his lips.

A Quiet Man of the Mute Prophets, sitting right next to him, shoulder-to-shoulder.

"To another successful escape," Gethrey said, holding up his glass to toast.

Tyvian obliged him, grimacing. "And to many more."

The *Argent Wind* was an affront to shipbuilding—a great, fat, four-masted lunk of lumber, a hull more circular than elliptical, and a fore- and sterncastle so gaudily gilded and so massively constructed that it was a miracle of buoyancy that the vessel didn't sink under its own weight. It was a twelve-year-old dunce's idea of a luxury yacht—all gold, glitz, and expense, but with all the refinement and practicality of a nickel-plated kite. As they passed beneath the bowsprit, Tyvian marveled at its incredibly poor taste—it depicted not just a single figure, but rather an entire tableau of nautical themes,

NO GOOD DEED   183

each clashing with the last. There was the selkie king with his trident astride a great seahorse, there were pegasi, there were dolphins, there were topless beauties fanning themselves with scallop shells, and all of them arranged in a kind of profane explosion of design elements. Tyvian could see the sculptor's pain in the work—it was wrought in the face of each figure, a kind of mute anguish that said, *Why was this asked of me? Whom did I wrong to deserve this?*

"Isn't she something?" Gethrey observed, grinning at the monstrosity his wealth had commissioned. "I spared no expense."

"I certainly believe it." Tyvian did his best not to gag. Gethrey had always been afflicted with a certain gauche style, but this . . . this was . . .

Gethrey's servant—a sailor in a mocked-up soldier's costume—rowed them both (*and the Quiet Man,* Tyvian told himself, *don't forget the Quiet Man!*) alongside to a boatswain's chair that would hoist them aboard. Tyvian elected to climb up the cargo netting with the sailor while Gethrey sailed up to the deck like a debutante on a porch swing.

"Oh Tyvian," Gethrey chuckled as the smuggler rolled onto the deck, "you really have fallen from grace, haven't you?"

Tyvian picked himself up and dusted himself off. "Whatever do you mean?"

Gethrey laughed again, rolling his eyes as though to say, *Don't say you don't know!* He motioned Tyvian belowdecks. "Come along! This way!"

Tyvian found himself standing in a room that might have been separated into five or six cabins on a regular luxury vessel but combined here into a single audience chamber. As had been the case outside, the interior was dripping with gold leaf and baroque woodwork. A crimson carpet the thickness and consistency of a well-maintained lawn stretched from wall to wall. It had sweeping staircases, a gaudy fountain, and windows in all the wrong places. It offended Tyvian's eyes, so he looked instead at Gethrey, with his blue hair and ship-hat, whose appearance he found marginally less painful.

Artus and Brana were there. Artus was seated on big fluffy cushions and sipping some kind of wine from overlarge wineglasses. "Hey there, Tyv!" Artus said, his speech mildly slurred. "Join the party!"

Brana said nothing—he was curled into a ball, asleep. In his human shroud, this made it look a lot like he was dead. His tongue was hanging out at an odd angle, too, which completed the illusion.

Gethrey grinned at Tyvian and waggled a finger at him. "Having me followed, eh? Do you really think so little of me? You must have known I'd notice!" He let himself sink into another giant cushion-chair.

Tyvian shrugged. "The thought crossed my mind, but I had to be sure."

Gethrey snapped his fingers and one of his servants stepped forward with a bottle of wine for Tyvian to inspect.

Tyvian inspected it—it was a Kholdris '16, arguably

one of the most expensive wines in existence. It wasn't for drinking, though—it was expensive because it was the last year this Verisi vintage grown by a pirate king on his own private island had been harvested before the Akrallian fleet burned the entirety of the island to ash and salted the earth. It was a collector's item. Tyvian was horrified, therefore, to see that the servant had a corkscrew stuffed in his belt.

"Had to be sure of what?" Gethrey asked. He waved to another servant—a big lout who barely fit in his livery, who dragged a cushion out of a trunk and deposited it behind Tyvian, completing the circle of sleeping gnoll, drunk boy, and tasteless fop. "Sit, please. I'll have the wine poured."

Tyvian winced. "That would be fine, thank you." He sat, removing Chance and laying it carefully beside him. The cushion had been perfumed, so the act of sitting enveloped him in a noxious fume of flower petals and plant extracts.

Artus giggled. "Isn't that cool? It, like, makes you smell flowery!"

Tyvian grimaced. "I've encountered it before." He left out where, though, which was in middle-rate Illini whorehouses.

Gethrey kept grinning at Tyvian as his lummox of a servant pried the cork from the bottle of Kholdris with all the grace of a bear with a crowbar. The man tossed the cork out a porthole and sloshed the wine into two expensive crystal glasses. When Gethrey got his, he stuffed his nose inside and inhaled deeply, as though he intended to go for a dive in the stuff. "Ahhh . . . the smell of history, don't you agree?"

Tyvian sniffed his own wine cautiously. It had clearly passed its peak—he smelled something that singed his nostrils and not much more. "I must confess to not spending much time smelling history, Geth. Now, I sense a sales pitch coming on—what is it?"

"Ah-ah!" Gethrey held up one finger. "Not before you answer my question—you had me followed because you had to be sure of *what*?"

Tyvian looked around the room and sighed—no point putting it off any longer. "If you, Gethrey Andolon, were in the employ of the Mute Prophets."

Gethrey's face froze, the smile fixed in place. "I beg your pardon?"

Tyvian rolled his eyes. "Oh, come *on*, Geth—you had a Quiet Man fish me out of the damned gutter and you thought I wouldn't notice? Give it up, man. Come clean."

Gethrey's smile gradually crumpled into something shriveled and bitter. "Well, good for you and your oh-so-impressive brain. I fail to see how having me followed would—"

"You forget, my friend—I've had a lot more experience with underworld types than you have. The Mute Prophets have a certain pattern of operation common to many crime syndicates. They prefer to *use* people rather than kill them. So, there were three possibilities in my sending my protégés after you: First, you would do nothing and be followed to your home, in which case you would be the same old hopelessly, clueless failed socialite you always were—"

Gethrey's face reddened, even over and above the blush he was wearing. "'Failed' socialite? *Failed?* I'll have you know—"

"Oh, and you'd have me believe your inviting me to the club wasn't a desperate ploy to improve your social image? I doubt all those people crowding around me today were there to shake *your* hand, but there you were, arm locked in mine and beaming like you'd just struck gold in your garden. The only reason I'm sitting here— the only reason you're trying to beat me over the head with your garish wealth, Gethrey—is because I'm your only hope for a respectable life." Tyvian held Gethrey's gaze, and gradually, Gethrey's indignation cooled to some kind of embarrassment. His eyes dropped to his wine and he swirled it around like a sullen child.

Tyvian pressed on. "You might have killed Artus and Brana here—that was the second option—in which unlikely case you'd become a significantly more vicious and independent fellow. You didn't and haven't become such, naturally. Instead, you sought to co-opt them, just like the Prophets co-opted you somehow. That told me everything I needed to know."

"What?" Tyvian looked over to see Artus climbing unsteadily to his feet. "You mean you sent me and Brana after a guy who coulda *killed* us and I didn't even get to bring a *weapon*?"

Tyvian scowled. "Don't be dramatic, Artus—I just explained that—"

"*Don't be 'dramatic'?*" Artus's face was flushed crimson—Tyvian knew that face well. He tried to rise in time to meet the boy's charge but didn't get halfway up before Artus threw his body into Tyvian's midsection in a full-body tackle, roaring as he did so. He might have dodged the attack, but he let it happen. It was a good opportunity to slip an envelope into the boy's jacket pocket, and he couldn't guarantee he'd get another chance.

This meant he wound up on his back, his head half buried in an odious Illini whore-cushion. Tyvian tried to twist out of Artus's grip, but Artus—even tipsy Artus—had learned too much from Hool to be easily thrown. In the blink of an eye Artus was straddling Tyvian's chest, his knees pinning Tyvian's arms and his right fist cocked to break Tyvian's nose. "*YOU LOUSY SON OF A BITCH!*"

Just then Brana's arm locked under Artus's chin and wrenched the boy off Tyvian. "No, Artus!" Brana snarled. "Bad!"

The two juveniles began to brawl, throwing each other around like so many bags of sawdust in a Rhondian gymnasium. An end table broke, rugs were scuffed, and the two of them growled at each other like animals, cursing in both Trade and gnoll-speak in equal measure.

Tyvian drew back from the melee and did his best to straighten his shirt. Gethrey was laughing at him. "That was a sight, Tyv. I shall cherish it forever."

Gethrey's liveried thugs moved in on the brawl,

each trying to get ahold of the other. Brana had his mouth open and his tongue out, clearly enjoying himself. Artus was still swearing and trying to shake himself free from the brutes' meat-hook grasp.

Gethrey crooked a finger at Tyvian. "Shall we repair to my study? For business?"

Tyvian retrieved Chance and banished the blade so he could slip the weapon up his sleeve. He then followed Gethrey up the stairs and into another large chamber—this one occupying the sterncastle of the ship. The décor here was still mired in gold leaf and asinine cherubic woodcarvings. Aside from a vast desk too large to be functionally useful save, perhaps, as a portable badminton court, the room was dominated by an enormous four-poster bed draped with delicate lace and fitted with leopard-print sheets. The sight of it nearly made Tyvian physically ill.

Gethrey positioned himself behind the desk. It took a while for him to walk around it. "Tyvian, I believe you and I can help each other."

"Oh?"

Gethrey nodded. "Oh yes, oh yes—very much so. Look, Tyvian, I've always known where I stand in polite society. I'm not a dunce. My family is poor, nobody has attained a staff in a hundred years—the Andolons are a laughingstock. A bunch of good-for-nothing dandies who own a swath of worthless swampland, right? That's half the reason you started hanging around with me, wasn't it? Just to spite your mother."

Tyvian snorted. "More than half, to be honest."

Gethrey chuckled. "Have it your way. But one thing has changed in all that time, Tyvian—I'm not poor anymore. I'm filthy, stinking rich."

Tyvian blinked. "You *don't* say? And here I was thinking this ship was rented."

Gethrey's smile got sharper—the smile of a little dog about to bite. "The Mundane, Tyvian—a clever man, a man who doesn't mind getting his hands a little dirty, a man with a few connections—can make an absolute *killing* on the exchange. When my father died, I sold the estate and sunk it all into investments. Doubled my money in two years. Kept doubling it, too. A decade of that, and here I am—the richest single man in Saldor."

Tyvian rolled his eyes. "Oh, please—the old sorcerous families have fifty times your wealth."

Gethrey nodded. "Yes, yes they do—because of the Secret Exchange, Tyv. *That's* where the real money is made and kept and held up. Everything we make on the Mundane, all those fools flitting about on the third floor of the club—everything they make trickles *up*, not down. The magi make money on top of the money on top of the money. It's obscene."

Tyvian yawned. "I keep waiting for this to involve me, Geth."

Gethrey got very still. Tyvian knew the posture—every time Geth was about to ask for something he was worried he wouldn't get, he got like this. In his youth, it had the effect of making him look like a scared deer. Now, he seemed more like a snake, coiled to strike.

"I'm going to knock the magi off their pedestal, Tyv. I'm going to make them see a new world, with me at the center of it."

Tyvian pursed his lips. "You're going to crash the Secret Exchange somehow and then short-trade a series of stockpiled commodities to corner much of the Mundane. If it works, the mayhem will bankrupt most of the wealthiest sorcerous families and firms in Saldor, and you'll be the only person left standing for them to turn to in the wreckage."

Dead silence followed. Gethrey looked as though he had his finger caught in a mousetrap.

Tyvian smiled at him. "Am I close?"

"How did you figure it out?"

Because the Chairman of the Secret Exchange told me as much. Tyvian thought, but said, "Does it really matter? Where do I come in?"

Gethrey shrugged. "Investors are, ultimately, gamblers. The thing is that the magi, with all their scrying, feel like the gamble is a sure thing. So, while the Mundane sees peaks and troughs as we mere mortals scurry from unreliable tip to unverifiable rumor, the magi are unused to uncertainty. Not much scares them." He grinned. "Not much *except you.*"

Tyvian nodded. "You need me to start a panic. That's all?"

"I'll pay you a handsome percentage—say fifteen percent?"

Tyvian regarded his old friend and said nothing for a moment. The amount of money he was being offered right now was . . . was incredible, frankly. Tens of millions of gold marks—enough to buy his *own* private island and grow his *own* substandard red wine until Akral burned it all down. In all his smuggling career he had never been made such an offer. He had always been a custom importer—dealing in small shipments of specific and rare items to expensive clients. It was lucrative, but on the scale that Gethrey was talking about, it was nothing—a drop in the bucket. Gethrey was, in essence, offering him a significant percentage of the wealth of every mage in Saldor. It was enough gold to buy a thousand *Argent Winds*, fit them for sea, and sail their fat hulls around the known world, handing a bucket of silver out to every whore in every port from here to Sandris.

And the ring hadn't even given him a pinch. Not so much as a dull throb.

"I'll need an answer now," Gethrey said, hands gripping the armrests of his chair.

"What's the catch?" Tyvian asked. Something was gnawing on the edge of his nerves. Something about this didn't make sense. "Why me? You have the Prophets helping you—why not use them?"

Gethrey sighed. "Because you're special, Tyvian—is that what you want to hear? Because in all the bloody world, only Tyvian Reldamar can trick his own brother into letting the market crash around his ears. Happy now?" The fop took a deep breath. "Don't be a fool, Tyv—this offer won't come around again. Not for either of us. The amount of money you'll have is—"

"Yes, I *can* do arithmetic, thank you." Tyvian rubbed his chin. Wasn't this what he wanted? Obviously Gethrey couldn't be trusted, and *obviously* the Mute Prophets were going to double-cross the preening dandy when it became convenient for them. There was nothing stopping Tyvian, though, from profiting, however temporarily, from Gethrey's ambitious little designs. He'd have a shipload of gold and be well out to sea by the time Geth's corpse was found floating in the harbor. It would solve all his ring-related troubles forever. He could finance a fleet and search for the Yldd at his leisure.

But then again, something about this deal stank. Namely, that it all seemed too easy. How did a self-important dimwit like Geth get into this position? Tyvian had his suspicions. It was, again, too convenient, too prepackaged. It stank of a setup, just like Myreon, just like that patsy in the club this afternoon. How convenient that Gethrey just *happened* to be in his coach to pick him up when he needed the help. Yes, convenient indeed.

"No." Tyvian stood up. "I don't think so."

Gethrey's plucked eyebrows shot up. "Oh? Don't feel I'm being generous enough?"

Tyvian took a scan around the room—no guards, no weapons. Good. "It isn't that, Geth. It's that you're not planning a money-making venture, you're planning financial apocalypse."

Gethrey shrugged. "What do you care? Are you trying to tell me that you'll feel bad for the plutocrats who have run the world this past century? Your whole career has been building to this moment, Tyv. This will be your masterwork."

Tyvian laughed. His *masterwork*? Cheating half the world just to sleep on a pile of money for the rest of his life? He kept laughing.

Gethrey stood up, frowning. "I don't really see what's so funny, Tyv."

Tyvian, though, couldn't stop laughing. "If . . . if I wanted to . . . to exploit the financial system of the West . . . I would have become . . . a *bloody mage*!"

Gethrey's frown deepened. "The time of the mage is almost over, Tyvian. My plan will work with or without you. Choose now."

Tyvian gradually got ahold of himself. He took a deep breath. "I'm afraid my particular brand of mayhem will not be contracted by you, Geth, nor by your . . . associates."

It was as though he had slapped Gethrey in the face. He blinked, adjusted his hat, and then smiled bloodlessly. "Very well, *Mr. Reldamar*." He motioned to the door. "Let us get you a boat."

Tyvian nodded. "Yes, let's."

CHAPTER 14

A DRAMATIC EXIT

Tyvian looked over the side of the *Argent Wind* to the longboat that rested there for his use. He felt like he was forgetting something. Oh, right—Artus and Brana.

The two of them were standing on deck, their clothing mussed. Brana was all smiles, but Artus had his fists clenched and his face screwed up into a scowl. Tyvian jerked his head over the side of the ship. "Artus, Brana—in the boat!"

Brana yipped and moved to obey, but Artus put a hand on the young gnoll's shrouded arm. "We're staying."

Despite himself, Tyvian blinked. "What?"

Artus pulled himself to his full height. "I figure we should stick around with Andolon some more—and so should you, not that you'll listen. We stay, and there's no more dirty work, no more carrying stuff, no more getting yelled at. What do you got to offer, huh?"

Tyvian shrugged. "Daring escapes and a life of adventure?"

Artus rolled his eyes. "A couple weeks ago I was almost eaten by a plant monster. No thanks."

"There, Reldamar—you see? Even the boy is reasonable." Gethrey put his arm around Artus. Tyvian noted with some satisfaction that the boy clearly didn't enjoy the touch of his new employer, but had the sense not to say anything. Gethrey nodded toward the longboat. "You leave this ship, and I can't guarantee your safety, Tyv, not even for old times' sake. You should reconsider."

Tyvian ignored him. Instead he looked at Brana. "What about you? Your mother will be angry."

Brana seemed to consider this for a moment, and then he also threw an arm around Artus's shoulders. "We brothers. Stay."

Tyvian nodded. "Well, keep your eyes open, then." He bowed slightly to Gethrey—the bow a nobleman would extend to a commoner of exceptional reputation, or, in other words, a small bob of the head. "Thank you for your hospitality, Geth. It's a shame your plan for world domination is doomed to failure and all. I feel pretty rotten about it, honestly."

Gethrey snorted. "Not at all, Tyv. Perhaps I'll remember *you* when I'm sitting atop my endless pile of money. Who will be the pitiful one then?"

Tyvian cocked his head. "You know, you never mentioned what it was that the Prophets had on you to reel you in."

Gethrey's blue hair seemed likely to stand up on end. "That's none of your . . ." He took a deep breath and shook his head. The fop released Artus then and made a good show of rearranging his cuff lace. "It wasn't my intention, Tyvian. I sort of just . . . fell into it."

Tyvian watched his old friend carefully—it took a moment for him to remember all the facial cues, but then he had it, as readable as an open book. He clapped his hands. "That's *it*! Claudia!"

Gethrey's mouth snapped closed. All the color fled from his cheeks, so that beneath his powdered makeup he looked very much like a corpse. "What?"

"You always were infatuated with her, weren't you?" Tyvian rolled his eyes, laughing, "Oh, but for the Prophets to get their hooks in you, it would have to be more than infatuation, wouldn't it?"

Gethrey's voice dropped an octave. "Tyvian, watch yourself."

Tyvian was agog. "You fell in *love* with her, didn't you? Oh, Gethrey, Gethrey . . ." Tyvian couldn't help but grin. "Was there a ring involved?"

Gethrey clenched his teeth, his cheeks coloring as he spoke. "I think you'd better go."

"Blackmail, then." Tyvian nodded, swinging one

leg over the side of the *Argent Wind*. "You take collections for the Prophets, and they don't spill news of your doomed love affair with a Crosstown mistress to the upper echelons. My my, Gethrey—how the mighty have fallen. Having to play pimp for your lady love—my, my, my . . ."

Brana cocked his head. "Pimp?"

"I'm not a . . ." Gethrey wrung his hands. "Get off my ship, you insolent lout! I can see you're no different than you ever were—hell-bent on ruining your own damned life. Our trajectories have switched, though, Tyv! You used to drag me down, but now I'm on my way up."

"Well," Tyvian sighed. "I suppose I'll just have to find solace in my good looks, elegant taste, and average height."

Gethrey scowled. "Get off my ship."

Tyvian needed no further invitation, as spending one more moment aboard that ship was likely to permanently injure his eyesight. As it was, he expected to be seeing gold leaf on everything for days. He hopped the rail and started down the ladder.

Gethrey came to the rail as he descended. His voice cracked with anger. "For all your posturing and despite that vicious reputation of yours, deep down I know you're still that little boy who cried over the body of Ryndal Gathren after you ran him through! You're a romantic, Tyvian, and the world is too hard for you! That's why you're walking away!"

Tyvian took one last look up and shook his head

slowly. "This from the man who proposed marriage to a whore."

Then he was down in the boat and he was off, rowing himself quietly across the busy afternoon harbor. He plotted a course between a few fat Illini cargo galleys, their hulls black with pitch and speckled with barnacles. He still felt like he was forgetting something. Something important.

He ticked off his goals for the afternoon on one hand. Check in on Artus and Brana? Done. Find out what Gethrey's angle was? Done. Find out where Gethrey was headquartered? Done. Figure out who sent the Quiet Man after him in Derby? Done.

"Ah!" Tyvian snapped his fingers. "Right! The Quiet Man!"

At that moment a shadow fell over him. Tyvian twisted to look, but something thin and sharp—a garrote—wrapped around his throat and he was pulled backward.

It was the Quiet Man. He had been sitting in the longboat the whole time, but Tyvian hadn't noticed he was there.

He struggled and thrashed, but the Quiet Man had a good hold. The world was dimming around him; the blood pounded in his ears. Above him the impassive expression of his murderer floated as though in a dream. With his last conscious thought he realized he had only one shot at survival. He threw all his weight to one side, tipping the boat. The seawater rushed in as the boat capsized and both of them fell overboard.

The Quiet Man's grip slackened as they hit the water. Tyvian threw his arms up, driving both of them deeper underwater and causing the Quiet Man to let go altogether. Tyvian looked up through the murky blue-green water, expecting to see the Quiet Man swimming upward. He was wrong.

The Quiet Man, his cloak billowing behind him like the black wings of a Perwyn manta, dove on top of him, a dagger glinting in one hand. Even now, in this alien environment, Tyvian still couldn't make out anything definite about his would-be killer—he was a shadow in a world of darkness, a murky spot in a murky river.

Blocking was not an option; Tyvian grabbed the Quiet Man's knife blade with his left hand. It sank deeply into the flesh of his palm, striking bone. The pain was cold. Blood mixed in with the water, making the world crimson.

He needed air, but the Quiet Man clung to him, trying to recover his knife for another strike. Tyvian grabbed the man by the throat and the two of them thrashed, gradually rising to the surface with their own natural buoyancy. The world spun, and all Tyvian could see was crimson water and white froth. The world narrowed as his lungs shuddered, in need of air.

The Quiet Man pulled the knife back from Tyvian's hand and stabbed again, this time taking Tyvian in the shoulder. It bit deep, but again the water and Tyvian's thrashing prevented the blow from sinking to the hilt. The Quiet Man had his arm around Tyvian's head.

They rose above the water for an instant—enough for a half breath for Tyvian—and went down again, this time with the Quiet Man's cloak over Tyvian's head.

Something hard bumped into his right palm as he struggled—Chance. Tyvian let it slide into his hand and pressed the trigger crystal against the Quiet Man's chest. Doing this let the assassin withdraw his knife again and ready himself for another strike—this time at Tyvian's face. Tyvian opened his mouth and shouted into the water: "BON . . . CHANCE!"

Chance appeared, striking up through the Quiet Man's chest and back through his spine. The featureless man went rigid and then limp. Tyvian, bloody and half blind with pain, managed to withdraw his sword and banish the blade before his assailant's body sunk into the depths.

One-armed and exhausted, he swam upward. The surface, though, was far away. Too far away. He felt the blood leaking from his wounds; he grew cold. Above him the sun seemed distant, uncaring. The world closed around him in darkness, and Tyvian let himself drift.

When Tyvian had told Hool to meet him "on the waterfront somewhere," he failed to mention just how *much* of Saldor was made up of waterfront. Two mouths of the Trell River emptied within the city limits, creating two harbors, and *from* these harbors and rivers branched dozens of canals, wharves, and who knew what else. Hool found herself floating along with a never-ending stream of humanity as it flowed everywhere and nowhere, trying to find a place that would get her a decent view of most of the waterfront.

The city was so full of scents that parsing any one of them in particular from the riotous bouquet of sweat and tar and fish and roasting meat was virtually impossible. Even worse than all that, almost everything she sniffed had the nostril-searing edge of sorcery to it. This city was so thick with magic it practically glowed, and the fact made her skin crawl. Wearing the shroud had been bad enough, but now to smell the taint of sorcery on the streets, on the people, and in the *air*, was too much. Not even Freegate, for all its filth and congestion, had come anywhere near this bad.

At long last Hool found herself standing on a bridge overlooking the main harbor, not entirely certain where she was in relationship to where she had been—any scent of her passing was washed away by the hundred thousand feet of passing humans. She had an urge to urinate on something, just to claim it as her own, but Tyvian had explained to her that such activities would ruin her disguise at once.

Here, however, she could at least see and smell things with some degree of clarity. She could see a group of men hoisting a waterlogged body out of a river—this was, evidently, something of a profession in Saldor, as she had seen a number of people engaged in the practice. Given how much water there was, she guessed it wasn't much of a surprise that people drowned all the time.

Hool watched them work for a moment as they

stripped off the man's boots and were rifling through his pockets. Something about the pale man looked familiar. She sniffed the air.

It was Tyvian.

Hool bounded to the dock in under a minute and tromped down the gangway toward where the men were haggling over Tyvian's things. Before she could get there, though, one of the group blocked her at the end of the ramp.

"Oy there, my beauty!" The man was fat, wearing a leather vest that was too tight for him over a shirt that was too loose. He leaned against the railing of the gangway and smiled. "No business for ladies down 'ere. Can I help you with something?"

Hool glared at him. "Get out of my way."

She moved to slip past him, but the fat man put himself in her path again. "Now now—no need to be frightened, beautiful! I didn't mean no harm! What's your name?" The man took off his cap and clutched it to his chest. "Ladies of quality shouldn't be walking by their lonesome through a neighborhood like this."

Hool looked around. This neighborhood didn't look much different than the other neighborhoods she had wandered through. Hool guessed the man was just making things up so he could look useful to her. She decided to let him off gently. "You're ugly and I don't like you. Go away now."

The fat man's flabby cheeks reddened at this and his eyebrows drew closer together. "Too good for me, eh, missy?"

"Yes." Hool smiled—finally, a human who understood.

The fat man grabbed Hool by the arm and tried to drag her behind a stack of empty shipping crates. He hadn't been expecting her to weigh more than he did, so when he yanked, his hand slipped off and he fell back onto the dock. "You bitch!" He struggled to rise. The men who were stripping down Tyvian started laughing.

Hool cocked her head to one side. "What are you doing?"

"Yer coming with me, understand?" The man got up and pulled a knife, and then Hool did, indeed, fully understand.

She put her fist so far into his paunch that she hit spine. The man's feet lifted three inches off the ground and his eyes crossed. The knife clattered to the dock. Now Hool dragged *him* behind the shipping crates. His mouth worked but no sound was coming out besides a hard wheeze. Hool knelt on his chest and grabbed him by the sideburns. "I am tired of you ugly, stinking men staring at me! Do you think if I rip off your head and wear it around my neck the others will leave me alone?"

The fat man blubbered, shaking his head, snot leaking from his nose. Hool wasn't sure whether that was a *No, they won't stop staring* or a *No, don't rip off my head.* As she was considering this, somebody hit her in the back with a club. It hurt, but not really as much as the man swinging the club probably thought. When she turned around, the two men standing there—two of the men who had pulled Tyvian out of the river—had looks of surprise on their faces.

One of them recovered from his shock quickly enough to snarl at her. He had a length of chain he was swinging around, though Hool couldn't imagine why. "You just got yourself in a lot of trouble, pretty."

Hool considered killing them all but then remembered what Tyvian had said about the Defenders being able to see the future. She'd probably get arrested for killing three people. Or maybe not—did they let pretty women get away with killing people?

As she was considering this, the man with the chain swung it at her, so she caught it with one arm and yanked it away from him. "Why a chain?" she asked, dropping it to the ground. "Why not a knife or a rock or something? Chains are stupid."

Before the attack could escalate further, though, another man's voice called from across the dock, "Oy! He's alive! The blighter is alive! Scatter, mates!"

The men beat a hasty retreat, giving Hool some nasty looks in the process but not stopping to explain what they meant. Hool ignored them and went to Tyvian's side. He was on all fours and coughing up a gallon of saltwater. One arm was bloody from two deep stab wounds—one on the shoulder and one on the hand. Hool folded her arms. "What happened?"

Tyvian looked up at her, squinting in the afternoon sun. "Your son took a job with the other side, Hool."

"What?" Hool grabbed Tyvian by his sodden shirt and dragged him to his feet. "What do you mean 'a job'!"

Tyvian pushed her away and sat down. "Easy, Hool, easy—I'm injured, dammit. Give me . . . give me a moment . . ." The color drained from Tyvian's face, which Hool knew meant he was about to pass out. She slapped him hard enough to knock him on his face, but it woke him up. "Damn! I'm . . . I'm surprised I'm alive."

Hool took a bloodpatch elixir from beneath her shroud and pulled out the stopper. "Drink this. Then talk."

Tyvian upended the small vial. The magic in the sticky liquid quickly stoppered his bleeding and shrank the wounds a bit, but he was still clearly hurt. He sat on the dock, breathing heavily and leaning against a piling.

"Those men were trying to rob you," Hool announced.

Tyvian chuckled. "Not robbery—salvage. Enough bodies get found floating in the river, removing them and turning them in for bounty money is a good living for the unscrupulous. Anyway, if they were thieves, the joke's on them—I haven't got any more money." He looked around at the remnants of his clothes that they had stripped off. "The bastards did take my boots, though. Honestly, how much money can you get for a pair of waterlogged leather boots?"

"They were trying to get your ring off. It didn't work."

Tyvian looked at his hand. "Good thing you got here when you did. Otherwise they might have started chopping." He sighed and patted himself down. He found Chance in its sleeve holster, and this seemed to make him relax a bit.

Hool figured she'd waited long enough. "Tell me what happened to Brana."

Tyvian explained, and, as he did, Hool grew more anxious. "Brana is working on a *ship* that sails in the *ocean*?" She could scarcely form the words.

"Well, *I* wouldn't sail the *Argent Wind* much beyond sight of shore, but basically yes."

"Brana is afraid of the water."

Tyvian sighed and wrung the seawater out of a stocking. "No, Hool, *you* are afraid of the water. That isn't the same thing as Brana being afraid of it. You've been underestimating him."

"Don't tell me about my own pup!" Hool sat on a crate. "I know my own pups!"

Tyvian shrugged, though it made him wince. "I don't know much about gnolls, Hool, but as a former rebellious young man turned rebellious adult, I do know a thing or two about adolescent behavior. Brana is infatuated with Artus—he thinks Artus is the best thing on two legs or four."

"So?" Hool snorted. "Artus is just a human."

Tyvian set about ripping part of his remaining clothing to fashion a makeshift sling. "Brana is how old?"

"He has been alive four winters."

"And he's spent over half that time surrounded by humans, Hool. He's used to them, and he sees Artus as his brother. Artus, meanwhile, is a teenager who resents being told what to do all the time, and so he's managed to get himself a job where he thinks he'll be respected. This should hardly be earth-shattering news." Tyvian looped his sling over his shoulder and gingerly rested his wounded arm in it.

Hool wanted to shake the smuggler until his head fell off. She wanted to howl at the world. Her pup? On a boat? *Working* for a human? How could she have let this happen? How could she *not* have seen what the human world was doing to Brana? Was doing to *her*? "We need to get them. We can't let them stay there!"

Tyvian put his good hand up in surrender. "Hool, calm down—the boys are perfectly safe. Well, safer than they would be with us, at any rate. Andolon is working with the Prophets, and the Prophets don't like squandering assets. Right now they see Artus and Brana as an asset."

Hool scowled. "Why would you do this? Now they are working for evil men."

Tyvian shrugged. "I'm not such a sweetheart myself, despite what you think. Anyway, Artus is smart enough to know when he's being given a raw deal—he'll figure it out. When he does, Brana will be back with us, too." He gave Hool a wink. "And as long as they stay over there, we've got ourselves a pair of spies."

Hool considered. "You are putting a lot of trust in Artus. He doesn't like you very much anymore, you know."

Tyvian nodded. "Trust is what all great manipulations are based upon, Hool. What happened in the Famuli Club while I was upstairs talking to my brother?"

"Somebody whispered in the ear of the boy who tried to stab you when you came down."

Tyvian grunted. "Obviously. Was it Andolon?"

"No." Hool described the person she had seen—a woman, thin and old, reeking of magic and wearing a blue shawl over a blue dress.

Tyvian nodded, but if he knew who it was, he did not elaborate. "Now, let's find ourselves a boat and get out of here before a mirror man comes sniffing around."

"I am *not* going in a boat!" Hool stomped her foot. Tyvian sighed and then jumped into a small boat with a mast. Hool felt her pulse quicken as she watched the whole vessel rock back and forth in the water.

Tyvian stepped into the bow, leaning against the mast with his wounded side. Hool noted that he seemed to have no problem balancing. He held out a hand. "I promise it won't sink, Hool."

Hool scowled at him. "Why can't we walk?"

"If I set foot on shore, the Defenders will be able to scry my location, and then we'll both be arrested. On water, which is always changing, no location is ever the same, so they can't scry here." Tyvian smiled at her and beckoned with his hand. "Come on, Hool—trust me."

Hool took his hands. "There are times when I hate you."

"I know." He yanked her aboard and guided her to a place to sit. "Just be still. Everything will be fine."

CHAPTER 15

TO GLAMOURVINE

Tyvian seemed to think Hool hated boats because she was worried about drowning, but that wasn't it—she could swim well enough to keep her head above water and she knew that boats didn't usually sink. What she hated was the way the water moved. She couldn't get her balance, she felt perpetually off-kilter. She also didn't like how boats were able to move somebody from one place to another without making much of a sound and without leaving a trail—the whole thing was a strange, uncomfortable way to travel.

She huddled in the middle of the little boat, knees

under her chin, while Tyvian tugged on various ropes with one arm and moved the stick at the back to make the sail work. He made Hool handle some of the ropes when two hands were needed, which she did without complaint. They headed north, away from the city. Though they sailed upstream, the current was slow and the breeze coming off the ocean was good. They moved at a good pace.

The city of Saldor lined both sides of the river for several miles—an endless series of docks, boathouses, and mills seemed to line up. There were small, half-naked boys fishing in the river in places, water taxis rowing important-looking people from one wharf to another, and several huge stone bridges, under whose arches their little sailboat easily slipped. Eventually, though, the urbanized shoreline gave way to marshy grass and enormous cypress trees, whose roots dipped beneath the water in a hundred places. The water lost the greenish-blue tinge of the ocean and gained more of an emerald to brownish-green tint. The air stopped smelling of salt and smelled, instead, of moss and mud. Mosquitoes buzzed around their heads in packs.

"Where are we going?" Hool asked at last.

Tyvian grimaced. "To Glamourvine—my family estate."

There were still people on the river—people in broad, flat-bottomed boats that slowly drifted downstream, as well as people living in tight little villages on the shoreline, their houses all built on stilts. The air was heavy, quiet, and humid. Hool didn't say anything;

she only sniffed the air for sorcery. She knew when she smelled it, they would be close to their destination.

She was right. Sometime in the late afternoon, after they seemed to have been aboard the little boat for a lifetime, Tyvian steered to a dock that jutted out into the river. This dock was no ramshackle affair—it was built to withstand all the storms the sea could throw and look good doing it—big, thick pilings larger than the massive cypress trees of the swamp were sunk into the river bottom, boards of sorcerously treated black wood laid in perfect lines to the shore. Tyvian clambered out and tied up their boat.

He pulled his torn, salt-stiffened clothing on with some discomfort and tried to straighten out his shirt collar. "Follow me. Do *not* stray from the path."

He led Hool through a tunnel of vegetation—old trees covered in lively green moss, the ground thick with soft, lush grass, the sky above obscured by the dense interweaving of branches. The dying light of day bathed the path in a joyful yellow-green glow, but Hool smelled sorcery all around them, heavy and intense, and grew ever more nervous as they walked. Tyvian didn't speak—perhaps, she thought, he could sense it, too.

The path ended at a huge, perfectly round door. It was overgrown—or, rather, *looked* like it was overgrown, with flowering vines—but when Tyvian touched the golden knob at the center, the door flew open, revealing a small courtyard edged by glorious rosebushes taller than Hool in her natural form. At the center of the courtyard was a fountain featuring an alabaster statue of a cherubic boy with a sword in one hand and a rose in the other, feathery wings arcing from his back. Water sprung from his eyes as though he were weeping.

Hool felt her hackles rise at the sight of the thing. "I don't like that statue."

Tyvian sighed. "You're not supposed to. My mother is sending me a message."

Hool frowned, still staring at it. "What's the message?"

Tyvian took a deep breath and walked toward the huge, ivy-covered house that stood beyond the courtyard. "The message is 'I told you so.'"

Glamourvine had been the family home of the Reldamars for seventeen generations, built at a time when the nations of the West were in a state of near constant war and the world looked a lot more like Eretheria than it did presently. Saldor had begun to emerge from its vassal-state status as merely "the region surrounding the Arcanostrum," and the magi were becoming less like isolated monks and more like active members of the world at large. The other nations of the world didn't like this—they saw it as the clear threat it was—and there was much rattling of sabers and swearing of bloody oaths. Glamourvine, therefore, was built primarily for defense.

What separated it from the other defensive buildings of the world—a veritable smorgasbord of keeps, holds, castles, and forts—was that it was built for defense by *magi*. This meant the building itself—an elegant, stone-and-lumber villa, covered in flowering ivy and filled with windows—was comfortable, spacious, and filled with sunlight. The woods and gardens surrounding it, however, were a different matter. Glamourvine was effectively invisible to the outside world save for a few predesignated pathways, such as from the house to the dock on the river and another to the main road that led back to the city. The rituals that had made this so were of the ancient sort—sorcery done with time and meticulous care rather than by more modern magecraft—and as such were as firm as the ancient stones of the house itself. If Tyvian was safe anywhere in the entire world, he was safe here.

Assuming his mother didn't turn him in.

The door was open but no one met them. Once there had been a great many servants in his mother's employ, but over the years she had gradually reduced the number of actual living humans present in her home. That, of course, didn't mean his mother no longer had servants—far from it—just that they weren't usually human. Or living.

The River Hall—as the entry hall by the river entrance was named—had vaulted ceilings and cast iron and silver chandeliers of the most delicate workmanship. A sweeping staircase dominated the room, its balustrades carved from dark wood in elaborate pastoral patterns—vines, flowers, hares, and foxes. Everything in the hall was in perfect order—not a speck of dust, not a corner ignored. The décor was as tasteful and ornate as Tyvian had remembered it—full without being cluttered, impressive without being gaudy. It made the *Argent Wind* look like a carnival tent.

"This is very pretty," Hool said. It was enough to make Tyvian do a double take—compliments were not Hool's strong suit.

Tyvian eyed the life-size portrait of his great-aunt Daria over the stairs. "Don't gawk, Hool—it will only encourage her."

Hool sniffed in its direction. "The picture? Is it magic?"

"No—my mother. She's watching us. There's nothing that happens in this house that she doesn't know about."

Tyvian spotted a card atop a table by the door, no doubt left there by his mother some hours ago, as she was expecting them. He picked it up and read the note, penned in the flowing, beautiful hand of Lyrelle Reldamar.

> *Dinner is at seven; the clothing you ordered has*
> *been delivered to your room. Please attend me in*
> *my solarium at your earliest convenience. Though*
> *I know you will refuse it, the fountain by the River*
> *Gate is enchanted to heal your wounds.*

Tyvian sighed—she even knew about his wounds. "You know, Hool, there's no reason you need to keep that shroud on here. It isn't as though my mother doesn't know what you really are."

He had barely finished his sentence before Hool had it off. She shook her mane and breathed deeply. "I'm hungry—how long until dinner?"

Tyvian pointed to the antique spirit clock in the corner. "It's at seven—figure it out. I don't plan on attending, myself. I'm going to bed. You'd better come with me."

Hool fell into step behind him as he plunged into corridor after corridor of pure, unadulterated nostalgia.

A boy in Glamourvine was a boy born under a fortunate star. Tyvian's childhood had featured every comfort, every courtesy. The ancient villa, with its long corridors and labyrinthine chambers, its wood-carved gargoyles and secret passages, was the perfect environment to hone such important boyhood skills as hiding, sneaking, exploring, and filching dessert an hour before suppertime. As Tyvian walked, he and Hool's footsteps muted by the lush rugs into chapel-like silence, he went back to that time. The faint smells of wood polish and dry mustiness of sun-worn tapestries brought it all back to him in crashing waves of memory.

Gods, he should have been a happy boy. At the absolute edges of his memory, Tyvian could see his mother's smile as she leaned over his bed, hear her soft voice telling him a story as the sun went down and the shadows grew long across the gardens. He really couldn't tell when that had changed or what had happened. As he grew, the warm smiles of Lyrelle Reldamar had grown colder, sharper. She did not tell him stories anymore, but rather lectured him. *You are a bastard, Tyvian,* she had told him once, *and that means you must take your life twice as seriously as anyone else.* That had been uttered on his tenth birthday, when his mother informed him that there were to be no more birthday parties.

"What is wrong with you?" Hool asked as Tyvian paused by a door—a door he hadn't opened in over a decade.

Tyvian shook his head. He felt foolish moping over a loss of birthday parties, when there were boys like Artus, whose own mother had banished him to a foreign country so he wouldn't have to go to war at the age of thirteen. "This is my room," he said.

Tyvian's chambers were as spacious as they were comfortable—anaglypta wallpaper in baroque swirls, thick velvet curtains for the broad windows, a balcony overlooking one of the gardens, a bed the size of a wagon, satin sheets, mattress stuffed with down. Nothing seemed to have changed except Tyvian himself.

Hool grunted. "How many of your brothers and sisters slept in that bed?"

Tyvian laughed. "If Xahlven had tried to slip into bed with me, I would have murdered him."

Hool shook her head. "No wonder you don't like people. Rooms like this made you think you were important without you even doing anything."

Tyvian shrugged—thanks to his injured shoulder, the gesture hurt a great deal, but he swallowed the pain. "Yes . . . yes, well, I'd best get out of these rags. Some privacy, if you don't mind?"

Hool's ears went back. "Why? I've seen you naked before. I can handle it. Besides, you might need help with your shirt since you were stabbed all those times."

Tyvian scowled. "Just get out, will you please?"

She left.

He tried taking off his shirt, only to discover how right the gnoll had been—the experience was excruciating. Were it not for the rather impressive pain tolerance he had developed while burdened with the ring, he might have screamed aloud. As it was, he resorted to drawing Chance and using the blade to cut the shirt off rather than try to remove it normally. In his armoire he found the clothing he had purchased that morning in the Old City. He pulled on a fresh shirt—a weirdly easier process than getting one on, though still painful.

Feeling halfway normal again, Tyvian sighed and walked out on the balcony. The garden beneath him was a museum-piece of sorcerous horticulture— flowers of impossible colors growing in perfectly geometrical beds among slender dwarf yews clipped into improbable curves and spirals, trellises of wisteria vines in full bloom, their chains of lavender blossoms dangling artfully over groomed pebble paths. The scent of damp soil and flowers was so thick, the air was like soup. In the distance he could see a beefy gardener—one of the few remaining servants, apparently—clipping a hedge. The man looked familiar, but Tyvian couldn't place him and didn't remember the names of any of the gardeners from when he'd left. It was doubtful the man had worked here fifteen years ago anyway.

It was a strange thing to be standing there again. He had sworn he would never come back—he wanted to be rid of his mother's schemes and manipulations. He had wanted to choose his own path, not live in a house where his path was already laid out. It was typical adolescent nonsense, in its way, but it had shaped his life. He knew that his fate was his own, that all the choices he made in his life could be of his own free will, and to that end he had abandoned the wealth and prestige of his family in exchange for the seedy underbelly of the world, where things were more fluid. Standing there, looking down at those beautiful gardens while two stab wounds throbbed in his arm and shoulder, he wondered for a moment if he had chosen wrong.

But only a moment.

The bed called to him, the rich summer air and the exhaustion of the day weighing down every part of him. He gingerly slipped himself beneath the blankets, careful not to jostle his arm too much, and had barely laid his head on the pillow before sleep took him.

For the first time in over a decade, he slept without his sword at hand and without checking to see if the door was locked.

CHAPTER 16

MOTHER

Tyvian's eyes shot open. Somebody had been in his room—the click of the door closing had awoken him. He sat up bolt straight, flailing for Chance and suddenly aware of how stupid he had been to let his guard down. He rolled out of his bed, half tangled in sheets, and managed to snatch his sword from the bedside table.

There was no pain.

He flexed his left hand—nothing, not even stiffness. He felt his shoulder, clean and smooth as though no knife wound had pierced it. There wouldn't even be a scar.

This was his mother's handiwork. He should have expected it. He suddenly felt very silly, crouching on the floor like a cornered animal. He took some deep breaths and let his paranoia cool.

How long had he been sleeping? He glanced out the window—the sun was low on the horizon, its light barely splitting the tree branches. He had been asleep less than an hour, maximum. He was still exhausted, still a little foggy from his ordeal that day, but there was no sense in putting off the inevitable anymore. It was time to see what Lyrelle wanted from him.

He stood and began to dress. He felt as though he were dressing for battle. In a very real sense, he supposed he was.

The solarium was an enclosure of pure mageglass—a decorative dome etched with frosted, arabesque patterns reminiscent of a tree canopy. The design mirrored the growth of actual vines, which, by some clever sorcerous manipulation of the mageglass surface outside, had found purchase and grown up and over various sections of the dome. Inside, the dying light of day was filtered into a mix of verdant greens and frosty whites, which played off the mageglass furniture nicely, their own design in keeping with the motif of the room. The floor was of spotless eggshell tile; the air was as filtered and cool as that of a mountaintop in Galaspin. Tyvian entered the room wearing black with gold accents, Chance at his hip. Lyrelle, of course, wore white.

Lyrelle Reldamar was well into her sixties, but looked not a day over forty-five, thanks, no doubt, to a lifetime of sipping *cherille* and a variety of clever and almost invisible cosmetic glamours placed upon her person. To say she was beautiful would be too simplistic—there is a great variety of beauty in the world, and not all of it comparable. Lyrelle was beautiful like spun glass—elegant, smooth, perfectly proportioned, but also *hard*. Lyrelle, with her golden hair arranged in a sophisticated array of pins and curtailed by a wide-brimmed sun-hat, was not a woman men wished to hold or kiss; hers was a beauty that stopped men dead and demanded their rapt attention. Her eyes—piercing blue, as was the Reldamar family trait—peered down a porcelain nose at her son, taking him all in with a single sweep and a flutter of full eyelashes. "Tyvian. How nice to see you again."

"Mother," Tyvian said. He could think of nothing else to say at that moment; he felt entirely on his guard, as though Lyrelle had pulled a knife on him by saying hello. He wanted to relax—he wanted to pretend as if the past fifteen years of no contact whatsoever hadn't happened and he could sit down and chat with his mother like a normal person. He couldn't, though. He stood there like a soldier under review.

Lyrelle looked over his shoulder, as though expecting somebody else. Pure affectation, of course—Tyvian's mother manipulated with gestures as much as with words. "And where is your gnoll friend?"

"It's your house; you know perfectly well where she is."

Lyrelle let that pass and patted the chair next to her. "Come, sit. We'll have some tea."

"A bit late for tea, isn't it, Mother?" Tyvian pulled out the chair across from Lyrelle and slumped into it, forcing himself to attempt an image of the blasé young man even if he didn't feel it and wasn't really young anymore.

Lyrelle's eyebrow arched at Tyvian's posture. "Hospitality can never be tardy, Tyvian. Besides, you're frightfully thirsty, aren't you, dear?"

Contradicting her would be pointless, so he didn't bother. "You seem to be maturing at a modest pace—my congratulations."

Lyrelle smiled. "*You* look as though you intend to tie a damsel to the spirit engine tracks and cackle." When Tyvian grimaced, she patted his shoulder gently. "Oh, don't despair, dear—it's a good look for you. Not all my children could have inherited Xahlven's jawline. I think your whole ensemble is rather dashing, in that villainous-rake kind of way. You could do with a good moustache, though."

Tyvian's ring hand tingled, but he noted that it wasn't the ring that was doing it, but rather himself. He was suddenly very conscious of it—the ring was an anchor waiting to be dropped at the wrong moment. He didn't want to sit here and chitchat with his mother about Xahlven's cheekbones and his facial hair. "Mother, I'd like to discuss the reason I've come."

The warm smile slipped from Lyrelle's face like the prop it was. She sat back in her chair as invisible specters brought in the tea and poured it for each of them. "Why Tyvian, you didn't come—you were *summoned*, dear."

Tyvian took a breath to steady his anger, which was building far too quickly to be rational. "Very well—allow me to rephrase. Why have you 'summoned' me here?"

Lyrelle sipped her tea. "I've always been very fond of Myreon Alafarr. It's a gross injustice, her imprisonment. That trial was a sham."

"That's an incredible thing for you to say, Mother, considering that *you're* the one who framed her."

Lyrelle snorted. "I did nothing of the kind—poor Myreon was the victim of being too good at her job. I merely made certain *you* heard of it—and here you are, come back to rescue her."

Tyvian scowled. "I'm not the rescuing type."

"Have it your way." Lyrelle shrugged. "Why *have* you come back, then?"

Tyvian said nothing. He tried to determine what it was his mother wanted him to say—to sever her interminable ability to know exactly what it was he would do and why. He got nowhere, just chasing his own thoughts around and around inside his own head, a puppy perpetually after his own tail.

Lyrelle raised her teacup to her lips and sipped, watching her son over the rim with a steady, insect patience. "I trust you met with Gethrey Andolon?"

"So that's what this is about? You summoned me back here to do what—stop him?" Tyvian searched his mother's face for a reaction.

There was none. "You may assume that if you

wish—I deny it. Poor Gethrey works under the assumption that his plans are invisible to us, but they could not be more transparent. Xahlven is well aware of his doings and will handle the situation. Your interference is not needed or warranted." She snorted. "Such a caricature of a villain, that man—your influence, I should think. Shame your sense of taste couldn't have rubbed off on him, too. Have you seen his ship? Gods, what an eyesore—it is one of the few vessels that I feel might be aesthetically improved by a good naval engagement."

Tyvian shook his head and pressed on. "Well then why summon me? Why use Myreon? What does this have to do with Andolon?"

"Is that you asking a question, Tyvian?" Lyrelle chuckled lightly—the mature, throaty amusement of a predator examining hapless prey. "I thought I was an irredeemable temptress and liar whose every answer to a question was as reliable as a desert mirage. Has something changed?"

Tyvian grimaced at the echoes of his own words, spoken in this very solarium fifteen years ago. He, a young man of scarcely twenty, enraged at the fruits of his mother's latest manipulation, screaming at her in a way he never had before. The anger was still there, too—smoldering, barely contained. If this conversation took but one wrong turn, he would be screaming at her again. "I haven't come back because I wanted to. I'm not going to apologize."

"Oh, and what *are* you here to do, then?" Lyrelle was grinning. She held out her hand. "Let's see it."

He felt his cheeks burning, but it wasn't with embarrassment. He wanted to strike her—had a vis-
ceral need to do something she *didn't* expect, that she
hadn't made happen. He wanted to prove he wasn't
a puppet. He clutched his hands together, running a
finger over the ring, which still seemed to tingle with
anticipation—perhaps also with a warning not to
strike his own mother.

Lyrelle rolled her eyes. "Now I've gone and made
you angry, have I? Really, Tyvian—have you matured
at *all* in the past decade? Grow up and show me the
ring; I'm curious to see it up close in any event."

"Can you get it off?" Tyvian asked.

"To determine that, I'll need to see it, won't I?"
Lyrelle beckoned him with one finger. "Come on."

Tyvian slapped his ring hand in his mother's palm,
face screwed up in what he imagined was a singu-
larly juvenile sulk. It occurred to him that perhaps
his mother was right about him—he had not matured
much. This, of course, made him even angrier.

Lyrelle turned his hand over, peering at it intently.
Tyvian felt the air shift slightly as his mother's will
shaped the ley of the room. Good sorcerers could use
just their hands to work spells, great ones could just use
their voice; Lyrelle Reldamar only had to will it, and it
became fact. This reminder of his mother's power was
suddenly sobering. He took a deep breath.

"It can be removed," she said at last. "There would
be dire consequences, though. In my opinion, it would
be unwise to remove it."

Tyvian's heart doubled its pace. "Do it anyway."

Lyrelle shook her head. "The ring is no longer a distinct entity, Tyvian. It works as a kind of capacitor for your better self—drawing those parts of your soul that appeal to your better angels, if you'll forgive the poetry, into itself and concentrating them. To remove it would mean removing much of what is good in you, which would likely drive you mad or even kill you. At minimum, you'd become a monster and a sociopath."

You mean like you? Tyvian wanted to say the words, craved the cathartic release they would bring, but didn't. He clenched his teeth. "So you won't do it?"

Lyrelle patted his hand gently and spoke very softly to him. "Tyvian, why would I remove the ring when I went to all that trouble to get it put on you in the first place?"

It seemed as though time had stopped. Tyvian couldn't breathe, couldn't even manage to speak. The words echoed in his mind like commandments from an angry god: . . . *when I went to all that trouble to get it put on you in the first place.*

At last, he managed to get something past his lips. "What? What did you say?"

Lyrelle released his hand and folded her own hands on her lap. She sighed. "What choice did you give me, really? My son, a smuggler and a thief, carousing with pirates and vagrants—it was intolerable."

"You . . . you *did this* to me?" Tyvian held up his ring hand like evidence before the court. "H-How?"

"The Iron Order is a cell structured organization,

but a poorly done one. Members, once they reach a certain level of redemption, are supposed to go about being Initiators, but they have no guidance or support to do so. I've studied them for some time—fascinating group, if naive. Whoever set the whole affair up had some romantic notions about knights-errant, questing about the countryside righting wrongs and bringing new members into the fold. In practice, it hardly ever works that way."

Tyvian stood up and stumbled back in his haste to retreat. "So, what—you tracked down that thug, Eddereon, and enjoined him to slap this boil on my moral backside?" He snorted out a cynical little laugh. "Was there a sales pitch? Did you *practice*?"

Lyrelle didn't smile, but her eyes sparkled in the dying light. "Yes. And yes. The hoary old brigand was very pleased with the opportunity, to be honest. I got him away from the League, where they were planning to dissect him like a diseased frog."

"Tarlyth." Tyvian shook his head. "You knew about Tarlyth."

Lyrelle rolled her eyes. "You met the man—do you really think he was a double agent by dint of his guile? Please. I had been feeding that ridiculous idiot false information for years. I'm rather disappointed you killed him—he was extraordinarily useful."

Tyvian rubbed his temples—the complexity of his mother's plot (how many years could it have taken to execute?) was unbelievable. "All this? Just to . . . to . . . shackle me to this thing?"

Lyrelle snorted. "There we are again with your cries of 'freedom' and 'self-determination.' Spare me, Tyvian. I gave you your freedom—I left you alone for fifteen years, the prime of your youth, and what did you do with it? Hmmm?" His mother's eyes were like spikes. "Pray tell me what you have done with your precious freedom? What have you to show for it? You're *homeless,* Tyvian. You're a wanted criminal whose only friends are impressionable adolescents and wild animals. Now, if you'd gone off and become a blacksmith or a tailor or married some sweet farmgirl somewhere, maybe this would be a different conversation, but you didn't, did you? Take a good hard look in the mirror, my son. If you like what you see, you aren't half as intelligent as you think you are."

Tyvian found himself shouting. "Why do you care? Why must you constantly warp my life to fit your aims? Why *do* this?"

Lyrelle rose—she was tall, straight-backed. Her voice was flat and even as a calm sea. "Because, Tyvian, I am and your mother, and I love you."

"Kroth take you and your bloody 'love!' " It was all Tyvian could stand. He stormed out of the solarium, regretting only that there was no door to slam.

Like everything else in Glamourvine, the kitchen was a work of architectural elegance unrivaled by anything Hool had seen with her own two eyes. With its low stone arches and fat brick ovens, it was a strange combination of fancy and cozy—like a warm den, but cleaner

and prettier. Maybe it was the scent of the garden drifting in through the open top half of the Eddon split-
door, or maybe it was the taste of centuries of cookfire
ash embedded in the cool stone floor, or even just the
quiet of the summer evening, and that certain magic
that fell over the world between the time the sun set
and the bugs came out—whatever it was, Hool dozed
contentedly before one of the wide brick hearths, calm
and at peace for the first time in months.

The cook—one of the few humans Hool had seen
since arriving—had surrendered her dominion over
the kitchen to Hool, and she had taken advantage of
it. The ham that had been intended for dinner existed
now as only as a faint aroma and a polished bone left
on a broad, sticky tray. She had then looted the stasis
chamber of a great array of red meat and wolfed it
down raw, grunting her approval—it was fresh, as
though just slaughtered. Hool knew it was sorcery, but
for once she didn't care.

Eating in the human world was a difficult thing for
a grown gnoll. In the Taqar, a pack of gnolls would
take down a few bison and eat their fill in one grand
feast. It would take hours—after the initial drinking
of the hot blood (a distinction reserved for the hunting
party), the animal would then be butchered into meaty
hunks and gulped down with great enthusiasm. The
bits that escaped the initial feast would be roasted and
then savored by the pack leaders and elders—cooked
meat was a delicacy—while the young and the meek
licked and cracked the bones. The inedible portions

(the bowels, mostly) would be left for the jackals or the birds, and then everyone would sleep for the rest of the day. All told, Hool typically would ingest around twenty pounds of fresh meat per kill, and then would be able to go without food for several days. It was an efficient and enjoyable way to live.

Humans, Hool had concluded, ate like bison—they grazed, a little at a time, *all* the time. They ate several meals a day of very small portions, which meant they basically spent all of their waking hours either eating, preparing to eat, or cleaning up after having eaten. Hool had spent the better part of the last few years being in a perpetual state of mild hunger thanks to this nonsense. Now, for the first time in a very, very long time, she had been permitted to eat her fill. Her stomach shuddering in gluttonous joy, she lay listening to the crickets' lullaby and imagined she was sleeping under the million stars of the Taqar sky with nary a human being in sight.

Tyvian stormed in and slammed the door behind him. "Bitch! Kroth take her!"

Hool sat up, her ears erect. "What happened?"

Tyvian looked her in the eye, and Hool was fairly certain she had never seen Tyvian angrier in her life. His face looked like it was going to split at the seams and run around screaming. "Don't trust her, Hool! Don't buy into the act, you understand?"

"Who?" Hool cocked her head. "Your mother?"

Tyvian threw up his hands, pacing the kitchen. "Who *else* would I be raging about?"

"Why are you mad at her for lying?" Hool snorted. "You lie and cheat people all the time. You like doing it."

"This is *not* the same. I do what I do to be free, and she does what she does to clap people in chains, Hool— she'll do the same to you, if you let her, understand? She isn't a mother, she's a *slave mistress*, dark-hearted as the blackest Kalsaari fleshmonger!"

Hool laid her ears back. "Don't talk about your mother that way!" she barked. "She loves you!"

This made Tyvian's face turn practically purple. "*That*," he snarled, jabbing a finger in Hool's direction, "is *complete* bullshit! Pernicious, *fatuous* non-sense!" He then stormed out the Eddon door and into the garden.

Hool watched him go and shook her head. "If he were my pup, I would beat him. Stupid humans," she muttered in gnoll-speak. She lay back down, turning herself around a few times to get the position just right, and put her head on her hands.

But she couldn't sleep. Hool knew it instantly—sleep would not come. It would not come because Tyvian was about to do something very stupid, and she was the only one who could possibly prevent it. Worse still, if she didn't prevent it, she would wind up alone here, in this hostile land full of sorcery and hordes of smelly humans, and have no way of getting Brana and Artus back from whatever foolish trouble they had gotten *themselves* into. Hool sighed—being the voice of reason was never a rewarding job.

She got up and took the door into the garden. Outside, the dusk dulled the wondrous flora into submission, letting fireflies take the stage as they drifted lazily on a humid breeze. She caught Tyvian's scent among the riotous array of smells wafting from the garden and set about following it.

Tracking him, she soon found herself in a hedge maze lit by strange, phosphorescent flowers sprouting from the hedges themselves. Abruptly she realized Tyvian's scent had vanished—sorcery. She might have called out, but that would only reveal where she was— that was a stupid, human thing to do. She was a gnoll; she was a hunter. She put her ears back, crouched low in the manicured grass and stalked her way forward.

There were no human sounds in the maze—just the sound of the crickets and, farther away, an orchestra of swamp frogs seeking a mate. A minute later, taking a few turns on instinct, Hool found herself in a wide-open space at the center of the maze. It was dominated by a broad, perfectly circular pond in which floated hundreds of lily pads and water blossoms. Fireflies buzzed around the pond's placid surface, granting the whole place an eerie starlight glow.

There, sitting on a stone bench at the edge of the pond and glittering like the moon, was a beautiful woman who smelled so strongly of magic it made Hool's eyes water—it had to be Lyrelle Reldamar. The sorceress looked at her with Tyvian's eyes. "Finally I meet the mighty Hool—I've been waiting for you."

Hool didn't know how to react—she had never seen a human so unconcerned by her presence before. It was unnerving. "What do you want?"

Lyrelle motioned for Hool to sit on the bench next to her. "To talk, that's all. One mother to another. It is so very rare that I am hostess to a great gnoll of the Taqar."

Hool approached slowly, a few steps at a time, her hackles raised. "You are a sorceress—I don't like that."

If Lyrelle heard her, she gave no sign. "How would you describe your experience as a human female? I understand you've been going about in a shroud for some time now, correct?"

Hool's eyes narrowed. "How would you know that?"

Lyrelle shrugged and smiled sweetly. "Sorceress, remember?"

Hool settled on her haunches about three paces from Lyrelle. "Human men are idiots. They have no discipline. They are spoiled. I don't know how you let them boss you all around."

Lyrelle laughed; her voice was like music. "Oh, but not all of us do, dear Hool." She passed her hand, palm downward, over the pool of water and gazed into it. "Of course, those of us who do not obey draw the ire of the men who seek to dominate us. They call us names—witch, temptress, liar . . ."

"I know. Does this have a point? I am looking for Tyvian." Hool edged closer, trying to see what Lyrelle was looking at in the pool, but from her perspective it just looked like still water.

Lyrelle fell silent for a moment, then took a deep breath. "Your son—your pup—what is his name?"

"Brana. Why?"

"You are upset with him, aren't you?"

Hool didn't like where this was going; her body tensed. "How do you know that? Can you read my mind? Stop it."

Lyrelle sighed. "All creatures desire one thing above all other things—freedom. They wish to be free to determine their own path, to shape their own fate. This is true, yes—you've felt it, I've felt it. All of us. It's very sad, really."

"Why? What do you mean?" Hool shook her head. "You are trying to confuse me."

Lyrelle stood up and stepped to the edge of the pond. She looked Hool in the eye. "When was the last time you were truly free?"

Hool thought, despite herself. She thought back to life on the Taqar, running with the pack, the breeze through her fur. Was that freedom? Maybe not—she was bound by various obligations to the pack even then. "You are trying to trick me."

Lyrelle smiled. "Your son, my son, you, me—all of us want to be independent of the world around us. We all buy into the fiction that we make our own decisions, but we do not." She touched a finger to the surface of the water, sending ripples out in every direction. "As mothers, we understand this, don't we? As soon as you look into the eyes of that screaming little thing and it looks back at you . . ." Lyrelle closed her eyes, breathing deeply. " . . . you know your choices are no longer your own. You are bound, more keenly than any sorcerer ever bound any demon."

"You're saying that Brana doesn't understand this. Neither does Tyvian." Hool nodded. "What does that have to do with me? Why are you bothering me with it?"

Lyrelle opened her eyes. "Do you think I'm a monster, Hool?"

Hool snorted—that was some question to be asked by a *human*. "No. There are no monsters."

Lyrelle laughed again. "Oh, there are—there very much are, my friend, let me assure you. But I am not one. I have simply recognized my place in the world—I am not free, not any more than you are. I am bound to the things that make me who I am. Those who call me witch simply misunderstand my guile for cruelty."

Hool frowned. The woman was talking like a lunatic. "Why are you telling me all this?"

Lyrelle laughed. "I'm distracting you, Hool."

Hool stiffened. "What?"

Lyrelle nodded. "I need to keep you out of the way long enough so that the Defenders don't encounter any surprises while arresting my son."

Hool stood. "*WHAT?*"

Lyrelle, though dwarfed by the size of the gnoll

before her, seemed entirely at ease. "Why yes—haven't you noticed the maze has changed?"

Hool lunged for Lyrelle but passed through where the sorceress ought to be. There was nothing there—only the fading shadow of the great sorceress's simulacrum. Her voice floated on the wind. *"It is for the best, Hool. It is best for our sons, too."*

Hool spun around, looking for an exit to the clearing—there was none, or none easily seen. "No!" She rushed to the hedge, trying to force her way through, but the enchanted plants pushed her back out. "NO!"

Above, in the distance, Hool heard the cry of griffons on the wind.

CHAPTER 17

ARRESTED

Tyvian knew who the gardener he had seen through the window was. He knew it in his bones.

He stormed past the perfectly coiffed flower beds and the artfully arranged wisteria vines; he pushed his way through a hedge (a childhood shortcut, now overgrown), skipped across the stepping-stones in a reflecting pool, and found himself at the gardener's shed. There was a fire burning inside, throwing a cheery light through the single, vine-wreathed window. Tyvian didn't bother knocking. *"Eddereon!* Come out here! Face me!"

The door opened and there stood Eddereon, but not the hairy mountain-dweller Tyvian had first met. He had shaved and cut his hair; he wore a simple white shirt and blue canvas trousers, but they were clean and well-kept, as though regularly laundered. But for his size and the wild, black chest hair curling out from beneath his collar, Tyvian might never have recognized him. Eddereon smiled his toothy smile. "Well met, Tyvian Reldamar."

Tyvian resisted the urge to slug him in the guts. "Don't give me that storybook bullocks, Eddereon. How did you know I would be here? How long have you been waiting for me?"

Eddereon rubbed where his beard used to be. "Well, it's been almost a year since your mother hired me. Ever since that stunt in Galaspin with the ballista and the schooner—lost track of you there, so I came here."

Tyvian scowled. "Thick as thieves, you and Lyrelle, eh?"

Eddereon closed his eyes and nodded, sighing. "She told you. Please—won't you come in?"

Tyvian eyed the shed—it barely looked large enough to contain Eddereon, let alone both of them. "Astrally expanded?"

Eddereon shook his head and went inside. "I'm just a simple man with simple needs."

Tyvian scowled but followed him. There was a small hearth with a clutch of small logs, cheerfully aflame. Beyond that, there were two chairs, a trunk, and a hammock hung out of the way but clearly intended to be strung from one corner of the shed to the other. On the walls there was an array of hoes, shears, spades, rakes, and saws hung neatly between precisely placed wooden pegs. Eddereon sat down to face the fire; when Tyvian sat down across from him, their knees were touching. Tyvian tried crossing his legs, but that would mean roasting either a foot or a knee over the fire. He resigned himself to pressing his knees together, like a virgin at church.

"Do not be too angry with Lady Lyrelle, Tyvian," Eddereon said, poking at the fire with a stick. "She did what was best for you—she did what was best for all of us."

Tyvian had almost forgotten how aggravating it was having a conversation with this man—his "Initiator." He steeled himself against unneeded profanity. "Tell me how to get this Kroth-spawned bastard off my bloody hand, you hairy pit-spawned barbarian."

Eddereon smiled. "I've already told you—you must become Redeemed."

Tyvian punched the wall, which made a rake fall from its place and nearly hit him in the head. "Kroth!" He ducked, wrestled with the thing, and then tossed it into a corner. "What does that *mean*? What the hell does 'Redeemed' mean—stop telling me riddles, you moron! Out with it!"

Eddereon raised his hands. "Please, please—calm yourself. I am not being unclear because I'm trying to mislead you. I was told by *my* Initiator that joining the ranks of the Redeemed was the only path to removing the ring. He did not say what that meant—I do not think he knew, and he died before he found out, Hann bless him. What I tell you is merely what I have been told and have reasoned out for myself."

Tyvian frowned. "And you have no contact with other members of this . . . this Iron Order?"

Eddereon shrugged. "I've met a few over the years, adventured with a couple for a time, but never for long. None of them knew any more than I, even those who gained the ability to bestow the ring on others."

"Why do it? Why shackle others to this fate? Surely the ring hasn't addled your brain so much that you forget who you were before it tortured you into . . . into whatever you think you are now."

Eddereon smiled. "Do you still think you would be better off without the ring in your life, Tyvian?"

"I do not think—I know with certainty." Tyvian looked at the ring—*his* ring—in the firelight. It glittered darkly, a pool of shadow on his right hand. "This object is the stupidest way for someone to improve their character I can think of. It doesn't make you better, it makes you a naive idiot."

Eddereon considered this, sitting back in his chair so his shoulders almost touched the wall. "The Thembra of the Eastern Sea have a saying: 'Only the innocent can save the world.' I think on it often. I think that, perhaps, becoming more naive is the only way to make us better men."

"You mean *deader* men. The world doesn't need innocence and guileless platitudes, Eddereon—it needs wisdom and intelligence, neither of which the ring considers when it doles out its judgment. Everything has context—try and save the world, and you wind up dooming it in a hundred ways you never considered."

Eddereon frowned. "Was that the case with Sahand? If you had not acted, he would have destroyed three cities worth of people and then invaded the rest. You saved millions of lives."

"That was dumb luck." Tyvian snorted. "Besides, I didn't defeat Sahand at all—Myreon Alafarr did. The wages for her victory? She gets framed for a crime she didn't commit and is a statue in some penitentiary garden somewhere, and all because my mother wants to play head games with me. Believe me, Eddereon—no good deed goes unpunished."

Eddereon stared into the fire, as though trying to witness the moment of combustion itself. "You mustn't believe that, Tyvian. We can't believe that."

Tyvian sighed—what was the point of this conversation anyway? The idiot knew nothing. It was almost pitiful. Still, he kept talking. "My mother implied that the ring was some kind of filter for our better selves—it collected our 'goodness,' so to speak, and we could later draw upon it. That was the gist of it, anyway."

Eddereon nodded, his eyes still far away. "Much of what I know I have learned from your mother and, before that, from the Sorcerous League and Tarlyth. I sought them out to try and unlock the ring's mysteries, but I only wound up with more questions."

Tyvian looked at his fellow victim of the ring as if seeing him with fresh eyes. He noted that, without the beard, he could actually place Eddereon's age—in his mid-forties, most likely. "How long have you had the ring?"

"A decade, perhaps a bit longer." Eddereon shrugged, "When I was first bestowed with it, I did my best to forget my pains. I drank and whored for a long, long time, deadening my senses with booze and ink and tooka."

"I've learned there's a way to get it off, you know," Tyvian said quietly. "Cleanly. Without undue side-effects, or so I was told."

Eddereon stiffened. "If that were true, you would have done it."

Tyvian shrugged. "I can't find them. I scoured every book of history and mythology I could get my hands on, and I don't even know where to start looking. An Artificer told me about them—they are called the Yldd. He claimed he had done me some disservice—they sound like unpleasant fellows, whoever or whatever they are."

Eddereon shuddered. "You must put it out of your mind, Tyvian. The ring seems a burden at first—this I know—but it changes you for the better. I know I am a better man, but I needed to learn to cast off the man I once was. You must do this, too. You cannot live the same life you led before."

"Not a chance." Tyvian smirked. "That reminds me—do you have any lamp oil in here?"

Eddereon looked away from the fire. "I've got a whole jug—why?"

"I would be most appreciative if you would pour the whole jug all over me—focus on the doublet and shirt, if you wouldn't mind."

"Why?"

Tyvian smiled, "I'm about to be arrested."

The initial stages of Tyvian's arrest had involved somewhere between ten and a dozen different mirror men kicking him in the stomach over and over again as he lay on the ground in the fetal position. Following that, everything was smooth and orderly. Within twelve hours he had been returned to the city via griffon-back, charged, processed, and installed in the dungeons beneath Keeper's Court—an ancient castle at the center of the Old City in which the legal machinery of Saldor was now housed.

As dungeons went, this one was downright comfortable. There was a canvas cot in good working order, a small stool, a chamber pot, and fresh straw. There was even a little barred ventilation shaft that admitted the sunlight from above. Too small to squeeze through, but just large enough to admit a little bit of a breeze and the scent of street vendors selling fried fish. Tyvian lounged on the cot, hands behind his head, and smiled. So far, things were going smoothly.

The Defenders had thoroughly searched him, but of course had not found anything of interest other than the fact that he reeked of lamp oil. When they asked him about it, he just said he had spilled some on himself in his effort to escape. The ring had given him a bit of a squeeze for that, but the momentary pain had been worth it: everything was proceeding according to plan.

A Defender rapped on the door. "Hey! Someone here to see you!"

Tyvian brushed some garden turf off his clothes and sat up in time for the door to swing open. Xahlven was clad in the black robes of his office but had been compelled to leave his magestaff outside. His fingers, though, were bedecked with a half-dozen rings featuring amethysts, emeralds, and garnets—every one of them, no doubt, contained a potent enchantment. It was always important, Tyvian knew, to remember that no one who had achieved the rank of archmage could ever be anything other than extremely dangerous.

He smiled at his brother. "Xahlven! Pull up a stool!" He kicked the tiny, three-legged thing across the floor.

Xahlven rolled his eyes. "Gallows humor?"

Tyvian shrugged. "You never know—I might get off. They're charging me with a murder I didn't commit."

Xahlven nodded. "And several murders you very likely did commit."

"I deny them all," Tyvian said, wincing as the ring clamped down on his hand. "I can be very persuasive."

Xahlven shook his head and pointed at Tyvian's hand. "Not with that you can't." He sighed. "Would you like help with your defense? I can testify for you."

Tyvian looked up at his older brother, all dashing with his dimpled chin and golden locks. Yes, he bet Xahlven *could* testify for him—probably even give him a fighting chance at acquittal. "No thank you. Very kind of you—most brotherly—but no."

Xahlven scowled. "Tyvian, don't let your idiotic pride get in the way of—"

"My pride? *My* pride?" Tyvian laughed. "You're enjoying this, aren't you? You've been waiting for this to happen for years—*years*! Now here it is, your moment of glory: step into your brother's cell, make him an offer, watch him swell with gratitude. Big brother to the rescue and, by the way, 'I told you so.' "

Xahlven's sunny face darkened. "Unlike you, Tyvian, I have concerns and beliefs that deal with matters larger than *myself*. You have always taken exception to that—you have never understood."

"Oh, I understand." Tyvian shook his head. "I understand that you are so far under mother's influence that you don't even realize how she's shaped you. You're a mini-Lyrelle, do you know that?" He sighed. "You *must* know that—how could you not? That was why you condescended to me all those years. You were jealous."

Xahlven laughed. "Jealous? Why?"

Tyvian stood up and got in his brother's face. "Because, unlike you, I *escaped* her. I went off and lived my life on my own bloody terms, and you had your whole life planned out—the tutors, the schooling, the Arcanostrum, the Black College, even the bloody office of archmage! Tell, me, Xahlven—have you ever, even *once*, made a decision for yourself? Hmm?"

Xahlven didn't even blink. "I am not here to dig up old feuds, Tyvian. I'm here to help you. I take it you know Andolon's plot?"

Tyvian stepped back, trying to calm his pulse. "What—the market crash he thinks he can pull off? Yes, obviously. He tried to hire me. I assume you have a counterstroke."

Xahlven nodded. "As a matter of fact, I do—you."

Tyvian sat on the cot and leaned back against the wall. A little tingle wafted through his body—a tingle of triumph. "Ahhhh—so *that's* it. You want me to offer the court Gethrey in exchange for leniency. Even if they don't go for it, I will draw their attention toward him—he's only lasted this long because nobody besides you and mother have noticed him."

Xahlven nodded. "Just so. Well?"

"Why should I?"

"Because you don't wish to be turned to stone and left in a garden to molder for the better part of two decades."

Tyvian smiled at his brother, reveling in the fact that, for once, he knew something that Xahlven didn't. "No thank you."

"Tyvian, the entire Western economy could collapse! The damage it could do . . ."

Tyvian shrugged. "You forget, brother—I'm a smuggler. Financial chaos is good for me. Sounds fun."

"You would bankrupt our family out of spite?" Xahlven shook his head.

Tyvian glared at him. "Spare me! Don't pretend you and Mother haven't moved to sidestep this little crash already—hell, you could warn the investors in the Secret Exchange yourself, if you wanted to, but you'd rather it be done like this, since if you said something it would become immediately obvious you were withholding information that could destroy the very banking system that keeps the magi and the sorcerous families on top of the world. And then," Tyvian motioned to his cell, "and then you would get to experience this cell for yourself."

Xahlven looked down at his brother, his hero's face fixed in a half frown. "Very well, have it your way. Good luck today, Tyvian. I mean that."

Xahlven called for the guard. In the second before the door opened, Tyvian yelled at his back, "Don't count me out yet, big brother. I'm smarter than you realize."

Xahlven left. He did not look back.

CHAPTER 18

THE TRIAL OF TYVIAN RELDAMAR

The courtroom had five sides, which, to Artus's eyes, made it one of the stranger rooms he had ever been in. Well, maybe not stranger than that temple where he had almost been eaten by rotting vegetables, but still pretty weird.

Artus was seated between DiVarro on his right and Brana on his left. They were squeezed tight, too, since the benches that made up the gallery were packed to the walls. Word of Tyvian's arrest had spread like a pox and the trial had rapidly become the social event of the season. Artus could scarcely see the floor of the court thanks to all the giant, feathery hats; the air had been rendered an olfactory battlefield as scores of complex and expensive perfumes—many of them sorcerous—warred for the attention of Artus's nostrils.

Until this moment, Artus and Brana's new duties in their "job" had involved sitting around the *Argent Wind* and indulging themselves. They hadn't seen much of Andolon—after Tyvian left, he got some kind of news that had him frantic and he was off to shore like a shot, DiVarro in tow. While he was gone, Artus and Brana had the run of the ship and exploited it, exploring every bolt-hole and crevice until Brana's insatiable boat-related curiosity had been sated. Then the word of the arrest came and with it a noticeably happier Andolon. They had come to Keeper's Court straight away.

Andolon was sitting behind Artus, grinning and occasionally rubbing Artus's shoulders. He smelled like wine and lavender and his hands were weirdly soft against Artus's hard muscles. "DiVarro," he whispered, "the numbers."

The sour-faced Verisi rattled off a series of figures. "It could be worse. Fear and Hope are only down by ten percent at the moment, but there should be a rally after the trial. With Reldamar safely out of the way, there is no reason to expect much more volatility before the pear shipment comes in."

Artus took a deep breath. "Doesn't doing this bother you at all? Tyvian is your friend."

Andolon rolled his eyes. "Tyvian *was* my friend—he was my friend fifteen years ago. Circumstances change, my dear. If it makes you feel any better, I'm not especially enjoying this. Then again, it isn't like I forced Tyvian to run off and become an international criminal mastermind."

Artus snorted—he couldn't help himself. "No, you just became a local one."

Andolon gently tugged on one of Artus's earlobes, which made Artus flinch. "Now now, Artus—no second thoughts, understand? I'm relying on you. We are *all* relying on you."

Artus shrugged him off. Andolon's soft, perfumed hands made his skin crawl. "I won't lie for you."

Andolon mimicked a laugh. "That's the beauty of it, Artus, my sweet—your sworn testimony will be nothing but the unadulterated truth. When they call your name, just tell the truth, and let justice take its course."

Artus's stomach rumbled at that—indigestion. He reached into his pockets—maybe he had stashed a roll somewhere. Instead, his fingers brushed against an envelope. He knew exactly who had put it there, too. He froze.

"Something wrong?" Andolon whispered. "Come, come—this is the only way, Artus. You wanted to be free, and I'm giving you the chance, right? You testify against our old friend, and I make you and your brother filthy rich. A fair deal, isn't it?"

Artus shrugged. "I guess."

DiVarro raised a single finger, cocking his head to one side. "Sir, a word if I may. Movement on the exchange . . ."

Andolon took his attention from Artus and dove into a secret conference with DiVarro, their whispers masked both by the ambient roar of the assembly and some kind of little abjuration the augur threw up to foil eavesdropping even from Artus's distance. Artus took the opportunity to look over at Brana.

The gnoll was wearing his shroud, but any physical indication of his humanity was counteracted by the way he was cocking his head and darting his eyes back and forth across the assembly. He looked nervous—the gnoll still didn't do well in crowds. "You okay?" Artus whispered.

"Tyvian here?" he asked.

Artus nodded. "Yeah. Yeah he's here."

Brana wiggled his backside in his seat. "We save him?"

Artus felt his stomach clench—was this how Tyvian felt every time the ring gave him a jolt? He tried to think of something to say to Brana, but no words came. How could he explain to the gnoll pup that he was being asked to testify against Tyvian? Even assuming he could get him to understand the concept, Brana would never understand why.

Still, Artus meant to do it. Tyvian had hung him out to dry plenty of times—*plenty* of times. He was only returning the favor. Even *Tyvian* would understand that.

Reaching into his pocket again, he brought out the envelope. Holding it in his lap, he opened it and hoped Andolon and DiVarro were too distracted to notice.

Inside were two items: a sparkstone—the little kind you used to light pipes and cigars and such—and a small notecard. The note was written in the flowing, immaculate handwriting of Tyvian himself. It read: *You'll know when.*

Artus scowled. The jerk was in irons and he was *still* ordering him around like he was some kind of trained animal. He grunted and stuffed the note and the sparkstone back in his pocket.

A bell sounded, and the heavy doors at the front of the courtroom opened. Five Defenders, firepikes at their shoulders, took positions around the fat black stone everybody was calling "the Block." Two more then entered, leading Tyvian Reldamar himself, still dressed all in black, his hands and ankles shackled together. Even thus confined, he struck an impressive figure—his dark clothes and fiery hair made him look every inch the brilliant villain he was reported to be, especially when surrounded by the white and mirrored silver of his captors. Artus had no doubt that the visual effect was entirely intentional.

Tyvian looked up at the gallery and winked. The crowd went wild. There were jeers, but there were also just as many shouts of encouragement and cheers of solidarity. Artus overheard a young woman giggling to her friend: "I think he winked at *me!*"

Tyvian grinned at the attention, nodding politely to the Defenders as they removed his shackles and cuffed him by the wrist via a mageglass chain bolted to the center of the Block. He blew a kiss to the gallery with his free hand. The young woman near Artus swooned and had to be carried out.

Brana stiffened when he saw Tyvian chained up. He looked over at Artus and nudged him with his shoulder. *"Rescue?"* he whimpered in gnoll-speak.

Artus gave Brana a tight smile. His stomach, though, started doing flips.

"Courage, my friend," Andolon whispered, giving him another limp shoulder rub. "Courage."

"Don't worry about me," Artus snarled, shaking him off again. Was he really going to go through with this? He found himself hoping against hope that Tyvian would escape before he had to testify.

The judges arrived, stepping in from a door behind their pulpits, each clad in a white wig and a robe colored for the energy they studied. The lead judge represented the Dweomer—she wore deep blue and held an orb of swirling azure. She held it aloft and it flashed with blinding sapphire light. *"Order in the court."* Her voice was amplified so that it echoed off all five walls, drowning out the commotion in the gallery with ease.

Everybody settled down.

The judge laid some kind of ledger on the podium before her. *"I, Kendra Forsayth, Master of the Dweomer, do now undertake the solemn responsibility of standing in judgment of this case, the eighty-second of this season: Tyvian Reldamar!"*

"Yes, your honor?" Tyvian's voice was clear, but small and distant. Artus craned his neck to get a better look at him.

"*You stand accused of thirty counts of trafficking in stolen magecraft, twenty-eight counts of possession of proscribed magecraft, eighteen counts of grand theft, twelve counts of conspiracy, ten counts of criminal mischief, and seven counts of murder. Are you aware of the charges and have they been made clear to you?*"

"Yes, your honor."

"*How do you plead to each charge?*"

"Not guil . . . ah . . ." Tyvian's voice skipped and his body tensed. "Not . . . guilty!"

The ring, Artus thought. That was it—maybe Tyvian could use the ring to give him the strength to break the mageglass . . . No. That couldn't work—mageglass was unbreakable. Artus didn't know much about magecraft, but he knew that much. Even if it weren't, how would Tyvian escape the courtroom? He was surrounded on five sides by armed men, the only door to escape through was barred closed, and the only other way out would require him to scale a twelve foot wall all while avoiding being skewered or blasted by firepikes. No, there was no possible way to escape. Strangely, this made Artus feel a little better. He couldn't help Tyvian even if he wanted to.

Judge Forsayth looked at the gallery. "*Will the representative of the prosecuting authority step forward to make his or her case against the accused?*"

"I will, your honor!" A loud voice from the back of the gallery. Artus, along with everybody else, twisted on their benches to get a view of the newcomer. It was a Mage Defender clad in gray robes—striking black mane of hair, clipped goatee, the shoulders of a smith, and a smug smile on his face. Artus found himself hating him immediately.

The judge of the Lumen nodded in the young mage's direction. *"The court recognizes Mage Defender Argus Androlli, representative of the Defenders of the Balance and the Gray Tower."*

Androlli strolled up to the witness's pulpit. He pulled a folio out of his robes and laid it on the podium. "I'm prepared to stand as witness against Tyvian Reldamar." He smiled up at the judges.

Tyvian folded his arms. "Who the hell are you?"

Androlli looked down at Tyvian. "I'm here to offer evidence of your wrongdoings in Akral, Ihyn, Tasis, and Galaspin."

Tyvian shook his head. "But you weren't *in* Akral, Ihyn, Tasis, or Galaspin. None of your order's unjust and baseless actions against my legitimate businesses in those locales involved you—I would have remembered you."

Androlli smiled tightly. "Are you so certain?"

Tyvian nodded. "I never forget an arse."

The crowd erupted in laughter. Judge Forsayth raised her orb for order. *"Magus Androlli, were you the individual to secure the evidence you are hereby asked to present?"*

Androlli looked appropriately contrite. "No, your honor. The evidence was collected by Mage Defender Gavin Holt . . ."

"Dead," Tyvian announced with a visible wince. "Mugged, I believe. In his . . . bed."

Androlli scowled. "By Master Defender Tarlyth . . ."

Tyvian ticked off another finger. "Dead. Fell off a mountain. Hiking—*owl*—accident. He was also a traitor."

Androlli's voice intensified in volume. "And Mage Defender Myreon Alafarr."

Tyvian sighed, wringing his hand. "And, forgive me if I'm wrong, but she's a convicted criminal—for smuggling, no less."

There was a smattering of applause. Somebody threw an apple core at Tyvian, but they missed by a mile and hit a Defender in the shoulder instead. Judge Forsayth frowned at Androlli. *"Is what the accused says true?"*

Androlli heaved a heavy sigh. "Yes, your honor. We have, however, scrying and auguries that verify the facts."

"Auguries and scrying can be altered, your honor, especially by unscrupulous persons like Alafarr and Tarlyth." Tyvian shook his head, chuckling. "This evidence is suspect, at best."

The judge of the Ether—a rail-thin man in overlarge midnight robes—stood. *"In light of this, I'm inclined to dismiss any evidence that does not have a living corroborating witness. Agreed?"*

The judges nodded to one another for a few moments, muttering under their breath in what Artus assumed was some kind of sorcerous private conference. He wished he could read lips better, but he'd never acquired the knack no matter how many times Tyvian had shown him.

Brana whispered in his ear. "Somebody wrestle Tyvian?"

Artus blinked at him. "What? Oh! No, Brana—this isn't a trial by combat. They're gonna argue about facts and stuff. It's how they do it here."

Brana considered this. "But . . . liars?"

Artus frowned—this hadn't occurred to him. "I dunno what happens if somebody lies. I guess maybe *then* they wrestle?"

Androlli was speaking. "The accusers call Artus of Jondas Crossing to testify as witness to the accused's crimes."

Then, just like that, everybody was looking at Artus. Andolon gave the back of his neck one last rub. "Remember, son—be your own man!"

The crowd shuffled to let Artus by. Everybody was whispering to everybody else—much of it was about how his vest didn't fit well and that he was wearing breeches two seasons out of fashion. He subconsciously adjusted his collar as he passed. He'd never felt so much pressure in all his life—it felt like the eyes of the entire world were burning fiery holes in his back.

Then he was there, at the fifth pulpit, looking down on a chained Tyvian. From this height he looked smaller than Artus always thought he was. He knew he'd grown a lot the past year, but Tyvian always seemed larger than life. It occurred to Artus that he had never had so much power over the smuggler before, not even in Freegate. One word from him, and Tyvian would be a statue in a garden for a long, long time.

Androlli was there, his hand extended to shake. Androlli—the mirror man, the Mage Defender—wanted to shake his hand. Artus took it and shook. He felt a little dizzy. One of the judges was speaking to him. *"State your name for the record."*

Artus realized he was standing there with his mouth hanging open. "Uhhh . . . Artus. Of Jondas Crossing. It's in the North—Benethor."

The judge—the Fey judge, if her vermillion robes meant anything—smiled at him. *"How do you know the accused?"*

Artus looked down at Tyvian and saw that the smuggler was looking at him intently, as though angry, but . . . but he wasn't frowning. The look made Artus forget the question, so the judge repeated it. "I . . . uhhh . . . I've been traveling with him for a few years now."

"He is your employer?" the judge asked.

Artus frowned. "Not exactly. We're . . . uhhh . . . partners, I guess."

Tyvian coughed. Artus looked down to see Tyvian still staring at him. The smuggler jerked his head to the side, as though twitching. Artus frowned. "What?"

Tyvian rolled his eyes. "Why do I waste my time?"

Artus found himself yelling. "We *are* partners—that was the deal, remember? *I* remember! I remember nursing you back to health after you got chopped up by Gallo! I remember the time I saved your arse back in Ayventry, too. If it weren't for me, you woulda had to carry all your crap from Freegate to here. We're partners, dammit!"

Tyvian shook his head, "Artus, that's not . . ."

"No!" Artus kept rolling. "No—you need to hear this, you stuck-up jackass! You respect Hool's opinion, you let Brana do whatever he wants, but what about *me*, huh? It's always 'go here, Artus,' 'go there,' 'do this,' 'carry this thing,' 'you walk into the poison gas room first!' It's a load of Kroth-spawned slop, is what! If you'da listened to me and not come back here, you wouldn't be in this mess—how about that? I betcha feel bad for not listening to me now, don't you?"

Tyvian groaned and shook his head. "What do you want—an apology? Hann's boots, boy, are you aware of just how sullen you've been lately? You're quick to point out just how important you are to me, but when was the last time you considered how important *I* am to *you*? Eh?"

The judges exchanged glances. The Fey judge chuckled. *"I believe the court can confirm that they know each other."*

Artus wasn't listening. "You? Are you kidding? What do you ever do for me anyway? You don't care about me at all—I'm just a tool for you to use. Just like *everybody* is a tool for you. You're some kinda . . . kinda . . ."

"Sociopath?" Tyvian offered.

"Yeah! A sociopath! You treat people like tiles in a *tsuul* match, and me worst of all. I'm basically your slave."

"Order in the court!" Judge Forsayth raised her orb.

Neither Artus nor Tyvian were listening, though.

Tyvian was too busy yelling. "I fed you, I clothed you, I taught you to read, I've saved your life a dozen times!"

Artus held up one hand. "Five times! Five bloody times! Not a dozen—*Hool's* saved me a dozen times! Hell, at least three of those times you was *pissed* you had to do it, too! You hate me!"

"ORDER!"

Defenders ran over to restrain Tyvian, but he jumped up on the Block. "What a load of utter nonsense! Hate you? Are you kidding? If I hated you, I'd have left you to die a dozen—"

"IT WAS FIVE!" Artus screamed, shaking his fist at Tyvian. "And the ring *made* you! MADE YOU!"

"Oh, and do you like your new job better? Does that weasel Andolon give you everything you ever wanted, huh? He pay you enough gold to forget about our partnership? What about Brana? Does *he* know what you're about to do to me?"

At this point Artus found his voice silenced by some kind of sorcery. Tyvian was yanked off the Block by two Defenders and wrestled to the ground. Judge Forsayth's voice boomed through the chamber. *"That is quite enough of that. Any further emotional outbursts, young man, and I'll find you in contempt of court—three days in the stocks!"* She looked down at Tyvian. *"And as for you, Master Reldamar, you are making a poor impression on the court, and it will be reflected at time of sentencing. Is that clear to both of you?"*

Artus found himself released. "Yes ma'am."

Tyvian snorted. "Gods, I'd hate to make a poor impression." He struggled to his feet and gave Artus that same, strange, intense look again. "Say, Artus—can I have a smoke?"

Then everything clicked. Artus slapped his forehead—the look! All those hours spent on nonverbal cues had practically vanished from his mind, but now they came flooding back. This one meant: *I need your help.*

Artus looked behind him. Androlli watched him carefully, his hands wrapped around his staff. Behind and beyond him, a gallery of hundreds followed his every movement. In the back he saw Andolon give him an enthusiastic thumbs-up. He took a deep breath—decision time.

It turned out making the decision wasn't very hard at all.

He reached into his pocket and pulled out the spark-stone Tyvian had given him. "Sure, okay." He flicked it at Tyvian. The little alchemical device bounced off Tyvian's jacket with a little flash of sparks.

Then Tyvian's entire torso burst into flame.

CHAPTER 19

ON FIRE

It is one thing to concoct a long-term plan to have one-self set on fire in the midst of Keeper's Court. It is quite another thing to be actually lit on fire. This Tyvian realized as the flames engulfed his body, flicking up around his face and ears with hot, red tongues, and he began to scream uncontrollably. It took him a second to realize the enchantment on his clothing kept him-self from actually being burned (though it was doing a good job of singeing his hair). He kept screaming—his panic was part of the plan anyway.

All around him people were in various stages of

shock. The Defenders on the floor seemed uncertain how to proceed, though Androlli was shouting orders at them: "Get a bucket!" and so on. The gallery was in a frenzy, split pretty evenly between howling for his decease and weeping for his salvation. The judges, for their part, looked on with academic interest—one of them took notes. Clearly they'd never seen anybody burn to death, and this was to be an educational experience.

Tyvian yanked with all his strength against the mageglass chain that held him to the Block but did so while screaming his loudest, so as to disguise his intent as merely the death throes of a man in agony. The mageglass didn't bend or give so much as a quarter inch; that was the thing about mageglass—completely immune to acts of physical force. You could hit this chain with a twenty-pound siege maul for days on end and all you'd do was break the maul or, possibly, your back—mageglass was the Dweomer rendered physical, it was order personified. It would never break.

It did, however, melt. Not to sunlight, not to mild heat—no—but fire? Fire was as pure a form of naturally occurring Fey energy as you were likely to find, and when the Fey and the Dweomer started rubbing elbows . . .

Pop! One link of the chain winked out of existence, and Tyvian was suddenly free. He immediately dropped the screaming routine and charged the Defender coming at him with a bucket of water. The prospect of being bear-hugged by a flaming criminal caused the Defender to stagger backward—he dropped the bucket, but Tyvian wasn't interested in dousing the flames just yet. What he wanted was the other thing the Defender dropped: his firepike.

He snatched it up and whirled on the other Defenders on the floor of the courtroom and began discharging the enchanted weapon in random directions, sending blazing bolts of Fey energy streaking across the room. The Defenders, following their training, dropped to one knee and ducked their heads. This was a good idea if facing sorcerous weaponry—the mageglass of their helmets and arms would protect them from a lot. What probably nobody realized was that men in this position made excellent stepping-stones.

Tyvian charged the closest Defender, leapt onto the man's shoulders and, just as the fellow was getting up to throw him off, leapt again, aiming toward the edge of the nearest pulpit. From there it was a simple pull-up and there he was—standing in the pulpit of Judge Kendra Forsayth, while on fire, while holding a firepike.

To all outward appearances, the Master of the Dweomer seemed to vanish in a puff of smoke, but Tyvian knew better—she'd just sped herself up and run off faster than the eye could see. He could tell because the door she fled through had just banged open as though hit by a charging bull. The judge had just provided him his escape route *and* left her ledger where it was—between Tyvian's legs. He snatched up the ledger and stuffed it underneath his flame-resistant doublet before it could singe. He then took one moment to survey the gallery, even as firepike blasts from below hit the walls around him, and blew them all a good-bye kiss. It was received with the kind of gaping astonishment he had anticipated.

Then came the hard part.

As soon as he left the courtroom, the ring clamped down on his hand hard enough to make him wail in pain. This was, largely, what the firepike was for—it was a crutch to lean on as he staggered through the judge's chambers and into the adjoining corridor, blinded with the righteous fury of a ring that wanted him prosecuted for the crimes that he very much *had* committed.

He kept moving, as steadily as he could manage, his right hand curled into a palsied fist as he burned both from within and from without. He banged into tables, tapestries, and door frames, leaving behind him a trail of fire that, while unmistakable to pursuers, would make their pursuit itself rather hazardous until they could wrangle a mage up there to douse the flames.

Tyvian heard shouts behind him, but they were the panicked cries of people trying to escape an old castle that was fast on its way to burning to the ground. He pressed on, his vision shrinking into a tunnel of fire, smoke, and the shadowy contours of the stone walls around him. His breathing grew labored. "I can do this," He muttered. "I planned for this."

Of course, when he had been lying awake in Derby the night after he poisoned that first Quiet Man, this entire plan seemed less painful. How did one rescue somebody turned to stone? You got inside Keeper's Court to steal their Rite of Recovery from the sentencing judge's ledger. How did one get inside Keeper's Court? Well, you got yourself arrested and brought to trial. How did you get yourself out of the courtroom and not turned to stone? Well, you lit yourself on fire.

But how did you keep the ring from ruining the whole affair by torturing him into submission?

Well, he hadn't thought that part out yet. The current plan called for just toughing it out. That part of the plan wasn't going well.

Tyvian felt the heat building beneath his jacket—the enchantment placed there was almost ready to give out. He was currently near the ancient south tower of Keeper's Court, which was his destination anyway. He threw himself on a stone staircase and stripped off his burning doublet, casting the thing in the direction of a large and antique rug, which promptly caught on fire.

The ring kept up its assault on his body, making it feel as though he actually was on fire. He had to check his hand to make sure, given how much of this place was going up in flames. It wasn't—just the ring's old tricks. Tyvian took a deep breath and tried to rise, ledger still stuffed under one arm. The ring cramped his joints with agony and he sank back to the stairs. Smoke was growing thicker and thicker in the air. The burning rug was now an inferno, catching on some of the support beams from the floor below, he guessed. The air became thick and hard to breathe.

"Dammit," he growled at his hand. "What, you're going to make me *die* here? What about Myreon, eh? Doesn't *she* deserve justice, you bull-headed trinket?"

Nothing changed. Somewhere nearby, Tyvian heard shouts, but these were organized—the shouts of military personnel. Defenders come to battle the blaze. Slowly, he began to drag himself down the stairs, one by one, headed for the base of the South Tower. It was slow going. They would catch him long before he got there at this rate.

"I'm trying to save Myreon, you stupid ring!" he screamed. "Release me!"

His answer was nothing but more pain.

Tyvian pitched himself into a roll—if he couldn't walk down the stairs, he'd fall down them. He wound up bruised and battered at their base, deep in the basement of the South Tower—the oldest part of Keeper's Court.

Even though he was so close to his goal, he could not rise. The ring bound him to the floor with cramps that bunched his muscles and ligaments into painful, inert lumps. Above him, he heard footsteps on the stairs. They were nearly on him.

What the hell did the bloody ring want from him? Was this it? It wanted him turned to stone alongside Myreon, left to rot until a decade after everyone forgot his name? If his mother was right, and the ring was some kind of storage unit for his better self, what kind of better self was this? What was it missing?

He wracked his brain for a way out. *Why am I escap-*

ing? Why am I doing this? If it's just for me, then the ring won't let me go, is that it? It wants to know I'm sincere about saving Myreon—that I'm doing it for her and not for myself.

"Fine!" he groaned, "It's for her, okay? Are you happy now? I'm saving another damsel, dammit! Isn't that what you bloody want?"

No, Tyvian realized, that isn't what it wants. *That isn't what I want. It wants me to make a decision: what do I, Tyvian Reldamar, think of Myreon Alafarr? Are my intentions pure?*

The steps drew closer—some mirror man, sword drawn, advancing carefully toward where a dangerous criminal might be hiding. Not much time left to dither.

Tyvian had never been much for deep introspection, particularly in personal matters. He was a man of action, not of thought. He tried to calm his racing mind and purge the adrenaline from his limbs. He had to think calmly.

Ever since he heard of Myreon's arrest and punishment, the ring had been there, throbbing slowly in the background of his daily life, like an old stubbed toe. That, though, wasn't why he had come—he'd learned to put up with such petty discomforts so that he barely noticed them. Then there was the knowledge that this was all a lure to bring him back, and he had told himself that he'd come to spite his mother and nothing else, but that also wasn't true. Instead, for him, he recalled that moment when he found Myreon's body in Daer Trondor. He tried to feel what he had felt when he kissed her—when he felt a portion of his life flow into hers like liquid fire. What was that thing that had given him that power?

Respect. Perhaps even admiration. Perhaps something harder for him to pin down, something that defied his description: the simple, sure knowledge that a world without Myreon Alafarr was a world lessened, and not just generally—lessened for *him* specifically. "Is that too selfish of me, ring?" Tyvian gasped, trying to crawl away from the approaching steps. "To want her alive and free? Is that too much to ask?"

Tyvian's pain crested some invisible ridge and began to slide away down the other side. Strength flowed back into his limbs in a torrent.

He sprang to his feet in time to see a mirror man with a rapier poised to attack. Tyvian snatched a feylamp from the wall and threw it at him, then turned to run, snatching up the ledger as he went. His legs seemed to be weightless—he felt like he could fly.

The South Tower of Keeper's Court was a fat, ancient structure dating to the days when the courthouse had been a keep for the Saldorian Kings of old and the Block was a big stone that sat in the open air before the keep's walls. It now served as the court's archives, and this made it two things: firstly, it was designed to be fireproof, and secondly, it contained a siege cistern in the depths of its ancient basements. That second part—that was his objective.

Tyvian fled downward, deeper into the old tower. He flew down old spiral staircases and threw up trapdoors, going deeper, ever deeper, into that ancient keep.

"Reldamar!" Androlli shouted from somewhere above. "There's no escape! Give up!"

He got to the lowest point—he could feel the dampness on his fire-baked skin. Here there were no scrolls and no books, only ancient shelves of dust and forgotten artifacts. Tyvian raced past them, kicking off his boots as he went. He grabbed some oilskin from a shelf, originally intended to protect paper from mildewing, and wrapped it tightly around the ledger to prevent water from ruining its pages.

"Reldamar!" Androlli's voice echoed in the distance. There it was—a cistern, the surface of the water black and calm. It would be a hell of a swim, and mostly underwater, but if he made it, he would come out beneath the docks along the Narrow Mouth. He tucked the ledger into his shirt and took several deep breaths. Ordinarily, this would be madness—suicide by drowning in some ancient black tunnel. The ring, though, would give him the edge. He would make it; the ring loved it when he played the hero.

He dove in and the cold blackness of the water surrounded him. There was no light, but the thought of his coming triumph, burning ahead of him in his mind's eye, was brighter than any sunshine.

CHAPTER 20

TRUTH OR CONSEQUENCES

Artus dove into the panicked courtroom crowd, using his lanky frame to slide between poofy gowns and lacy collars and delivering sharp jabs with his elbows to anybody who didn't slide aside. Brana met him somewhere in the fray and pulled him to an open spot. "Where's Andolon?" Artus asked.

Brana aped a fair approximation of a shrug. "All gone. Run away?"

Artus scowled. "Doesn't sound promising. C'mon, let's get out of here."

"Find Tyvian?"

Artus shook his head. "He's on his own."

The smell of smoke was building in the chamber— the pulpit where Tyvian had made his escape was now almost entirely on fire. A few Defenders were lobbing buckets of water up at it from the floor, but they were doing little more than slowing the spread. Androlli had taken command of the scene, barking orders from a pulpit and throwing spells around to slow the spread of the fire. For once Artus was glad to be forgotten.

Defenders tried to organize the crowd into a more orderly manner of egress. Artus and Brana kept their heads low, blending in with the masses as best they could and going with the flow out of the courtroom. Artus got a glimpse of Androlli scanning the crowd with some kind of magic, but whatever it was either didn't work or he wasn't looking for them anyway. Alarm bells were sounding. While everybody around Artus was nervous—Brana included—the spectacle of the chaos Tyvian had caused kept making him chuckle.

"You incredible bastard," he muttered under his breath, grinning. "How'd you know I'd throw that spark-crystal, anyway?"

Everybody was ushered out the main gates where, to most of the visitors' shock and indignation, their coaches were not waiting to receive them. Again, so-called polite society made for a good cover for Artus and Brana, since every visible guard was receiving a piece of some merchant heiress's mind or being accused of ineptitude by Baron von Whoever. It was a simple matter to slip out into the street.

The question of where to go, however, was barely considered before Andolon's massive coach-and-four clattered to a halt in front of him. The door popped open and the Saldorian fop glared at them from beneath a hat comprised of a coiled, smoke-belching dragon. "You two—*get in!*"

Brana hopped right in, as requested. The shrouded gnoll looked over his shoulder. "C'mon, Artus—ride!"

Artus looked to his left and right. Crowds of people had gathered along the streets to watch the ancient citadel of Keeper's Court burn. Troops of Defenders ran to help combat the blaze, and everywhere he looked there seemed to be another mage in mirrored armor marching around with a staff. If he stayed here, he was as good as stone himself.

Artus stepped forward, reluctant. Somebody made the remainder of his decision for him—he was grabbed by the collar and hauled inside like a bale of hay by a strong hand. With a sharp whistle to the driver, Andolon ordered the coach forward.

Artus tried to figure out who had grabbed him—not Andolon, surely. He squinted around the interior of the spacious cab. Brana was beside him, DiVarro and Andolon were squeezed next to one another on the other side, and across from him was . . . was a man. A man Artus couldn't fully see or rationalize—a shadowy outline of black, hooded and sinister. Above the corner of his mouth was a small tattoo that Artus couldn't quite make out.

The unseeable man pressed a long double-bladed

dagger against the inside of Artus's thigh, less than an inch from his codpiece. Unlike the man, the pressure of the blade against his leg was something that he could perceive quite clearly. He held very still.

Andolon smiled at Artus. The smile was confined to his lips only. "I suppose you think you're very clever, don't you? Oh, bravo, boy—well done. You've saved your master only to doom yourself."

Artus looked at the knife and looked over at Brana. The shrouded gnoll had his head stuck out the window of the coach as they sped through the streets of the Old City, his arse wiggling back and forth in excitement.

Andolon tsked. "You'll be spilling your life's blood all over the inside of my coach long before your idiot brother can help you. And then, after you die, he'll be next."

Artus licked his lips. "Look, I didn't know he was going to light on fire—"

Andolon produced the notecard with Tyvian's handwriting on it. "Spare me, please." Artus grasped at his vest pocket, eyes wide, as the fop chuckled at him.

"You know," Andolon said, "people don't think I'm dangerous. I suppose it's my sense of fashion—I enjoy a bit of whimsy in my dress, is all—but just because I like bright colors and beautiful hats doesn't mean I'm some kind of fool to be pushed around." He leaned forward and looked Artus in the eye. "Do you know I could have had you killed *at any time*? While you were following me to my ship I could have had your throat cut in an alley. While you were having grapes stuffed in your greedy little mouth, I could have poisoned you. While you were sitting in the bloody courtroom just now, my man here could have choked you dead and nobody would have noticed the body until after the trial."

Artus licked his lips again. "What, and that's supposed to impress me? You wanna hear all the times I could have had *you* killed? There's a lot of them—you might wanna take notes."

Andolon sat back and laughed, clapping his hands. "There! That was pure Reldamar! I mean, not as clever by any means and clearly false, but *that's* my old friend talking. You have learned a few things from him, haven't you?"

"What do you want from me?" Artus tried to look at the man with the knife but found his eyes drawn away by the trees passing by the windows, by Andolon's stupid hat, by DiVarro's crystal eye. It was if there was nothing of the assassin to see.

"Where is Reldamar going now?" Andolon held up a finger. "And don't presume to lie to me, boy. This coach is in need of reupholstering anyway."

Artus frowned. "I don't know."

The knife pressed hard against his leg, cutting through fabric. Artus inhaled sharply and tried to sit up straighter, but the knife-man pressed him back against the wall of the coach with his free hand. Andolon smiled. "Let's not do this, eh? I'm only asking you because you seem to be capable of speech. I can always just kill you and ask the moron."

DiVarro, who had up until this point had his real eye closed and was muttering to himself, suddenly stirred to life. He cleared his throat. "Andolon, there's something—"

Andolon rounded on him. "How are the markets?"

DiVarro frowned. "The timetable has advanced—we can't wait for the pear shipment. The moment to strike will be tomorrow morning and no later. That wasn't what I was going to say. It's about the—"

"Tomorrow? Tomorrow *morning*? You're certain Reldamar's escape will shake things up that far?"

While Andolon was distracted, Artus grabbed Brana by his illusory belt and tugged him back inside the coach. The gnoll had that stupid, wide-mouthed grin on his face. "Lots of fish smell!"

Artus growled in gnoll-speak, *"Brana, trouble—get ready."*

Brana stiffened instantly and sniffed the air inside the coach. His head cocked to one side. *"Who?"* he snarled back.

Andolon froze in mid-conversation. "I'm . . . I'm sorry, but were you just *barking* at each other?"

Artus took a deep breath. Was he actually going to do this? Really? His stomach started doing flips as he spoke. He desperately hoped his voice wouldn't crack. "You're finished, Andolon. Your plan will never work now."

Andolon blinked and then began laughing. "Don't be ridiculous, boy—my plan is *inevitable*, understand?

The only thing that changes is the timetable. So what if I become the richest man in the West tomorrow instead of next week? There's nothing Reldamar or you can do to stop it."

DiVarro tapped his employer on the shoulder. "Andolon, there's something you should know about the boy—"

"Hush!" Andolon glared at the augur, then turned back to Artus. "Tell me where Reldamar is or die where you sit."

Artus smiled. "You can't kill us here—the Defenders' augurs will have already scryed it, and then you'll be arrested the next second."

"Ha!" Andolon looked at DiVarro. "Do you believe this?"

DiVarro, though, had his eye fixed on Brana, who had a toothy grin from ear to ear and staring at Andolon. "Sir, the boy! He's a—"

Andolon rolled his eyes. "Really, DiVarro—the boy's grinning at me like an idiot. He *likes* me!" He turned back to Artus. "As for you, don't you think the Mute Prophets would have found a work-around to Defender scrying by now?" He patted the walls of the coach. "Not only is my coach warded against scrying, but my half-invisible friend here is *wholly* invisible to scrying. A Quiet Man's life and all his acts are unknowable to any augur anywhere, so if I want him to stab you both to death in my coach and dump your bodies in a gutter, the only thing the Defenders will ever find is your corpses."

Andolon sat back, folding his arms. "There—now what do you think of that, boy?"

Artus grinned. "Sounds like that kind of warding works both ways, don't it? Brana, *sic 'em*."

Brana took off his shroud. At that moment it became very evident what Brana's "goofy smile" actually represented: a hundred fifty pound gnoll bearing every single tooth in his large snout.

Then all hell broke loose.

Brana lunged for Andolon but was intercepted by the Quiet Man, who would have put his knife in Brana's eyeball had Artus not grabbed his knife hand. Brana's jaws latched onto the Quiet Man's arm and bore down—there was a snapping noise as the arm broke, but no scream.

Andolon, eyes wide in panic, fumbled for something around his neck but thought better of it. Instead, he pulled a slender dagger out of a sleeve and worked at stabbing Brana, who was forced to release the Quiet Man in order to dodge in the tight confines of the coach.

All DiVarro did was scream, but even then his face didn't alter much from its perpetual frown.

Artus, though, didn't have time to think about the augur for more than a fleeting second. The Quiet Man was on top of him, a shadow made real, the knife bearing down at his chest with all the man's weight. Artus brought his knee up to try and push him off, but the space was too tight and he couldn't find any good spot to kick. All he could do was press both his hands against the wrist of the Quiet Man and try and hold him off. The Quiet Man, though, was stronger and heavier. The blade inched downward, slowly, until it was grazing Artus's chest.

Brana fared better. There was a thump and a squeal of pain from Andolon—Brana had gotten the knife away from him and used it to pin the fop's arm to the ceiling of the coach. He then started hitting Andolon in the stomach with a series of rapid jabs. "Ha!" the gnoll growled. "Take it!"

"Brana!" Artus yelled, his arms quivering.

The gnoll's ears swiveled toward his friend, and seeing the knife about to fall, he put his feet against the opposite side of the cab and drove himself forward in a lunge that knocked Artus and himself out through the door of the moving coach. They hit the cobblestones hard and rolled, Artus knocking over a group of children and Brana winding up in an apple cart. The world spun for a moment as stars danced in Artus's eyes and he struggled to get back his breath.

Eventually he sat up. The Quiet Man hadn't pursued them, apparently—or had he? Artus looked around at the crowd, trying to spot him. It was hopeless. If he was here, he and Brana would never be able to tell.

Somebody helped Artus to his feet. It was Brana, who had somehow replaced his shroud. The crowd of onlookers dispersed shortly thereafter, with one or two people saying they should report that coach to the Defenders. Artus smiled his thanks but his heart was racing too fast to come up with something to say.

He sat on the curb and Brana sat next to him. He had no idea where he was—somewhere overlooking one of the harbors. The mazelike streets of Saldor all seemed the same to him, and every angle on the harbor looked alike. He guessed they were both lost.

Brana turned his golden eyes to Artus and whimpered in gnoll-speak, *"I want to go home."* He leaned forward, nudged Artus's shoulder with his forehead and gave his hand a little lick.

Artus looked out across the harbor and at the forest of masts that glowed red-gold in the light of the setting sun. Thousands upon thousands of people, all of them far from home, brought here by the promise of gold. Thousands upon thousands of people, all hoping to get home—the only place where gold really mattered.

Artus put his arm around his adopted brother. "I want to go home too, Brana." For once, though, he realized he wasn't thinking of Jondas Crossing, or of his family farm, or of his mother. He was thinking of Tyvian in the common room of a roadside inn, his feet up beside the fire, sipping a glass of wine. He thought of laughter over roast rabbits caught on the road, the smell of Hool's fur after a light rain, and the gleam of Tyvian's smile in the lamplight.

Home.

CHAPTER 21

JUSTICE UNDONE

Petrification had not been and was not painful, not in any physical sense. It was cold and dark. Time seemed to both collapse and expand at equal rates—a moment could be a year, a year a moment. There was no way to tell. Myreon felt no hunger, no thirst, no fatigue. She was adrift in the abyss of her own memories.

At first she remembered her life well: her time as a little girl in her family vineyards, ducking and hiding among the trellises, all of them pregnant with the heavy weight of ripe grapes. She remembered the smell of spring rain, going to the river for the Festival of Arrival and dancing around the maypole. She remembered the panic of the fire—the sound of her uncles shouting, and the sight of the bandits, blades bare, as they ran among the storehouses.

And afterward: poverty in Saldor. Bereft of home and family, her father drifted from job to job, often working on the river. She remembered a stay on a riverboat for a year, hauling goods from Freegate to Saldor, sleeping with her father in a tiny bunk meant for one man, the sound of his breathing in the night after a long shift poling the boat around shoals. The smell of tar and sweat.

And afterward: Her attending school in Saldor. Years of study—history, religion, natural philosophy, magecraft, mathematics. Her teachers smiling at her. Then the Arcanostrum.

Those eerie spires loomed large for Myreon in her dark exile. She remembered learning as an initiate, being famulus to Lyrelle Reldamar, attaining her first mark and being accepted as apprentice, remembered earning her second mark and being granted her staff. She remembered Archmagus Lyrelle taking the time to congratulate her just before she, herself, was set to retire; she remembered sipping tea in that incredible woman's chambers, talking about her future.

She also remembered Tyvian. His damned grin—so self-satisfied, so confident. His face in pain, above hers—the feeling of his lips, so hot they seemed to still burn her. She remembered the heat of a hundred suns coursing through her, raising her from the grave itself.

What was the genesis of that power? She had always wondered. Now, with infinite time to think, she did not wish to think on it. The thought of it frightened her more than anything else; she pushed it away, only to have it rise again. It seemed as though Tyvian's lips were always there, hot against hers, blowing life into her from the bottomless depths of his soul.

As time went on, her memories bled into one another. There was Lyrelle at her family vineyard, purchasing wine from her father. There was Tyvian, an initiate in the Arcanostrum, like her—he was thin and slight, but had the same wry grin, the same intelligent eyes. They never spoke.

She saw the Dellorans on the riverboat, her father fighting them. She recalled seeing her uncles die at the hands of a bloody, nude Banric Sahand. She saw Hool at the Festival of Arrival, flowers in her mane, dancing to music she could only half hear. Fact and dream combined into a seamless flow of images and sensations, all of them dulled by the veil of her bodiless existence.

And also that damned kiss. Always with that damned, stupid kiss.

She found herself, all at once, missing the sound of her pumping heart. Missing her humanity. Would she be mad when she at last emerged from this prison? How long had it been? What would become of her?

Focus, she cautioned herself. *Control your thoughts or lose yourself.* She had seen it a hundred times—a warlock performing the Rite of Release upon a prisoner, and that person emerging listless, dumb, and blind. It took some months to recover themselves, and even then they were never fully restored. Many wound up on the streets of Saldor, halfhearted beggars panning for loose change. Most of those died within a year.

That was not her. That *would not* be her. She ran herself through mental exercises, carefully filing and annotating her life into a little mental biography only she would ever see. The concentration it took was nearly unbearable. The human mind, she decided, was not meant to work like a library, ordering itself into neat piles. The harder she tried to cling to the threads of her memory, the more wildly they scattered.

The case, she told herself, *focus on the case.*

She thought of Gethrey Andolon, the Saldorian gentleman. A man in gaudy clothes, jewels embroidered into every surface of his doublet. A cane with a jade topper carved into a toad and wearing shoes with five-inch heels, Myreon could still see his powder-blue hair and his elaborate hats. *Yes! Focus on him!*

For what seemed to be forever, Myreon lived and relived her investigation of Andolon. The mysterious cargoes that went missing without a trace. The bodies found in the river, tied only loosely to him. The frustration at knowing something was wrong, but being unable to prove it. She nurtured a hot, blazing anger toward him for as long as she could—she would have her revenge, she told herself. He would face justice.

But even that, in time, was not enough.

Too much darkness now. Myreon could not remember the sound of her name in the lips of others. The world was fading. Everything seemed distant, abstract.

Had there been a man named Gethrey Andolon who had wronged her? Myreon told herself it was true, but it did not seem so anymore. The perfumed man with his gaudy clothes and his sweaty palms seemed more like a caricature of a chapbook villain than a real person.

She had begun to believe that there was no real light. There was no real time. Her dreams and memories had almost entirely faded, losing the vivid color that had once been their hallmark. The smell of spring rain and the smell of tar and sweat merged together. Her father's face became indistinct. Had she been able, she might have wept, but she could not. Even that was denied her here.

With glacial slowness, she knew she was losing herself. Bit by bit, piece by piece, until nothing in the end would remain. Thoughts of vengeance seemed pointless, even if considered dispassionately. She was stone—why not truly become it? Why torture herself with things that were no longer for her, no longer of her world?

Maybe none of that had ever been real anyway. Maybe this was the world as it was meant to be—quiet, dark, cold, unflinching. She could go on forever like this, just a mote in the stream of eternity, and what would be lost?

Since there was no true pain, there could be no true suffering. There was peace at last.

It remained this way for what might have been a moment or what might have been a century. Myreon wondered if she had been forgotten, but she could not, in truth, remember who there would be to forget her. It was just her. It had always been just her, alone in the dark and cold.

Then, a light—a *real* light, faint but pulsing ever closer. There was warmth building, starting deep inside. *Boom-boom.* Her mind grew quiet before the noise, waiting. *Boom-boom.*

Her heart. She was coming back to herself. Her body was reverting to its flesh once again. Her sentence had passed.

Her sentence had passed!

The process seemed to take years. Every beat of the heart was a lifetime apart, every gradually increasing note of sensation took shape in a process that began with numbing cold, then a tingling, almost painful storm of sensory static, then, eventually, full and complete awareness. She was hungry. She was tired and sore. Her fingers were stiff and cold; the first time she bent them in who knew how many years was pure, blessed agony. Myreon found herself loving the pain, reveling in it.

Then, at last, her face—her lips (dry, cracked), her ears (the screaming noise of crickets, so cacophonous as to make her cover them with her stiff, unwilling hands), her nose (the smell of grass and roses and horse manure and river water), her eyelids (stiff and ready to open).

She opened her eyes.

There, leaning over her, his arms wrapped around her, was the face of . . . who? A handsome man . . . she thought she knew him . . .

Tyvian Reldamar. *Tyvian!* When he smiled, his teeth were whiter than the stars above. "Hello, Myreon. Back with us, are you?"

He was as she had never seen him, never imagined him to be—filthy, wet, stripped to the waist like a common longshoreman. His torso was a tightly maintained core of smooth muscle crisscrossed with small scars, like the hull of a pirate's sloop. He was warm and breathing. She knew that this was real—the first real sensation she had experienced for three years. She opened her mouth to speak but no words could form.

Tyvian rose, and she realized he was carrying her. "Don't worry—time enough to talk soon enough. Save your strength."

Myreon decided she didn't need to speak. She wrapped her arms around his neck, pulled him close and kissed him deeply. Tears ran down her cheeks, fogged her vision. Even after the kiss had broken, she clung to the smuggler's muscular neck like a woman drowning.

She fell into a blessed sleep, years in the making.

She did not dream.

Morning sunlight and the smell of dusty linen greeted Myreon. The mattress beneath her was down-filled, but beaten flat by years of use. The quilts seemed to weigh a ton; she was hot, sweat pooling in the small of her back. The sensation was glorious.

The largest woman Myreon had ever seen leaned over her. When she smiled, it looked as though her teeth had been fighting with each other. Her dark eyes twinkled beneath caterpillar eyebrows. "Good morning, magus . . . oh, well . . . Miss Alafarr, I suppose." The woman sighed. "Don't seem proper, addressin' you like that, do it?"

Myreon groaned and searched for her voice. She found it; it creaked like a rusty hinge. "Who are you?"

"My name's Maude, dearie." Maude poured water from a clay pitcher into a wooden mug on the bedside table. Then, bizarrely, she planted a kiss on Myreon's forehead. "Cripes, you're hot as karfan under there!" She hauled off the heavy quilt with a single sweep of a muscular arm. Myreon felt like she could breathe again.

"I told you she'd get hot, Maude." The voice was a knife in her ribs. Tyvian.

She sat bolt upright, fatigue forgotten. There he was—sitting in a simple wooden chair, sipping tea from a cracked cup and weathered saucer. "You! What the hell are you doing here?"

Maude chuckled. "I'll leave you two alone, eh?" She gave Myreon a wink. "Give 'im hell, lassie."

Tyvian snorted. "Thank you, Maude."

Maude waved over her shoulder and pressed a small knot in a wooden support beam. A secret panel in the wall rotated open and she disappeared through it. After she had gone, the panel closed again. It was then that Myreon noticed the room had no other door.

"Who is that woman? What are you doing here? *Where am I?*"

Tyvian gave her a half grin. "That woman is Maude, an old friend. You are in a hidden saferoom in the basement of the Cauldron. You are here because this is where I took you after rescuing you last night."

Myreon blinked. Her thoughts were like congealed fat in a tube—barely moving, barely working. "What . . . what did you do? My sentence . . . was it commuted?"

"No." Tyvian sipped his tea. "Well . . . in a manner of speaking. I commuted it by breaking you out."

"How? What . . . what did you *do?*" Myreon threw the sheet off, only to realize she was only dressed in a thin cotton shift. She pulled the sheet immediately back over her. "In order to release someone from petrification, you need to access their Rite of Release in Keeper's Court! You didn't . . . did you?"

Tyvian nodded. "I did. I broke in, stole your rite, and set much of the place on fire. A simple thank-you will suffice."

"You've made me a *criminal!*" Myreon flexed her fingers.

"To be perfectly fair, Myreon, you already *were* a criminal. Now you're a fugitive."

Myreon found herself casting a spell before she knew it—the Shattering burst from her hands with a thunderclap and reduced Tyvian's chair to flinders. She rose from the bed and fairly flew across the room, tackling him. She had him by the shirt-laces and started shaking him. "You son of a bitch! You miserable, self-centered, insane—"

Tyvian put up his hands in surrender. "Myreon, Myreon—how can you call me self-centered? I just *saved* you!"

She slapped him. "No! You are obsessed with me—you are a sick, twisted psychopath! You heard I was helpless and couldn't wait to charge in here to steal another kiss!"

Tyvian put his hands behind his head. "I believe *you* kissed *me,* this time. We're even. Besides, I'm not the one currently straddling the other's body in my underclothes. Who, mademoiselle, is obsessed with whom, eh?"

Myreon punched him in the chest and got off him. She wobbled on her feet and nearly fell, but Tyvian was there, holding her by the arm. She shook him off. "Don't touch me. Get out—I need some time alone. I need to collect my thoughts."

Tyvian shook his head. "I'm afraid you're going to have to collect your thoughts with company."

Myreon's eyes narrowed. "What?"

"Allow me to remind you, Myreon: you are a criminal now. I am also a criminal. We two criminals are wanted by the Defenders, but that is only the first of our problems." Tyvian held up another finger. "Second among our problems is that whoever framed you for the crime you so *obviously* did not commit will now know you are released, which means they will want you silenced."

"Gethrey Andolon." The name felt foul in Myreon's lips. She could still picture his stupid blue head and his ring-studded fingers, going through his elaborate charade of not knowing what was happening to all his shipments of *cherille* and karfan and good Akrallian brandy, and on and on . . .

Tyvian twiddled his third finger. "Gethrey is working with the Mute Prophets. The Mute Prophets own this establishment, and while Maude is a friend, Claudia—her co-owner—is not. If I leave the room, Claudia or one of the employees herein loyal to her may see me, and then the jig is up."

Myreon glanced at the door. "I assumed this was a safe-house of yours."

Tyvian shrugged. "Used to be. Now it's more of a safe-*room*."

Myreon waited for the punchline, but Tyvian merely looked at her with that stupid half smile, hands in the air as if to say *Sorry*. She considered the merits of punching him. "So, what—we're going to live here now? Is there anything more to the plan, or have the last few years rotted your brain?"

"Years?" Tyvian laughed. "Myreon, you've only been petrified for perhaps six months, if that. It's the twelfth of Kromonth, the twenty-fifth year of Polimeux II. Ozday, if you must know. As for how long we have to stay here, I'd estimate no more than a few days. Then we'll be more or less free to go."

"What do you mean? What about Andolon and the Prophets? What about the Defenders?"

Tyvian smiled. "Don't you worry about the Defenders. They were too busy putting out fires to even notice the lack of a single judge's ledger, I'd wager. By the time they figure out I've sprung you and find out where we are, we'll be gone. As for Gethrey, he only wants you and me dead because he's worried we'll ruin his plans. The solution to that problem is incredibly easy: we don't ruin his plans. Once he succeeds, which I imagine will be soon, he won't give a damn about us, and we can be on our way."

Myreon couldn't help but gape at him. " 'We'? Who is 'we'?"

Tyvian Reldamar, inveterate lothario and black-hearted scoundrel, had the audacity to *blush*. "Well . . . I'll need to collect Artus and Brana, of course. Hool, I expect should catch up soon. And then there's, well, there's *you*."

"Me?"

"I can't very well leave you here. Do you know how much trouble I went to rescuing you?"

Myreon beckoned Tyvian closer with one finger. "Come over here, please."

Tyvian blinked, but came closer and sat next to her on the bed. He grinned. "No need to thank me, but— OW!"

Myreon's knuckles stung where she clocked Tyvian in the jaw. It was a gratifying feeling. "Let us establish one thing, sir: there is no *you* and *me*, understand? I am not going anywhere with you."

Tyvian was now sitting on the floor, rubbing his face. "Understood. Fine. But if you get caught again, you're on your own. I'm not burning down Keeper's Court a *second* time for you."

"Fine."

Tyvian nodded. "Good."

"Agreed."

Silence. Myreon noted that her heart was beating far too quickly. What was she afraid of, exactly? Tyvian? Certainly he was dangerous, but that wasn't it. She was still angry—still violently angry—that he had interrupted her sentence. Yet, another part of her knew that having already lost her staff and her position in the Defenders, there wasn't much worse that could happen to her. What did she have to lose by letting Tyvian help her? Why was her pulse racing?

She took a deep, steadying breath—what a glory to be able to breathe again—and tried to clear her head. What she needed to do was regain her strength, escape this room, and . . . and . . . what? Turn in Tyvian to the Defenders as a means to commute her further sentence? Stop Gethrey Andolon, whatever it was he was doing? Turn herself back in? Her head spun—she needed time. Time to think. Time to plan.

For the time being, she was stuck here. With *him*.

Myreon looked around the room—a bed, an armoire, a single shuttered window, a tiny fireplace, a seaman's trunk. "Where will you sleep?"

Tyvian smirked. "Well, since you just destroyed the only chair . . ."

Myreon's eyes shot open. "No. No way in hell."

Tyvian sat on the bed next to her, but not too near her. "I promise to be a complete gentleman."

"I promise to lode-bolt you into an icicle if you so much as brush against me. You sleep *on the floor*."

He held up his right hand to show her where the ring still rested. "When I say I'll be a perfect gentleman, it isn't as though I have any choice in the matter, you know."

"You still sleep on the floor." Myreon pointed to the ground. "You can have the quilt, if you like."

"Kind of you." His tone did not convey much in the way of gratitude.

Silence. Tyvian turned away from her, and she found herself examining his profile, remembering the strength of his arms around her. She needed to change the subject desperately. "What is Andolon planning? I assume you know."

"Oh, that?" Tyvian brightened. "He's going to crash the Secret Exchange and buy up the wreckage. If it works, he'll own a quarter of all of the Arcanostrum's wealth. The whole economy of the West will fall into chaos. Well, assuming it works."

Myreon felt like ice water had just been poured down her shift. "WHAT?"

Tyvian blinked at her. "What's wrong?"

"And you aren't going to stop him?" She threw her pillow at him. "Not even *try*?"

Tyvian shrugged. "What do I care if that taste-less weasel robs the Arcanostrum? I'm a smuggler—

economic chaos is good for business. Besides," he said, waggling his ring hand at her, "not a pinch. Not so much as a tingle—how about that?"

Myreon felt heat rush to her cheeks. "Tyvian, a collapse like that would lead to half the city starving within the year! Eretheria would drop into all-out civil war! Gods, it would be a worldwide disaster! You can't be serious about just *leaving*!"

"I've never been more serious about anything in my life." Tyvian sighed. "Shall we keep arguing, then, or would you like a nap first? You look terrible."

Myreon glared at him. Had she the energy, she would have lit his hair on fire right there and then.

Tyvian smiled, nodding. "Arguing it is, then."

CHAPTER 22

SEEING AND BELIEVING

Hool woke up to the sound of birds and the heat of the sun on her back. As she often did, she was struck with the possibility that she was on the Taqar again; that all this had been a dream. She clung to it for a few moments longer before, inevitably, she needed to breathe in. The scent of Glamourvine and its pervasive sorceries dispelled all illusions.

Hool rolled to her feet. The hedge maze was still closed to her. Somewhere, not too far away, she heard the gardener clipping the funny little trees that lined some of the paths. She did not remember falling asleep.

At the edge of the pool, sitting in a mageglass chair before a small table, Lyrelle Reldamar was sipping tea and paging through an old, iron-bound book. She wore a great, wide sun-hat and a dress of warm hunter green and white lace. On her nose were perched a pair of orange-tinted spectacles.

Hool's hackles rose. "You betrayed your own son."

Lyrelle glanced at her and then back at the book. "And what? Now you intend to kill me? Are you certain that's entirely wise, given your situation?"

Hool displayed her teeth and stalked closer, her weight resting evenly on all four limbs. "You are a liar. Why should I listen to anything you say?"

"Whether I lie or whether I tell the truth is completely inconsequential. Everybody fails to understand that—very frustrating. I need only reference last night—I misled you, and yet I achieved my aims. It would seem that 'truth' is, at best, an indifferent motivator of other people's behavior. At the very least, it is certainly no more persuasive than falsehood."

Hool pounced with a roar, her hands set to seize the sorceress by the neck and crush her. Instead, she met only air and tumbled onto the ground. When she rolled to her feet, Lyrelle was located in a slightly different part of the clearing. She hadn't bothered to look up from her book. "Now, consider your current situation, Madam Hool: did I *move* myself using sorcery, or was I never where you thought I was to begin with? In other words—was the scene the truth or a lie? Does it really matter now? The effect, as you see, is identical."

Hool grabbed a great stone vase from the ground and hurled it at Lyrelle. It passed through her with a flash, and again Lyrelle was somewhere else in the clearing, still sitting and reading her book. The sound of the vase smashing apart on the ground did cause her to look up, though. "Really? Was that entirely necessary?"

"Where is Tyvian?"

Lyrelle fished a circular, ticking brass device out of a hidden pocket and consulted it. "If I know my son, he has recently escaped Keeper's Court. After swimming through some greasy canal, perhaps with a dagger in his teeth, he emerged to rescue his lady love from her prison and is now fighting with her in some little bolt-hole he's got squirreled away in Crosstown."

Hool blinked. "How long have I been sleeping?"

"This is the morning of the second day since Tyvian's arrest."

Hool laid her ears back. "You enchanted me!"

Lyrelle smiled. "No, the *ham* was enchanted. You merely ate it."

Hool snorted—lousy sorceress. She decided to change the subject. "You knew Tyvian would escape?"

Lyrelle pulled down her spectacles to look Hool in the eye. "Are you trying to tell me you cannot predict the behavior of your own children? Come now, Hool—how many pups do you have?"

"Four . . . no." Hool felt Api's loss again in that instant. It was like a knife to the heart. Her hackles lowered and her ears drooped. "Only three."

Lyrelle nodded, pursing her lips. "My condolences. Forgive me, however, if I press you on my point: what is Brana doing right now?"

Hool thought. "Brana is wherever Artus is."

"And where is Artus?"

"Doing something to make Tyvian angry because Tyvian doesn't pay him enough attention." Hool sighed. "They fight like roosters."

Lyrelle smiled. "There, you see? It isn't all that hard, now is it? A solid understanding of individuals is the basis of all manipulation."

Hool sat on the ground. "Why are you telling me this? Why did you call the Defenders on Tyvian if you knew he would just escape?"

Lyrelle laughed lightly. Hool didn't see what was so funny. Hool didn't like this woman, who was never quite what she seemed. She considered just running away, but she had a feeling that Lyrelle's sorcery would keep her there in that garden until she was done with her. "Hool," the sorceress said, "if I made a habit of telling any given gnoll my plans, where would I be?"

"I don't want to talk to you anymore," Hool announced. "I want to find Tyvian and Artus and Brana and get away from this terrible city and never come back."

Lyrelle nodded. "That's exactly what you're going to do, my dear, so don't fear. I must show you something first, though, or you might not destroy the right people when you go."

Hool folded her arms. "Who said I was going to destroy anybody?"

Lyrelle pushed her spectacles back up. "I did."

Hool growled. This time, instead of pouncing, she walked up to the table and stood over the sorceress. "I am not your slave! You don't tell me what to do!"

"Of course I don't—that's the whole point. You, my dear, are going to do whatever your heart desires. Just not yet." Lyrelle motioned to the seat across from her. "Would you care for some tea?"

Hool looked at the chair and then back at Lyrelle. "Won't I just fall through it?"

"Don't be silly," Lyrelle said. "Please—sit. If not tea, then water? Something to eat?"

Hool sat. The mageglass chair felt cold and hard beneath her. "I want bacon. Bring me some bacon."

Lyrelle smiled broadly, her teeth gleaming in the afternoon sunshine. "That's the spirit! How lovely! Now, why don't you tell me a little bit about yourself? I'm just dying to hear more of what a gnoll makes of our mad little world."

Hool folded her arms. She didn't want to talk, she wanted to *act*. Every moment sitting there while her pup and her adopted family needed her was enough to make her mad with frustration. She thought of Tyvian floundering in black water, of Artus getting stabbed by assassins, of Brana lost and alone. It took all of her self-control not to howl and roar. But that would be just what Lyrelle Reldamar expected, wouldn't it—another dumb animal for her to trick into doing her bidding.

No. Not her.

Hool did not talk to Lyrelle, and the sorceress did

not talk back. They sat in silence in the garden for hours. Lyrelle had bacon brought out by some invisible spirit, and Hool ate it all. It was delicious, but she didn't say so. Lyrelle didn't inquire.

Hool imagined that they were engaged in some kind of battle of wills, but she was at a loss as to what the stakes were. At one point she stood up and Lyrelle looked up at her, evidently surprised. "Planning on going somewhere?"

"I want to leave. Show me what you wanted to show me!"

Lyrelle pointed at the chair. "Not just yet, I'm afraid. Sit."

Hool thought about flipping the table over or something, but there was so much sorcery in the air, she knew it wouldn't work and she would just look foolish. Scowling, she sat back down. Beyond the chirp of the birds and the rustle of the breeze through the cypress branches, the only sound was the dry flip of the pages of Lyrelle's book.

The sun began to set and Hool decided to take nap—she was tired of sitting in a chair, and, other than the stink of magic everywhere, the garden grass was lush and comfortable. When she slid onto the ground, Lyrelle (or the simulacrum of Lyrelle—who knew?) did not look up. Hool snorted, turned herself around, lay her head on her paws and closed her eyes.

There were dreams, but they were indistinct—the sound of Brana howling in danger, Tyvian laughing, and tangled streets of Saldor, wet with blood and filth.

Hool . . . Hooool. . .

Her eyes popped open.

Nightfall had again descended upon the garden. The archsorceress Lyrelle was again clad in glimmering white and silver, the fireflies floating about her golden hair like a halo. She knelt before the still waters of the pond, a staff in one hand. She waved Hool closer to her. "Come. Look."

Hool sniffed the air. "Time is strange here—why is it so dark already? Did you enchant me again?"

Lyrelle pointed to the perfectly circular pond. "This is a power sink—similar in form to the one you saw beneath Daer Trondor, but much smaller, much younger, and much less . . . well . . . let's say *tampered* with."

Hool glared at the pond. Now that she was looking at it in that light, she noticed many similarities between it and the great fiery pool beneath the mountains—its seeming depthlessness, for instance, and the strong reek of sorcery. "What does it do?"

Lyrelle ran a hand across the surface of the pond, but rather than ripple, the water grew still, like a mirror. "Power sinks are just collecting pools for the Great Energies. They are built along ley lines and slowly accrue power. A sorceress can then tap into those stored energies to enhance the efficacy of their arts. This one I use when scrying, which channels the Astral a great deal. The side effect of all this Astral energy flowing around is that you and I are currently within what I like to call a 'hiccup' in time. Hence the nightfall."

Hool's nostrils flared. "I don't like it."

Lyrelle motioned toward the surface of the pool. "Look."

In the pond, floating below the surface where Hool expected to see her own reflection, she instead saw Artus walking down a shadowy corridor lined with doors, a double-edged dagger drawn. "The Cauldron," Hool grumbled. "What is Artus doing?"

Lyrelle nodded. "Shhh. Listen."

From one of the doors in front of Artus, Hool could hear a fight. A man was cursing and swearing. Hool recognized the voice: Gethrey Andolon. *"You LOVE him, don't you? DON'T YOU? SAY IT!"*

Artus was at the door. It was slightly ajar, and he leaned against the wall to peer through the crack. Hool found that she and Lyrelle peered with him. There, lying on the floor, blood pouring from her nose, was Claudia Fensron. She was clad in a black silk robe that was bunched around her hips. Her pale skin flickered beneath the light of a fireplace. She spat blood on the floor. *"I never said I love—"*

But Andolon didn't let Claudia finish—he kicked her in the stomach four times, each blow punctuated by a single word: *"NEVER! LIE! TO! ME!"*

"Pleasant fellow, don't you think?" Lyrelle whispered. Hool didn't answer.

Andolon's voice cracked. Artus could see tears welling in the fop's eyes. *"After . . . after all I've done for you, Claudia, and this is how you betray me? Haven't I protected you from the Prophets? Haven't I given you anything you wanted? HAVEN'T I?"*

Claudia dragged herself into a chair, wheezing. *"You stupid, stupid boy. The same stupid boy you always were, Gethrey—in love with a whore. Age just made you vicious, like it does with everybody."* She laughed. *"What are you crying about? You think I haven't been beaten before, and by bigger men than you? Reldamar isn't here, and even if he were, I'd never tell you where."*

Andolon loomed over her, hand on his sword. *"You want me to call in the Quiet Men? They'll turn this place upside down. How do you think it will look, having the Prophets' muscle busting in on wealthy young gentlefolk in the midst of their jolly-time? What do you think will happen to this little whorehouse then?"*

"Go to hell." Claudia spat on the floor. *"Kroth take my whorehouse anyway."*

Andolon grabbed her by the hair and slammed her head into the mirror of her vanity so hard it broke. He hissed in her ear. *"Listen to me, you lying slut: this isn't your business, it's the Prophets' business! You aren't allowed to not care, understand? You and all your little two-bit harlots live and die at my recommendation! I know he's here—you and Maude are the only two friends Reldamar has in this city. You don't want to tell me, then fine—I'll find him anyway, even if I need to burn the place down!"*

Lyrelle shook her head. "Poor Gethrey—always such a sensitive boy."

Hool snorted, her ears back. "He doesn't look very sensitive."

"Oh yes," Lyrelle whispered, "Only a man with deep feelings can harbor such rage. He loved Claudia once—still does, in a way—and her refusal of him is too much for his fragile ego and hopeless affection to take. She poisoned his heart, and in her he sees the physical evidence of all his failings and troubles. Sad, really. Also incredibly useful for people like me."

As Andolon brutalized Claudia, Hool could tell Artus was working up his nerve for something. He had his dagger pointed at Andolon's back and slowly, very slowly, opened the door to Claudia's room wide. He stepped upon the threshold of the room.

"*No!*" A new voice, half strangled with emotion, came from behind Artus. He whirled to see Maude, standing rigidly upright, her chin raised, her hands by her sides and bunched into fists. "*Behind you!*" she managed.

Artus turned back . . . and froze, his face bright with shock. He was bleeding from his chest—a knife plunged into his heart.

"NO!" Hool screamed at the water. "NO! NO!"

There was no assailant Hool could see. Blood fountained up from Artus's throat. He fell to his knees.

Andolon turned from Claudia, his face wound up in a red-eyes sneer. "How many men are going to die for you tonight, Claudia? Make up your mind."

Artus fell to the floor, facedown. The image faded.

"ARTUS!" Hool howled. She whirled on Lyrelle, "You can see the future! Why didn't you save him! He was just a pup!"

Lyrelle smiled softly. "But Hool, that *was* the future. One of them, anyway—a likely one. There are others—some show my son dead, others show Myreon Alafarr screaming in pain. Not all of them will come to pass. Nevertheless, there is a very real chance that Gethrey Andolon will have Artus and my son murdered before the sun rises."

"Who stabbed Artus? Were they invisible?"

"After a fashion. The Quiet Men of the Mute Prophets have no identity—no destiny, no fate—and as such do not appear in my scrying or anyone else's. They are difficult to see, since there is fundamentally nothing *to* see."

Hool felt fire in her limbs and a trembling urgency in her heart. "How long?"

Lyrelle smiled. "What we just witnessed won't happen for another two hours. Possibly three."

Hool's legs tensed—she was ready to fly, if necessary. "I need to go!"

"You will need a weapon." Lyrelle pointed to Hool's feet. There, snugly fastened inside a leather holster with a shoulder strap, was a heavy spiked mace with a flarewood shaft. As Hool looked at it, the mace's head seemed to . . . *move.* It flowed slowly, like thick mud or clay.

Hool held out a hand to pick it up, but hesitated. "What is it?"

"An artifact of great power, once used against my family many centuries ago. It is called the Fist of Veroth. A parting gift—a peace offering for my detaining you here so long."

Hool picked it up—it was heavy, but the holster fit

comfortably around her shoulders so that the weapon rested just behind her head. "I need to go *now!*"

Lyrelle smiled. "The time has come. Remember, Hool: know the game and have the confidence to play it well. You know what humans will do as well as any predator—use that instinct."

Hool didn't wait for Lyrelle to finish speaking. She took off at a dead run, rocketing out of the maze on all fours. She left via the main entrance, which led to the road, which in turn would lead her to Saldor, still many miles distant. She howled into the night, sprinting for all she was worth. It felt good and right. She gloried in the feeling of the night air rushing over her fur.

Hool had been running for almost a half hour before she realized one horrifying fact: she was doing exactly what Lyrelle Reldamar wanted.

She clenched her teeth; she went anyway.

CHAPTER 23

INTIMATE NEGOTIATIONS

Myreon threw a book at Tyvian, which he only just managed to dodge. "No, no, no!" she yelled. "You have a responsibility, dammit! You're *involved*!"

Tyvian retrieved the book and threw it back—Myreon deflected it with a quick guard spell, but her mouth popped open in indignation. "Don't look at me like that!" he snapped, thrusting a finger in her direction. "You threw a book at me, so *I* threw a book at you—fair's fair! Furthermore, if we follow your asinine plan, we're going to wind up back where we both started—Keeper's Court, chained to the bloody Block! If we keep a low profile, if we just—"

"Coward!" Myreon spat. "Chicken-livered little—"

Tyvian rolled his eyes. "Why do you, against all sense, want to charge into danger to protect the very people who took your staff away!" He picked up the judge's ledger. "Look at this again! Tell me Forsayth and who knows how many other judges had you petrified on the merits of the case and *not* because Andolon was lining their pockets with silver! You might be stubborn, Myreon Alafarr, but you just aren't that naive!"

Neither of them had slept. Tyvian was exhausted, having swum for an eternity in perfect darkness, navigated a flowing river, and then dragged her deadweight body there under cover of night. He couldn't imagine Myreon felt any better, but they kept arguing without stop. He wasn't sure they could stop. Honestly, he wasn't sure he wanted to.

Myreon was lecturing again, "If we don't stop Andolon, the West will descend into—"

"Chaos, violence, starvation—I know, I know. Gods, you're like a bloody maypole with that bit—round and round and all wrapped up!" He sighed and ran a hand over his increasingly shaggy face—Maude, it turned out, did not possess a razor. "Myreon, even if we *did* do something to stop Andolon, somebody else would come up with the same trick eventually. The Secret Exchange is riding a bubble—it can't get bigger forever. Why save it if it's doomed anyway?"

Myreon glared at him but didn't say anything for a few moments. "Andolon shouldn't be the one."

"What?"

"He's an odious, self-absorbed little troll, Tyvian. You've agreed as much. Suppose there is bound to be a crash sooner or later—I'm just a poor Defender and don't claim to understand it, so I guess I'll take your word—but why should Andolon be the one to clean up? There has *got* to be a better option, right?"

Tyvian shook his head. His mother's plan was becoming all too clear now. How to get him to save the exchange? Easy—stick him in a room with an inconveniently beautiful woman with a stubborn streak the size of the Eretherian Gap. This had been the plan all along, damn her, and here he was, almost on the brink of agreeing to it. And, after it was all over, Lyrelle would have lost nothing and no one would have any idea she was responsible—just how she liked it. Still, there were pieces missing. "His plan probably won't work anyway, Myreon, and even if it does, the Prophets will just kill him and eat up the leavings."

"I'm telling you that we need to make *certain* Andolon's plan doesn't work. We need to go to your brother and offer to have you testify . . ."

Tyvian groaned. "Not this again."

"*Listen to me, dammit!*" Myreon punched the bedpost. "Testify against Andolon on condition of immunity. I'll vouch for you—I still have friends in—"

"Myreon!" Tyvian got down at her eye level. "You. Are. A. Criminal. They aren't going to listen to you—they're the ones who let you get set up! They aren't going to give me *immunity*—not after I set Keeper's Court on fire. It won't bloody work!"

"So that's it? You're just going to surrender?"

"There's more to this than you understand, Myreon. Gethrey's just a pawn in a game of *couronne*—we *all* are. The game is rigged and the only way to win is not to play at *all*."

Myreon threw up her hands. "So you keep insisting, but you refuse to explain!"

"If I explain, that becomes *part* of the game, dammit!"

"So why did you even *come* here, Tyvian? Why even bother saving me if all we're going to do is sit here fighting?" Myreon arched her eyebrows. "Well? When you busted me out, what did you think would happen? You'd sweep me onto a white charger and ride off into the sunset?"

Tyvian snorted. "Of course not."

"Then *what*? Why am I even here?"

Tyvian's whole body ached. It seemed like the only things that could change the course of their conversation were the very things he swore he'd never say. "This will never work if you won't listen to reason."

Myreon folded her arms. "I might say the exact same thing to *you*."

The secret door swiveled open, bringing the muffled roar of a busy night at the Cauldron with it. In came Maude with a tray in one hand. She was wearing her boots and bracers. "Busy night, my duckies. Would have come in sooner but for some pisser who took a swing at Jari." She gave them a big wink. "Settled him quick, never fear. His friends collected his teeth and cleared out."

"Is Jari all right?" Tyvian asked. He had a vague recollection of a bartender, Rhondian, tall and dark.

Maude set a tray of roast chicken on the bed, pulled a demi of Akrallian white from somewhere in her blouse and handed it to Myreon. She added two wooden cups to the tray. "Not the best stuff, mind, but nothing that will be missed neither."

Tyvian inhaled the aroma of the chicken—not a culinary masterpiece, but the hint of rosemary and garlic was enough to set his mouth watering. "That is more than adequate, thank you."

Myreon echoed the sentiment with a weak smile, which made one of Maude's eyebrows wrinkle. She looked at Tyvian and back at Myreon. "Now, you two'd best leave off the shouting for a while—just have a go with each other and have it over with. Beds're built for using, eh?"

Myreon nearly dropped the wine bottle. Tyvian opened his mouth to reply, but Maude gave him a peck on the cheek, a wink, and retreated, locking the door behind her.

Tyvian found himself eye-to-eye with the steel-gray gaze of Myreon Alafarr. He found himself unable to read her expression, but he gathered it wasn't positive, given how her eyebrows were pinched together. He smiled at her and did his best to sound nonchalant. "So, care to have a go?" He cocked his head at an angle popular with dandies and gave her an overblown, rakish wink.

Myreon's face got somehow even *more* tense for a

moment before bursting with great, whooping guf-faws. Tyvian found himself joining her, and they laughed together for a full minute, one picking up the levity when the other ran out of breath, until both of them were leaning back against opposite sides of the bed, smiles on their faces. Silence fell over them, and it felt, for the first time, to be a comfortable silence. A silence between friends. Maybe. He reflected he was probably fooling himself.

"However did you earn the loyalty of that woman?" Myreon asked, shaking her head.

"Maude is a fine specimen of person," Tyvian said, realizing he was reacting more seriously than was his wont. "The finest, actually."

"Oh—I don't mean the question as a slight, no!" Myreon smiled at him, "She's wonderful. She reminds me of some of my aunts. Well, if my aunts were gigan-tic and terrifying."

Tyvian looked up at the ceiling. He found himself talking. "I used to come here a lot when I was young. I'd sneak out of the town house or sneak a horse out of Glamourvine or something and come here—popular place with the rich kids. The food was rustic and tasty, the wine list serviceable, and the whores were high quality. No place a boy of fifteen with a chip on his shoulder would rather be, believe me."

Myreon frowned. "I heard about you back then. Nothing good—you had a reputation for a temper. Fought a lot of duels. Heard you killed a boy."

Tyvian nodded slowly, remembering that moment—

the blood, the saliva bubble the boy had blown before he died, the dead weight of his body on top of him. "I did. You asked about Maude, though. This was after the whole killing thing—when I had a *really* dangerous reputation. Funny thing about a reputation, actually—you work so hard to get it without realizing what happens when you do. I had every suck-up and gay-blade in Saldor nipping at my heels. I fought a duel twice a week or so. They were mostly just foolishness—a nick here, a little poke there. Nobody seriously hurt."

Myreon poured the wine. "What's all this have to do with Maude?"

"I decided pretty early on that I liked prostitutes." Tyvian saw Myreon stiffen, and added, "Look, I won't lie to you—I, ah, sampled the wares. What teenage boy with silver burning a hole in his pocket wouldn't? That isn't quite what I meant, though. I *liked* them. I knew all their names, I liked to hear their stories."

Myreon snorted. "You were paying them, Tyvian. It was just an act—"

"Please, Myreon—a little credit? I *knew* the act. Through them I got an education in manipulation and deceit no tutor could ever teach me. Maybe they never liked me—very probable, actually—but I didn't much care. I visited often, tipped generously, and became *quite* popular. They also gave me plenty of excuses to pick fights, which I actively relished back then. Some fop gave his jenny a slap, and I was there, ready to make him regret it. Champion of the Night Ladies, that was me." Tyvian rolled his eyes. "I was their personal gods-damned savior. And I loved every minute of it, I assure you."

Myreon was watching him closely, her eyes searching his face. "I assume the gay-blades didn't especially like that?"

Tyvian nodded. "One fellow—a vicious little prick named DeVauntnesse—took exception to his whore for the evening extolling my virtues. He beat her, and rather severely. Now, the DeVauntnesse family was too rich for Maude to do much about it, but I, on the other hand . . ."

Myreon gasped. "Hann's boots! Is this *Faring* DeVauntnesse?"

Tyvian grinned. "I suppose you know where the story goes from there."

"*You* did that?" Myreon laughed. "I never guessed you would have cut off a man's balls for beating a jenny. Never in a million years."

Tyvian shrugged. "I was a nicer person back then." He sipped the wine—not good, but passable. The fact that it was in a wooden cup nearly ruined it, but it was better than nothing. "I gave all that up, though. As much as I enjoyed stabbing my peers, in the end I came to realize nothing good ever comes from saving people from themselves. That particular instance is a good example: the girl I'd fought for went back to comfort Faring as soon as he was on his feet again. It was his last visit—his worst fears were confirmed, I suppose. He beat the girl again. Anyway, that's why

Maude loves me—Tyvian Reldamar, retired defender of the defenseless." He raised his cup. "Cheers."

Myreon raised her cup. "I would have cut off his balls, too."

Tyvian grinned at her. "That's what makes us such a good team, I suppose."

"Right." Myreon rolled her eyes. She was quiet a moment, then, "Who was the girl?"

"Does it matter?"

"I'm curious."

Tyvian sighed. "Her name is Claudia Fensron."

Myreon's mouth popped open. "But—"

"She hates me, yes." Tyvian took a long sip of wine. "The wages of gallantry, my dear. Remember them well."

They ate in silence—a kind of truce, Tyvian supposed. Myreon seemed deep in thought and Tyvian opted not to disturb her. Besides, he was having a hell of a time figuring out how to eat a chicken without utensils or napkin and without getting grease all over his only shirt. As he refused to lick his fingers like a dog in front of a lady, he was forced to surreptitiously wipe them on the bedspread when Myreon wasn't looking. The whole affair was incredibly uncivilized. It reminded him of eating with Hool.

One way or another, there wouldn't have to stay in Maude's saferoom much longer. Andolon's plan was likely almost at fruition. Tyvian guessed his escape from Keeper's Court had made that possible for him, on some level. Anyway, the markets were ripe.

Here, in the depths of the summer, trade was at its peak in the Secret Exchange—the Eretherian campaigns were in full swing, and the war chests of petty nobility would need bolstering. Calls for loans would be high, which meant interest rates would be high, and a lot of rich people would be hedging their bets for a good harvest come the start of autumn. The risk would be high as well, given the interest on the loans they took to keep Baron What's-his-name out of their realm, and so they'd seek ways to secure the value of their harvest, hence they'd be purchasing derivatives from wealthy sorcerous families in Saldor who, in turn, would be packaging those derivatives into the complex derivative products for sale on the Secret Exchange. Akral, as Eretheria's other major trading partner, would be bound to Eretheria's financial fate. Galaspin was bound to Saldor's. Ihyn depended on all of them. And on and on and on.

If the Secret Exchange went belly up, the Saldorians wouldn't be able to pay out their derivatives, which would, in turn, mean the Eretherians would have no guarantee for the price of their grain. This wouldn't normally be a problem, since a good harvest would still mean they'd have an abundance of grain to sell and, perhaps, just break even instead of turning a profit. That, of course, was how the Saldorians used auguries to guarantee their own speculation—they *knew* (or thought they knew) that the harvest was going to be good, so playing free and loose with money they didn't yet possess wasn't too risky. If the Eretherians had a *bad* harvest (like, for instance, because Quiet Men with bags of poison were going about causing trouble) or if the prices of certain key commodities dropped precipitously (like, for instance, by Gethrey Andolon releasing a hidden stockpile of goods to force prices down), the petty nobility would go belly up, default on their loans. Those who lent to them (Akrallians as often as not) would go belly up, too, since they needed that money to guarantee their *own* loans. The whole chain of dominoes would fall, and though nothing in the world really changed from the perspective of the average farmer, his local lord would be raising taxes to make his loan payments. That farmer, already living on a narrow margin, would find himself starving inside of a year.

Of course, all of that depended on the auguries of the hundreds of magi who traded on the Secret Exchange to be wrong. The theory of Gethrey's plan was sound, but the execution would require something extra—something even the Prophets would have difficulty providing. Gethrey thought he could panic the Secret Exchange into hemorrhaging a significant percentage of its money in a single day's trading. It just wasn't likely, flighty as investors could be.

Unless . . .

Tyvian had called both Myreon and himself pieces on a *couronne* board, but *couronne* was played by two players. If his mother had manipulated events to get Tyvian in this room, at this time, to *stop* Andolon . . . who was she playing against? Tyvian's mind raced through the possibilities, but only one of them made sense.

"Xahlven." Tyvian felt his stomach flip. "Oh gods— it's Xahlven."

Myreon put down her wine. "What is?"

Tyvian stood up. "He's the one backing Gethrey. He's using Geth to crash the market, and then using the Prophets to remove Gethrey, and then . . . then he'll just seize Gethrey's assets in the investigation. Gods, it's brilliant."

Myreon climbed to her feet. "Your *brother* is the one who framed me? I thought he told you to turn Andolon in at your trial!"

Tyvian felt dizzy. "Of course he did! Of *course!* I've never done *anything* Xahlven has asked me to do! Not since we were children! He was just playing me. Gods, he's been playing us both!"

Myreon grabbed his arm. "Tyvian, listen to me: I am going to stop Xahlven. Alone if I have to. I can't let this pass."

Tyvian looked down at Myreon's hand wrapped around his forearm. Her touch—so soft after the regeneration of her skin, post-petrification—tingled through his whole body, like his own bones were singing with excitement. When she moved to take it away, he laid his hand over hers and held it in place. "Xahlven is too dangerous to take on alone."

Myreon nodded, staring him in the eye, their faces so close that he could smell the faint touch of wine on her breath. "That's why I need your help."

Tyvian felt pinned in place by her eyes, her touch, the smell of her in the stale air of the saferoom. He felt short of breath. "I should warn you, Ms. Alafarr, my consulting fees are quite steep."

Myreon smirked. "Really? Is my credit good?"

Tyvian smiled. "Well, you *are* a felon."

She pushed him away. "I'm serious."

"I am, too." He shrugged. "I always help a felon in need. Even the crazy ones."

Myreon's face broke into that rarest of expressions—the full, ear-to-ear grin. She opened her mouth to speak—

There was a banging on the wall—the savage, angry banging of a man too drunk or too angry to understand his own strength. A muffled voice shouted from the corridor beyond the saferoom. *"I know you're in there somewhere, Tyvian Reldamar! Come out! Come out now or, so help me, I'll start cutting throats!"*

It was Gethrey Andolon.

Tyvian turned to tell Myreon where she could hide, but she had a trunk open and was rifling through clothing, searching for something to wear. "What are you doing?"

She scowled at him. "Sneaking out the window. You coming?"

Out in the hall, Tyvian heard a bellow that had to be Maude. *"There's nobody here, you blue-haired bastard! Leave her be! Just leave her— Oooh!"*

The ring clamped down on him as Tyvian heard Maude cry out. It couldn't have been Gethrey doing that—the skinny fop probably couldn't throw a punch hard enough to make Maude giggle. That meant one thing: Quiet Men. "No," he said to Myreon. "I'm not coming."

She frowned. "You can't seriously want to go out there? He'll kill you!"

"*Five minutes, Tyv! Understand?*" Gethrey shouted.

"What are you going to do?" Myreon hissed, staring at the secret door.

"The only thing I can do." Tyvian waggled his ring hand. "Play hero. Again."

CHAPTER 24

DRINKS WITH DAGGERS

Tyvian kept his back turned as Myreon dressed, but only partially because he was a gentleman—he also didn't want to look away from the saferoom's secret door.

Myreon took a deep breath. "Any last minute advice?"

Tyvian didn't look back. "Do *not* confront Xahlven directly."

The rustle of clothing stopped. Myreon's voice had that old edge of suspicion. "Why?"

Tyvian tried to think of a good way to explain, but

nothing came to him at that moment. "Just . . . trust me."

Myreon was quiet for a moment. "How do I know I can trust *you?*"

Tyvian grunted. He might have lied, but for some reason he did not—he found himself telling her one of the first things Carlo diCarlo had told him when he asked the old pirate the same question fifteen years ago in this very dive bar. "You don't. You cannot know this; this is life."

He heard Myreon go to the window. "Good luck, Mr. Reldamar." Tyvian gave her a smile over his shoulder. She smiled back, but with less certainty. Then she squeezed through the window; Tyvian went out the door.

He hadn't been out of the saferoom five seconds before he felt a knife at his back from a corner he had originally thought empty. "Ah," he said. "Didn't see you there."

The Quiet Man said nothing. He prodded Tyvian in the direction of the bar, so Tyvian went. The common room of the Cauldron was bustling, as ever, an equal mix of the powder-wigged or dyed nobility and the hat-wearing, greasy-haired common folk. A Verisi with a concertina was playing some kind of nautical dancing tune, and a collection of young bravos were dancing unevenly with a variety of half-drunk women, only some of whom were Claudia's employees. Tyvian, though, did his best not to notice this. He focused, instead, on that which would ordinarily be unnoticeable.

Seeing the Quiet Men themselves in a crowd like

this was nearly impossible, but he could pick out people who were frightened. This turned out to be easy: the employees were terrified. Not so much the whores—they didn't seem to be aware of what was going on—but the barstaff, the serving girls, and Maude herself had the ashen expressions of people contemplating their own mortality. A little staring and a little concentration, and Tyvian got a glimpse of why: Quiet Men, scattered throughout the room, their blades drawn. One of them stood right behind Maude, a knife to her throat. Nobody noticed but Tyvian. That meant they wanted him to notice. He had never seen so many of them in one place before—the Prophets were pulling out all the stops, it seemed. The whole group of them would work as one coherent unit, sharing thoughts and feelings as intimately as if they were the same being. There was quite literally *no* way to get the drop on them this way, no way to take them down one by one—nothing he could do.

His own Quiet Man piloted him to a corner table, where bloody-faced Claudia sat with Gethrey on her right and a featureless individual who had to be a Quiet Man to her left, also with a drawn blade. Its dirty, jagged point was laid against the pale flesh of Claudia's long, elegant neck.

The Quiet Man turned the last chair around so Tyvian would have to straddle the back and leave his kidneys easily exposed to a blade from behind. Tyvian sat and folded his arms. "Well well well—you always did have a way with the ladies, Gethrey."

"Oh, indeed. Perhaps next time I will try cutting off someone's testicles—that always worked for you." Gethrey was dressed in his usual finery, his blue hair fetchingly restrained by a diamond-studded clip to form a ponytail, and just a hint of rogue on his cheeks. His hat was on the table in front of him, a sorcerous tableau of clocks and hourglasses.

Tyvian caught the eye of one of the terrified serving girls. "My dear, how about a bottle of *chleurie* for the table, eh?" He met Gethrey's eye. "On Mr. Andolon's tab, naturally."

Gethrey half smiled, half snarled. "You had to come back, didn't you?"

"Had I realized my presence was such an imposition upon your petty criminal activities, I certainly would have reconsidered." Tyvian shrugged. "Yet here we are."

"Don't pretend like you didn't know," Gethrey sneered. "You knew. You knew perfectly well, but you came anyway. Why? Haven't you done enough to me?"

Tyvian blinked at him. "I have no idea what you're talking about." He looked at Claudia. "Do you know what he's talking about?"

Claudia's voice was icy. "Your misplaced sense of chivalry."

The *chleurie* arrived in a crystal decanter and three glasses. Tyvian poured. "If I misplaced it, I certainly had no intention of finding it."

Gethrey shook his head. "You know what the big difference is between me and you, Tyvian? You could leave places like this behind you—anytime you want, just trot back to Glamourvine and live a charmed life— but you *choose* to associate with this rabble of your own free will. I, meanwhile, am *trapped* here, forced to look my shame in the eye every damned collection day, when all I want to do is brush these people off, once and for all."

Tyvian took a sip of the Akrallian brandy and pointed at Claudia's bruised and bloodied face. "Is that what 'brushing off' looks like? Seems strenuous. You likely broke a nail."

"I used to think you had it all figured out, do you know that?" Gethrey picked up his brandy and drank deeply. "To hell with all the high-class twits and their pointless dinner parties, right? Life was on the fringes, you used to say—here, in New Crosstown, where the slime of humanity ruts and vomits its way through life. I rolled around in it with you, and then you . . ." Gethrey struggled for the word. Eventually he blew on his hand as though scattering dandelion seeds. " . . . vanished. I stayed; I fell in *love* with . . . this." He gestured toward Claudia. "I got stuck, Tyv. For all my wealth, I wound up stuck here, living in the muck."

"How awful." Tyvian rolled his eyes. "Think of all those dinner parties you've missed now."

Gethrey slammed his drink on the table. "That's just *it*, Tyvian! You were *wrong*! *I* was wrong! The dinner parties *are* life—a good life! A *successful* life! You know what the friends we grew up with are doing now? They've got families and *land* and *dignity*. They take vacations to Eretheria on the spirit engine, they charter cruises through the Ihynish Archipelagoes. They have mistresses and hunting engagements and on and on and on. That could have been *us*, Tyvian! That could have been *me*! All our friends are there, living it—they've surpassed us!"

"Friends?" Tyvian stared into the crystal of his glass. "I didn't have friends, Geth. I was the bastard son of a woman everyone was too scared to hate openly, so you know what they did? The hated *me*. You know why I wound up killing Ryndal Gathren? Because the Kroth-spawned arse wouldn't leave me alone. He was two years older than me, thirty pounds heavier, and he thought his miserable swordsmanship would be a good way to push me around. He was wrong. Don't tell me about friends, Geth—you were the one with friends. Don't blame me for throwing your own life away either. You did that when I wasn't even here."

Claudia snorted at that. "Please. It was three years before your little crowd stopped coming around, asking after you. You set a fire under those boys' arses, Tyvian Reldamar. You were their very own Perwynnon. You—"

"Shut up!" Gethrey backhanded Claudia across the mouth, his signet ring cutting her cheek deeply. She didn't so much as squeak. She looked steadily at Tyvian with those shimmering brown eyes, her expression unreadable.

Tyvian forced a smile. "So, what now, Geth? Do the

Quiet Men drag me into a sewer and murder me? Will that solve your problems?"

Gethrey smiled. "No, I had something more interesting in mind." His eyes traveled up past Tyvian to someone else in the bar—someone who had been expecting this very summons. Tyvian turned.

There, perched on a barstool in fashionable maroon riding leathers and gold embroidery, was none other than Marcom DeVauntnesse, nephew of whore-beating eunuch Faring DeVauntnesse, and proud owner of a wine-bottle-shaped bruise that covered much of the right side of his face. Marcom's drinking buddies—a veritable who's-who of beardless Saldorian dandies, with the pastel hair coloring and feathery hats to match—got to their feet along with their boy-liege as he sauntered across the floor to stand in front of Tyvian. None of them, Tyvian wagered, noticed the Quiet Men standing right there, knives drawn. Tyvian could barely notice them himself.

"Hello, Marcom." Tyvian grinned. "How's the skull?"

Marcom DeVauntnesse took off his glove one finger at a time and then slapped it hard across Tyvian's cheek. "To the yield, Reldamar." His dim-witted goons spread out around Tyvian in a half circle around him, one of them actually jostling a Quiet Man aside. "There's no window for you to jump out of this time."

Tyvian shrugged. "Alas, I haven't got a sword, so . . ."

Gethrey laid his rapier on the table. "Oh, by all means use *mine*, Tyvian."

Tyvian, grimacing, reached over to take the blade. When he did, Gethrey grabbed him by the wrist and pulled him close. Whispering in his ear, he said, "You lose this duel, Tyv. You let DeVauntnesse here cut off your balls and gut you in front of everybody, or all the girls have their throats cut right here, right now. Understand?"

Tyvian nodded. "How very theatrical of you, Gethrey."

Gethrey raised his glass of *chleurie* to him in salute. "I learned from the very best, didn't I?"

Myreon channeled the Fey into a feyleap that brought her up behind the chimney of a restaurant and paused for a moment, listening. Somewhere in the distance she heard the shouts of a Sergeant Defender bringing a platoon on the march—the third such she had encountered since she left the Cauldron. They were closing in on Tyvian and, possibly, on her. The augurs of the Gray Tower were no doubt directing the whole weight of the Defenders in her direction. Bridges would be blocked, major intersections would be watched, and patrols would be frequent. She only hoped it was Tyvian they were really after and not her.

With one finger she drew the Sigil of Danger on the bricks of the chimney, warm with the smoke of a night of good food and the good cheer it brought. It was enough of a Lumenal ley to give the Sigil life, and

Myreon watched it intently as it glowed and flickered, counting in her head. One, two, three, four, five . . .

It vanished with a sudden pop. Danger was close—too close to be the Defenders at the moment. That meant the only other group who might want to catch her: the Quiet Men. The Mute Prophets didn't earn their title for nothing—they could see the future almost as well as the Defenders could, and they would know she was on her way to stop them from winning more riches than even they could have foreseen ever having. She took a deep breath and erected a variety of guards and wards around herself—bladewards, bowwards, telekinetic guards, a Dweomeric enchantment to strengthen her clothing to the hardness and tensile strength of chain mail.

She really could have used a second pair of eyes, but her only ally (ally?) had just sacrificed himself to the Mute Prophets in order to protect a bunch of whores and drunks. On some level, Myreon still couldn't believe Tyvian had done it, ring or no ring. It was . . . well . . . it was one of the most selfless things she had ever seen anybody do. Part of her wanted to rush back and help him—every step away engendered a little pang of guilt in her stomach. How would she feel if he died?

Myreon pushed all that away and focused on making it to the Old City. Besides the Defenders everywhere, the streets were strangely quiet—even without their own augurs, the people were cagey enough to know trouble was afoot. This made things complicated. Had there been a crowd to hide in, she would have stuck to the streets, using any tail's own cover to thwart them. The second option would be the sewers—very difficult to scry, but slow going and Myreon didn't know them well enough to not get lost.

That left the rooftops, and at that Myreon excelled. Once she was atop the nearest building, much of the rest of her journey simply involved watching her step—the buildings in New Crosstown were close enough together so she could skip from roof to roof with barely more than a short running start, and for anything farther apart, she could feyleap. She got winded quickly, though—a side effect of being petrified for several months, she wagered—and had to stop to rest frequently.

During those rests, she would stop to consider her next move. Tyvian didn't want her to confront Xahlven directly, which, to her mind, was all the more reason to do so. He might have saved her and he might—*might*—have changed, but that didn't mean she was going to listen to the man. She'd fallen for his tricks too often before, frankly. No, she was going to find Xahlven Reldamar, and she was going to force him to save the West from its own greed.

As for *how* this was to be accomplished, well . . . she still had a city to run across to think about it. Oh, and a probable ambush by Quiet Men to negotiate. That, too.

The Quiet Men were men without identity, somehow—stripped of individuality and voice by a sorcerous process as undoubtedly illegal and unethical as it was unknown to the Defenders. What they did left no sorcerous mark on the ley of an area, and no augury or scry could seek them out. Only general things—like the Sigil of Danger—could detect them, and then only indirectly.

So, the plan—the only plan she had—was this: since you couldn't see a Quiet Man coming, you couldn't help but be ambushed. The only choice one had in the matter was *where* the ambush would take place, and so she had determined the one spot where the Mute Prophets *knew* she would have to be in order to find Xahlven, and therefore where she would be ambushed: outside the Venerable Society of Famuli.

Myreon just had to get there before the Mute Prophets figured out what she already knew. For a full mage, that shouldn't be much of a problem, but she would have to pick up the pace. She smiled and made another feyleap that covered half a city block. For once *she* was the one making the plans that the other person was struggling to unravel. That felt good.

She leapt again, pushing herself, pulling as much of the Fey from the summer evening as she could. There was a *lot* of it—too much, even for a big, chaotic place like Saldor. It made her think of Daer Trondor and Sahand's systematic manipulation of the Trondor sink, only somewhat less intense. Chaos was brewing, that much was clear—she didn't need to be an augur to figure that out. Andolon's plan was about to bear fruit, and the brilliance of it was starting to become clear to her. Keeper's Court aflame, the Defenders swarming the streets, Tyvian Reldamar on the loose—it was a perfect storm of the chaotic and unpredictable. How the hell did a low-rate nobleman know this would happen when all the rest of the augurs in Saldor did not? Was his pet Verisi that good?

Or had it been Xahlven the whole time, just like Tyvian said?

Myreon made it to the Old City in record time, coasting on a ley of Fey energy that drove her feyleaps into the realm of the legendary—she cleared both the West Mouth and the Narrow Mouth each with one bound, and the walls of the Old City had scarcely been a challenge. The Defenders, it seemed, were not looking for her at all.

So it was that, still fortified with defensive enchantments and armed with a staff she had liberated from a drunk in a Crosstown alley, she slipped from the shadow of a cypress tree along a dark carriage lane in the Merchant Quarter just across from the Saldorian Exchange. She eyed the great columned halls, watching for movement. The cool damp of the summer evening filled her nostrils and made her shiver; her body ached. It was past midnight now and too peaceful. Bloody mornings should begin with more warning.

She took great care to not be seen as she walked the short distance from the exchange to the Famuli Club. Once there, she remained in the shadows, waiting for some indication of where the Quiet Men would hide. There was none. She etched the Sigil of Danger again, and only managed to count to two before it vanished. They—or someone else who meant her harm—were here, somewhere. She'd made very good time from New Crosstown, but she hadn't made it quite quickly enough.

If the Prophets wanted to stop her, they would have to divine how she meant to get to the Secret Exchange and cut her off. If she could avoid them, all the better. But how?

Tyvian had told her about the window with the weak latch that she could enter to sneak into the exchange. To her knowledge there were only three ways to that window. The first was through the club itself and then onto the roof, the second was climbing the ivy-covered walls, and the third was simply feyleaping to the roof. It stood to reason, then, that they would be waiting for her on the roof, hidden in the shadows surrounding the dome of the Secret Exchange.

There was an easy way to find out, of course. Myreon withdrew deeper into the shadows and, drawing the cool and the dark into her bones, worked a careful Etheric spell to craft a simulacrum of herself. A relatively simple thing—more glamour than substance—but worth it for the kind of fishing expedition she had in mind. With a thought, she impelled her illusory self across the street and to the walls of the club, where the simulacrum began to "climb," or at least simulate it with as much accuracy as possible, given the situation.

The simulacrum achieved the top, and Myreon

watched its progress with a farsight augury. It walked to the dome at the center of the roof and paused at the window—no one emerged to hinder it. Had that really been her, she could have slipped right in.

Myreon frowned—had she been wrong about all this? If they hadn't ambushed her on the city roofs, if they hadn't waited for her while she crossed over the city wall, and they weren't waiting for her outside the Secret Exchange, then the only feasible place they could expect her to be was . . .

. . . right here.

Her breath catching in her teeth, Myreon snatched up her staff, but in that moment somebody shoved a burlap bag over her head, drowning her in darkness.

They had been right behind her the whole time.

CHAPTER 25

NO GOOD DEED UNPUNISHED

As Tyvian stood up to face Marcom, voices around him whispered to one another in a half-dozen tongues: *That's Tyvian Reldamar. Heard he killed twenty men . . . Best swordsman in the West . . . Murderer and traitor. Burned Keeper's Court to the ground.* The effect on his self-esteem was not to be underestimated. He gave Marcom a winning grin. "Swords, to the yield, right here, and right now."

Marcom's flunkies began pushing tables out of the way and threatening patrons to clear out until there was a large area of filthy, sticky floorboards across which to duel. The patrons, for their part, were engrossed in the drama about to unfold. Whore, slumming gentlefolk, and skeevy barflies alike hung on Tyvian and Marcom's every motion. Marcom threw off a half cape and sank into the en garde position. "This time we do it for real. No more tricks."

Tyvian drew Gethrey's sword—a well-polished but infrequently used rapier with barely an edge left on it and a trifle unbalanced toward the point. He gave Gethrey a significant glare. His former friend was watching him carefully; their eyes met. Gethrey made a slicing gesture across his throat and smiled broadly.

Turning back to Marcom, Tyvian mirrored the young twit's en garde. "Ready when you are, sir."

Marcom pressed the attack, intending to test Tyvian's defenses. His technique was adequate but not sophisticated. Tyvian parried once, twice, without retreating a step, ducked a slash and then met the boy's lunge with a locking parry, bringing them *corps à corps*. Marcom pushed hard against Tyvian, but all his youthful enthusiasm wasn't quite equal to Tyvian's battle-hardened strength; he easily held the boy at bay.

Tyvian could have ended the duel right there—a quick sweep of Marcom's forward leg, a pommel strike to the fool's nose, and Marcom would be on his back with a blade at his throat. He couldn't do that, though. He had to lose somehow—the knives at Maude's and Claudia's throats and the ring on his finger made that a certainty.

He let Marcom push him back but parried the

boy's next two thrusts more out of reflex than intent. Marcom frowned. "You think you can trick me? I'm no fool, Reldamar!"

Tyvian countered with a few simple attacks at about half his normal speed, letting Marcom parry them while he tried to come up with a workable plan. "I should think you'd be pleased, Marcom—you're doing very well."

Marcom pressed the attack and the two of them skipped back and forth across the sticky floorboards, blades flashing. The bar patrons whistled encouragement and jeered on occasion, but nobody interfered. It wasn't immediately clear to Tyvian whether he was performing before a pro- or anti-Tyvian crowd.

Marcom made a wild slash—very sloppy—and Tyvian beat his sword out of his hand. The boy's face froze in terror, but Tyvian stepped back, hands up. Boos echoed throughout the room as the young DeVauntnesse scurried to retrieve his blade.

Tyvian took the moment's respite to look over at Gethrey—he was livid, his eyes bulging. "What are you doing?" he snapped.

Tyvian shrugged. "What do you want from me? The boy is as bad as his uncle ever was."

"End it," Gethrey growled, jerking his head. There was a sharp sigh and Tyvian's head whipped around to see one of the barmaids slump facedown on the bar, a river of red pouring from her slashed throat. The Quiet Man who had done it was gone; nobody noticed the girl was dead. Not yet, anyway.

The ring blazed with unconscionable fury, and Tyvian nearly dropped his sword. He stumbled back against Gethrey's table and his former friend gripped him in the shoulder. "For every touch you win, I cut a throat, Tyv—think about it."

Tyvian felt the ring pulse with power—it seemed to glow on his hand. "I am," he said, standing up.

Marcom *flechéd*; Tyvian parried and let Marcom run past, giving him a quick kick in the rear as he went. Marcom went stumbling into the laps of several whores, who laughed a bit too loudly and made a couple uncouth suggestions on what Marcom could do while there. Somewhere behind Tyvian, he heard a Rhondian voice shout, *"Olé!"*

Yes, this was definitely a pro-Tyvian Reldamar crowd.

Somewhere, though, another innocent was paying with her life. There was too much noise and chaos for him to know where, though. Tyvian's heart shuddered with anger.

Marcom got up, his pink hair mussed, his nostrils flaring. "You'll *bleed* for that!"

Tyvian offered no rejoinder. He couldn't keep this going—the Defenders would be surrounding the Cauldron at any moment, Gethrey would keep ordering the Quiet Men to cut throats, and sooner or later Marcom would get lucky and stick him somewhere uncomfortable.

As they fenced, Tyvian tried to see solutions, but he wasn't finding any. Had the duel been to first blood, he might have been able to let Marcom win without gravely injuring himself. Had it been to the death, well, at least then it would be final. To the yield was a bit more . . . unusual. It meant they would duel until one or the other of them surrendered. Tyvian, of course, could just yield at any time, but that wouldn't satisfy Gethrey one bit—that meant throats cut, no more Maude or Claudia. He also couldn't force Marcom to yield—throat-cutting, again.

The only way out was to get himself stabbed—and to make it look good—but without actually dying. He grimaced as he countered a particularly obvious feint from Marcom. *I can't believe I'm actually considering this.*

He advanced on Marcom and loosened up his form, leaving openings that even a novice like the young DeVauntnesse would see. Even so, it took the boy two exchanges to notice and another before he actually struck. Marcom's blade sunk three inches into the meat of Tyvian's thigh; the pain stole his breath and made him fall to his opposite knee. He felt the blood spreading, warm and sticky, inside his breeches. Somehow, he managed not to cry out.

Marcom held his blade to Tyvian's cheek, a tight little smile on his pug face. "Yield!"

Tyvian looked at Gethrey, who was watching over a crystal glass of *chleurie*. Gethrey smirked and shook his head slowly. The room was silent.

"Kroth take you, you little priss." Tyvian launched himself upward, pain flashing bright as lightning, and lunged at Marcom, blade thrusting wildly at the boy's chest. Marcom stumbled in his retreat and fell. For the third or fourth time in as many minutes, Tyvian refrained from ending the duel. Leaning heavily on his uninjured left leg, he waited for Marcom to rise. .

Marcom's eyes narrowed. "What game are you playing?"

Tyvian grimaced. "The same one you are, only I know I'm a piece and you think you're a player." Tyvian switched to his left hand and modified his stance to minimize the pressure on his injured leg. It didn't help much, and it also meant he had to start fencing Barrister, which was really better suited to a sabre than Gethrey's poorly balanced, dull rapier.

Marcom was ill-suited to the change in style. Tyvian attacked more forcefully with the edge of his blade, beating and striking Marcom's rapier out of line and advancing aggressively, though not as quickly as he might have with two good legs under him. Marcom battled but Tyvian again kept from ending it. He let Marcom struggle in *corps à corps* before letting Marcom push him over and onto his back. Marcom slashed with his rapier, putting a smooth, shallow cut across Tyvian's chest. Red blood bloomed across his white linen shirt. "Yield!" Marcom shouted, panting.

Tyvian looked again at Gethrey—the fop was chuckling. He shook his head and waggled his finger at him.

"Why do you keep looking over there?" Marcom pressed his blade to Tyvian's neck. "I have you! You *have* to yield!"

Tyvian's mouth felt dry; the pain of his injuries seemed to sing in his ears; the ring throbbed with the weight of oceans. "I don't have to do a damned *thing*." With his off hand, he grabbed Marcom's rapier by the tip and, feeling the blade cut into his hand, he pulled it aside and rose as quickly as he could. The room spun as the blood rushed from his head. He stumbled against Marcom, knocking the boy backward. There was a riot of movement and sound—people gasping, people cursing. He felt his hands push Marcom away, and it was then that he realized that he'd dropped Gethrey's sword.

His blood pressure gradually equalized and he found himself standing in the center of room, hands at his sides, unarmed. Marcom was three paces away, rapier drawn—in easy lunging distance. The boy, though, did not strike. Nobody spoke; it was as though the entire barroom had decided to collectively hold its breath.

Tyvian spread his hands. "Well? What are you waiting for?"

Marcom's eyes were wide—in confusion or fear, Tyvian couldn't tell. "Yield!"

"I refuse." Tyvian kept his hands spread. "C'mon, boy—take your shot. Kill me already."

Artus and Brana ducked into a doorway as another squadron of mirror men marched by. Brana growled softly.

"I know." Artus nodded. "There's a lot of 'em around."

Brana nodded—an exact mimic of Artus's own nod. "Looking Tyvian?"

"Yeah, but I wonder why they ain't kicking in doors and such." Artus thought about it. "Guess they're waiting for the right wizard to tell 'em which door to kick, huh?"

Brana growled, which told Artus all he needed to know.

"I know—we're almost there, okay? Just keep moving."

Getting to the Cauldron was proving to be complicated. They had spent literally hours finding a way to cross both the Narrow Mouth and the West Mouth without being questioned by a Defender. All the bridges were guarded, all the water taxis stopped and searched, and stealing a boat was among the last things he wanted to try again, despite Brana's enthusiasm for that plan. They wound up bribing a corpse salvager—a distasteful, toothless old man with knobby hands—to hide them each in a sack and take them across both rivers in his black-hulled boat. The little skiff had reeked of rotting meat and dried blood, and the inside of the sack had smelled worse, but they had made it. He had made a mental note to take some ilbane powder at the next opportunity, just to be safe, and then they hurried through the narrow alleys and twisting cobbled streets of New Crosstown, dodging Defender patrols along the way.

They made it to the Cauldron just a few hours before dawn—a time Artus was fast realizing had become like his natural habitat—and observed it from across the road, keeping an eye out for tails or Defenders snooping around. Artus saw nobody. Come to think of it, the streets were unusually quiet. Everybody was keeping their heads low, he guessed. People here had heard how Tyvian burned down Keeper's Court; they were probably waiting for the other shoe to drop. He could almost taste the unease in the great city's odd silence.

Wherever Tyvian is found, the mirror men will make that place pay. If Tyvian was found in the Cauldron, he had no doubt Maude and whoever else would get dragged back to the Block. He supposed the rich folks in the Old City would demand something be done about the rabble that would harbor such a criminal, and life over here would get harder—more Defenders, more augurs scrying your future, more trouble if you stepped out of line. He'd seen that kind of thing happen in Ayventry and in Freegate before that. No matter what happened, the smallfolk were always the ones left holding the bag.

The basement entrance to the Cauldron didn't open to his knock—not even the viewport slid back. "Is it closed?" Artus wondered, but he remembered seeing lights in the windows, and since when would a place like this close before dawn?

Brana cocked his head and sniffed the air. "Fighting inside. Blood."

"You smell Tyvian?"

Brana yipped in the affirmative and began to get excited, his whole body squirming inside his illusory suit.

Artus grabbed him by the shoulders. "Okay, we need a plan." He paused—he realized he had no plans. "Whaddya think?"

"Escape on a boat!" Brana said, nodding furiously.

Artus licked his lips. "Well . . . actually, that's not such a terrible idea. Where will we get a boat, though?"

Brana snorted. "Docks, stupid."

Artus sighed—of course. Then again, he didn't have a better idea. "Okay, fine—*I'm* going to go in here and spring Tyvian. *You* go down to that dock we went to the other night and get us a boat, okay?"

Brana *hurruffed* assent and then bolted away, moving with feline speed and grace into the Saldorian night. Artus, meanwhile, slipped around the side of the building and broke in through a window. After that it was just a matter of acting like he belonged—a skill that Tyvian had spent extensive time tutoring him in. He was pretty damned good at it, too. Though he passed at least two whores on his way down to the common room, neither of them so much as batted a voluminous eyelash at him. He slipped through the kitchens and came out into the common room behind the bar.

There was some kind of fight going on in the center of the barroom floor. Artus heard the clash of steel—a duel. People were stacked along the walls five deep, making room for the combatants. Nobody seemed inclined to move, and he barely squeezed his way to a spot atop the corner of the bar itself. There, through a fog of pipe-smoke, he saw who was dueling: Tyvian.

Odd fact: Tyvian wasn't winning.

Artus had seen Tyvian duel enough to know that he was good—very, very good. Indeed, their brief (and frustrating) fencing lessons had proven to him that Tyvian was capable of things with a sword that not only seemed impossible but that he had trouble seeing with his naked eyes. So, the fact that Tyvian was standing in the middle of the barroom floor with blood staining the front of his shirt and a nasty wound in his right thigh either meant he was fencing somebody equally as terrifying with a blade, or . . . what?

Tyvian growled something from the floor and grabbed the tip of his opponent's sword, pulling it aside with his bare hand. There was a scuffle and Tyvian pushed the other guy away, but dropped his own sword in the process. The bar fell silent. He spread his arms and looked at his enemy. "Well? What are you waiting for?"

"Yield!"

Artus took a good look at this master duelist. His voice was young; he had pink hair. He was maybe three years older than himself but certainly not any older than that. Artus didn't know much about fencing, but he knew enough to see that though the guy looked competent, he didn't have that easy, predatory grace that Tyvian had with a blade. What the hell was the game here?

Artus leaned forward on the bar, trying to get a

better look, and noticed that his hand was in something sticky and warm. He backed off and shook his hand, expecting vomit or old beer to go flicking off. It wasn't. It was blood.

One of the barmaids was dead, her throat cut, and lying on the floor behind the bar. Artus would have screamed but caution made him close his mouth. What the hell was going on?

"I refuse." Tyvian was wide-open and had no defense. "C'mon, boy—take your shot. Kill me already."

Well, that slots it. Artus grabbed the hilt of a double-edged dagger hanging in a sheath from a tap and began to shoulder slowly through the crowd. Tyvian might be willing to get run through for some damn fool reason, but that didn't mean he had to let it happen.

"You think I won't do it?" the pink-haired guy was saying, "You think this . . . *display* will be enough to save you? What kind of fool do you take me for?"

Tyvian rolled his eyes. "I don't see you killing me, do I? Do it, you limp-wristed pile of cosmetics!"

Artus slipped behind a bench of whores, all of whom were enthralled so deeply in the drama before them, you'd think it was tooka smoke. Two of the girls clutched each other's hands, their knuckles turning white.

"This is a trick," the boy-swordsman said. "Pick up your sword."

Tyvian shook his head. "I'd just as soon never wield that misshapen lump of steel again, thank you. Now, hurry up and kill me, or I'll call you a coward."

Artus spotted Gethrey Andolon in the corner with a black-haired woman to his left who seemed to have had her face kicked a couple times. Andolon was watching Tyvian with a cool smile on his lips, sipping some kind of brandy.

"Fight me! I want satisfaction!" Pink-hair stamped his foot.

Behind him a group of young gentlemen with all the hallmarks of pink-hair's goons began jeering at Tyvian. "Coward," they catcalled. "Whore-lover!"

Artus was close now, his dagger drawn. He had only to work his way past a few more rows of witnesses.

Tyvian threw up his hands, exasperated. "Fight you? Why? So I can let you poke me a few more times? No thank you."

Artus kept his attention on Pink-hair's back, keeping his blade low so people wouldn't notice it. He slipped past a Verisi sailor whose mouth was hanging open like his jaw was broken.

"Let me? *Let* me?" Pink-hair scoffed. "You can't—"

"Do you seriously think you were beating me?" Tyvian laughed. "Typical DeVauntnesse self-delusion! Boy, I could have not only won that stupid duel, I could have *killed* you three times by now. You're welcome."

Artus was behind DeVauntnesse's goons. Just another second and he'd have a knife between the fop's shoulder blades.

Pink-hair snorted. "And yet *you're* the one disarmed and injured, and I'm here, about to kill you."

"And taking your bloody time about it, too." Tyvian

sighed. "Would taunting you help? Here: your uncle Faring was a puffy-cheeked lummox with hands like plucked turkeys, and the only people he had the courage and the strength to physically abuse were women half his size whom he had to pay to let him punch them. Cutting off his balls was a public service, as had he ever reproduced, the collective reputation of the Saldorian gentry would never have recovered from the shame."

Artus saw DeVauntnesse's shoulders tense, saw his body coil—he was about to strike. Artus raised the dagger—one bull-rush past the pack of dandies and he was there.

"No!" A voice called from the crowd. Maude's? "Behind you!"

Artus looked behind him just in time to see the flash of a blade—a blade aimed directly at his heart.

CHAPTER 26

BRAWL IN THE CAULDRON

Strong arms dragged Myreon onto her back. She thrashed against her attackers—two of them, she guessed—and managed to get one off her by smashing the back of her skull into what felt like a nose. Four hands pushed her back down. A dagger—a wicked, crooked thing that caught the streetlight for an instant—was plunged into her chest, only to rebound away sharply as it struck her sorcerous guard. Myreon knew from experience that having your blade ripped away like that hurt like hell, but the attacker made not a sound—not even a grunt.

Another blade touched her throat and was dragged across with a kind of professional savagery that was chilling to experience. Her bladeward held nicely—what should have ended her life only made her gag a bit. She found she had a hand free, and used it.

Murder in the dark had enough ethereal energy laced through it that invoking a basic rot-curse was easier than breathing. Myreon flung it at one of the Quiet Men standing over her, but he ducked out of the way and her curse went upward into the tree branches. She found herself pinned again, and the Quiet Man still standing over her pulled a long thin wire out of his cloak—a garrote.

A tree branch fell on his head, having rotted off the bole by her curse. He fell over her and the branch—a huge bough, actually—covered all of them. Myreon found herself free from human hands but now ensconced in leafy ones. It was a contest to see who could wriggle their way out first.

She was thinner than her assailants, it turned out, and got all the way out while her foes were only halfway free. She looked down at them—weirdly nondescript faces, black empty eyes, and little tattoos of buttons over the corners of their mouths. They looked at her with the exact same expression: murderous hatred.

She looked around. The street was no longer empty. Five men, all as blank and dark as the other two, and hard to see, stood in a half circle around her, their black cloaks concealing their features as well as their weapons. They closed in as one entity, smoothly and without signal.

Myreon felt all the anger she had felt on the courtroom floor all those months ago flow through her—these were the men who had seen her trapped in stone, who had almost driven her mad. These inhuman bastards were the reason she had lost her staff and been made an outcast. Now it was *their* turn to feel her pain. She pointed to the tree bough and focused her rage into Fey energy flowing from her fingertips. *"Burn."*

The branch burst into flame all at once. The Quiet Men still pinned beneath it contorted with agony but made no sound. They struggled madly against the inferno, their cloaks catching fire. Myreon turned back to the other five.

All of them were staggering with the pain of their fellows, clutching their bodies and writhing at the sensation of their partners' deaths. This close together and this many of them dying in agony at once had overloaded their senses. Myreon smirked. "A bit of a design flaw, wouldn't you say?"

The first sign that the Quiet Men had been compromised was Claudia smashing the crystal decanter of *chleurie* over Gethrey's head and screaming, *"MAUDIE!"*

Marcom DeVauntness made his lunge and Tyvian sidestepped and advanced, putting him nose-to-nose with the overextended pink-haired fool. Tyvian landed a solid haymaker on his bruised head, knocking the boy to the floor. He stepped on his sword. "Missed your chance, Marcom."

Maude moved through the crowd like a whale coming up for air, knocking patrons aside with barely a pause. She was making a direct line to Gethrey Andolon and cracking her knuckles as she went.

Tyvian would have dropped a knee into Marcom's guts, but he had no real guarantee he could stand up again thanks to his injured leg. Instead, he kicked the boy just below the breastbone, hard, and forced him to roll away. Then he flipped Marcom's bejeweled sword into his hand with a practiced kick of his good leg.

Behind him, Tyvian heard Gethrey squeal, "Now, Maude . . ." before there was the sound like a hammer hitting a sandbag and Gethrey's air whistling through his teeth. In front of him, he saw Artus wrestling somebody disinteresting with a dagger—no, a Quiet Man!

Marcom was back on his feet, flanked by his armed sycophants. He had Gethrey's sword. "En garde."

"I've had about enough of this," Tyvian snarled, and slipped into en garde with a blaze of pain from his leg.

Tyvian beat the boy's first attack out of line, advanced once, and then ran Marcom through the guts with a lunge. Tyvian grimaced as he watched the color drain out of the boy's face, memories of another duel, too much like this one, popping into his head. "Sorry. You really were asking for it."

Marcom toppled to the floor, clutching his stomach and groaning. The flunkies advanced, swords out, and Tyvian disarmed the closest one with a lighting fast move that put the fellow's sword in his off hand. He now had two rapiers pointed at two different men. "I want you idiots to think very, *very* hard before you do anything rash. I didn't kill young DeVauntnesse here, so long as he sees a doctor in the next hour. I do *not* extend the same offer to you lot."

The flunkies froze. Behind Tyvian, Gethrey howled as Maude proceeded to give him the beating of a lifetime. This seemed to settle it—swords clattered to the floor. One man knuckled his forehead. "Terribly sorry, Mr. Reldamar, sir."

Tyvian surveyed the bar—the outbreak of disorganized violence had escalated into a full-scale brawl. People seemed to have noticed the Quiet Men in their midst, as they were all writhing in some kind of pain so intense it broke their usual veil of inconspicuousness. The reactions followed two trends: all-out assault on the assassins or terrified flight. People clogged the only exit, beer mugs flew through the air, and whores beat a hasty retreat upstairs or dove behind the bar.

"Artus!" Tyvian yelled. "You all right?"

Artus had his Quiet Man in a headlock and was sitting on the assassin's back. "This guy almost killed me, but then he, like, froze!"

Tyvian nodded. "Carry on pummeling."

Maude screamed. Tyvian whirled to see the big bouncer back on her rear end, clutching her face as blood poured down. Gethrey leaned against the table, a crimson-stained stiletto in one hand. His face looked like five pounds of ground beef, his nose flattened sideways against his bruised cheek, both his eyes swollen, his blue hair horribly mussed. His breathing came unevenly.

Tyvian pointed both his rapiers at his former friend. "Nobody left to hide behind, Geth. Let's see how well you've kept up your footwork, eh?"

Gethrey spat a tooth onto the floor. "You . . . you think this is the only trick I've got up my sleeve?" He laughed hoarsely, reached beneath his collar and drew out an amulet of some kind of dull, polished metal. He touched three fingers to it and spoke a word: *"Avorra."*

Tyvian's blood ran cold. "Kroth—how they hell did he get one of those?"

The ceiling above Gethrey buckled upward, as though pressed by a massive fist, until it broke apart entirely, raining down wood and plaster and dust. Through the wreckage, Gethrey rose ten feet into the air; interlocking plates of mageglass solidified, formed a cage around his body and then formed a body of their own—arms, legs, shoulders. An instant later Gethrey Andolon was standing within the chest of a headless, fifteen-foot-tall mageglass giant that glowed like ice and starlight and was planted in one corner of the Cauldron's common room. Tyvian had heard of these devices but never seen one in action—they were war-machines, used by the armies of the West against Kalsaari manticores and war elephants. It was called a "colossus," and he honestly didn't know any way one could be destroyed.

When Gethrey spoke, it was amplified to the

volume of ten men. *"Just one of the little perks of being a good friend to the Prophets, Tyvian. Not so confident behind your little swords now, are you?"*

The sight of the colossus only intensified the panic inside the bar. Those struggling to leave struggled harder, trampling one another while making for the exits. Those who had been in the midst of fighting suddenly realized they had somewhere else to be, and joined in the retreat.

Gethrey laughed at them all. *"Scurry, scurry, scurry my little rats!"* He stepped forward and the colossus stepped forward also, ripping beams, supports, and debris aside with easy sweeps of its mageglass arms. He stomped on a pair of drunken sailors too slow to retreat; blood spurted across the floor.

Artus was beside Tyvian. "What do we do?"

Tyvian pointed at Maude's unconscious body. "Help me with Maude; head for the kitchen!"

Screams and the sound of the collapsing first floor echoed through Tyvian's ears as he crouched before Gethrey's colossus to help Artus drag a stunned Maude to safety just before a support beam came crashing down. Dust was everywhere, as was smoke. Something was on fire. Gethrey shuffled awkwardly through the rubble, chuckling. *"You know, Tyv, I always hoped it would come down to this. Well, not this, specifically—who would have guessed I'd get a colossus as a personal security measure?—but I mean this situation: you, protecting some girl, being ground beneath my boot heel."*

Hidden from Gethrey for the moment behind a pile

of rubble, Maude got her wits about her. Her face was red with blood. "Gonna lose the eye," she said. Artus grabbed her by the elbow and dragged her toward the kitchen, darting behind the bar while Gethrey was distracted by more screaming bar patrons.

Tyvian moved to follow but found the ring inexplicably clamping down on him. "What now?" He looked around: there was Marcom DeVauntnesse, lying on the floor in a pool of his own blood, left completely alone.

He reached a bloody hand out to Tyvian, his face a rictus mask of pain. "Help . . ."

Tyvian took a step toward the kitchen, just as a test, but the ring gave him a sting that made him finch. "Bloody hell! You have *got* to be goddamned kidding me!"

"Tyvian!" Artus yelled. *"Let's move!"*

"Coming! Right behind you!" Tyvian dumped his stolen swords, crouched down next to the wounded young man, grabbed an arm and a leg and threw him across his shoulders. His leg screamed with pain. "If you bleed to death on me, Marcom, I'm going to kill you, understand?"

Gethrey spotted him and kicked a pile of half-crushed tables and chairs his direction, but they made the door to the kitchen in time. Crouching beneath the remainder of the ceiling, Gethrey crawled on his construct's hands and knees, trying to reach Tyvian before he darted out of sight, but only managed to collapse the stone arch of the kitchen doorway.

The kitchen in the Cauldron took up a full quarter of the footprint of the building, with a massive hearth big enough to have six pots boiling at the same time—and an equally massive chimney, one with a whole network of brick and tin ductwork that linked all the little fireplaces and cookstoves in the house to the central chimney. Maude was leaning against a butcher-block table, panting. "He'll kill us all, the bastard!"

Tyvian threw DeVauntnesse on the table. "Artus, put out those cookfires! Now!"

Artus grabbed a basin of water and threw. "We're going *up* the chimney?"

Tyvian gestured around the underground kitchen, whose only windows ran along the edge of the ceiling and were only about five inches high. "Got any other ideas?"

The wall behind them buckled inward from a swipe of the colossus's claws.

"Come out, come out, wherever you are!" Gethrey boomed, chuckling. *"I'll take the whole place down if I have to, Tyv!"*

Artus looked up the chimney, which stretched up four stories to the night beyond. "We'll never make the climb! Your leg is too hurt, that pink-haired jerk his half dead, and Maude's eye is . . ."

Maude looked like she was ready to pass out again, but she rolled her head back and fixed Tyvian with her good eye. "Spice . . . locker . . ."

BOOOM!

Half the kitchen imploded with a full-body charge by Gethrey. Had the chimney not been between him and them, he would have killed them all. Instead, his

shoulder rammed into the bricks and the whole structure shook with the impact.

Tyvian, the ring fueling his strength, threw
Marcom back over his shoulders and ran, Artus close
behind, Maude behind him, all of them stumbling
through the dusty darkness of the collapsing building. The spice locker was a small door in the back
corner of the kitchen that connected to a dry, dusty
hall, which then connected to a small room full of
shelves and dried spices hanging from rafters. Here,
though, between the supports, a trapdoor led to the
alley behind the Cauldron. Artus unlatched it and
crawled through. He reached down for Tyvian, who
passed DeVauntnesse through, then he turned to
Maude. "C'mon!"

Behind them, Gethrey continued to rummage
around the kitchen, crushing any possible hiding spot.
Maude was looking back that way. "Where's Claudia?"

"Dammit, Maude—come *on!*"

Maude looked panicked. "Did you see her get out?
Did you see what happened to her?"

"Tyvian!" Artus yelled from above. "We've got a
problem!"

"Add it to the bloody list!" he shouted back. "Maude,
I'm sure she's fine—let's *go!*"

Maude headed back toward the kitchen. "I've gotta
go back. She could be hurt. She could . . . could . . ."

Tyvian grabbed her by the shoulder. "Maude! Leave
her be! If she's back there, you can't help her, understand? There's nothing you can do!"

"*Real* problems here, Tyvian!" Artus yelled.

"Shut *up*, Artus!"

Maude looked down at Tyvian and favored him with a bloody, snaggle-toothed grin. "Don't you worry for me, boy. Rolled too many shits like Gethrey Andolon in my time to step back now."

Tyvian could scarcely believe he was hearing this. The ring fairly screamed on his finger, *Don't you let her go!* "Why, Maude? It's bloody suicide!"

Maude took a deep breath. "You come back to certain death for your lady love, let me do the same for mine, eh?"

Tyvian felt as though he'd just been gut-punched. It took him a minute to find his voice, but then he didn't know what to say. Then Maude *actually* gut-punched him. Her fist was like a cantaloupe propelled through his intestines; all the air rushed out of his lungs and he fell to his knees, trying to wheeze his objections.

Maude patted his cheek. "Sorry 'bout that, but this is so's you don't follow me. Don't feel bad." She gave him a kiss on the forehead. "Always were a good lad, no matter what they said. Go on and be a hero to someone else now."

And then she left, running into the smoke and dust of the ruined cellar, with Gethrey's colossus still smashing everything in sight.

Lady love? The ring burned, but he scarcely felt it. By the time he got the wind back in him, Maude was long gone into the smoke and fire and cacophonous racket of Gethrey's colossus.

Tyvian climbed through the trapdoor and into the alley, still a bit numb.

Artus had Marcom leaned up against an empty crate. "Took you long enough."

"What the hell are you whining abou—"

At that moment a host of tattlers swarmed around Tyvian's body, illuminating the whole alleyway. At either end, standing shoulder-to-shoulder with their shields and firepikes at the ready, were the Defenders of the Balance. An amplified voice echoed through the night air. *"Tyvian Reldamar! You are under arrest for crimes against the state! Kneel on the ground with your hands behind your head or face the consequences!"*

Artus put his hands behind his head and knelt. "How can our situation keep getting worse?"

"Story of my life." Tyvian sighed, and also knelt. The motion hurt like hell.

CHAPTER 27

STEPPING INTO HIS PARLOR

Myreon considered killing the Quiet Men right here, right now. Her fury still coursed through her veins, powerful enough to light volcanoes with the Fey she could channel. She raised her hands and prepared to burn the sorcerous monstrosities to ash . . . and stopped.

Was this how it started? Was this how Tyvian Reldamar had gone from the defender of the weak to the ruthless criminal she knew best? Was this what the ring kept him from becoming—a slave to his own darker urges, chained there by a series of bad choices and worse luck? No. She was a lot of things—perhaps even a criminal—but a butcher she wasn't.

One of the Quiet Men crawled toward her, clutching at the hem of her borrowed dress. She kicked him away and, stepping over the prone, agonized forms of the others as their fellows still burned, she feyleapt to the roof of the club and pulled out Tyvian's spare set of lock picks. There was the briefest of moments when she wondered whether he was all right, or whether he would escape from the Prophets and the tightening cordon of Defenders. It was a strange, alien feeling to her—when did she start caring? If he was made of stone, would she come back and save *him,* just as he had done for her?

Tyvian Reldamar came back to rescue you! The thought thundered in her mind, nearly blinding in its strangeness. She had to stop and take a deep breath—there were much more important things to focus on here.

The latch on the window slipped easily—so easily it made Myreon nervous. Another trap? Taking a deep breath, and wishing her staff weren't smoldering beneath a bonfire in the street, she stepped onto the floor of the Secret Exchange.

The gleaming white walls of the great dome glowed with a luster that blinded her midnight-adjusted eyes. She hugged the wall for a moment, letting herself acclimate. The air was cool and dry, with no discernible odor. There was no sound whatsoever—it was so quiet, she could hear her heart booming and her joints creak as she moved. To Myreon, who had never been to the Secret Exchange, it seemed like she had entered a temple.

While the exchange was open—sunrise to sunset—she would have expected to see dozens of magi there. There would be masters in the Blue, Black, and White Colleges of the Arcanostrum; some of those who were retired would be currently serving as judges. Representatives of every wealthy sorcerous family in Saldor and proxy traders from foreign governments, all magi of one of the four colleges. For all the magestaffs to be seen, though, not a one would belong to a Defender—Mage Defenders, the joke went, might be the only magi paid a salary, but they were also the only poor sorcerers in the West. If you were from a wealthy sorcerous family, you didn't go into the Gray Tower—you went into one of the four colleges, treating sorcery as an academic pursuit, and made all your money by investing daddy's coin in the markets. Make your own hours, nobody to give you orders, and retire rich and comfortable. It was, essentially, the exact opposite of a Defender's lot.

For now, however, the exchange was closed, the vast checkered floor empty, making the whole place look like one massive *couronne* board, stretching off in all directions. Xahlven Reldamar was alone, his black robes pooling around his feet like bleeding shadows, his hands lightly clasped about his silver magestaff—he was patiently waiting to receive her. He was tall and handsome in a kind of breathtaking way that Myreon realized would make it difficult to look him in the eye while speaking to him. It struck her that she was about to confront one of the most powerful sorcerers in the entire world—the Archmage of the Ether, the Chairman of the Black College, the *youngest* person in recorded history to achieve the rank of Master. Myreon's mouth went a little dry.

But she hadn't made Mage Defender by being meek either. She squared her shoulders, fixed her eyes on Xahlven's dimpled chin, and marched straight across the floor. The heels of her boots echoed through the whole exchange, seeming to carry on forever. She must have been a sight to behold—hair wild, soot on her face, skirt tattered, the scent of fire and blood wafting from her skin. "Xahlven Reldamar! I must speak with you!"

Myreon and Xahlven met each other by the edge of the great scrying pool at the center of the Secret Exchange. He looked at her with open concern. "Myreon Alafarr? You ought to be in a garden, shouldn't you?"

"I was framed," she spat back. "As if you didn't know."

Xahlven's golden eyebrows shot up. "Framed? Why?"

Myreon scowled at him. The nerve of this jackass, denying it to her face! "Don't play stupid, Reldamar. We've got it all figured out—we know what you're trying to do."

"We? Are you, perchance, referring to my brother the wanted criminal?" Xahlven shook his head. "What has he got you believing, Myreon? Let me guess: that

I'm the center of some elaborate, nefarious plot of some kind. That you have to stop me to save the world." He smiled. "Am I close?"

"This isn't about Tyvian—this is about *you*." Myreon pointed at him. She found herself wanting to punch him in his perfect nose.

Xahlven smiled. "Oh, no doubt. I'm certain my brother was very convincing—that is his talent, you know. Tell me, when he was explaining my evil plot to you, did he provide any evidence?"

Myreon stepped closer to him. "My being petrified for a crime I didn't commit is evidence enough! I know all about Gethrey Andolon, all about his plot, and therefore I know all about *you*! Only you have the connections to pull something like this off."

Xahlven raised one finger. "Correction—only a *Reldamar* has the connections to pull something like this off. Namely myself, my mother, or Tyvian." Xahlven gave Myreon a little shrug and shook his head, as though genuinely sorry he had to bring this up. "Now, of those three, who is the most likely to engage in a plot with Gethrey Andolon?"

Myreon faltered. She felt suddenly sick—what if . . . ? "You expect me to believe that . . . that . . ."

"Does my brother sound like the kind of person who would turn down Andolon's offer?" Xahlven smiled, but his eyes—Tyvian's shade of searing blue—were full of sympathy. "I'm the Archmage of the Ether, Myreon. Give me a little credit, hmmm?"

"No." Myreon set her jaw and pressed on. This was

smoke and mirrors. This was simple misinformation—how many *times* had Tyvian outsmarted her operations with things like this? "Tyvian couldn't have had me framed. Tyvian wouldn't have broken me out of petrification if he was working with Andolon—it doesn't make sense. Your mother has no motive. You, meanwhile . . ."

Xahlven nodded, considering this. "Ah. And what is my motive, supposedly?"

Myreon snorted. "If you crash the exchange and use Andolon to bail them out and then kill him, you can gain control of the Secret Exchange for yourself."

Xahlven chuckled and turned his back on her. He began to pace around the scrying pool, glancing into it from time to time. "Really? And I suppose Tyvian sent you here to talk me out of it? To, what, *threaten* me into not doing this?"

Myreon followed behind him. "Actually, he specifically told me to *not* confront you."

Xahlven shot her a look over his shoulder. His eyes were twinkling, "A rather *significant* specification, don't you think? Get you to assume I'm guilty and then make certain you don't talk to me. Convenient."

"I keep waiting for you to deny any of these charges." Myreon stopped and readied her defenses in case Xahlven attacked. "Call your little operation off or I'll expose you."

Xahlven held up one finger. "Let us refrain from casting about threats for the nonce and return to the original assertion of my guilt, please: you, through my brother, insist that I am doing all this to gain control of the Secret Exchange, is that not correct?"

Myreon's stomach tightened—she didn't like this. She didn't like the way this conversation was going. It felt like a conversation with Tyvian—old Tyvian, *original* pre-ring Tyvian—only more polished, more prepared. For all Tyvian's brilliance at scheming, much of what he did relied on a certain degree of inspired improvisation. With Xahlven, Myreon felt as though he had rehearsed this same exact conversation several times before. She and he were playing out a little skit, written by him, meant to elicit the outcome he sought. She tried to think of a way to break it, a way to escape his expectations, but what? Tackle him?

When she didn't respond to his set question, Xahlven answered it for her. "Such is your supposition. Now, as I am Chairman of the Secret Exchange, how exactly would *controlling* the Secret Exchange in any way expand the powers I already possess?"

Myreon clenched her hands into fists. "I . . . I don't know."

Xahlven nodded, smiling. "Indeed. I *already* essentially control the Secret Exchange—I or my agents approve all transactions. So, if I am currently in possession of the two things I stand to gain by crashing the exchange—those being material wealth and financial influence—why in the name of all the gods would I bother risking my position, reputation, and future by conspiring to defraud the markets?"

Myreon felt frozen. Oh no, she certainly didn't like

this—something about Xahlven, something about his easy confidence, his knowing smiles, made her feel as though she were a child. He was talking down to her, like some aspiring apprentice. "If you know about Andolon, then, why haven't you stopped him yet?"

"There is something very useful about having a person expose the weaknesses of a system you manage, especially if you can curtail them from doing real damage at any time. Andolon is troubleshooting the markets for me, my dear, and when he gets to the point where he must be stopped, he will be. I have a troop of Defenders standing by for exactly that purpose."

Myreon didn't want to, but she had to admit that Xahlven, for all his sanctimonious airs, was making a lot of sense. "Explain the Quiet Men trying to stop me from seeing you, then!"

"The answer is right in front of you, Ms. Alafarr, though you are oddly unwilling to see it. Who has the contacts of a Reldamar yet lacks money or financial influence? Who is old friends with Gethrey Andolon? Who was offered a lucrative job by his old friend—the man who framed you? Who has existing contacts in the underworlds of five major Western cities?"

Myreon's mouth was dry. "Tyvian."

Xahlven nodded, his voice grave. "Tyvian."

"Gods . . ." she breathed. "You're right. Oh . . . oh gods!"

"It is my brother who plans to double-cross Andolon and snap up all his riches. It is my *brother* who hopes to secure a substantial portion of the West's wealth. His ring has made him unable to exist in his former shady world of smuggling, theft, and piracy, and so he's decided to foray into the more morally ambiguous world of finance. You, my dear, are designed as a distraction."

Myreon looked at Xahlven and felt her world spinning around her. Of course. *OF COURSE!* Tyvian had played her—rescued her, been kind to her, shown his so-called "good" side—and all so he could send her here to hassle his brother even as he was probably off somewhere making the *real* plot happen. It had been a lie! It had *all* been a lie! "That bastard!"

There was a heavy footfall behind her from an individual that weighed far more than any human being. Glancing over her shoulder, Myreon saw a white marble golem, silver inlaid in arabesque patterns on its chest and arms, looming over her. "Now," Xahlven was saying, "while this chat has been very illuminating for me and no doubt for you as well, your crimes have unfortunately rendered you forbidden from the floor. The golem will see you out the way you came in. You understand, of course, that I will be informing the authorities of your trespass here."

Myreon turned back around. "No, wait—"

The golem, though, wasn't about to wait. It grabbed her around the waist with two animated stone hands and threw her over its shoulder like a sack of potatoes. Myreon struggled to escape, but she might as well have been trying to kick over a mountain. The golem thrust her out the open window, depositing her roughly on the roof.

She sat there, head in her hands, as her mind spun from both the roughness of her ejection and the shock of what Xahlven had suggested. How could she have been so stupid? So naive? It had been Tyvian the *whole time*! Myreon sat on the roof, head in her hands, trying to think about what she should do next. How could she stop him?

That, as it turned out, didn't require as much thought. Myreon was on her feet, anger once again firing the Fey energy in her. She leapt into the wind, vengeance burning behind her eyes. Tyvian Reldamar had a reckoning coming, and this time there was nothing that bastard could say to save himself.

CHAPTER 28

CROSSTOWN RUMBLE

The Defenders lost no time in putting Tyvian and Artus on their faces and kneeling on their backs. Two others were gently transporting the death-pale Marcom back somewhere—to a healer or doctor, perhaps. Maybe a priest. At the moment, Tyvian had neither the time nor inclination to worry overmuch.

"Can I say something?" he managed through the half of his mouth that wasn't kissing Crosstown cobblestones.

A man in a mirrored mageglass helm shouted in his ear, "Shut yer hole!"

Manacles clamped around his wrists and he was hauled upright. "You're really going to want to hear this."

The Defender grabbed him by the hair and pulled his head back so the light of the tattlers clearly illuminated his face. "Here he is, magus. He won't shut up neither."

Tyvian found himself looking at a rather tired but still smug Argus Androlli. "Not blowing anybody kisses now, are we, Mr. Reldamar?"

Artus was hauled up next to Tyvian. "We got this one, too." The Defenders sounded excited—nearly giddy. Tyvian understood. It was like a fishing trip, and they'd just hauled in the One That Got Away.

Tyvian eyed the smoke billowing from the windows of the Cauldron behind them and felt the rumbles in the cobblestones and decided to cut through all the wordplay. "Magus, we need to get out of here right now."

Androlli looked at the Cauldron over his shoulder. "Do you burn down *every* building you go into?"

"He's not kidding, magus!" Artus nodded. "We gotta run for it! Trust us!"

Androlli snorted. "Don't worry, we're leaving, but not before I ask you—"

The Mage Defender didn't get to finish his sentence. Behind him the Cauldron—which had been producing a stream of soot-covered, terrified patrons and employees out of every possible door and window for a few minutes now—shuddered as though it were an egg about to hatch. Androlli trailed off, looking back toward the building. "What in all the hells is this?"

The wall of the Cauldron closest to them collapsed forward in an avalanche of stone, lumber, and plaster. The Defenders closest to the wall were crushed beneath the rubble; Androlli would have been, too, but for a last minute guard he managed to erect, which spared him and those behind him—namely Artus, Tyvian, and their two arresting Defenders.

Before the dust had cleared, Gethrey Andolon, still ensconced in his colossus, emerged from the gutted interior of the whorehouse. His mageglass hide was covered in a thin sheet of plaster, coating his shoulders and torso like snow. Gethrey shook it off with a quick twist and then looked down at Tyvian. His voice boomed through the alley. *"Surprise, surprise!"*

Androlli craned his neck upward, mouth agape. "Hann's boots!"

Tyvian felt his bowels contract in fear. Nevertheless, he couldn't pass up the opportunity: "I told you so."

Tyvian's adrenaline banished his weak-kneed terror faster than it did for anybody else. The first thing he did was kick Androlli in the direction of Gethrey, who tried to step on the Mage Defender and splat him into so much smug Rhondian goo. Androlli threw up another guard—this one powerful enough to force Gethrey to stumble backward into the Cauldron.

The Defenders on either side of Artus and Tyvian leveled their firepikes and began blasting at the colossus, but the eldritch war machine had been specifically designed to handle such punishment well—the fiery bolts pattered off his torso plates like so many incendiary raindrops.

Tyvian was about to pick their pockets for the keys to his manacles when he had those keys thrust into his hands by Artus, who was a half second ahead of him. "What do we do?"

"Run for our lives!" Tyvian grabbed him by the shirt and tugged him into a limping sprint down the alley. Behind them, the rumble of collapsing architecture indicated that Gethrey was close behind.

They shot out of the alley and into the street, only to find themselves staring down a firing line of twenty Defenders, their firepikes blazing. "Oh Kroth!" Tyvian dropped to the ground, pulling Artus with him, just as the Defenders opened up in a blaze of Fey energy that lit the night. The blasts were aimed at the colossus, but the basic inaccuracy of the firepike meant bolts of fire scattered over a wide area, hitting the Cauldron, the building next to it, scorching cobblestones, and also bouncing off the colossus's armored hide.

Gethrey charged into the street, totally ignoring the Defenders in favor of hunting down Tyvian and Artus. The two of them dodged one heavy footfall and then scrambled into the nearest building—a four-story tenement just recently set alight by a volley of firepike blasts. Tyvian didn't pause to talk to Artus until they were in a corridor on the second floor. It was then that they actually had time to remove the manacles from their wrists, too.

"How do we stop that thing?" Artus gasped, his eyes wide. "Fire melts mageglass—can we set him on fire?"

"Does he look especially flammable to you?" Tyvian growled.

The building shook as Gethrey plunged a huge mageglass hand into the tenement structure and swept it across in a lateral direction, destroying whole apartments and probably killing or injuring a dozen people. Tyvian caught a glimpse of the colossus peering through the gaps in the wall. *"Tyvian, this grows very tiresome. Where are you?"*

The screams of people hurt or just terrified caused the ring to give Tyvian such a wrench that he gasped. "Artus, we split up—he's after me, not you. Find Hool, find Myreon—help her if you can."

"Myreon?" Artus blinked, "You mean you *actually* rescued her?"

Tyvian scowled, "This is not the time, Artus!"

Artus nodded. "I sent Brana to grab us a boat—we can escape that way when you're done!"

Tyvian blinked. "That's . . . that's actually an excellent idea."

Artus broke into a wide grin. "Really?"

People's heads popped out of their front doors and into the filthy second-floor hallway. More screaming. Tyvian waved Artus away. "Yes really! Just go, dammit!"

Artus gave him a firm nod and went. Tyvian turned back toward Gethrey. Did he have a plan? *Was* there a plan here? The ring burned, not caring—he had to deal with this.

Tyvian went up to the third floor, fighting a panicked flow of humanity rushing downstairs, shoeless, with their children tucked under their arms. A mageglass fist thrust through the wall and into the central corridor, its fingers fumbling around for something to hold onto. It grabbed a pantless man around the waist and squeezed. The sound was like a large beetle ground beneath a wagon wheel. Blood splashed the ceiling. *"Was that you, Tyv?"*

The fist pulled out, causing even more destruction on its exit, so that Gethrey could examine his grisly acquisition. A whole room fell off into space to Tyvian's right. He kept running upstairs, his wounded leg's fiery pain masked by the throbbing of the ring urging him on.

"Hmmm . . ." Gethrey remarked absently. *"Probably wasn't you, was it? You'd have pants on."*

Tyvian tore past the third floor and went straight to the fourth, pushing past even more fleeing people. For the first time, he realized just how *many* of the poor made their homes here. It had to be near to hundreds. Gods.

Gethrey struck the building again and again, this time seeking to knock the place down more than finding Tyvian. It was working. The whole building swayed, threatening to fall against its neighbors. Tyvian found himself standing in the half-ruined attic, a hole torn open by a hurtling block of stone cast carelessly by Gethrey's rampage. Beneath him, he could see Gethrey punching and striking at various stubborn stone chimneys that supported much of the building. If they went, the whole structure would go. The ring throbbed with worry, but Tyvian didn't need its reminder. "I have to draw him away," he said aloud.

Around Gethrey, a cordon of Defenders blazed away, worrying the back and sides of his armor like a swarm of bees. The colossus's armor was strong, but it couldn't take that indefinitely. Sooner or later that much Fey energy would make certain plates destabilize and vanish. Perhaps they already had—just not enough to get at Gethrey inside.

Tyvian had an idea. A really, really stupid idea, he thought. Nevertheless, he took two steps back from the opening in the wall and got ready to run. Looking at his ring, he said, "Wish me luck, better self," and took off.

He leapt out of the fourth story of the half-ruined building to wrestle a fifteen-foot war colossus without so much as a paring knife for a weapon. He knew it was, to date, the craziest thing he had ever done. He was forced to reflect on the way down, however, that the night was still young.

He hit the top of the colossus with a bone-jarring thump. The mageglass plating was like a wall of solid steel; he was surprised to still be alive.

Gethrey, ensconced within his war-construct, looked up at him through translucent crystal plating, his mouth agape. *"Are you out of your mind?"*

Tyvian would have said something pithy, but his mouth was full of blood—must have bit his tongue or lip or something when he hit. He was clinging by his fingertips to the small cracks between the moving plates of mageglass, spread-eagled atop the colossus like a cat atop a galloping horse. It occurred to him, much later than it really should have, that he ought to be devising a plan to survive this. Nothing immediately came to mind.

Gethrey was laughing. *"Fine—this just makes things easier."* He shook the colossus's torso back and forth. Tyvian's feet came loose from their precarious toeholds and slid back and forth with the force of momentum. He put his head down and clung for dear life. The world spun as Gethrey spun, blurring into a collage of fire and smoke and darkness.

Tyvian knew he should have fallen—he should have flown into space by now—but he hadn't. Come to think of it, the fall should have at least knocked him unconscious. *The ring!*

It pulsed with a kind of power Tyvian hadn't ever experienced before—well, perhaps *once* before, deep in the tunnels of Daer Trondor, when he brought Myreon back to life. When he had sacrificed himself for the lives of countless innocents, just as he was doing right now.

There were shouts—sorcerously amplified shouts—coming from below. *"Surrender or be destroyed, by order of the Defenders!"*

Gethrey stopped shaking and faced the firing-line of Defenders, all of them set and ready to shoot. Tyvian, head still spinning, could see the sergeant with his sword raised, shouting orders to his men.

Tyvian suddenly realized where they were going to fire and where, exactly, he was clinging. "Oh . . . Kroth!" Adrenaline surging, the ring practically shining with power, he managed to scramble off Gethrey's "head" and onto his back just in time for the firepikes to spit their blazing bolts of energy into the colossus's chest. They hit with a great blaze of heat and flame, causing Gethrey to stumble back a pace, but the mage-glass armor of the colossus still held back the onslaught.

With a roar of frustration, Gethrey snatched up a massive timber that had fallen from the Cauldron and hurled it at the mirror men. They had prudently activated some guards incorporated into their armor, so they weren't all crushed, but instead knocked sprawling as the sorcerous defense flashed with energy. It was the opening Gethrey was seeking—he charged their position, kicking or crushing any Defender that stood in his way, and ran through another four-story building as though he was pushing his way through undergrowth.

The masonry of the home crumbled around the colossus like it was made from hollow plaster—wood and stone were crushed or pushed aside by the war-construct, and with the roar of its destruction were joined the screams of the people living inside. Tyvian clung to the colossus's back, again only able to stay on by dint of the ring's power, and saw a little girl, no older than eight, fall from her crushed bedroom to the street below. The sight of her, the sound of her scream, shook his heart. His mind cleared; he knew what had to happen now.

They emerged onto a parallel street in a puff of dust. Gethrey was still chuckling. *"Now, time to settle you, Tyv. Hold still now."*

Gethrey fumbled for Tyvian, but the colossus moved much like a person did, and it didn't have the ability to grab the middle of its own back. Tyvian stayed put, trying to figure out how to pry the construct open while Gethrey struggled like a man with an itch he couldn't scratch.

Mageglass was impenetrable, yes. Enough fire and enough heat would melt it, true—the firepike blasts had probably weakened the armor a fair amount. He knew he just had to find the gaps in that armor and somehow exploit them.

Gethrey threw himself backward into the wall of another building. Tyvian, anticipating, scrambled back onto the colossus's shoulders, this time standing on his own two feet. From the side of the building extended an iron bar meant for throwing a rope over to hoist furniture to the upper floors, rather than bother with the narrow spiral staircases these places had. Tyvian grabbed it with both hands and pulled, snapping it off the side of the house like a tree branch.

Gethrey stood and, seeing Tyvian's new weapon, laughed. *"Gods, you don't quit, do you? All this to protect some pointless commoners? You really are mad."*

The colossus's open palm slapped down where Tyvian was standing, but Tyvian nimbly danced to one side and Gethrey only managed to slap himself in the face rather than crush him. The force of the blow knocked Gethrey off-balance and he stumbled backward again, smashing into another building. Tyvian held on.

Selecting the widest of the gaps between the mageglass plates—the fissure between the breastplates and back plates that ran along the top of the construct—Tyvian raised his iron bar and drove the end of it into the opening as far as it would go. He managed a couple inches of depth, which he hoped would be enough.

"What in blazes are you doing? Stop that!" Gethrey shook his torso around, running farther down the street as he did.

Tyvian clung to his bar for dear life, staring daggers through the mageglass at his former friend. "I used to like you, Gethrey."

"You're the one who changed, Tyvian." Gethrey dropped a shoulder and charged through a low-hanging footbridge, hoping to smash Tyvian flat, but Tyvian was too quick and adjusted his handholds to shift position and hang from the crystal-plated back again. Stone and mortar exploded, showering the street below. Tyvian could hear people screaming. Bells were ringing. He smelled smoke.

Gethrey looked back and forth until he spotted Tyvian again, crawling back to his shoulders. *"You used to understand the relationship we had with these* commoners—reveled in it, even. We didn't slum it at the Cauldron all those years because we liked the people, we slummed it because we had power over these people—we were free of all the restrictions of polite society because nobody could stop us!"

Tyvian grimaced at the words—Gethrey was right, in a sense. It had started that way. He honestly couldn't say when that had changed. He gripped the iron bar and began to pull, trying to pry the plates apart. Even with his ring-altered strength, nothing budged.

Gethrey laughed. "Who do you think you are? Landar the Holy? Saint Handras? Don't be ridiculous." He put both shoulders down and this time charged headfirst into a slender Hannite chapel. The stone belltower shuddered from the impact, and the force of it caused Tyvian to lose his grip. He flew off the colossus's shoulders and wound up skidding across the chapel's steeply angled roof. His head spun as he flailed around for some purchase on the lead shingles. He managed to grab a gargoyle before he plummeted into the alley below.

"I really don't understand why you turned down my offer, you know." Gethrey moved into the alley so he was just beneath Tyvian and rolled his shoulders, preparing for the kill. "Who cares what happens to these pointless little people? I'm sure they'll survive somehow. Gods, Tyvian— the only thing they do is survive. They survive to leech off of the rich, and we pay them to amuse us."

Tyvian climbed to his feet on the roof of the chapel, looking down at his former friend. He broke a heavy stone gargoyle off from its perch and hefted it like he meant to throw. "You make them all sound like whores."

Gethrey smiled and nodded. *"They are whores, Tyv. Every commoner who takes a copper for my custom is my whore, to do with as I please. It's the way of the world. You, of all people, should understand."* He shook his head. *"But seeing as you don't . . ."*

Gethrey raised both colossal mageglass hands above his head and formed a huge fist, intending to drop it and crush Tyvian in one titanic blow. Tyvian waited for it to fall and, at the last moment, put all the power the ring had into one last leap. He sailed over and past the colossus's fists and came hurtling down on Gethrey's head.

Or, more accurately, on the iron bar he had placed as a wedge. The gargoyle—which had to weigh at least a hundred pounds—hit the bar square, with all the momentum of gravity and Tyvian's own bodyweight behind it. The mageglass plates themselves might have been impenetrable, but the telekinetic force holding them all together couldn't be—not if the thing was able to move. All it took was the right amount of force in the right spot.

Tyvian split open the top of Gethrey's colossus like an oyster. Another pry, and Gethrey—wide-eyed, caught in mid-laugh—was clearly visible in the flesh. Another second and Tyvian knew that Gethrey would beg for his life, weep for forgiveness, and the rest of it—and the ring wouldn't let him kill him.

With Hendrieux, he had waited and lived to regret it. Some people deserved to die, no matter what the ring thought about it. He pulled the iron bar loose from the opened colossus and raised it over his head.

"Tyv, I—" Gethrey began.

Tyvian plunged the blunt end of the weapon down with all his strength, crushing Gethrey's skull in a grisly demonstration of mass and inertia. The colossus stumbled forward with Gethrey's last convulsions, throwing Tyvian atop the church hard and knocking his head against a stone buttress. Then the colossus faded from existence, vanishing into the alley below along with the murder weapon and the body of Tyvian's former friend.

The ring's power abandoned him then, leaving Tyvian weak and injured, on his back. He stared up at the stars and wondered by what destiny had he been born that forced him to kill so many of his friends.

There was a white glow from somewhere. Myreon was standing over him, light pouring from a tattler at her shoulder. He smiled at her, "M-Myreon? Thank the gods . . . I . . . I thought I was dead!"

Myreon's eyes were hard as stone. "You're going to wish you were, you son of a bitch."

CHAPTER 29

ARROWS WELL-AIMED

Hool reached the outskirts of Saldor well after dark, but she did not slow her pace. She blazed down the cobbled streets, making no effort to disguise her passing. Those who got in her way were bowled over—it wasn't her fault that the humans were too slow and too stupid to move, and she wasn't about to let up just to spare them some bruises.

She had counted the moments from when Lyrelle told her Artus was going to die but had no idea if she was too late or not. She had never quite gotten the hang of human timekeeping, especially at night, where the moon was a traitor and did not tell you how late in the evening it was. Her every heartbeat was a wish for her feet to go faster, for her journey to end, for her to be *in time*.

Artus did not think so, but Hool knew she was responsible for him. He thought he was very grown up, of course—human pups all did at that age, just like gnoll pups when they reached six or seven and were almost full grown—but Artus had a lot to learn about the world. Like most males, Tyvian was useless for this kind of task. Artus needed a mother, and Hool was it.

And she would *not* lose another pup. Never again. Not even if she needed to kill every single human between here and the Taqar to prevent it. In the front of her mind, visions of Api's tanned hide mingled with the sight of Artus's blood in the Reldamar witch's premonition. They were so horrifying they nearly made her blind with anguish, and she howled into the night to release the pain. The pain, though, would not go. It stayed with her, a knot just above her heart that only having Artus and Brana safe in her arms could untie.

She reached the first squad of Defenders along the banks of the Narrow Mouth as she was about to cross the bridge into Crosstown. They had heard her coming and they thought her a monster. They bustled themselves into rows, their magic spears pointing out at her, squinting into the gloom of the summer evening.

Hool paused atop a roof, looking down at them. They blocked the bridge—there was no other way across without going another mile down the river. She could not jump over—their spears were long and she might be stabbed. Fine then. She would go through.

She drew the mace that Lyrelle Reldamar had called the Fist of Veroth. The iron head was fashioned in a complex, swirling pattern, like that of flames frozen in black metal. She could feel its weight as a kind of destiny, ready to fall. It wanted to be struck; it craved battle. The smell of sorcery made her nostrils flare—this weapon had an evil feel. But then, she supposed all weapons did. This one would do.

The Defenders stood, waiting, eyeing every shadow. Their leader—their *sergeant*—stood at the edge of the column, holding his sword aloft, ready to give the signal. Hool resolved to kill him first.

She charged them from their left, leaping from a rooftop, the Fist of Veroth above her head, roaring for all her worth. From beneath, she imagined they could see the outline of her body and the glitter of her eyes in the dim light but nothing more. The effect was as she had hoped—they froze, if only for an instant.

An instant was all it took to kill the sergeant. She brought the Fist of Veroth down on his head, crushing him all at once, as though he had been hit by a boulder. There was a flash of orange light—like flame, only angrier—and the ground shuddered beneath her feet. Many of the Defenders fell down, the others staggered back. Hool raised the enchanted mace again, and a fiery light bloomed from its heavy head—the iron was no longer iron, but molten fire, burning and stirring like a piece of the sun itself. The Defenders, their eyes wide, fled before her weapon and her wrath. This suited her fine—she darted over the bridge.

Three more times was she forced to confront the Defenders, and each time the Fist of Veroth crushed their bodies and scattered their defenses. What its head touched was destroyed utterly. A Defender roadblock of two overturned wagons was reduced to flinders with one blow, its guardians scattered to the ground like bowling pins. Hool was an unstoppable juggernaut— humans fled before her wrath. Warning bells rang.

At last she caught scent of Artus. It was mixed with the smell of ash and fire, and she wondered if it was the fist throwing off her senses, but no—there was fire and ash ahead, too. She put all her strength into covering those last few blocks.

The Defenders had Artus tied, hand and foot, and were carrying him between two of them. A mage with a staff stood at the head of a column of seven or eight men in mirrored armor stained with dust and cinders. Her heart seized—was he alive or dead? Was she too late?

Then she heard the most blessed thing: Artus cursing. "Kroth take you stinking mirror men! I can walk, dammit! You didn't need to bind my bloody ankles, you pack of filthy arses!"

Hool emerged from her hiding place, growling, "Let the boy go."

The Defenders took up their weapons. The mage raised his staff. "Stand back, beast!" he said in a clear voice. "You are no match for me!"

Hool brandished her enchanted mace. "If you do not let him go, I will kill you all."

The mage's dark eyes widened at the swirling, molten head of the weapon. "My arts are quite powerful! I warn you!"

Hool got closer and the Defenders backed up, along with the mage. Then she noticed something—the flames at the tips of the magic spears were mere flickers, barely alive. The mage's eyes were ringed with dark circles, his every step a labor, and his joints were stiff. These men were exhausted, their weapons nearly spent. The mage, if he could have worked a spell to hold her, would have done so already. They were no match for her, especially not with her weapon.

She found herself raising the fist, ready to strike, her legs tensing to charge and crush them all in one mighty blow—she had barely thought of it, moving as though by instinct. It would be the easiest thing in the world. What's more, she wanted to feel the heavy thrum of the fist's power as it was expended. She wanted to watch the shockwave of force as it destroyed them. She craved these things as she craved a good slab of antelope meat. She took a step forward.

"Hool?" Artus said. "Hool! Don't do it, okay?"

"What?" Hool asked, advancing forward, swinging her weapon to and fro.

The mage invoked some kind of blast of white light, but Hool felt it rebuffed by the aura of the mace. Two Defenders charged, their pikes out. Hool knocked the first weapon aside and, spinning, brought her weapon into contact with the man's shoulder. He disintegrated into a shower of charred gore and bone with a meaty *THROOM!* The second man was knocked sprawling by the shock wave. Hool kept advancing.

Artus's voice seemed far away. *"Hooool!"*

Firepikes discharged, but their flaming bolts were drawn in by the swirling heat of the Fist of Veroth and it seemed to grow angrier in Hool's hands. More restless. She struck another blow, and three men died for it, their bodies pulped beneath their shields. Hool snarled in satisfaction. Good—they deserved to die. She just didn't remember quite why.

Men fled before her, and soon there was only a boy, bound hand and foot, cowering before her. The Fist of Veroth impelled itself aloft, ready to strike the final blow. Ready to secure her ultimate victory.

The boy was yelling at her. *"Hool! Snap out of it!"*

Hool's nostrils flared—how dare he make demands of her? Some lowly human who smelled of—

"Artus!"

Memory came flooding back, and with it self-control. Hool dropped the enchanted mace onto the street; it landed with a heavy thump, embedded in the stone. Hool looked around her—she stood at the center of a blackened expanse of street, the buildings around her all sporting broken windows. The twisted, misshapen remains of several Defenders lay about the ground, unmoving.

"Dammit, Hool—what the hell got into you there? Kroth, I thought I was dead! You were gonna . . ."

Artus's complaints were muffled by Hool's fur as she picked him up and hugged him. After a time, she let him go. "I thought you might die."

Artus nodded, incredulous. "Yeah, me too! Are you okay?"

Hool glared at the Fist of Veroth, which stood cooling in the center of the street, awaiting a wielder. "She lied to me," she said at last. "This was what she wanted. She wanted me to be a monster. But I'm not. She is wrong."

"Who?"

Hool's lips curled back. "Tyvian's mother."

Myreon grabbed Tyvian by the shirt and dragged his torso out over the edge of the roof. She stood over him, shaking him up and down. "You son of a bitch! You lied to me! I should . . . I should *kill you*! Tell me what the plan is! Tell me, or so help me Hann, I will drop you to your death, you scum!"

Tyvian, strangely, seemed unmoved. His initial surprise degraded into that same damned infuriating smile "Been talking to Xahlven, have you?"

Myreon spat in his face. Her arms trembled from exhaustion. "Don't smile at me, Reldamar—your brother explained everything to me. You've been behind this the entire time, haven't you? You even arranged to have me framed—you had me *turned to stone* just so could swoop in and rescue me! And to think . . ."

found tears welling in her eyes. She blinked

them away—they only made her angrier. "I ought to kill you right now!"

Tyvian spoke carefully and slowly. "Myreon, I want you to think about this. I didn't do this. I am not behind this plot. I have not been lying to you." He held up the ring for her to see. "See this? I couldn't do that to you if I *wanted* to."

"All these years—all these *years* of your vicious little plots!" Myreon was full-on crying now. She wasn't sure how much longer she could hold Tyvian like this. She felt her fingers slipping from his bloody shirt lapels. "I am so *tired* of your lies, you miserable spoiled rich boy bastard!"

Tyvian nodded. "You're right. I'm a liar and I'm spoiled and, yes, I am, quite literally, a bastard. But Myreon, this is how my brother works—he uses people, and he's even better at it than I am. You stormed in there and confronted him, and he told you the absolute most effective thing to get you off his back—*he* played you, not me."

"How do I know?" Myreon blinked her eyes, trying to see Tyvian's face clearly. "How can I possibly know?"

Tyvian heaved a heavy sigh, even though he was slipping ever closer to falling off a church roof. "Because . . . well . . ."

"*Tell me!*" Myreon roared at him. She was barely holding him by his fingertips.

A tear leaked from Tyvian's eye—from *Tyvian Reldamar's* eye—and when he spoke, his voice sounded wooden, as though he could scarcely make it ob him. "When I found you beneath Daer Trondor

"Don't you *dare!*" Myreon spat. "No!"

Tyvian grabbed her by the wrists. "You were *dead*, Myreon! Dead, you understand? It nearly killed me to know that! I didn't think so then, maybe—I was too caught up in things—but it's bloody true! I . . ." He paused, his voice nearly cracking, "I couldn't live with myself to know you had died. I *couldn't*."

Myreon barely found her voice. "Why?"

Tyvian looked her in the eye. "Because . . . because you are the best person I know."

Their hands, slick with sweat and blood, slipped from one another. Tyvian slid off the roof with a shocked grunt. Myreon leapt to her feet. "No! Nooo!" She dove to the roof's edge and reached out with all of her Art. On the fly, she inverted a feyleap and thrust it at Tyvian, stopping him mid-fall and propelling him *up* at her.

He arced, ungainly, up through the air, and then fell into her arms. His weight pushed both of them onto their backs on the tile roof of the church. She found herself staring down into his eyes and found him staring up into hers. He gave her a shy smile. "Don't look so horrified. This is hardly the first roof I've been thrown off today."

Myreon grabbed him by the shoulders and pulled him close. "You goddamned idiot!"

This time, for the first time, they kissed each other.

CHAPTER 30

ONCE MORE, WITH FEELING

Tyvian kissed Myreon more than once on that rooftop, which, in retrospect, was a bit of a tactical error. The sun would soon be rising and, therefore, the markets were about to open.

Myreon looked as though she had just committed a crime. "I can't believe I just did that."

"We. I was involved, too." Tyvian looked across the rooftops of Crosstown. A fire was burning—probably starting near the Cauldron—that was eating a whole city block. Alarm bells were ringing from all over town. The swath of destruction Gethrey had wrought stretched out over several blocks as well. It seemed everywhere Tyvian looked and in every direction, chaos and fear was ruling the day.

"Is that it, then? With Gethrey dead, will the markets crash?" Myreon asked, surveying the city.

"No. They'll be crashing anyway—my brother would see to that, somehow." Tyvian stretched, wincing at the wound in his leg—which was only now reasserting itself after the ring had deadened it for him during his fight with Gethrey.

Myreon nodded. "We need to get back across town. But how?" She motioned to the chaos. "The Defenders will be everywhere. The Old City will be locked up tight as a drum."

"Hey!" a voice called from below. Tyvian looked down to see Hool looking up at them. "Your blue-haired friend is dead in this alley. Sorry."

Tyvian grinned. "Good old Hool—regular as the sunrise." He then called over the side, "We're coming down. Did you find Artus?"

Hool's ears were laid back. "Yes. But he has a plan I do not like."

Saldor harbor was cloaked in mist in the predawn light. The boat Brana had secured was meant to be rowed by two people, which meant both Myreon and Tyvian were at the oars—nobody else knew how. Tyvian's bandaged leg still screamed at him with every stroke, but they were making good time.

Artus was in the bow, keeping a lookout. "You sure they won't spot us?"

Myreon shook her head. "Relax, Artus—even if the Defenders *could* scry over water, they're far too busy right now. The only challenge will be when we make the docks by the Foreign Gate."

Tyvian turned his attention to the matter at hand. "So Andolon Gethrey to crash the market *today,* and probably laid the groundwork last night after you and Brana left him, Artus, but *before* he tried to kill me."

Hool's shroud was back in place and she was sitting in the stern of the boat, her hands tightly folded in her lap. "So who do we kill now?"

Myreon shuddered. "Gods, I will never get used to your voice coming from that face, Hool."

Artus snorted. "Wait until you see her hit somebody."

Tyvian whistled to get everyone's attention. "Focus, dammit! We can't just *kill* anybody. The crash, I am sorry to say, is probably inevitable—Gethrey was right about that. What we need is a plan to stop my brother from achieving whatever he hopes to achieve by aiding the crash, and we need it quickly. It's practically dawn, and once the markets open, things are going to get ugly quick."

"Dock ahead," Artus whispered. "Mirror men waiting for us."

Myreon worked the Cloak of the Mundane to keep them all nondescript. All except Hool. When they arrived at the dock, she leapt out of the boat and confronted the lead Defender. She waved Tyvian's signet ring under the guard's nose. "I am a mighty sorceress, and if you don't let us through, I will turn you into a fish."

The Defender took a good look at the statuesque Hool in the predawn light, took a good look at the ring, and did the mental arithmetic needed. His eyes bugged out. "Yes! Yes, archmagus, of course—go right ahead!"

Moments later they were in a coach heading through the Foreign Gate and into the Old City. Hool pulled off the ring and threw it at Tyvian. "If we can't kill anybody, then what is the plan?"

Tyvian rubbed his temples. His mind was like a series of rusty gears at the moment—the pain in his leg and chest and . . . well, *everywhere*, was muddling his thinking. Not to mention Myreon. He found he couldn't look at her without grinning like an idiot, and that nonsense had to stop right away. There would be time for it later, assuming they lived and made it out of the city undetained. Unfortunately, how they were going to do that remained a complete mystery to him.

Artus had his face screwed up in that frown he made when he was thinking too hard. "You said your brother was playing Andolon, right?"

Tyvian groaned. "Yes, Artus—try to keep up."

"Right, but *how*? Like, if he's the one who put Andolon up to this, how was he doing it? With who?"

"It could be anybody." Tyvian shrugged. "The Prophets, the Defenders, Andolon's damned sister—anybody."

Artus straightened. His face split into a grin. "It's DiVarro."

Myreon frowned. "What do you mean? Andolon's augur? He's in Xahlven's employ?"

Artus shook his head. "No, no—Xahlven *is* Di-Varro. It's a shroud."

Tyvian cocked his head. He felt the wheels beginning to turn. "Wait—how do you know?"

Artus pointed to his eye. "That crystal thing he's got, right? That's the same as Carlo's, isn't it? It's supposed to see through anything, right?"

"Yes? And?"

Artus grinned. "He never noticed that note you slipped me, now did he? Or, if he did, he didn't tell Andolon nothing about it—that either means he don't have a working crystal eye *or* he wasn't working for Andolon at all."

Tyvian thought back to his conversation with Xahlven on the floor of the Secret Exchange. He remembered Xahlven watching DiVarro intently and even working some sorcery on him. Tyvian had assumed it was an augury of some kind—spying on DiVarro—but DiVarro hadn't been *doing* anything at the time. He was just standing there.

He had been a simulacrum!

"Dammit, Artus," Tyvian breathed, "I think you're right! It all makes sense now—Xahlven was feeding Gethrey the precise information needed to crash the Secret and Mundane Exchanges all this time. Gethrey assumed the vast sums of money he probably paid

DiVarro were sufficient to guarantee his loyalty, too. Gods, it's the perfect cover."

Artus grinned. "Not too shabby, eh?"

Hool snorted. "That doesn't help us. I hate this." She groaned and adjusted her dress—an act that made Myreon laugh out loud. Hool scowled. "I hate humans."

Tyvian looked at Artus and Myreon. "I think I have an idea."

Artus frowned. "You gonna tell us about it?"

Tyvian smiled, nodding. "Oh yes, Artus—everybody is going to hear all about it, *especially* you. You still have that good pair of eyes in your head?"

Artus smiled. "Sharp as ever, boss."

"Good—for this to work, all of us need to be *perfect*."

By all outward appearances, Gethrey Andolon was a man busy transcending himself. The oceanic floor of the Saldorian Exchange and its armies of sharp-eyed, early morning traders had become a constellation of moons orbiting around the gravity of his wealth. His surprise offer of karfan beans had been well-received, but when he started selling silk and *cherille*, the floor had exploded with activity. Everybody knew he was up to something, but nobody knew what it was.

The chaos of the last few days—the Specter of Reldamar—had distilled itself into something ineffable and yet inexorable on the floor of the Mundane. There was a kind of panic in the air, and Gethrey Andolon—

the most successful trader the Mundane had yet known—was at the center of it. He stood on a stool among a sea of faces, all waving paper tags in his face with the marks of their houses and masters. He took orders carefully, a self-writing quill recording them. He was hemorrhaging goods like a man about to go bankrupt, and the exchange sensed that if they didn't get a piece of it now, they would regret it later—they were guiding Andolon's wealth like a great ship, and, like good pirates, they were going to get that ship into port and strip her down to her planks.

Of course, none of them knew that Gethrey Andolon was now several hours dead. And also none of them knew that there were commodities flooding the market had been planted by Andolon himself, guaranteeing the price would drop. They thought they smelled blood, and they were right. They just didn't know the blood was theirs.

As all this happened, the swirl of activity was being closely monitored by the Secret Exchange, who also were in the midst of a panic of their own. Their auguries were reading massive volatility in the markets—so much that some were swearing the prophesies were wholly unreliable, the result of an unnaturally high Fey ley and the mysterious appearance of a glut of goods on the Mundane. For the first time in ages the old sorcerous families began to realize the risk they were exposed to in the case of a mistake. Soon, mage by mage, the Secret Exchange began to slide into a downward spiral of sell-offs and panicky trades.

On the lips of every man and woman on the floor of either the Secret or the Mundane was one name: *Reldamar.*

It was during this financial panic that Tyvian Reldamar, dressed in a long cloak of forest green and leaning on a cane, disembarked from a coach and stepped onto the floor of the Mundane. He was flanked by two women—one a stunning beauty with auburn hair in a green dress, and the other an intimidating blonde marred with ash and soot.

Tyvian stood there for a moment, letting the effect of his presence sink in, and then nodded Myreon and Hool forward before the Defenders could be called for. "Ready?" he asked them.

"Are you sure this will work?" Hool asked, staring down a few men who dared to gape at her.

Tyvian nodded. "Once Artus gets it to you, wait until they are at their most frightened, and then start buying things."

"Which things?" Hool asked.

Tyvian shook his head. "It won't matter—if someone makes an offer, just say yes and slap hands."

Myreon, her eyes scanning the crowd for trouble, nodded in the direction of the man who was the spitting image of the late Gethrey Andolon. "There he is. Ready?"

Tyvian shot her a wink. "I've been ready my whole life for this." He broke away from them both. "Keep a low profile until the proper moment, you two."

They nodded; Tyvian made a beeline for the specter of his dead friend. The crowd parted around him as though he was still on fire. He wondered how many of them had been present to witness that. He wondered if it had been as impressive as he'd hoped.

"Gethrey" spotted Tyvian from twenty paces off. He doffed his absurd hat—a miniature mountain with a working waterfall and field of wildflowers—and waited for Tyvian to arrive. He gave Tyvian a winning smirk. Tyvian would have known that smirk anywhere.

"Hello, Xahlven," he said, coming to stop a few paces away. "Still like to play dress-up, I see."

Xahlven grinned from beneath his shroud. He spoke loudly enough that everyone nearby could hear. "Plan to stick a dagger in my eye, Tyv?"

Tyvian smiled. "Much worse—I came to talk."

Gethrey/Xahlven didn't move, but something significant was happening to the ley of the room—Tyvian felt chills and hot flashes travel up his spine; winds picked up and died. Finally, it stopped. "You're warded. Quite competently, too," his brother observed.

Tyvian shrugged. "Mage Defenders are trained to fight other magi, first and foremost. You should have thought of that before you framed her." He cocked an eyebrow at the traders surrounding them, who were looking on with intense curiosity even as they kept trading with one another. "Can they understand what we're saying?"

Xahlven shook his head. "They are hearing you threaten Gethrey Andolon with death—that's all. Any moment now and the Defenders will be on you. Was there something you wanted to say before they drag you off?"

Tyvian fished Gethrey's amulet from around his neck and held it where Xahlven could see. "Oh, I'm not much worried about the Defenders just now, Xahlven. Sic them on me and you'll have a colossus rampaging through here—I doubt you want *that* much chaos. You can't collapse the markets if the marketplace is collapsed, if you follow my meaning."

Xahlven smiled tightly, which didn't look right on Gethrey's face. "Really, Tyvian—that's rather violent, even for you."

"Xahlven, you have no idea the violence I am capable of right now." Tyvian dropped the colossus amulet. He eyed the crowd. Business was already taking shape—whispers passed from person to person and courier djinns dispatched even as everybody kept an eye on them.

And while *nobody* kept their eye on Artus.

"Very well—a private chat, then." Xahlven snapped his fingers and the boiling human chaos of the Mundane fell away, replaced by a perfectly circular room with no doors. The walls were of polished ebony, the ground covered by a lush purple rug. There was a *couronne* board on a small table and two chairs. Xahlven stood across from him, shroudless, hands folded around his staff. "An illusion. To keep our conversation private. Everyone else will think we walked off, but they will forget where."

Tyvian snorted. "Obviously. I'm not an idiot, Xahlven."

"Really? That's a statement in need of justification, I feel."

"This won't get anywhere if you keep insulting my intelligence. You're DiVarro and I know it—you're behind the whole damned thing. You wanted me to believe it was Mother, but that doesn't wash."

Xahlven nodded. "You always did have a hang-up over mother. It was an easy enough diversion. It kept you out of my hair for a few days while I planned my counterstroke."

The lies came quickly to Tyvian's lips. After the night he'd had, pretending to look shocked was easy. "What do you mean? *Didn't* you frame Myreon? Didn't you *bring* me here?"

Xahlven sighed, shaking his head. "You're always a step or two behind, Tyv. Very frustrating. I didn't bring you here, no—Mother did. She framed Myreon."

Oh, very good, Xahlven—keep thinking I'm stupid. "Why?"

"To contest me, of course. She is as capable of manipulating Gethrey as I am. I created him, in a sense—I gave him the resources to do what he is about to do—but Mother was able to steer his thought process through her control of the Mute Prophets, in which Gethrey so desperately wished to advance, as you know. When Alafarr was framed, Gethrey felt he was safe, but rumors, when precisely fashioned, are as accurate as bowshots. She gave Andolon the idea of trying to hire you, knowing you would hate him, and therefore knowing you would disrupt his plans."

Tyvian didn't bother trying to follow the convolutions of Xahlven's fictitious plot; he focused on looking confused. He wasn't here to parley, he was here to buy time. Just enough time for Myreon to work a little weakness into Xahlven's illusory room—just a *little* one.

He kept up the charade. "But . . . when you visited me before my trial, you told me to give Gethrey up . . . so . . ." Tyvian slapped his forehead. "Of course."

Xahlven chuckled. "Tyvian, you are far too predictable. What better way for me to prevent you from doing something than to tell you to do it?"

Tyvian pressed on. "But *why*, Xahlven? Why crash the Secret Exchange? How does it help you to get all that money?"

Xahlven shook his head, toying absently with the pieces on the *couronne* board. "What is the point of this conversation, Tyvian? Do you honestly expect me to reveal my endgame? No—not a chance. What is *your* endgame, hmmm?"

Behind Xahlven there was a small alteration in the illusion—a door, not large, but big enough to admit a person's hand. Myreon had done it, Hann bless her.

Tyvian advanced on Xahlven slowly, putting subtle menace into his limping steps. "My endgame is to stop this, obviously. Don't let the market crash. It's madness. The whole West will suffer. You'll embolden the Kalsaaris. You'll . . . you'll make another tasteless, rich twit like Gethrey, and I don't think the shipbuilding industry could handle another *Argent Wind*."

If Xahlven had one weakness, it was his lack of *physi-*

cal guile. He backed away from Tyvian smoothly, closer and closer to the little door. The little door that was now opening. Xahlven raised his free hand. "You talk as if the market crash is something that can be stopped, Tyvian. It isn't, though—*you* made that possible."

That one took Tyvian a bit off-guard. "What?"

"What makes markets flow, Tyvian?" Xahlven stopped just before the wall and leaned on the mantel of the illusory fireplace. "Fear. Uncertainty. The real challenge to Gethrey's plan was to foster false confidence and then pull the rug out—with my agents working on his behalf, he did quite well. He just needed a tipping point. He was originally going to use various crime syndicates, but then he stumbled upon a better option, or so he thought—namely you. That was Mother's doing and, but for my interference, it would have worked to prevent the crash. You would have stopped Gethrey, end of story."

Tyvian frowned. "What did you do?"

"I knew you'd escape from Keeper's Court, if you wound up there." Xahlven shrugged. "After that, the auguries were pretty clear. It would end with a war-construct rampaging through Crosstown, a monster assaulting Defenders all over town, and you—known criminal mastermind—barging in here and insisting upon a private audience with Gethrey Andolon in the midst of his apparent attempt to commit financial suicide."

"That's the tipping point—me, here, now. I'm causing the crash. You've won. But . . . why?" Tyvian stared at his brother. This part—this singular part—might just be the truth. Xahlven knew this conversation was going to take place. Did he, though, foresee Artus's hands under his cloak?

Xahlven was smiling. "I don't have to tell you anything. 'Why?' is not a question pawns like you get to ask, Tyvian."

Tyvian smirked. "I should think I would at least rate a shepherd."

Xahlven kept smiling. "I'm glad you and I agree that I've already won and we're down to debating semantics. I thank you for your service."

The illusory chamber dropped away and Tyvian was left face-to-face with Myreon and Artus, both of whom gave him curt nods and stony expressions. He clapped his hands together and faced the glares of scores of confused-looking traders. "Well, must be going—Defenders and whatnot. Enjoy making your fortunes, everybody!"

Xahlven cocked his head. "Wait . . . what are you . . ."

Tyvian, though, did not pause—he and his companions vanished into the crowd, losing Xahlven-as-Gethrey behind a few massive pillars. It wasn't until they were clear on the other side of the exchange that he dared ask Artus. "Well, did you make the switch?"

Artus grinned and held out a hand. There, stacked neatly in sweat-stained bundles, were all the trade receipts Xahlven had collected that day as well as his ledger and autoquill. "Jackpot," he said.

CHAPTER 31

TO REAP THE WHIRLWIND

Hool stood at the center of the seething chaos of the floor with all the regal tranquility of a predator among prey. The analogy was apt, even to her—there were many times on the Taqar when she had stood among the fleeting antelope and watched them scatter, terrified beyond the capacity for thought. This place, this "exchange," was not unlike that. Like all good predators, she stood still and silent and waited for the right moment to pounce.

She left her hands folded behind her back. No one approached her, no one paid her any heed—that was normal, Tyvian had said, since she was unknown here. In a few moments, however, she was going to make them remember her name. For once, the collected masses of humanity would beg her attention and hang on her every word. She would defeat them at their own stupid game. She liked the idea of it.

Look for the moment. Hool studied the crowd, still waiting. A lifetime of studying the body language of large animals had given her an exceptional capacity to cold read others. After several years among humans, she had fine-tuned it into a tool that could be used to predict what humans were going to do just before they did it. She could do this without sorcery and without magic hats or crystal balls or power sinks or whatever else humans used. She was a gnoll; she did not need sorcery to be powerful and smart. Lyrelle Reldamar had been right: she knew them better than she thought.

Around her, the people shouting to each other and slapping hands were growing more frantic. The numbers people were shouting got lower and lower and lower. Soon now—soon she needed to act. From across the exchange she saw Artus, Tyvian, and Myreon watching her carefully. She nodded to them, holding her human posture upright and serene, as she had seen Lyrelle Reldamar do.

"Now, Mama?" Brana asked at her side. Unlike her, he was a bundle of nervous energy, his eyes flitting to every bustling human as though ready to chase them down.

"Wait," Hool cautioned him, and then looked

toward where the shrouded Xahlven stood, his hands also folded behind his back. He had no idea that the paper tickets hidden in his robes were, in fact, blank. The real tickets—the only true record of his trades for the day—had been passed to her by Artus and were nestled securely underneath Hool's shroud. Xahlven, in his arrogance, hadn't even checked them yet. Even if he did, he could not reveal himself—for one thing, that would mean acknowledging that he was pretending to be Andolon, which was a crime, and it would *also* require him to show everybody he was a mage on the floor of the exchange, which was *also* a crime. There was nothing he could do but call in the Defenders.

And now it was too late.

"Buy!" Hool barked at the nearby men. "Buying karfan! Buying *cherille*! Buying all the things!"

The traders' heads cocked in her direction, but they hesitated.

Hool fixed them with her copper glare. "What are you waiting for? Buy, stupid!"

Above her, floating near the center of the exchange, rotating illusory numbers of the current day's trading showed the dire straits of the markets—the warnings were clear, and the traders on the floor were rapidly adapting their strategies to try and salvage themselves from bankruptcy. Though she did not fully understand the numbers in front of her, Hool knew enough to expect the wild surge of humanity that swarmed her, waving their tickets at her in the vain hope she could save them.

As Tyvian had instructed, she bought every ticket waved in her face, each purchase recovering what Andolon/Xahlven had sold just a short time before. Those goods? They were borrowed—pinned at their original high price from the original stakeholders. For every pile of goods Hool purchased now, she made a huge profit at the expense of the men who had loaned the goods to the false Andolon that very morning when the prices were high. Hool did not have a head for math, but the speed with which she was slapping hands with sweaty-palmed fools was such that she had no doubt the profits would be exceptional. Stupid as it was, she felt her adrenaline surge at the thought of having power over these humans—of being able to finally do as she pleased without their incessant judgment and foolish notions of propriety.

For the first time, she thought she might be coming to understand wealth.

"We're doing it, Mama!" Brana shouted over the din, slapping palms with another man and exchanging tickets.

"Yes." Hool nodded, but didn't let herself get carried away—something was wrong. She glanced over toward where Xahlven should have been. He was not there. "Almost time to go," she yelled to Brana. She noted also that Tyvian and Artus and Myreon were likewise gone—they knew their time was short as well.

"Buy!" Brana called. "Karfan! Wine! Salt!"

They slapped more hands.

Suddenly, everyone stopped. Hool blinked at them all, "What?"

No one answered. They were all staring at the center of the Exchange, where a massive wraith of none other than Archmage Xahlven Reldamar floated. Around him the numbers of the day's trading so far floated as well—even Hool could tell they were dire, worse than dire.

"*In the interest of the health of the Domain of Saldor and its allies,*" Xahlven said solemnly, "*trading is hereby suspended for the day, possibly longer, while we look into what caused this loss.*"

One trader couldn't believe his ears. "What? WHAT? He can't do that! Who does he think he is, doing that? This is *business*! This is *money*! He can't just *stop it from happening!*"

The man—hopeless, wild eyed—cast his gaze around at the other traders on the floor, most of whom were standing stone still, in a state of abject shock. Gaping at the wraith of Xahlven, they looked like rows of animated corpses wondering what happened to their souls.

"We don't have to listen to him!" the man screamed. "Keep trading! Keep going! Selling karfan—cheap! Sell! SELL!"

Nobody listened. Everyone was too busy cleaning up the ashes of their own financial empires to hear an angry little man scream. Hool noted that Xahlven had slapped hands with this man several times early in the run. She walked up to him and found the tickets with the man's smell all over them—they smelled like fish oil. "You owe me for these," she said simply.

The man sagged as he looked at his own handi-work. "Who . . . who in blazes are you?"

"I am the richest lady you know." Hool looked down her human nose at him. "Now, pay me or I will rip off your arms."

The *Argent Wind* sailed out of Saldor Harbor with most everyone ashore assuming Gethrey Andolon had skipped town to avoid his debts, assuming Tyvian's plan had worked as he'd hoped, though they hadn't tarried long enough for him to confirm it. In any event, the ponderous vessel sailed along the coast, heading west toward Eretheria. There was no sign of pursuit.

Hool was the unofficial new owner of the vessel, a fact that she did not seem to enjoy. It was, on some level, piracy, but Gethrey's former crew of thugs and brutish sailors didn't seem to mind so long as Hool's newfound wealth paid them for the voyage—which it did, and amply.

Brana spent most of his time in the rigging, working with the sailors. He nattered on to anybody who would listen about everything he was learning about ships. His Trade was improving markedly, though it was now healthily spiced with various maritime curses that made Hool grumble. The journey, all things considered, was going well.

Tyvian was sitting at the table in the wardroom the ship gently rocking to and fro. Across from him was Hool, looking miserable as usual, and Myreon, who had her boots up and was reading one of Gethrey's vast array of books that had clearly been selected based on the impressiveness of their bindings and not the intelligence of their contents. This particular book was an Eddoner bildungsroman about a young Wardenrider seeking to avenge his father's death at the hands of gnolls, of all things.

"Hool," Myreon asked, "do gnolls drink blood?"

Hool's ears went back. "Does that stupid book say we drink blood?"

"It does indeed."

Hool snorted. "Well . . . we do. Sometimes."

Myreon flipped across a few pages. "Do you also howl at the moon?"

"Why would we do that?"

Myreon read a short passage. "It says here because you think it's a god."

"It's not a god. It's the moon." Hool put her head on the table. "Stop asking stupid questions."

She shrugged. "I've just never had the opportunity to read one of these with an actual gnoll present, is all."

Hool snarled something rude in gnoll-speak and left. Myreon kept reading. Tyvian said nothing. "Well?" she asked at length.

Tyvian felt a stab in his guts; he knew what was coming. "Well what?"

"Is this how you usually celebrate a stunning victory? Moping and staring off into space?"

"I'm still not convinced we won."

Myreon shook her head. "It's been two days—nobody is following us. We've made it."

"Escaping with your life isn't the same as winning," Tyvian said. He looked at her—the salt air and sunshine had washed away the pallor petrification had left in her cheeks. She was radiant, frankly. He could scarcely believe she was trying to cheer him up. Him, of all people.

Myreon reached out and grabbed his hand. "You couldn't have prevented the crash. None of us could. I see that now. At least we stopped Xahlven—we did that much."

Tyvian gave her a thin smile and kissed the back of her hand. "You're the best person I know."

Myreon's eyes sparkled. "And you're the worst."

He withdrew, climbing up on deck. He found Artus staring out to sea on the quarter deck, the wind tousling his mop of hair. Gods, Tyvian thought, eyeing the boy's attire, he's already grown out of those damned pants.

Artus nodded to him. "Hey."

"Artus." Tyvian said, standing next to him.

They said nothing for a moment. Then Artus cleared his throat. "I'm sorry."

"What?"

Artus looked at him. "How'd you know I'd throw that sparkstone at you?"

Tyvian shook his head. "I don't know."

Artus nodded and looked off at the sea. "Thought

you'd say that. Me? I think it means you trust me. Don't you?"

Tyvian nodded. "I suppose so."

Artus grinned. "So, what's the plan now?"

Tyvian rubbed the ring and looked out at the sunset. "Artus, for once, let's have no plans at all."

Artus nodded, breathing deeply of the salt air. "Sounds good, partner."

Tyvian put his arm around Artus and held him there for a moment, but no longer. Then they stood together awhile, staring deep into the green swirl of the summer ocean.

EPILOGUE

Lyrelle Reldamar knew, within a quarter of an hour, when Xahlven would come to see her. She wore a gown of cornflower lace and pearls and waited for him in the solarium at Glamourvine. Outside, a thunderstorm brewed, rumbling on the horizon and flashing over the cypress trees.

Xahlven came in as a specter might—no sound, his midnight robes trailing behind him like smoke. "I suppose you think you're terribly clever, Mother."

Lyrelle made a show of stirring cream into her karfan. "Don't be obtuse, Xahlven—I spent too much on tutors for you to be this slow."

Xahlven's eyes flashed with anger—insulting his intelligence never failed to get him riled. "He has no idea what you've shown him, old woman. He never will. Tyvian cares only about his next fine meal and his next suit of clothes."

Lyrelle smiled at her eldest son and sipped her kar-fan—it was still too hot. She channeled some of the Dweomer and cooled it to her tastes. "He knows, Xahl-ven, or suspects at any rate. You underestimate him, as you always do." She pointed to the chair across from her. "Won't you sit down? You look tired."

Xahlven scowled. "I am never tired. I am too busy."

"Trying to destroy the world?"

"Trying to save it." Xahlven shook his head. "And there's nothing you can do about it either. I *won* mother. I now have control of both the Secret and the Mundane Exchanges—I'm the *savior* of the West's economy, snatching it from the jaws of oblivion."

Lyrelle raised an eyebrow. "But, I note, with just *enough* oblivion present to make them think they still need you as overseer of both markets. Bravo, my boy. I'm very proud, of course."

Xahlven took a deep breath. "I came to give you one final warning—stay out of my business."

"My children's business is my business by default," Lyrelle countered, sipping her karfan—ah, there it was: the perfect temperature.

"Why do you persist in this 'caring mother' fiction? You never cared about me—you only wanted a tool by which to bind father to your will, and so here I am. Must we continue the charade now that he is thirty years dead?" Xahlven came to stand over her, Etheric energy pulsing around him in black waves that Lyrelle could more smell than see.

She set her karfan down—that much Ether had likely

turned the cream now. Such an inconvenience. "Xahlven, darling, I love you despite your faults, not the least of which is a complete inability to believe yourself lovable."

"If you interfere with me again, I will kill you."

Lyrelle laughed. "I should like to see that! You, the boy who was afraid of *wisteria vines*, threatening my life? Quite amusing."

The sunlight vanished behind a black cloud, and Xahlven seemed to loom larger in the room. His eyes glowed red with power as he channeled more and more of the Ether. Outside, the flowering vines that grew up along the outside of the solarium began to wither and die. *"This is your final warning,"* he hissed, his voice reduced to a scratching sound.

Lyrelle looked up at her son and patted him on the cheek, her own Lumenal wards easily nullifying his Etheric transmutation of himself. "Oh, Xahlven—you don't need to warn me, my midnight child. You needn't concern yourself with me either—I've already defeated you. It's only a matter of time."

Xahlven scowled. "You mean Tyvian? Even if he does understand his recent defeat, he doesn't threaten my plans at all. He is not my equal, Mother."

Lyrelle laughed lightly. "Of course not, Xahlven—you're a *monster*. Tyvian, on the other hand, is a hero."

Xahlven rolled his eyes.

Lyrelle nodded at him. "Oh, of course he is—he just doesn't realize it yet."

"I see I'm wasting my breath," Xahlven said, stepping back. "You've been warned."

Lyrelle nodded. "As have you."

The young archmage withdrew, leaving his mother to her karfan. After calling for a new cup and fresh cream, she summoned Eddereon to the room.

The big Northron bowed to her. "Yes, milady?"

Lyrelle pointed to the vines outside the solarium, now all but dead. "Be a dear and see about replanting those vines for next season, will you? Xahlven has ruined them in a fit of pique, it seems."

Eddereon rubbed where his beard used to be. "Of course—I'll do it right away."

Lyrelle looked out the solarium toward the approaching clouds. "Oh, I'd wait on it, if I were you. Seems a storm is rolling in."

On the horizon, the lightning began to flash.

ACKNOWLEDGMENTS

A special thanks goes out to my friends, John Serpico, John Fraley, and John Perich, who, sometimes without their knowledge, helped me understand financial markets enough to write this book. I have every confidence that I screwed it up anyway, but am immensely grateful, nevertheless. I also wish to extend a heartfelt thanks to Rebecca Lucash, for stepping in as editor when needed and doing an absolutely wonderful job. Finally, I wish to thank all those who read this continuation of Tyvian's adventures. It is my grand prediction that we will all get to see some more of him, but time will tell. Auguries, as Tyvian is so fond of saying, are not destinies. Until then . . .

ABOUT THE AUTHOR

On the day **AUSTON HABERSHAW** was born, Skylab fell from the heavens. This foretold two possible fates: supervillain or scifi/fantasy author. Fortunately he chose the latter, and spends his time imagining the could-be and the never-was rather than disintegrating the moon with his volcano laser. Auston is a winner of the Writers of the Future Contest and has had work published in *Analog* and *Escape Pod*, among other places. He lives and works in Boston, Massachusetts.

Find him online at www.aahabershaw.wordpress.com, on Facebook at www.facebook.com/aahabershaw, or follow him on Twitter @AustonHab.

Discover great authors, exclusive offers, and more at hc.com.